W. Lawton Brown

CLASH

OF

SOULS

**We weren't born to hate, so why do we?
In this stunning new age thriller
this monumental question is answered.**

NEO Books   Lynnwood, Washington

Published by:
NEO Books, P.O. Box 2402, Lynnwood, WA 98036-2402

Printed in the United States of America
First printing: September, 2005

ISBN: 0-9769588-0-5

Library of Congress Control Number: 2005927297

Senior Editor: Diane Houston
Cover design by Bruce DeRoos
Layout and design by DIMI PRESS

Dedication

On April 20, 2002, Ann Brown,
my best friend, lover, spouse and soulmate,
passed on to the next dimension.
This book is dedicated to her loving memory
and to Joni and Alison,
my lovely and wonderful daughters.

Acknowledgments

A great many individuals contributed to this book. Their contributions ranged from supplying technical advice, reading the manuscript, editing, evaluating, proofing, design and layout. I have tried to include everyone, however if I have omitted anyone, please accept my apologies. My deepest thanks go out to the following kind souls:

Diane Houston, Beverly Delich, Margaret Devinny, Michelle Mahler, Barbara Davies, Temera the Psychic, Emily Baumbach, Litta Ross, Carol Bendinelli, J.G. Thompson, Nic Lundborg, Barbara Taylor, Lani Kesler, Doris Von Marenholtz, Patty Fyhr, MaryJane Cavanagh, Crystal Wendekier, Ann Marie Legere, JP Van Hulle, Janet Forrest, Brenda Lee Rogers, Gia Freeman, Karen Lofurno, Victoria Marina, Jose Stevens, Ph.D., Gracie Thompson, Jeanne Scolaro, Jessica Morrell, Louise Flanagan, Marcy Angel, Mary Alice Brown, Michelle Inishi, Susan Crawford, Helga Kahr, Susan Newton, Detective Kim Turner, Mary Harris, Ph.D., Bruce DeRoos, Dick Lutz, and Mary Lutz.

Chapter 1

A n eerie feeling of unease gripped me. I felt a sense of danger that contradicted the festive sights around me. Something seemed wrong, but I couldn't put my finger on it. I slowly scanned the area around me, but couldn't spot anyone that might be sending out the negative vibes I was picking up.

I snapped out of my sixth sense reverie when Joni, my twenty-six year old daughter, spoke, "Dad, what do you want?"

"Uhhh, I don't know. I guess just a regular coffee. You order something for me."

Turning to the clerk, she said, "One Grande Non-fat Latte and one tall Americano."

Life in Seattle has gotten too complex. At fifty-two, I'm old enough to remember when coffee was just coffee. It came black and you could add cream or sugar or both. Now it seems like you have a hundred and two different options and I don't understand ninety-nine of them. It's amazing that a guy who was once fearless enough to skydive for fun could be so intimidated just walking into a Starbucks.

While we waited for our drinks, Joni, oblivious to the negative vibes I was picking up, said, "Dad, did you know this was the first Starbucks store?"

"No, are you sure? I thought it was near the downtown Nordstrom store."

Behind me a gravelly male voice spoke, "Nope, she's right. It sez right here Starbucks started here in the Pike Place Market in 1971." I turned to see a small wiry sixty-something man with a short scruffy white beard jabbing his gnarly right index finger at the wording on a large polished brass plaque.

Irritated at having someone eavesdrop and butt-in on our

conversation—and not in a mood to strike up a conversation with some grungy stranger—I acknowledged his remark with a brusque "Oh yeah...I see" then turned away.

Outside, Joni and I lingered for a minute in a small crowd of people forming a half-circle around a talented black quartet called the Apostles, singing gospel songs on the sidewalk for donations. They were doing a good job of getting the mid-morning crowd at the Market in an upbeat mood.

The Pike Place Market has been a Seattle landmark since it opened as a farmer's market in 1907. Now it's a diverse shopping center featuring fresh seafood, produce, arts and crafts, street entertainers, plus a variety of shops and restaurants that keep locals and tourists alike flocking to it year round.

Today was one of those rare late-March days in Seattle. Not only was the sun shining, it was a Saturday.

That meant a big crowd of pale-skinned Seattlites at the Market, most squinting like moles venturing outside and braving the blinding daylight. Seattle's sun-deprived populous jumps at any opportunity to be outdoors without rainwear.

Joni was in town visiting for a few days and wanted to take in the Pike Place Market. While she was busy looking for things to buy, I was enjoying her company and partaking in people watching. But as we strolled along the narrow red brick street towards Pike Street where the main entrance to the Market was situated, the feeling of impending danger returned, sending all my senses into a state of high alert.

A crowd was gathered around the always popular fish vendors who were putting on a show of yelling and tossing fish back and forth. Catching a wet, slippery two feet long fish is not easy and the crowd cheered and applauded every catch.

As we approached, I noticed the old man with the white beard was standing on the outside perimeter of the crowd about twenty feet in front of us. The short hairs on the back of my neck bristled.

Suddenly, I was bumped into and roughly pushed sideways by a man who was intent on getting somewhere quickly. In the split second that I recovered my balance I spotted the gleam of a knife blade he was holding behind his back in his right hand.

He was dashing straight for the white-bearded man. I yelled out, "He's got a knife! Watch out!" The old man instantly spun around. His left hand grabbed the wrist holding the knife while his right hand threw his hot coffee into the assailant's face. Screaming in pain, the attacker dropped his knife, broke free and bolted through the startled crowd into the Market and down the stairs leading to lower level shops—a perfect escape route.

For a split second time seemed suspended. The crowd around us was stunned, frozen in place, not knowing how to react. Everything happened so fast that those who had witnessed what had transpired saw only a white male wearing a navy blue sailor's jacket and a black stocking cap pulled down over his ears pushing his way through the crowd and then getting coffee thrown in his face. Most of the crowd was so intent on watching the fish-throwing performance that they were oblivious to what had happened. I looked down and saw the knife, a chrome six-inch long hunting knife with a leather handle. The white-bearded man quickly bent over, grabbed the knife, and shoved it into an outer jacket pocket.

"Just some crazy kid on drugs folks. No harm done," he said to the startled onlookers. Then he grabbed my elbow and said, "Let's get out of here fast. We need to talk."

Twisting my elbow free from his grasp, I said, "What the hell's going on here? Who are you?"

Looking squarely into my eyes he said with a sense of urgency, "Please. This is of the utmost importance. Please follow me. You'll be safe."

Still skeptical, but not seeing any danger in following him, I nodded my head. I grabbed Joni's hand and we struggled to keep up as he weaved his way through the crowded Market. He abruptly stopped in front of the Athenian Inn, a popular Market eating and drinking establishment. There was a line of fifteen to twenty people waiting outside for seating, but the bearded man whispered something in the ear of the hostess and she motioned us inside and pointed to the upstairs balcony accessible by a narrow stairway with black wrought iron railing. Once upstairs we were led to a far corner table tucked behind a support pillar but still with a panoramic view of Elliott Bay. The little man took a seat with his back to the wall and facing the way we had entered.

"Okay, now will you tell me who you are and what this is about?"

"Call me Mike. As far as what's going on, you just participated in a little game the Universe worked out so we could meet."

Apparently I had a puzzled look in my eyes, so he added, "I appear to have jumped ahead of myself. Let me rephrase it. You and I were destined to meet this lifetime and the Universe created the little drama that just occurred to make it happen. Actually we met momentarily in Starbucks but you chose to ignore me, so plan B—the knife attack—had to happen."

I looked at Joni. She had her skeptical face on and I could read her mind, she was thinking "Dad, this guy is nuts. Let's get out of here."

I looked Mike straight in the eyes and said, "You mean to say that someone staged an attempted knifing *just* so we could meet? That's crazy."

"No, no, no," Mike said, "Nothing was staged. The attempt to kill me was real. If you hadn't intervened someone else would have. I know it sounds crazy, but you and I were destined to meet this lifetime and work together on an important project. You're a writer aren't you?"

"Yeah," I said cautiously. "I am, but how did you know that? I haven't even told you my name."

Our conversation was suspended as a frazzled middle-aged waitress wearing a name tag that said Dottie appeared, plunking three glasses of ice water down on the table and saying, "The usual for you Mike?" Mike nodded and she turned to us, "How about you folks?" Joni, still clutching her Grande Non-fat Latte, and anxious to leave, said "Nothing for me." Having lost my Starbucks Americano during the knife attack, I said, "Just black coffee for me."

As the waitress turned and left, Mike moved his left arm, revealing a 6-inch tear in the padded sleeve of his dirty tan parka. "No," he said, "This was for real—not play-acting. That punk was trying to kill me." He unbuttoned the top two buttons of his red-plaid shirt, revealing a Kevlar bullet-proof vest—the type usually worn by the police. "This saved me two other times." Then, as he lifted the white hair on the right side of his head, just above the ear, I could see an ugly purplish-red four-inch scar—apparently from a bullet that grazed his skull. "This," he added "happened at the same time I took one in the vest last October."

By now, my curiosity was really piqued. Yet I felt a sense of fear by being so near to a guy who obviously was a walking target for somebody. As I nervously turned my head to look around, Mike reassured me, "Don't worry. We're safe for the time being. That punk is long gone for today."

"Look" I said, "a few minutes ago you said I was a writer and we were destined to meet so we could work on some project. Well, I'm not looking for a partner nor a project to work on. I've got plenty on my plate now and I'm in the middle of writing a book. But I do want to know how you knew I was a writer. Was it a guess or did you overhear us say something about writing when we were in Starbucks?"

"Neither. You're aware that some people are more psychically gifted than others. I'm one of those people and like other psychics I have an ability to tap into knowledge that comes from another dimension. Some metaphysical books refer to that dimension as the Akashic Records, the place where all knowledge, past, present and future, is stored."

Mike continued, "When I woke this morning I had a strong feeling I was going to meet an old friend today who would play an important role in my life's mission. Then the moment I saw you at Starbucks I picked up the energy pattern emanating from you and knew you were the person I have been waiting for—for over two years. My friend, you and I have known each other in many past lifetimes, including your last one."

I scrutinized Mike closely. He could easily pass for an old, slightly crazed homeless person. He was wearing a dirty crumpled canvas all-weather hat similar to what fly fishermen wore. His weathered skin was a ruddy red with deep pronounced crinkle lines around his deep-set brown eyes. His large sunburned and peeling Roman nose had a slight twist to the right halfway down that looked like it was caused by a right hook from someone's fist. Like Abraham Lincoln, his upper lip was devoid of facial hair, while his short scruffy white beard made his chin look like it jutted out—daring someone to take a swing at him. His big bushy white-brown eyebrows had a wild unruly look and were joined in the middle forming one solid eyebrow that looked like a fat caterpillar. Peering directly into Mike's intense eyes I had a strange feeling of familiarity. I had a feeling I had known him before. Was it real or just the power of suggestion?

With my elbows on the table, hands folded together under my chin, I looked at him skeptically and said, "Okay. Then tell me about my last lifetime."

Decades earlier, when I first started studying many different types of metaphysical subjects, I had dabbled briefly in automatic writing. Supposedly, when I would hold a pen in my hand, I could get messages coming in from another dimension. My hand would write without my conscious control but I could never determine what was causing it, or if it was real, until one day I asked about my most recent past life. The pen started writing and spelled out where I had died, in Denver when I was a twenty-two year old male. The month, day, and year were given, November 9, 1909, as well as the fact that I had been shot by my older brother for playing around with his wife.

It was a fascinating story but was it real? I needed proof. Since the lifetime had supposedly ended in November 1909 in Denver, Colorado, I realized that the story was unusual enough that it more than likely would have been recorded in the Denver newspaper. So I visited Denver, went to the library and pored through the microfilm archives. When I got to the day following my supposed death, November 10, 1909, there it was—the story of my being shot the previous day. The short hairs on the back of my neck bristled as an eerie chill swept over me. I instantly knew I was the person in the article. The odds on me coming up with the month, day, year, and place of death, plus the fact I was a twenty-two year old male shot by his brother, were astronomical. At that point, all doubt vanished from my mind. Past lives are real!

Since I had told almost no one about my past life discovery, I was putting Mike to the test. Would his story match mine? I was doubtful and mentally prepared to grab Joni and split, leaving this apparent homeless derelict to find some other gullible sap to fall for his weird story.

Mike, shaking his stubby beard from side to side, started to chuckle. "You were really stupid last time around. I was your best friend. Andrew was my name, but you called me Snuffy because I chewed tobacco then. I still do this lifetime but not as much because nobody has any spittoons around any more. Your name was Martin, or Marty for short. One night we had a few beers in a bar and you decided to visit your sister-in-law. I tagged along because you were raving about how beautiful she was and how I had to meet her.

"We got to your brother's place, and he was gone but she let us in. The next thing I know the two of you are in a passionate embrace in the kitchen. I was feeling uncomfortable so I excused myself and left. The next day I found out Johnny had come home later that night and caught you in bed with his wife and in a rage shot you. I was with you in the hospital when you died. You were only twenty-two."

Startled, I countered, "Where and when did this take place?"

"Denver, in 1909, and as I recall it was sometime in early November."

I needed no further proof! Mike, or Snuffy as I had known him last time around, was for real. He was a legitimate psychic. The same eerie chill swept over me once again. Joni might still be skeptical, but I wasn't.

At that moment the waitress appeared, armed with Mike's food and my coffee. His usual turned out to be an Oyster Omelet, a house specialty. Mike slathered some orange marmalade jam on the accompanying toast and dug into the omelet as if he hadn't eaten in days. Obviously knife attacks don't phase this strange little man's appetite. Between bites he looked up and asked, "So Marty, what's your name this lifetime?"

"You mean you don't know that? I was getting the impression that you knew everything about me."

With a twinkle in his eyes, he replied, "Sorry. I forgot to ask my Spirit Guides. I have been known to be wrong now and then. Actually, I figure I'm about 80% accurate. Psychic work, or what some people call channeling, burns up a lot of energy and since the information coming in has to be filtered through the human mind and human personality, mistakes can be made. And then there's Free Will. You chose to ignore me at Starbucks. That was Free Will. Remember the old saying, 'You can lead a horse to water but you can't make him drink.' "

"Well, my name this lifetime is Scott Hunter, and this is my daughter Joni."

Turning toward Joni he tipped his hat slightly revealing a high wrinkled forehead with thinning white hair combed straight back. "Delighted to meet you Ms. Joni."

Still skeptical, Joni mumbled a bland social response and forced a weak half-smile.

"As far as the book you're writing Marty—I mean Scott—it won't sell yet. It's too premature. It's about a past life you lived, right?"

"So, you even know what I'm writing about?"

"Just the basics not the details."

"It's about a particularly bloody lifetime I lived about two thousand years ago and the emotional baggage I've carried forward in time since then. I uncovered the lifetime while doing some past life regression therapy a few years ago. It's a fascinating story that can give people a real understanding of how past lives can have a powerful influence on our present life. It also explains how one can solve present day problems by going back into the past and confronting one's traumas and mistakes."

"Look Scott, it's a great idea to write about, and you're right, someday it will help thousands—maybe millions of people—improve the quality of their lives, but you've got the cart before the horse."

Mike continued, "Just think for a minute. Who's going to believe your book about a past life if they first don't believe in reincarnation? The majority of people with a Judeo-Christian-Islamic upbringing do not yet even believe in past lives, or for that matter even understand reincarnation and karma.

"Scott, I have the information you need to write a book that will get the public's attention and give them enough information to help them understand and accept what your reincarnation book is about."

Like most authors, I didn't like to hear someone tell me my book idea was premature and wouldn't sell well. I didn't respond to his comments. In my mind I was weighing his remarks against the hours of labor I had already put in on the book.

Finally, reading my mind, Mike broke the silence and said, "Look, I know you've already put a lot of time and energy in your present book, but will you let me explain my message before you flat-out reject working with me?"

"O.K. Mike," I said reluctantly, "I'll listen."

Chapter 2

"The message I have to share with the world comes from spiritual entities no longer living on the Earth Plane. They completed their cycle here lifetimes ago, having since evolved to a higher plane where their goal is to help those of us still on the Earth Plane. They have told me that we are in a time of accelerated spiritual growth and evolutionary changes on planet Earth. It's a time when old spiritual teachings are to be updated to align with our rapid technological advances.

"No longer are we in a primitive society where only a handful of people can read or write. Complex truths no longer have to be explained in simple parables or analogies. Judaism, Christianity, and Islam have been insisting for hundreds of years that people blindly trust, or take solely on faith, ancient teachings, whether they are right or wrong. And, unlike Santa Claus and the Tooth Fairy, we were never allowed to outgrow the old simplistic messages. Yet, if you can't challenge the existing message there can be no real spiritual growth."

I interrupted Mike. "Yeah, I know exactly what you're talking about. Decades ago, when I was a brash fourteen year old, I started to question the belief system I was being taught. When I would ask my Baptist minister questions about other religions and practices he was unable to give me sound answers. Instead I was force-fed his rote-memorized fire and brimstone rhetoric.

"I was upset with his attitude, which I considered arrogant and condescending, so I went to the library and started devouring books about other religions. I kept asking myself, is my minister right? Is it possible for a billion Chinese to be doomed to burn in Hell for all of Eternity solely because they had a different belief system? I was only a teenager at the time but it seemed like something was terribly wrong with that logic.

"So, while I realized something was wrong, I had reached an impasse. My faith was full of unanswered questions, and so were the others, leaving me, at the time, no place to turn to for the truth. Then, as I grew older, my interests shifted to sports, girls and preparing to enter the working world. As the years passed and I matured, I realized that a great deal of the information being spewed out by our most cherished institutions, like churches, governments, schools, and the medical field, whether by design or ignorance, was far from correct."

Nodding his head all-knowingly, Mike said, "That's amazing. Even at the young age of fourteen you were already questioning and seeking answers to the meaning of life. So, Scott, tell me, what happened to you around age twenty-eight?"

"Funny you picked that time period. At twenty-eight, quite unexpectedly, I went through an emotionally devastating divorce that forced me, in my search for meaningful answers, to re-explore the territory I had first entered fourteen years earlier. Only this time I didn't just limit my study to religions. My research took me into a myriad of metaphysical fields—astrology, automatic writing, the Edgar Cayce readings, channeling, hypno-regression, the I Ching, mental telepathy, numerology, past-life regression therapy, psychic recall, pyramid healing, the tarot and even UFO's."

"Did you come to any conclusions after all that studying?"

"Yeah, I did," I replied. "There's a wealth of information existing for the study of these subjects. However, first I learned caution. Like most fields there are both sincere, legitimate practitioners and those out for a fast buck. All fields of metaphysics make claims that are hard to prove. This becomes frustrating when you're trying to verify the accuracy of information, or even understand the validity of the underlying theory.

"After more than 20 years of serious study I learned to approach the field of metaphysics as an 'open-minded skeptic.' By this I mean, I try to be open-minded rather than close-minded and skeptical rather than gullible. The close-minded person who denies the existence of anything that's not in a government endorsed school text, or fits under the scientist's microscope, or a part of one's religious belief system, will only be limiting his or her intellectual and spiritual growth. The open-minded skeptic is not afraid to look, searching for ultimate truths rather than erecting a truth-obscuring brick wall around metaphysics."

"This is perfect," Mike said. Then lifting his glass of water, and looking upward, he added, "Thank you, Universe, thank you, thank you. You brought me the right person." Then looking at me, he said, "Scott, it's not a question of will you work with me. We're already destined to. Even though you didn't know it, you've been preparing for this moment since the time you were fourteen! I mean you have Free Will. You can always say no, but why would you? You're about to fulfill one of your major goals for this lifetime."

"Which is?"

"Scott, your major goal for this lifetime is to disseminate true spiritual knowledge to millions of people. Knowledge that will help them immensely in accelerating their spiritual growth."

"If that's true, Mike, then why wasn't I some spiritual guru in this lifetime? While I've spent the better part of this lifetime studying metaphysics, I've mostly earned my living in the business world, particularly in the area of advertising, marketing and communications—areas not particularly considered very spiritual."

"Exactly! Disseminating spiritual knowledge in this day and age requires job skills you could only get in the business world. Do you seriously think that if Moses, Muhammad, or Jesus were to reappear today they would simply rely on word-of-mouth to draw a crowd? No way. The world is too large. They would use all the modern means of communication to get their message out to the masses."

"But Mike, we already have plenty of spiritual laws. Why do we need more?"

"You're right. We don't need more. The Universe isn't look-ing for someone to create new spiritual laws. That's already been done. The job now is to get the *correct* knowledge out to mankind by presenting a modern explanation and understanding of the old laws.

"Remember, Scott, when you challenged your Baptist minister about not believing that one billion Chinese were doomed to Hell because they didn't believe in Jesus? He was operating off misunderstandings of ancient spiritual laws that are over two thousand years old, and in many instances first recorded hundreds of years after the various events took place. Facts get distorted over time. Memories tend to get fuzzy and stories get embellished. Translations are only as good as the translator. Parables can be interpreted a dozen different ways. One must remember that two thousand years ago very few people could read or write. The people who had those skills had an enormous power over others. I hope you're not naive enough to think that people never abused power in the past."

Mike continued, "So, let me summarize this—over a span of thousands of years a small number of highly evolved and gifted prophets appeared on Earth. This rather elite group includes: Buddha, Confucius, Jesus, Krishna, Lao Tsu, Mother Cabrini, Mahatma Gandhi, John the Baptist, Mohammed, Socrates, St. Francis of Assisi, Rama, the Hindu God, and Ra, the Egyptian Sun God.

"They each had a spiritual message to share with the masses. Each message was somewhat different from the others but, contrary to popular belief, they complemented rather than opposed each other.

"But, left in the hands of their partisan followers, and the leaders in power at the time, the original teachings were distorted and corrupted. The true messages have been altered enough to create the mess we have today. Instead of teachings supporting one another we have a world where each faction claims their way is the correct path and the others are wrong. Any history book can give you a list of the wars we've fought over whose version of the truth to believe. Millions of people have been slaughtered in the Holocaust, the so-called ethnic cleansings, racism, bigotry, and hatred that all too often exists simply because someone appears to be different from the group in question."

I could tell Mike was getting pretty agitated at this point. His voice had risen considerably and I noticed a few heads turning in our direction to see what was happening. I motioned with my hands for him to lower his voice which he quickly did.

"Sorry, Scott, I always get carried away when I think about the horrible injustices that have been committed in the name of some deity. But, let me ask you one simple question. Do you think all of this could have happened if everyone was following the correct spiritual laws?"

I knew he was right. The record of mankind is drenched in the blood of countless wars and battles fought over religious interpretations. Whether it's Jew against Muslim, Catholic versus Protestant, or Christian against Jews, Muslims, Buddhists, Hindus, and dozens of smaller sects. We only have to look at something as simple as ancestry, gender or sexual orientation to see that being different has commonly been interpreted as being wrong, or something of which to be afraid.

Joni, who had been silent up until now spoke up, "So what. We've been trying for eons to stop all the hatred but things are barely better now than they were before. What makes you think that you and my Dad can change anything?"

Joni had spent eight years working as a dispatcher for the Los Angeles Police department. Her earlier idealism, so typical of young college students, had faded as she saw the realism of life from her unique vantage point. Every single day she handled the 9-1-1 calls for help. Dealing with murder, rape, robbery, assault, arson, are all a part of her job. The spiritual messages teach love and kindness, yet the real world is just the opposite. I too wondered if we could make a difference.

"Because Joni," Mike replied, "we have to. There's too much at stake. The survival of this planet hinges on enough people becoming enlightened in time to reverse the current trend towards global annihilation. You're right, your dad and I can't single-handedly change everyone, but what if we could get our message into the hands of a few key people who have millions of followers or fans? For example, take Oprah Winfrey. She's a remarkable charismatic lady who's already well along her spiritual path. She's not just an entertainer, she's a highly evolved spiritual being. Every day she influences millions of people in a positive way. If she resonates with our message, she will be an enormously powerful force for planting the seed of truth in people. Find ten more people like her and you can change the world.

"Then Scott, as our message—actually the Universe's message—becomes accepted and integrated into our culture, people will start using the new terminology and doing so they will gradually start shifting from the old violent way. Situations that would have created hatred before will be viewed differently. For example, now when two strangers, one black and one white, see each other, there is often suspicion or hate. Imagine how different their feelings would be if they both were aware they had lived lifetimes as a member of the other's race. They would no longer see themselves as different but just playing reverse roles this lifetime. Solutions to problems will shift to align with the Universe's truths.

"So, Scott, when do we start?"

"I need some time to think it over first and talk to my wife. My big concern is for the safety of my family, and it's obvious that someone doesn't like what you're promoting. Who are the people after you and why do they want to kill you?"

"Scott, I truly understand your concern. Once I explain to you how the Universe is structured, and how we souls cycle through different lifetimes, you'll be able to understand at a much deeper level. For now let me just say we're dealing with some Baby Souls and Young Souls acting out the negative side of their soul age."

"Whoa! Not so fast Mike. What do you mean by Baby Souls? Young Souls? Negative side of soul age?"

"According to the knowledge I've received from higher dimensions, souls can be put into categories based on the number of lifetimes they have lived, lessons completed, experiences gained, and karma repaid."

"Wait. You're saying that all souls fall into different categories? I thought all souls were equal?"

"They are in terms of the bigger picture but souls evolve at different rates. As I'll explain in more detail later Scott, there are seven different main categories of soul age with seven sub-levels within each of the soul ages. Where you are in terms of your soul age can have a major effect on the type of issues you deal with in a lifetime. Whether you respond positively or negatively is up to you.

"The problem occurs when one particular group of people, all the same soul age, try to force their viewpoints and issues on the other soul types. This creates a clash of souls that's destructive to everyone. This clash of soul ages is responsible for most of the hatred and violence in the world today."

"Okay, I think I understand what you're saying, Mike. If a group of souls are all at the same point in their evolution they could think their particular viewpoints are right and other souls with differing views are wrong."

"That's correct, Scott. The punk that tried to knife me belongs to a group of people who are predominantly Baby Souls, called Defenders of God, or DOG. They're super right-wing religious fanatics determined to use terror to ram their viewpoints down the throats of everyone else. As best I can tell DOG is headquartered in southern Mississippi, with a loose network spread around the United States, Canada and Europe.

"Their leader is a man by the name of Calvin K. McCallum. We have learned that he is in his late 60's and an ex-military hero. He went from First Lieutenant to Captain in the Korean War, then to a full bird Colonel in Viet Nam. He earned enough medals to be on the fast track to becoming a General when his career was cut short by racial accusations that forced him to retire. According to my sources he deliberately assigned black officers and black enlisted men to the most dangerous missions in Nam. As a result, five times as many black soldiers were killed under his command as white soldiers. He shrugged it off by saying blacks weren't as good as whites. He would quote the original clause in the U.S. Constitution that implied blacks were worth 3/5s of what a white male was worth. McCallum sent a lot of courageous black soldiers to their death. He's an evil cold-blooded killer.

"The west coast regional DOG leader is a man named Wolfe Drake. He's a forty-something former house painter who served a few years in prison for some aggravated assault charges. Now he gets his followers, mostly young confused kids off the streets, to do his dirty work. The punk you saw try to knife me was one of his gullible stooges.

"Like the White Supremacists, he recruits these punks by making them feel important—convincing them that they are superior to blacks, Jews, and just about everyone that isn't a white Anglo-Saxon Christian. They take passages from the Bible and interpret them to support their views, so even whites are targets if they subscribe to a different spiritual interpretation than DOG's. By the time Drake gets through his brainwashing he's turned lonely kids, mostly social outcasts, into vicious little monsters thinking they are the only hope for the salvation of the planet.

"The Fed's have been tracking McCallum for several years but he's cagey. Apparently, a few years ago, McCallum thought DOG's West Coast operations had been infiltrated by the FBI so he ordered Drake to flush out the spy. Drake launched what he called Operation Chili Dip where he required each one of his people to kill an illegal alien crossing the Rio Grande from Mexico into the U.S. We got word that two of his men failed the test. They shot at Mexicans in the river but missed. Either they were spies or bad shots. Drake didn't care which. He figured either way he was better off without them. Both disappeared under mysterious circumstances and haven't been heard from since.

"Now that's become part of his rite of initiation. According to a defector, who is now missing, Wolfe Drake and McCallum like to pick on wetbacks because they're brown-skinned, Catholic, non-American, and entering the U.S. to steal jobs away from hard-working Americans.' I won't sugar coat the situation for you—these are very dangerous and very sick people.

"There are some other people who are trying to stop my message but right now DOG is the most active group.

"Now before you start thinking I'm the Lone Ranger taking on an army of bad guys, let me assure you there is a team of good guys out there helping me."

"Well, that's refreshing to hear" I said.

Chapter 3

I noticed Mike's eyes dart from me to the stairway. Then he gave a slight flip of his head indicating to someone to come over to our table. At first I thought he was calling the waitress then I turned my head and saw some huge grungy looking biker type with a pot belly swaggering towards us. As Mike scooted over one chair towards the window and the burly biker dumped his massive body into the chair, Mike caught the surprised look on my face and Joni's. "Folks, I'd like you to meet Pudgy Walters. Pudge, this here's Scott Hunter and his daughter Joni."

Joni gave a weak little, "Hi." It was obvious she was not feeling comfortable and not enjoying the stench of old dried sweat emanating from him. I extended my hand and found it engulfed in Pudgy Walters massive beefy paw and his vise-like grip. I figured Pudgy to be late forties, about six-five, three hundred twenty-five pounds. He had long scraggly brown-gray hair that hadn't seen any shampoo in quite a while. The top of his head was covered with a greasy scarf knotted in the back that appeared to be a small American flag. Betsy Ross was probably turning over in her grave. With all his tattoos and pierced rings Pudgy was a walking advertisement for body mutilation. From his tattoos I deduced he rode a Harley Davidson, liked cobras, loved his mother, the Grateful Dead and once had somewhat serious relationships with various women named Maria, Shirley and Olga, plus served in Nam. Beneath his worn, grease-stained black leather vest he wore a black sleeveless T-shirt that had imprinted in blood red the motto on the New Hampshire state flag, "Live Free or Die."

Mike, apparently sensing that Pudgy was not making a great first impression, quickly stepped in and said, "Pudge, is one of the good guys helping us. Last October when I was shot at he caught the two guys and did a number on them. Before turning them over to the cops, he managed to break one guy's jaw and three ribs on the other dude. You never saw any two punks happier to see the cops arrive."

Pudgy spoke, "Mike, I just heard about what happened. Hey man, you can't go out in public without having backup. You know that."

"It's okay, Pudge, this time my Guides told me to do it. You're looking at the reason why. Scott is the person who's going to help us get out the *Message*. He's a writer and the knife incident was simply the Universe's way of getting us together. I was in no real danger this time." With that he pulled the hunting knife out of his jacket pocket and handed it to Pudgy who looked at it carefully before sliding it into an outside knife pocket on his right boot.

Pudgy turned his piercing blue-gray eyes on me and said, "No shit. You the writer? Where the hell you been man? We been waitin' over two friggin' years."

Suddenly feeling a little intimidated I said, "Look I'm sorry. Until a half hour ago I didn't know anything about Mike and what he's up to. But, frankly I don't know enough right now to say yes. I'm already writing a book that should take me till the end of the year to finish."

"Listen up man" Pudgy replied while wagging his right index finger in my face, "We can't wait till next year to get the show on the road. There ain't no goddamned book more important than this one." Then, pointing at Mike he added, "See this man here? He's given his life to gettin' the *Message* out. This ain't about writing some lollypop-assed cookbook and spendin' your life at prissy little book signings and tea parties at some rich bitch's mansion. This is about gettin' out a message so damn powerful it can change the course of humanity and stop all the friggin' killings and hatred."

Sensing that Pudgy was about to tear my head off if I said no, I blurted out, "Okay, okay, just let me talk to my wife first."

"Talk to your wife first? What the hell are you man, some goddamned little pussy-whipped pansy?"

Pudgy was starting to irritate me. I was six feet tall, weighed 220 pounds, ex-military, and had played a lot of smash-mouth football, and semi-pro baseball, not to mention two years of jumping out of airplanes. So I didn't feel 'pussy-whipped pansy' was an accurate description.

Mike quickly reined in Pudgy by saying, "It's okay. Scott's with us. Let him discuss it with his wife. According to my Guides there won't be a problem." Turning to me, he added, "Scott, let me apologize for my friend's exuberance. Sometimes we get a little carried away and focused so strongly on our cause that we don't see anything else. It's of the utmost importance that your wife be involved and supportive. We can't guarantee that there won't be some possible danger, but there will be a team of people protecting you, not to mention the Universe. Today is Saturday. How about we meet Monday?"

His words calmed me down. As my blood pressure started dropping, I broke off my glaring eyeball-to-eyeball standoff with Pudgy. "Sounds okay to me," I said.

Pudgy responded, "Yeah man, I'm sorry. I just got carried away. It's just we been on the friggin' runway too damn long. It's time to get off the ground."

"Good. Everyone's happy" replied Mike, "Then Scott, let's you and me meet at Green Lake Monday around 10:00 AM. Pudgy will cover our backs during the meeting. Just be careful you're not being followed on your way to the Lake. If you're being followed, phone me and abort the meeting. Here's my cell phone number, take it and memorize it then destroy the piece of paper."

I glanced at the slip of paper, noting the Seattle area code of 206 followed by 555-6789. I repeated the number to myself three times then tore up the paper and handed it back to Mike. "Okay" I replied, "where do we meet at Green Lake?"

"We have to be careful. Drake's stooges sometimes look for me there. On the east side of Green Lake around 71st and Woodlawn, there's a bike rental place called Gregg's Greenlake Cycle. Go in there and rent an old-style one-speed black and red Schwinn.

"When you get over to the lake, you'll be near the Community Center. Get on the path there, going to your right, counter-clockwise around the lake. After going about 8/10ths of a mile you'll be at the Bathhouse Theatre. Approximately one hundred and fifty yards past the Theatre look off to your right. The terrain at that point slopes up to a grassy knoll about fifty yards off the path. On the top of the knoll you'll see two park benches. I'll be sitting on one of them wearing a faded red baseball cap and reading a newspaper. Don't stop. Just keep riding. Go all the way around the Lake again. I'll be watching to see if you're being followed. If you're being followed, I'll be reading the newspaper when you get back around. Don't stop, just keep going and call me later to reschedule. If you're not being followed, I'll have put down the newspaper. Pull off the path, lay the bike down and come join me. I'll have a brown paper bag with some sandwiches in it, and we can get started with the *Message*. Now, for security reasons let's leave here separately."

Pudgy jumped up, grabbed my hand and shook it hard. "Hot damn, now we can get the show on the road." Then he clanked away.

A minute later, Mike slid back his chair, stood up, dropped a ten and a five on the table and extended his hand. As we shook hands, he said with a twinkle in his eyes, "Scott, I'm counting on you. Don't do something stupid like screwing around with someone's wife this lifetime, and getting shot."

I laughed, "Mike, don't worry. I learned my lesson. It looks like you're the one getting shot at this time."

After he strolled away, Joni turned to me and said, "Dad, you're not going to do this are you? They were weird...and smelly. How do you know these guys didn't escape from some mental institution?"

Something inside me told me I was going to do it, but to placate my worried daughter, who didn't rely on intuition as much as I did, I said, "Don't worry, Joni, I'm going to check everything out before I commit to anything. Your plane leaves at 4:00 PM so we better get back home so you can pack." Joni is a beautiful tall slender brunette, five-foot nine, and I love her very much, but at times she treats me like I'm the child and I get frustrated with her. According to my past lives research, Joni had been my mother in my last lifetime and we are doing a common parent-child reversal this time around.

We left the Athenian Inn and as we headed for our car I stopped at a booth selling flowers and picked out a colorful spring bouquet for my wife Karen. I knew I had a tough selling job ahead of me. We caught the elevator in the Market that connects to a parking garage built on the side of the steep hill that runs from the Market down to the Elliott Bay waterfront. We located my seven-year-old Lexus ES300—my only visible reminder of my days as an advertising agency executive— and headed for the I-5 freeway. Even with 140,000 miles on it, the Lexus was still going strong. Once on the freeway, the thirteen mile drive to suburban Lynnwood went quickly. Karen and I, along with two cats and two dogs, live in a modest three-bedroom townhouse where we have turned two of the bedrooms into offices—one for Karen and one for me.

Four years earlier, I had met Karen at an advertising conference where I was one of the featured speakers. Karen was a top salesperson for a major Seattle printing company at the time. We were instantly attracted to each other. Later, we discovered that we had been together in many past lifetimes.

Two years later we married, her second and my third. We both were tired of our careers and longed to get into something more spiritually fulfilling, so we decided to leave the business world. I knew I wanted to concentrate on writing metaphysical books, particularly ones about reincarnation and past lifetimes, while Karen wanted to explore alternative healing. At age forty-three, she enrolled in the three year program to become a licensed Acupuncturist at the Northwest Institute of Acupuncture and Oriental Medicine (NIAOM). A very bright woman, she concurrently studied the latest German techniques in treating various symptoms with colored light. Additionally, we both explored very esoteric healing disciplines such as Auricular Medicine, SHEN, Reiki, Cranial Sacral work, Rolfing, and Intuitive Healing.

In spite of the fact that we both looked like two conservative straight-laced business types it would be a gross understatement

to say that we were your typical middle-aged mainstream sub-
urbanites. So, I knew Karen would at least listen to me.

When we arrived home, Joni immediately blurted out, "Karen,
we met some really weird people in the Pike Place Market."

Since Karen has been to the Market countless times, she
wasn't startled. After all, there are often a lot of strange and interesting people at the Market. As I handed Karen the flowers, I
countered Joni's negative comment by telling her to get packed
up so we could get to the airport on time. Then I said, "Yeah,
some very interesting people."

Joni, leaving the room, said "Dad, that's a gross understatement."

I quickly changed the subject by asking Karen if we had a vase
for the flowers. She said, "Scott, what's Joni talking about?"

Continuing to be evasive, I replied, "It's fairly interesting, but
let me go into the details when I get back from the airport. I've
got to get on the computer now and check out the freeways."
Seattle's freeways can become parking lots at the drop of a hat,
so I have learned to go in on the Internet, before any trip into the
city, and pull up the Washington State Department of Transporta-
tion freeway maps showing where the bottlenecks are.

Fortunately for me, there were backups on I-5 near the downtown Convention Center and at the South Center Hill, near the
exit for the airport. It gave me an excuse to get Joni out of the
house before she could influence Karen with her impressions of
Mike and Pudgy.

After a slow, hour and fifteen minutes drive we got to Seattle-
Tacoma International Airport. At the gate for her Alaska Airlines
flight to Burbank, I gave Joni a big hug and a good-bye kiss and
told her not to worry as she boarded. I reminded her to keep in
touch with her younger fifteen year old sister Alison, who lived
in Minneapolis with my last wife.

The drive back took half the time. Karen was in her office busy
studying various places to stick needles in people and making
me grateful that my days of doing school homework were long
gone. I disappeared in my office and played a few games of chess
against the computer. Not exactly in the same league as Bobby
Fischer, I played a lower level of the chess software program that

allowed me to win about 80% of the time, thereby stroking my competitive male ego.

Later, eating dinner while seated on the sofa, and watching some Discovery Channel show about droves of wildebeests trying to cross a raging river full of crocodiles, Karen asked, "What was Joni talking about?"

I replied, "I met a guy who wants me to write a metaphysical book. He'll supply the information and I do the writing. It sounds kind of interesting. I'm going to meet him Monday to learn more of the details about the subject matter and then decide."

"Well when would you do it? You're more than half done with your current book but it could take you four or five more months before you finish it. Will he wait that long?"

"That's hard to say. He maintains that my present book is premature and that writing the book with him first will help sell my book later. He thinks I have the cart before the horse."

"What do you think?"

"I'll find out more Monday and let you know."

"Joni said the people were weird. What did she mean?"

I countered, "You know Joni, she's always neat and well-groomed and they were a little scruffy looking and smelly. One guy, a biker type, had a real bad case of B. O. so she had a little trouble relating to them." I changed the subject by starting to cheer on a young wildebeest that was successfully struggling up the muddy bank escaping from the crocodiles.

Chapter 4

Monday, at 9:45 AM I parked my car and went in Gregg's Greenlake Cycle and picked out a red and black one-speed Schwinn. After leaving a credit card deposit, I hopped on the bike and headed over to the riding path.

Green Lake is a popular manmade lake located about five miles north of downtown Seattle. The path around it is close to three miles in length and is usually packed with hundreds of walkers, dog owners with their leashed pets, joggers, rollerbladers, bike riders, even fathers and mothers pushing strollers. Boat rentals, tennis courts, wading pool, baseball and soccer fields, indoor theater and community center, all add to the popularity of Green Lake. Throw in some Canadian geese, ducks, mud hens and an occasional loon, and you have one of Seattle's most enjoyable outdoor attractions. Walking around Green Lake you see everything from lean cross-country marathoners to obese office workers hoping to magically drop ten pounds before they hit the singles bars Friday after work.

Following Mike's instructions, I pedaled counterclockwise around the Lake. In no time at all I was at the Bathhouse Theater and approaching the rendezvous location. I spotted Mike. He was wearing a red baseball cap and reading a paper as he had said. I kept riding. The next time around, starting to feel a little silly like I was a ten year old playing cops and robbers, I spotted Mike. The newspaper was down so I pulled off the path, pushed the bike halfway up the hill, laid it down in the grass and walked the rest of the way to the top of the knoll. Plopping down next to Mike, I said, "Where's Pudgy?"

Mike turned so he was looking behind the bench, down the hill at a large parking lot partially obscured by trees. Through the trees, I could make out a guy who looked like he was soaking up some rays lying in the grass next to a massive Harley. "Pudgy has our back covered and as you can see we've got a great view of the pathway around the Lake. But if anything happens, we go in opposite directions. Got it?"

I nodded my head.

"You and Pudgy didn't seem to hit it off too well in the Market."

"Yeah, well I don't like having some big dumb fat Neanderthal question my masculinity."

"Before you go jumping to more conclusions, let me tell you some things about Pudgy. Appearances can be deceptive. He enrolled in Stanford as a gifted student at age sixteen with an IQ of 175. At nineteen he got his BA and his MBA at twenty. He was on the fast track to becoming some bright, and wealthy, Silicon Valley CEO. He got drafted and sent to Nam. He saw things there that are too horrible to talk about. He witnessed first hand man's inhumanity to man.

"He came back and tried to fit into society but couldn't stand what he saw and he didn't want to play the office politics essential to getting ahead in the white collar world. He dropped out and started playing the stock market. Some of his old Stanford buddies tipped him off to some hot Internet startup stocks that took off and he turned a small $10,000 inheritance into a million bucks. Now, he's probably worth three times that.

"To keep busy, as well as to keep tabs on the bad guys, he works nights as a bouncer at a blue collar bar in the Fremont district.

"Five years ago, he met and married a beautiful Asian lady by the name of Lee Chou. They live just east of the Green Lake area up near the Reservoir. When you see the place, you'll be blown away by the flowers. Pudgy grows award-winning flowers, particularly roses. His yard looks like a miniature Buchart Gardens."

Having visited the stunning floral displays many times at the world famous Buchart Gardens, on the outskirts of Victoria,

British Columbia, I was looking forward to seeing this other side of Pudgy Walters that I had never dreamed could exist.

Mike continued, "Look below the surface and you will discover a truly beautiful, spiritual person who has dedicated his life to our cause."

"Okay, I'm sorry. I take back the dumb Neanderthal remark."

At that moment, an aggressive little gray squirrel appeared in front of Mike, standing on its hind legs and chirping demandingly. With a loving smile on his face, Mike opened the brown paper bag sitting next to him on the bench, took out a small packet of unsalted sunflower seeds and rewarded the little guy. Once all the seeds were safely stuffed in his bulging cheeks the squirrel scampered away and up a nearby tree to impress his more timid mate with his success.

Brushing his hands together to get rid of the sunflower seed residue, Mike's face turned serious. He scrunched his eyes together making his long continuous eyebrow look like a caterpillar contracting it's body in the middle. "There's so much to discuss, I'm trying to figure out the best place to start," he said as he pulled two bottles of water from his bag and handed me one.

To get Mike moving forward, I said, "Why don't we start with Reincarnation? That was the thing you said the public needed to understand before they would be ready for my book."

"Good idea, Scott. Let's start with both reincarnation and karma—they tie together nicely and they make up what I call the 'Big Lie' that's been foisted upon the Judeo-Christian-Islamic world. Once we expose this lie, everything else will start to make a lot more sense."

I pulled out my trusty palm-sized Panasonic microcassette recorder and pushed the record button. I'd learned years ago that trying to take notes in longhand was not one of my strengths.

With his chin resting in the palm of his left hand, Mike started, "The simplest way to understand reincarnation is to think about a play. The soul is the actor, the character he or she is playing is the human body. The soul remains the same but, as the actor changes plays and roles, the soul changes human bodies."

"Mike, what you're saying really hits home. Only last winter

I had attended a particularly enjoyable play, and I remember my thoughts. As the curtain dropped the house lights came on and the audience rose, applauding a brilliant performance. When the curtain came up again the troupe of anxious actors scrambled back into the footlights to bow gracefully to the audience and then quickly exited into the wings. When the hoped-for applause continued and intensified, the actors raced back into the lights with the tension in their faces melting into smiles of gratitude and pride. As the beaming actors made their final exit the applause subsided and the audience filed out busily chattering about the performance.

"I sat in my seat reflecting upon what I had just witnessed. A few members of the cast were friends and I had always marveled at their ability to *become* their character and suspend reality for a period of time. They had told me that what makes an actor's performance great is his or her ability to become totally immersed into the role. To feel the character. To totally be the character for the duration of the play. I remembered Shakespeare's famous line from act II, scene 7, of *As You Like It,* spoken by Jaques, 'All the world's a stage, and all the men and women merely players. They have their exits and their entrances; and one man in his time plays many parts.'

"I had always thought his line was simply a metaphor, but then as I sat quietly contemplating, my mind went back to the performance I had just witnessed. I wondered if perhaps Shakespeare was not just using a metaphor. Was there a double meaning? Was it possible he was giving us a profound bit of knowledge of our earthly existence and I was too brainwashed by my own Christian upbringing to grasp the deeper significance of his words?"

"No, Scott, it was no metaphor. Shakespeare understood reincarnation. The dictionary defines reincarnation as 'a rebirth of a soul in a new human body.' If a person was raised in any of the most popular Western Religions the odds are excellent that they, like you, were told there is no such thing as reincarnation. However, if you were raised in an Eastern culture and religion you were more than likely taught the opposite—that reincarnation is a fact of life and we truly do live many lifetimes here on earth. Who's right? That question has been argued in theological circles for hundreds of years but generally speaking the public was never allowed to join the debate. Depending upon the culture you were raised in you were told which way to believe. Questioning what you were taught was not an option. After all, the religious leaders hundreds of years ago were among the very few who could read and write. What they wrote down on scrolls was passed down to later religious leaders and taught as the written truth. To the poor, ignorant peasant there was a spiritual mystique attached to the written word. It was sacred—something to fear and be in awe of—and since perpetuating that mystique was in the best interests of the religious leaders there was no good reason for them to rock the boat by opening the subject of past lives and reincarnation for public debate.

"While Western religions do not embrace the idea of past lives or reincarnation they do, along with virtually all religions in the world, acknowledge that *something* lives on after the physical body dies. So, at least we have agreement on one very important point—it's a starting point. If religions can agree that something called a 'soul' survives physical death, then we should only have to trace back in time to see where the divergence in thought occurred. Did the founding spiritual leaders of each religion preach the exact same message we are taught today, or was the original message altered by subsequent leaders who were less spiritual and more human? The latter appears to be the case.

"Records show that the earliest Christians, particularly the Gnostic sects, taught reincarnation as a part of Christianity. According to them, it was absolutely necessary to reincarnate in order to fulfill one's obligations under the Law of Karma. The next wave of religious leaders, men like Origen, AD 185-254, and Justin Martyr, AD 100-165, continued to teach the concept of reincarnation. Origen asked the rhetorical question, 'Is it not rational that souls should be introduced into bodies, in accordance with their merits and previous deeds?' He further stated that 'the soul has neither beginning nor end.'

"In his fascinating book, *Many Lives, Many Masters*, Brian L. Weiss, MD, a highly respected psychiatrist with impeccable scientific credentials, writes about many astonishing discoveries that he made, concerning the existence of past lives, while doing hypnotic regression on a patient named Catherine. When his results contradicted his own religious belief system he did some research and to his surprise found a wealth of information that contradicts his religious upbringing and supports the concept of reincarnation.

"He discovered that there were indeed references to reincarnation in both the Old and New Testaments. Yet why are followers of Judaism, Christianity and Islam the last to accept reincarnation? Dr. Weiss's research turned up a crucial bit of information—"In AD 325 the Roman emperor Constantine the Great, along with his mother, Helena, had deleted references to reincarnation contained in the New Testament. The Second Council of Constantinople, meeting in AD 553, confirmed this action and declared the concept of reincarnation a heresy."

"Mike, you're kidding! A Roman emperor and his mother changed Christianity? That blows my mind! Do you mean to tell me that in 1,500 years no one has gone back and dug up the truth? That we've been slavishly following a lie for all these centuries?"

"Sad to say, but that's exactly right" Mike said, "The information is out there—one only has to dig deep to discover the Truth. Reincarnation in Christian teachings did not become a problem until the politicians got mixed up in religion, and we all know how they can mess things up when they're given the slightest bit of control. From the day Constantine declared Christianity to be the official religion of the Roman empire, the true teachings of Christianity started to change to fit the political needs of the Roman emperors.

"When Justinian became emperor in AD 527, the Roman empire was rapidly crumbling. He had to deal both with military uprisings in the provinces and internal problems with the increasingly unhappy citizens of his empire. As a person with strong theological beliefs he decided it was necessary to enforce a uniform canon of belief—one that the masses would strictly follow—only he chose to side with the faction that opposed the original teachings. One hundred sixty-five bishops showed up at Constantinople, but Pope Vigilius, who opposed the Council, refused the Emperor's summons to attend and hid in a church nearby. The Council, without the Pope present, drafted 14 anathemas—official denunciations—banning the original beliefs. Since Justinian was Emperor, he enforced the anathemas even without the Pope's agreement. The Popes that followed Vigilius, from Pope Gregory on, simply accepted the Council's rulings without question."

"So, Mike, am I to assume that the underlying reason for the Emperors and bishops taking the action they did was simply a control issue?"

"That's right, Scott. They had the mistaken belief that if the ignorant, unwashed masses believed they would live life after life they would not have an incentive to obey the leaders, and instead would laugh at every order, even threats of death. You'll learn when we discuss karma why this is not the case, but now you know how two men with the title of Emperor, Constantine and Justinian, changed one of the basic truths of Christianity as originally taught by Jesus, and to this day Westerners are still being spoon-feed lies instead of facts."

Shaking my head and chuckling softly, I said, "You know, Mike, one has to admire the wisdom of America's founding fathers when they established a separation of church and state. If the U.S. government had the power to control what we could believe or not believe, it is not too much a stretch of the imagination to see that our religious teachings would have been altered even more to fit whatever political correctness was in vogue at different times in our history. There have even been a few Presidents whose personal actions would indicate that they would have rewritten a few of the Ten Commandments if they had the constitutional power vested in themselves."

"Now, Scott, here's where you have to be persuasive. Normally, explaining to people that they have erroneous information is not a problem as long as you have logic or facts to support your statement. After all, everyone wants to know the truth, but in this case—in the case of religion—which often contains deep emotional imprinting, from early childhood on, the mere act of questioning someone's deeply held beliefs can be quite tricky. People tend to admire and respect their religious leaders and accept what they say without questioning, but ultimately, it is not what the priest, pastor or rabbi says or thinks, but the truth that really matters. The leader can be wrong, as our leaders often are. So, it is important to get the point across that only the truth can set you free. It is far better to seek out the truth with a vengeance then to enact vengeance on he who brings you the truth."

"And I assume that last sentence describes you and what has happened to you."

"That's right on, Scott. The guys trying to stop me have no interest in seeking the truth. They are so locked into their false belief that they will kill anyone who questions them." Opening his brown paper bag, Mike took out a couple of fat deli sandwiches and handed me one. "I hope turkey's all right."

"Perfect," I said feeling the saliva in my mouth kick into gear. I hadn't realized how hungry I was until the smell of fresh turkey, dijon mustard, lettuce and tomatoes hit my nostrils. Mike ate silently for a while, looking off into the distance at a couple of eight man racing shells practicing on the smooth dark emerald colored water of Green Lake.

Chapter 5

I broke the silence by asking, "Mike, how do you prove reincarnation? Once a human body dies, it can't return in the same form. I know there are stories about ghosts and there are thousands of documented cases of 'Near Death' experiences, but 100% absolute proof doesn't exist."

"Scott, you hit on the problem. There isn't 100% proof available while we're in the Physical Plane of existence. Once we die, or drop this body, we instantly know, but that doesn't help us here. Instead, we have to rely on logic and all the anecdotal data that supports the concept. For example, Dr. Ian Stevenson, a highly respected Professor of Psychiatry at the University of Virginia Medical School, has written five books based on his worldwide research into case histories of children who, at a young age, appear to have retained memories of a former life. Dr. Stevenson's well-documented work shows that children between two and four are of the best age to remember a past life. Apparently, sometime between age five and eight children begin to forget their memories of past lives. His young subjects would oftentimes recall events, names of people, and even places where they had lived in the prior lifetime.

"While some cases were impossible to verify, Dr. Stevenson was able to substantiate a great many of his various case histories. Some children would point to a birthmark on their body and say that this was where they had been injured by a bullet, knife, or some other type of weapon, in the prior lifetime. Dr. Stevenson has examined over 200 birthmarks that children claimed were caused by a wound in a prior lifetime.

"There was a case of a boy in India who insisted that he had lived and died in another nearby village. When he was taken to the village, he identified his former wife, who was still living, and even told about something that he had buried in a secret location. He went to the hiding spot and dug up the item he had described.

"As Dr. Brian Weiss discovered, there is a wealth of information residing in books that support the concepts of past lives and reincarnation. One only has to be open-minded enough to look, and that's the problem we face. The information is out there but unfortunately it's not mainstream. It's buried in obscure books usually found only in small independent metaphysical bookstores. Scott, that's why you're here—to get this message out into the mainstream where it can be read by enough people to start making a difference.

"Try typing the word *reincarnation* into an Internet search engine. You'll be amazed at the thousands of online references waiting for you on the World Wide Web. You'll discover curious tidbits of information like the epitaph Benjamin Franklin wrote for his gravestone at the tender age of twenty-two. It reads:

'Here lies the body of Benjamin Franklin, printer.
As the cover of an old book, the content is teared
away and removed for all finery and binding. It is
lying here, as food for worms, but the work will not
be lost. Because it will come once again in a new and
more elegant edition, revised and corrected by the author.'

"While this epitaph never actually appeared on his gravestone when he died at age eighty-four, for whatever reason, it's apparent that Benjamin Franklin, one of the most brilliant minds among America's founding fathers, clearly was capable of thinking beyond the strict limitations of the prevailing religious beliefs of his time. However each person has to come to that understanding on his or her own. If our readers can accept the concept of reincarnation, then they should find the remaining information even more helpful in understanding and unraveling the mysteries of their lives.

"But, after you write the book, if readers still find the concept of reincarnation difficult to accept, don't worry. One doesn't have to believe in something for it to exist. Mankind existed for thousands of years believing the earth was flat and it didn't alter daily life one iota. When civilization had advanced to the point in time where knowledge of the earth's roundness was becoming more critical for our evolution, the knowledge appeared, as is always the case.

"When new knowledge is first presented it is usually rejected by the ruling powers of society because they have a vested interest in the status quo. The pioneers who discover new truths often are killed or persecuted, yet the truth ultimately prevails. So it is with reincarnation and the next topic, karma. Eventually everyone will believe in reincarnation and karma because they represent a universal truth. If we can convince some people and at least crack the door open a bit on others, we'll have accomplished a lot. Just getting people to consider the *possibility* can be a tremendous win particularly when we're dealing with such deeply ingrained beliefs that have been unrelentingly pounded into the minds of virtually the entire Judeo-Christian-Islamic world!"

"Mike, if you're not some wacko, and you really do have knowledge that will challenge traditional thinking, I assume you realize you're taking on, single-handedly, some of the most powerful institutions and vested interests in the world. No wonder you've been shot at and had several attempts on your life. This is big-time scary! Why are you doing this, Mike? What's in it for you?"

As he contemplatively stroked his white chin whiskers, gazing off towards the lake, he said, "I used to be an electrical engineer for a subcontractor working for NASA. It was a fairly decent job and I was doing okay. Then about ten years ago, come this May 15th, my wife Beverly, and my son Denny were killed in an auto accident. Some drunk crossed over the center line and hit them head on. They died instantly. She was forty-one and he was ten."

"Mike, I'm sorry. That had to be a tremendous emotional blow."

"At the time, we were living in Houston. I was torn up emotionally. Work was impossible. My will to live was fading fast.

"I finally packed up and moved to San Francisco—to a completely different environment to try and erase the memory. It didn't work. So I started experimenting with drugs. You name it and I probably did it. I hung out in the Haight district and started meeting people that had a totally different view of life than I had. I went to astrologers, psychics, aura readers, the whole gamut. As an engineer, I was skeptical at first but the longer I listened and the more I read metaphysical books the more I started changing.

"Between what I inherited from Bev and the life insurance money, I was okay financially, but I was still tormented inside by the deaths of Bev and Denny. I searched for some kind of answer that would explain it. All the Bible thumpers could say is 'God works in strange and mysterious ways' or 'God's just testing your faith' and crap like that. God was supposed to be all knowing and all loving so why would he take from me two of the kindest, most loving people I ever knew?

"The more I read about some of the Eastern religions and philosophies the more I realized they had answers Western religions didn't. I had been raised that they were Godless pagans worshipping idols—you know the story—the same bull your minister tried to feed you as a kid.

"I did the whole nine yards. I spent some time in an Ashram. I took trips to India and met different Gurus. Then I heard about a group of people in the Bay Area supposedly involved in channeling information from levels of higher consciousness. I decided to look at the possibility. That was ten years ago.

"For centuries there have been gifted people—whether you call them mediums, psychics, prophets or whatever, who could tune into some non-physical place or 'deity' and get information. More recently someone coined the word 'channeling' which is just another form of pulling in information from another dimension. Some mediums are good at contacting recently departed loved ones, while most of the channels I know claim they are communicating with specific entities on higher non-physical planes.

"The newsstand tabloids have had a field day with channels, often reporting their claims of being in touch with some five thousand year old Egyptian ruler, or something like that. There are a lot of fakes running around conning gullible people. Most of what they spew out is pure 'ethereal, feel-good, love thy fellow man' garbage that can't be challenged, let alone have any significant impact in your life.

"You walk away, along with two or three hundred others, having shelled out several hundred dollars to the channel. You feel good. The message was inspiring but the next day you're right back where you started—still mired deeply in the everyday muck of work and relationships. Was it for real? Who knows?

"What I discovered different about the group of channels in the Bay Area, was that they all claimed to be channeling information from the same source, and they didn't claim to have an *exclusive* connection like other channels I have encountered. Their information was more structured and verifiable to some extent through observation. Instead of useless 'feel-good' blather, they gave me information that made sense and could be applied both at work and in relationships.

"They claimed to be getting similar information from a group of approximately one thousand souls, going by the group name Michael. The group is located on a higher level called the Causal Plane. This group of channels is so non-exclusive that they will actually train anyone who's interested, in how to channel information from this entity called Michael.[1] That really piqued my interest and raised my confidence level that they were on the up-and-up. I took their training, and within a matter of months I was channeling. Mike is not my real name—I just like to use it because I'm channeling the Soul Teachings of the entity called Michael."

"So, Mike, what happens when you channel? Do you go into a deep trance like Edgar Cayce?" Cayce, who died in the 1940's, is widely recognized as America's greatest medium. He would go into a deep trance and come up with all sorts of amazing data. Some doctors even used him to diagnosis their most difficult medical cases. All of his work is documented and available for researchers to study at the Edgar Cayce Institute in Virginia Beach, Virginia.

1. See Appendix B for a list of Michael channels.

"No Scott, I've studied Cayce, and I don't operate like he did. All of the Michael channels I know go into a light trance and we all use our normal voices. There's no hocus-pocus where the channel suddenly changes their personality and talks in a weird spooky voice. In some of our future meetings I'll demonstrate how I channel.

"But, a few minutes ago you asked 'what's in it for me?' I don't need money. I'm quite comfortable. What I'm after is spiritual fulfillment. In the Michael Soul Teachings, all people fall into one of seven different roles. My role for this lifetime and a series of lifetimes, is that of a *Priest*. It doesn't mean I should be a priest in the formal sense, just that I have a message that I believe in strongly and my happiness comes from sharing it with others and enriching their lives. Your role is that of a *Scholar*. I'll go into your role and the other five roles later."

The roar of a Harley broke the tranquillity of the setting. Mike and I both turned our heads and looked down at the parking lot and saw Pudgy revving up his Hog.

"Trouble" said Mike as he quickly grabbed up the remains of his brown bag meal. "That's the signal someone's arrived. Get on your bike and leave. Don't panic. Just act normal. They don't know you yet. I'll contact you later." He disappeared down the hill, away from the parking lot.

I spotted an old maroon Dodge Caravan slowly circle the lot, then stop near the pathway leading from the parking lot to the Lake, about one hundred yards north of our location. Two men jumped out of the van, opened the rear door and pulled out two bikes. I quickly walked down the hill, picked up my bike and started pedaling counter clockwise around the lake.

After about a mile, I reached the Boathouse. I got off the bike and ducked into the men's room to relieve myself. When I came out, I could see the two guys approaching on their bikes. They stopped about one hundred feet away and were talking to some people walking around the lake, apparently asking for some kind of information. Then they headed straight for me. I suddenly recognized the lead guy as the lone attacker with the knife at the Pike Place Market. Would he recognize me? What should I do if he does? My heart started to pound. Where the

Hell are the cops when you need them? I slipped my sunglasses on and started to mount my bike.

Before I could pedal away he stopped his bike beside me and said, "Hey, Buddy, we're bounty hunters and we're looking for some bad-ass dude who jumped bail." His sunglasses covered his eyes but I noticed he was in his early twenties, shaved head, ears that stuck out too far, a thick bushy red mustache that drooped around the corners of his mouth. His teeth were yellow and badly stained. His build was muscular, about five foot eleven and one hundred eighty pounds. His attire today was much neater than the drab, nondescript outfit he wore at the Market. His sleeveless T-shirt was khaki colored and tucked neatly into his camouflage colored trousers which in turn were tucked into a pair of shiny black boots. He probably just got out of the military. Around his neck was a chrome-plated cross on a chain with two stainless steel dog tags.

His cohort, a shorter, stockier version, wearing a black turtle-neck with camouflage pants and black boots, shoved a piece of paper in my face. "This is the scumbag we're trackin' down. You seen 'em?" I looked at the paper. The heading said, WANTED. Under it was a fairly good hand-drawn likeness of Mike with the name David Ruben under it. So, Mike's real name is David Ruben. The subhead said something about unlawful flight to avoid prosecution. Prosecution for what it didn't say. It was obvious that it was not an official wanted poster. I held it in my hand for a moment and was about to send them on a wild-goose chase, but since I didn't know where Mike hangs out or where he was headed, I decided to play dumb. "Naw, I don't think so. He looks like a thousand other old men ya see everyday. What did the guy do?"

"We told ya—he jumped bail."

"No, I heard that. I meant what crime did he commit before he jumped bail?"

The first guy spoke, "Come on Ernie, this shithead doesn't know squat. Let's get going." Ernie grabbed the paper out of my hand and off they went. Since bikes all have to circle the lake in the same counterclockwise direction, I followed discreetly behind Mr. Knife and Ernie. Every so often they would stop somebody and show them the picture—apparently with no luck. When they got around to the Community Center they pulled off the path. The maroon Caravan was waiting for them in the adjacent parking lot. While Ernie loaded the bikes in the van, Mr. Knife and the driver walked over to an outdoor vendor's stand near the boat rental building and got three coffees. I stopped as close as I could, and sat with my back to them, on a raised concrete bulkhead separating the parking lot from the path. I pretended I was soaking up some sun. I could just barely make out what they were saying.

"Nobody knows shit man. Who gave us this bum tip?"

"It was this dumb broad Drake knows. She works around here somewhere. She said she seen him when she was takin' her jog around the lake."

"Yeah, well, she's full of shit."

"Hey man, you say that to Drake and he'll tear your fucking balls off. As long as he's dickin' the stupid bitch, you keep your mouth shut. I'm gonna call Drake and see what we do next."

I turned to see who was calling and spotted the driver with a cell phone in his hand. He was thirtysomething, about six two, lean build, probably one hundred seventy pounds. His hair was close-cropped and looked like it was growing out from having been shaved a few weeks ago. "Yo Colonel, this is Mitch. We're at Green Lake. Carla's tip didn't pan out. I checked all the parking lots and Reamer and Ernie went around the path showing the picture to everyone." After a long pause, Mitch said, "Okay. Got it. We'll stop there and check things out then be back at HQ at 1300 hours." As they jumped in the van and took off I noticed the van had an Idaho license plate.

Compared to the rather solitary life of an author, cooped up in an office keystroking away at a computer, this morning had been exciting. I had gotten some fascinating information from Mike—also known as David Ruben—had a run-in with the bad guys and even learned their names. Mr. Knife is called Reamer, and I have no desire to find out how he got the nickname. His sidekick is Ernie. Wolfe Drake has a girlfriend named Carla. Mitch, the driver, seems to be higher in rank than Reamer or Ernie. They drive a maroon Dodge Caravan with Idaho plates, and these guys are into playing soldier, both in their attire and their vocabulary.

I returned my rented bike to Gregg's Greenlake Cycle, hopped in my old Lexus, headed for the nearest on-ramp and was soon on my way to Lynnwood. Karen was in her office studying for an upcoming midterm so I just said Hi, gave her a soft kiss on her neck, and went into my office and turned on my Power Mac. I logged onto AOL, checked my e-mails, deleting all the usual online offers to meet 'naughty nurses,' 'sultry coeds with insatiable sexual appetites,' and 'hot teens in black leather.' I couldn't decide whether the sex e-mails or the endless mortgage refinancing offers were the most annoying.

Being an author means discipline. Since you usually work out of your home, you need enough discipline to get started every day and avoid the trap of getting sucked into doing chores instead of writing. After twelve years as an international award-winning advertising Creative Director and Copywriter, I had no problem with time management. In the advertising game, I always faced tight deadlines. There was no time to procrastinate or get writer's block. Clients and the agency account executives always expected miracles and I had a reputation for always getting my work done on time.

Away from the enormous pressures of the ad game, I allowed myself a slightly more relaxed schedule, but nevertheless I was a stickler for putting in time at the keyboard. My typical day consisted of getting up around eight, showering, shaving and downing a quick breakfast. If it was a day Karen has acupuncture school, I would usually drive her there. I'd be back home ready to write by 10:00 AM.

My daily target is one thousand words. I had once read somewhere that John Grisham, the best-selling author, wrote five hundred words a day. Since my life was not as complicated as his, I decided one thousand words would be an achievable daily goal, excluding of course, days when I had to go somewhere to do research. My weekly goal was five thousand words. If I wasn't at my goal by Friday night, I would do writing over the weekend to stay on target. I occasionally will log in a day where I can write over two thousand words. I can write, with only minor breaks, for five to six hours a day. After that, my brain becomes as mushy as a bowl of corn flakes left in milk all day.

Today, before I started writing, I had to decide whether to continue working on my past life book or start on Mike's book. As I mulled over the pros and cons, Karen stuck her head in my office. "So, my sexy husband, how did your meeting go?"

At forty-three, Karen was still a knockout. Five-foot five, one hundred twenty pounds and the picture of good health—trim with short blond hair and an infectious smile that revealed near perfect teeth. She projected an air of quiet competence and was well liked by almost everyone she met.

Having only been married two years, we still were in the honeymoon phase and were both determined to make it last forever. That meant being attentive to each other's needs and not taking each other for granted.

I beckoned Karen into my office. "Do you have a minute to talk?"

She responded with a tired sigh. "Yeah. I need a break. For the last three hours, I've been studying Zang Fu pathology and I still need to spend some time on acupuncture points and meridians. Let me go grab us some tea first."

A few minutes later she came back with two cups of steaming hot Tazo Green Ginger tea. Picking up the packet of tea, I noticed the slogan under the Tazo name, 'The Reincarnation of Tea.' Turning the packet so she could read the slogan, I said, "How prophetic. That was what I spent my morning discussing—reincarnation. Mike, the guy I told you about seems legit. His logic about writing his book first does make more sense than finishing mine now. I hate to stop mid-stream but I think it's the right thing to do."

"You refer to it as his book, but who gets the credit as the author and what about royalties and all that mundane stuff?" At times, Karen can be brutally practical and does a great job of waking me up when my left brain falls asleep.

"I don't know yet, he said he didn't need any money, but those are things I have to nail down the next time we get together. Our meeting ended before I could ask." I knew I had to tell her about the downside, but I had to do it carefully.

"Karen, the only problem I see is that the book's message is controversial and there are a few kooks who'll be upset when it's published."

"Well, isn't your book about past lives controversial?"

"Good point. The big difference is Mike's message is even more controversial and he apparently has already stirred up some of the crazies. And, it hasn't even been written."

I sipped my tea, staring off into space, "Karen, do you remember when I told you about my past? How, after six years, I gave up a promising career as a Merrill Lynch stockbroker, and I became a professional astrologer?"

"Yeah, you made one of the strangest career changes I've ever heard of. But what does that have to do with this situation?"

"At the time, I started an astrology association. To get it going I posted flyers around town promoting the first meeting to be held in a public auditorium that I had rented for the night. I got to the auditorium about two hours early to check everything out. Shortly after I arrived, I got a phone call. It was a bomb threat telling me to cancel the meeting. I had a choice, cancel and cave in to the threat or stand my ground. I found the building's custodian and determined that the auditorium had been tightly locked up all day so it would have been difficult for someone to plant a bomb. I then, all by myself, searched the entire auditorium looking for a bomb. I didn't find one so I decided to hold the meeting as scheduled. Nothing happened. It was a hoax.

"Later, I opened an astrology bookstore and school and about six months later the same thing happened. Another bomb threat. Since the store was locked when I wasn't there it would be difficult for someone to plant a bomb so my main worry was what might happen at night when the store was closed. It was possible someone would drive by and toss a molotov cocktail through the front window and burn the place to the ground. My decision was to stand my ground, so I spent the next several nights in the store in my sleeping bag, with a fire extinguisher and a gun at my side, ready to defend my property and what I believe in. Fortunately, it turned out to be just another false alarm.

"Both of us, you with alternative medicine, and me with metaphysics, have made a conscious decision to take a stand for something we believe in rather than caving in to what is currently politically correct. Forty years ago, acupuncture was not allowed in this country. Western medicine considered it a primitive and ineffective medical treatment—something from the Dark Ages. Nowadays, some HMOs are even offering it as an optional form of health care for specific ailments. So, progress is being made but as we've discussed many times, there are dozens of other forms of alternative medicine that are laughed at even though we have personally seen them work phenomenally well.

"Eventually, they will become mainstream, but in the meantime, a lot of practitioners are going to be persecuted."

"I understand all that, Scott. Where are you going with this discussion?"

"I want to write the book with Mike, but I need to be upfront with you and tell you there can potentially be some trouble because of the subject matter."

Karen got up from the chair she was sitting in, walked to the door, turned in the doorway and said, "Several gifted psychics and channels have told us that we are on the correct path towards fulfilling our life's purpose. So, if we're doing what we're supposed to this lifetime, I don't see how we can back down. We would have failed. No, I don't want to back down and I know you don't either. I'll support you no matter what."

"Thank you."

I knew I'd have to bring Karen up to date on the bad guys soon but for now I needed to start keystroking—transcribing today's notes from Mike on reincarnation.

Chapter 6

The next day, while I was driving Karen to school, I quickly brought her up to date on the bad guys who were after Mike. Commuter traffic on I-5 was at a crawl except in the car-pool lane where we were. By the time we reached the 50th Avenue exit, I had finished my abbreviated version of what had transpired to date.

"Has Mike talked to the police?" Karen asked with apprehension in her voice.

I responded, "I don't know, but if he hasn't I'm going to insist that he does."

"Good. I'll feel a lot better if the police start watching these guys before things get out of hand."

Minutes later I swung into the parking garage under the building NIAOM shares with Adobe and several other high tech companies. I always thought it rather ironic that an acupuncture school, teaching one of the world's oldest known forms of medicine, share a building with companies creating the newest technology. I dropped Karen off and headed back home.

Going North, against rush hour traffic, made this part of my twenty-six-mile round trip go smoothly. I had to consciously hold the Lexus down to five miles over the posted 60 MPH speed limit. As I neared the county line between King County, where Seattle is located, and Snohomish County, where we lived, my cell phone's irritating beep-beep, startled me out of my enjoyment of a Kenny G tune being played on the smooth jazz station I favored.

I answered the call and heard Mike's voice. "Scott, there's been some trouble. Can you talk?"

"Yeah, Mike, what's up?"

"I think DOG struck again. Early this morning—around 2:00 AM—on Capitol Hill, two gay guys, one black and the other white, were badly beaten up. One's dead and the other is in intensive care at Harborview Hospital. He gave the cops a description that makes me think it was Drake's goons."

Capitol Hill is a combination commercial and residential district of Seattle east of downtown. Broadway, the main commercial street, runs north-south, and is a hangout for young adults, college students, gays, lesbians, and the body-piercing, pink hair, and tattoo crowd. One of the more liberal in Seattle, it has been a fairly safe place for people seeking and living alternative lifestyles.

"Apparently," Mike continued, "a dark colored van with five or six militia type skin-heads, drove along side and started yelling obscenities at the gay couple shortly after they left a cafe. After a block or so, they stopped, got out of the van and started a fight with the gay couple. In a matter of seconds the gays were on the ground being brutally kicked.

"The fight escalated with the black survivor, being pinned to the ground, knifed three or four times, and then castrated. Unconscious he was left to die. The white guy was found nearby with the black guys genitals shoved in his mouth. A shotgun had been rammed up his butt and the trigger pulled. By the time someone called 9-1-1 the attackers had disappeared, driving away without lights on so no one could get a license plate number."

"The residents of Capitol Hill and the Gay community are going ballistic. The Mayor and the City Council are all over the Chief of Police's back demanding immediate action. The Chief has called in the Feds to get some of the pressure off his back. It's being labeled a hate crime."

"How did you find out all this information, Mike? The police don't give out many details."

"That's why I'm calling you, Scott. I told you I had people supporting my efforts including local police and FBI agents. They tipped me off immediately and wanted to know if I had any information to help them nail Drake. I told them about yesterday at Green Lake and they want to question you. I said I'd set it up.

Where are you now?"

"I just pulled off the freeway and I'm heading north on 44th Avenue in Lynnwood. I'm almost home."

"Sorry to do this but you need to turn around and get downtown to the FBI office pronto. Their address is 915 Second Avenue—near Madison Street—in the Federal Building. I'll meet you in the reception area."

"I'm on my way," I said as I disconnected.

Twenty minutes later I pulled into a parking garage and walked a block to the Federal Building. Mike was right where he said he'd be. "You made that pretty fast."

"I got lucky."

"They're waiting for us, I'll tell them you're here," Mike said as he walked over to a receptionist, a young black woman with beautiful brown eyes, speaking into her phone. She told Mike in a soft warm voice, "Special Agent Connors will be right with you."

Almost instantly, two men, one white and one black, both dressed in conservative gray suits, white shirts and boring striped ties, came around the corner. The white guy appeared to be in his mid-fifties, about six three and two hundred twenty-five pounds. His steel-blue eyes were boring into me. This guy meant business. The black guy was younger, early thirties, about an inch shorter and thirty pounds lighter. He had a nice bright intelligent look about him that made me think of Denzel Washington, one of my favorite actors.

The white guy spoke first, "This the guy, Mike?"

"Yeah, Wes, this is Scott Hunter. Scott, special agents Wes Connors and Tyrone Willis, they're part of a special FBI Task Force tracking hate crimes."

After the customary handshakes and hellos, agent Willis led us to a nearby conference room. Mike and I sat on one side of a putty-colored metal table with a walnut laminate top. Nice for a government table but a notch or two below corporate America. Connors and Willis took the chairs opposite us.

"Mike tells us you might have some information that could help our investigation," Connors said as he pulled out a small narrow notebook and Cross pen from his inside jacket pocket.

Mike interrupted, "Scott, after our meeting broke up, Pudgy followed the van and saw you sitting close to the guys. He figured you might have overheard something."

"Yeah I did. First two of them got on bikes and went around the lake. They stopped me, and almost everyone else on the path, and showed an artist's sketch of you on some fake wanted poster. I got a good look at them. They met up with the van near the community center."

As Connors and Willis rapidly scribbled notes, I gave a complete description of the van and three guys.

Connors spoke, "Mike's buddy, Pudgy Walters, got the van's license plate number. We ran it and it turned up belonging to a retired couple in Idaho—up near Lewiston. Agents out of our Spokane office talked to the couple a few hours ago. They sold it two or three months ago to their nephew. Apparently, he never transferred the title with the DMV. He was in the Marines, stationed at San Diego, until he got in trouble and was booted out. The couple thought he was back in Southern California. The nephew's name is Ernest Goddard, nickname Ernie."

Willis fanned six mug shot photos in front of me. I immediately spotted Ernie and tapped on his photo. "That's him, and this other guy looks a lot like Mitch. I don't see the guy they call Reamer."

"Okay" Willis added, "We'll show you some more photos and if we don't have any luck we'll have an artist do a sketch."

Connors, looking at Mike, said, "The good news is, we can tie Goddard to the van and being in the Seattle area at the time of the attack. The crime lab was able to pick up a tire tread impression. There was some oily scum on the street and the van drove through it leaving a nice track on the dry pavement. For once, it didn't rain here last night." Turning to Tyrone Willis, Connors said, "Ty, I need to check with the Seattle PD— can you handle the photo ID with Scott?"

"Sure thing, Wes."

Connors left and Willis excused himself to get more photos for me to examine. Mike put his left arm on my shoulder and said, "Scott, this is why the world needs you to write the book. This hatred and violence has to come to an end. Once people understand the message we have, they'll realize that we have all been different races, practiced different religions, and almost all of us have lived gay lifetimes. When a soul lives several consecutive lives as the same gender, then switches gender, they often find the first few lifetimes difficult from a gender perspective. The natural tendency is to relate better to the former gender. If both the gay and non-gay communities understood this there would be no reason to hate one another.

"Over the course of several hundred incarnations the soul of each one of us gets to experience all the variations of human existence. In effect, we all get to play a huge variety of roles. These very scumbags who attacked the two gays could very well be gay themselves in a future lifetime. The white, skin-head, neo-Nazi might be Jewish in his next lifetime.

"The more we understand the Universal Laws, the sooner we will come to view people as souls playing different roles and gaining the experiences a particular role has to offer. The secret is knowing how to play your role.

"Sports is a good example. The competitors can be going at each other as hard as possible, according to the agreed upon rules, then when the contest is over they can shake hands and go out for a beer together.

"You'll often see two political commentators, one conservative and one liberal, aggressively arguing with each other. Then when the show is over, they laugh and resume their friendship. That is the way to play your role using the Universal Laws.

"There is so much more I'll share with you about how the Game of Life is played, but I think you can see how critical it is to change the mindset of the masses about reincarnation."

"You're right, Mike," I said. This old bullshit about my skin is a better color than yours or my religion is right and yours is wrong, has got to stop. What about Connors and Willis, have you known them for awhile?"

"Yeah, Wes and I go back about eight years. I've known Ty for three years. About two years ago they used me as a volunteer decoy to trap another group of Calvin McCallum's hoods. This was before DOG brought in Wolfe Drake to run the west coast operation.

"Wes was born in Hong Kong. His father was British, stationed in Hong Kong as a high British official in the government. His mother was American—teaching English at the University of Hong Kong. He was raised with a strong eastern understanding of reincarnation and karma so Wes doesn't have the usual Judeo-Christian-Islamic hang-ups about what I'm promoting.

"On the other hand, Tyrone Willis is still a little skeptical but open minded enough to give the concept a chance. The guy's credentials are something else. Ivy league with honors, law degree, ex-military, Gulf War Intelligence, and one helluva marksman; winning the regional FBI handgun competition three years in a row. He volunteered for the hate crimes task force. Wes won't give me the details, but said Ty has some past personal experience with right wing militia hate groups."

Willis walked back into the room with an armful of photos and files that I spent the next half-hour sorting through, without identifying Reamer. Willis picked up the phone and asked an artist to join us. While we waited, Willis surreptitiously handed me a manila file folder. "Wes said to give this to you unofficially. This is not exactly policy, but Mike has been a tremendous help to us, even risking his life once. So, since you're working with Mike you need some information on DOG and photos of the key players. It might help keep you alive."

I opened the file and flipped through the pages until I came to a photo of Calvin K. McCallum. He is sixty-nine, but looked more like a seventy-five or eighty years old man who had been exposed to the sun for too many years. His sagging upper eyelids formed little fleshy hoods shading his deep-set yellow-brown eyes, while the bags under his eyes hung down to his cheekbones. Deep-set wrinkles were formed around the corners of his eyes and long vertical wrinkles sagged down each side of his face, turning into jowls of flesh below a firm-set jaw line. A small scar ran from his thin lips to the tip of his chin. His slightly receding hair was a course, wiry gray-white. His unruly dark brown eyebrows were pinched together at his nose—a bulbous glob of flesh covered with purple spider veins common among heavy drinkers. McCallum had the look of a strong ruthless leader who had survived many a battle.

Looking over my shoulder, Tyrone interrupted my perusal of the photo and spoke, "I'd give a year's pay to nail that bastard. He's slippery. Every time we get close he manages to beat the rap. Usually the witness testifying against him disappears or has some fatal accident. It's a long shot but we're hoping we can get some of the local thugs to testify against both Drake and McCallum in exchange for no prison time. Unfortunately, most of his men are willing to do time. They have a lot of buddies already behind bars so when they do serve time it's like an Aryan brotherhood reunion."

There was a soft rap on the door and in walked the artist, a small, delicate man about forty. He wore thin wire frame glasses perched on a thin nose with light brown hair pulled back into a short ponytail. Tyrone introduced him as Larry Westcott. His limp handshake reminded me of squeezing a warm wet sponge. Larry quickly set up his drawing tablet and started asking me questions. I interrupted him to say, "I thought you guys no longer sketch the faces by hand. On TV the artist shows the witness thirty different looking noses, they pick the right one, and then do the same procedure for the other face parts."

With a feminine flip of his hand and a deep sigh, Larry said, "Yes. That's quite true Mr. Hunter. Most artists do it that way now, but I've been at it so long I guess I'm a little old-fashioned, besides the new ones would have trouble drawing thirty different noses. The art schools are absolutely hideous these days. Now, let's start with the overall shape of the face."

Within fifteen minutes, Larry had created an exact duplicate of Reamer. I had to admit I was impressed with his skill.

Tyrone said, "Thanks, Scott. You too, Mike. That's all we need now. We'll be in touch if we need more information. I've been told there is a crowd of reporters in the lobby so you two may want to exit through the garage."

As we got into the elevator and punched "G" Mike took out his cell phone and said, "I've got an idea, Scott."

He punched in a number and as the elevator reached the garage level Mike said "Hello? Hello? Is this Connie?"

There was a brief pause then Mike continued, "Can you join me for an early lunch? I have an important friend I want you to meet."

"Ivar's. Pier 54. Outside."

"I'm on my way there now."

"Don't bother. I just met with them. I can give you more information."

"Bye."

We exited the building and headed for my car. $8.00 later the Lexus was freed from the parking garage. I said, "I'm assuming I should head down to Ivar's, right?"

"Right. I asked a woman by the name of Connie Kamura to join us. She's a staff columnist for the Seattle Times who understands a lot about reincarnation and karma. She also has written some blistering articles about hate groups. It turns out she was waiting in the FBI lobby hoping to get some of the details about the attack on the gays. You'll like her. She's a very bright young woman. Her parents and grandparents were put in a Japanese internment camp in Utah during World War II. She got her Journalism degree from the University of Oregon and a Masters in Far Eastern Religions and Philosophy from the University of Hong Kong."

Getting from the Federal Building to the waterfront took only a few minutes. I found parking next to the railroad tracks directly across the street from Ivar's.

Chapter 7

L ocated on the waters of Elliott Bay, Ivar's has been a Seattle landmark since 1938. Now there are several indoor locations around the metro area, but I still like the nostalgia of the outdoor one at Pier 54. Far from fancy, Ivar's is a walk-up and order, fast-food operation.

I went for a cup of Ivar's famous clam chowder and halibut and chips. Mike chose the clam nectar with halibut and chips. We carried our trays over to an outside picnic table overlooking the water between Pier 54 and the next pier where two Seattle fire boats were tied up and gently bobbing up and down. Just to the South of us was Pier 52, the Washington State Ferry Terminal, where we could see ferries coming and going to Bainbridge Island, Bremerton and Vashon Island. Very picturesque. I took a deep breath, inhaling the unique smells of Ivar's—a mixture of seaweed, barnacles, ferry exhaust, clams, tarter sauce and deep-fat fried halibut.

No sooner had we sat down than a dozen gray and white seagulls descended upon us—some circling in the air only a few feet above our heads and others standing on the railing a few feet in front of us, cocking their heads from side-to-side waiting for a handout.

Mike, spotting a woman crossing the street, presumably Connie, waved his hand. She waved back, then headed over to the counter to order. A few minutes later, tray in hand, she joined us. "Connie, this here is Scott Hunter. Scott, meet Connie Kamura." We shook hands. Her grip was firm and her dark eyes had a look of slight curiosity in them. I'd guess she was thirty-five, five-foot four, one hundred ten pounds, and knew who she was and where she was going in life. A modern career woman who had achieved the delicate balancing act between femininity and aggressiveness in the business world. The lack of a wedding ring led me to believe that she was single.

Smiling, she spoke first, "Scott, how did you get involved with this crazy character?"

"Beats me" I replied. "I was just minding my own business when some guy tried to kill him. Next thing I know he's asking me to write a book."

"Ohhh, you're the author Mike has been looking for."

"Yeah, only right now, hanging around Mike, I feel more like a target for kooks."

"I know what you mean," Connie said. "I've been involved in a few scary moments myself."

Turning to Mike, she asked, "Mike, you said on the phone you might have some information for me about the gay attack early this morning. This is a big story—I could use everything you know."

"Okay" Mike said, "but first the usual agreement—no direct quotes or anything that will screw up my relationship with the FBI. I would suggest you start digging in your files for everything you have on the Defenders of God. There's a strong chance they're responsible as they've been doing some heavy recruiting of new members in the last six months. Calvin McCallum might have given Wolfe Drake orders for an initiation ceremony requiring the new recruits to attack and kill someone to make sure the recruits are not infiltrators for the FBI."

"Okay, thanks for the tip," Connie said, "I keep hoping they'll disappear and find something else to do. But no such luck!"

I noticed Mike was careful in what he said to Connie and didn't mention my involvement. I had no desire to see my picture plastered on the front page of the Seattle Times and the local TV channels.

"Connie, I have a favor to ask of you," Mike said. "Scott is working with me on the metaphysical book and with your extensive background in karma I'd like you to share with him information on the Law of Karma. Do you mind?"

With a light laugh, Connie said, "You mean I get a chance to dust off my old Master's thesis? Mike, I'd be delighted to help. Scott, what's your timeline?"

"As soon as possible," I replied. "How about after you get off work today?"

"Okay. I live on the North side of Queen Anne Hill," she said as she wrote down her address and phone number and handed it to me. "Call first to make sure I'm home. I might have to work late on the gay attack. A year ago I wrote a column on 'Hate Groups in the Northwest' so I'm sure my editor will want me to follow-up on this story."

After sharing half of our fries with the fat overfed seagulls, we said our good-byes. As Mike and I hopped in the Lexus he said, "Scott, you have enough information on reincarnation. Connie will bring you up to speed on karma, then we can tackle other material that you'll find extremely fascinating—how the Universe really works and how we pick our human bodies and personalities."

I dropped Mike off at Broad Street, near the Monorail station at Seattle Center. I quickly got on I-5 and once again headed for Lynnwood. Thirty minutes later I was busy keystroking.

Chapter 8

A t 6:30 PM I called Connie Kamura. She was home and told me to come to her condo. I interrupted Karen's studying long enough to tell her who I was meeting and why.

"Well," she said, "should I be worried? You're meeting a famous columnist and judging from her photo in the paper she's quite attractive."

I answered, "No. Yes. Yes. No, you shouldn't be worried. Yes, she is famous, and yes, she is attractive. And Mrs. Hunter, if you'll give me a kiss I'll be on my way."

Which she did with a long soft lingering kiss that I finally had to pull away from before becoming too aroused.

Taking I-5 to 50th, I followed side streets to the Fremont Bridge. A few blocks from the bridge I found her street and spotted the light blue building where Connie's condo perched on the south side of the street. The building was built into the northern slope of Queen Anne Hill requiring a hike up a long steep flight of stairs to condo number 304.

Connie opened the door holding a cell phone to her left ear, motioning me to come in and take a seat on the sofa. While she finished her call I looked around and saw a small nicely furnished condo. Her tastes ran toward soft and plush with light accent colors in yellows and greens. Overall the place was clean and tidy. The exception was a small white pine desk along one wall piled high with papers in a disorganized stack beside her laptop computer. Several back issues of newspapers were piled on the floor.

Wrapping up her call, Connie turned to me, "Welcome, Scott, excuse the mess. I was working on some research on our *friends*, the Defenders of God. She had switched from conservative business attire to a pair of tight-fitting black spandex shorts that left little to the imagination and a loose-fitting, low-cut teal top with spaghetti straps that revealed a pair of lovely breasts unencumbered by a bra.

"Would you like some tea, Scott?"

Fixated on her cleavage, I stumbled over my words but managed to get out a feeble, "yes."

In a few minutes, she returned carrying a tray holding a jade-colored tea pot and two matching cups. Placing the tray on the coffee table in front of me, she poured the steaming hot tea into the cups.

She took the seat across from me in a white stuffed chair, pulled her legs up under her, took a slow cautious sip of tea, and started explaining her background—particularly her post graduate years at the University of Hong Kong. I did my best to keep my eyes focused high—on her face.

"Scott, karma and reincarnation work closely together. Understanding this point alone will help millions of people better understand their lives as well as why certain things happen in life to some people but not others. Since the belief in karma has been, for all practical purposes, banned in Christianity for over fourteen hundred years, it tends to be thought of as a concept peculiar to only Hinduism and Buddhism. Nothing could be further from the truth. Each and every one of us is personally affected on a daily basis by the Law of Karma.

"Simply put, karma refers to the force generated by a person's action in life. One's action can be good or bad and will affect future lifetimes. The Law of Karma could equally be called the Law of Action and Reaction, or the Law of Cause and Effect. Remember the old biblical saying, 'An eye for an eye, and a tooth for a tooth'? That's just another way of explaining karma."

I interrupted Connie, saying, "You said good or bad. I thought karma was only bad."

"No, Scott, many people tend to think of karma as something bad and from a past life, but that is only a part of karma.

Everyday, in your present life, you are creating karma which is either positive or negative. Good deeds or actions will earn you good karma, bad deeds or actions will add to your tally of bad karma. The Golden Rule, 'Do unto others as you would have them do unto you' is really about creating good karma, only it has never been explained to you that way in Sunday School or your place of worship.

Connie continued, "The payback, whether good or bad, does not always happen immediately. Sometimes it can take lifetimes and the payback is not always exactly the same as the original karma. For example, let's say you volunteer weekends at a shelter serving food to two hundred homeless individuals. This is a very good deed and will earn you a lot of good karma. But, for an exact payback to occur you would have to be homeless in one or more future lifetimes and each one of the two hundred homeless people you helped would have to serve you to balance things out. Well, even for God, or whatever form of deity you recognize, that's a record keeping nightmare, and besides what if you don't want to be homeless in a future lifetime?"

I laughed to myself as I visualized Karma Headquarters in Heaven, staffed with thousands of accountants and ex-IRS workers posting entries in huge karma ledgers.

Connie pulled me out of my mental side trip, saying, "There can be surrogates who represent you in karmic paybacks as a way of simplifying things—a lot like our system of currency facilitates the exchange of goods and services. In earlier times a farmer might pay a doctor three chickens for medical help. Or one farmer might give another farmer one newborn calf in exchange for the breeding services of the first farmer's prize bull with four of the second farmer's cows.

"The direct exchange system only works to a limited degree," she said, "then one needs a better medium of exchange, whether nuggets of gold, or our modern currency system. An example might be a situation where you robbed dozens of people in a past lifetime. In this lifetime, a burglar might have broken into your home and taken enough things to equal out all your past robberies. The burglar, acting as a surrogate for the people you had robbed, could be a younger soul more willing to incur bad karma. Or let's take the case of a person who, as a mass murderer in a past lifetime, had killed twenty people. Murder is heavy duty karma, but the reality is the person would have to be killed in twenty future lifetimes which gets a bit too complicated, and the twenty people who were killed, no matter how just, might be loathe to commit murder themselves."

"So" I asked, "What's the answer?"

Connie paused, taking a long sip of tea, "The mass murderer could come back as a surgeon and save hundreds of people's lives. In effect he has balanced out his bad karma through his later good deeds. Don't take this example to mean that all surgeons were former mass murderers in a past lifetime, it just illustrates a possible way to balance bad karma."

"Connie, I just remembered I experienced a surrogate form of karmic payback a few years ago while I was vacationing in Amsterdam."

"What happened?" Connie asked.

"I was at the phone company making a call to the States when a man leaned around the edge of the open phone booth yelling at me in a foreign tongue. While I was trying to figure out what he was trying to communicate, an accomplice of his came up behind me on the opposite side and swiftly grabbed my wallet off the phone booth ledge, where I had placed it to access my phone calling card. The yelling man disappeared and I finished my call before I realized what had happened. I raced outside to see if I could spot the thieves but they were long gone. I started to feel anger at them and myself for being stupid enough to have let the theft happen, then suddenly about five minutes later a light bulb went off in my head. I had just experienced a karmic payback from some past lifetime! I instantly felt a wave of relief sweep over me—like the nice feeling you get when, after three years, you make your last car payment. I lost about $100 and had to go through the hassle of canceling out stolen credit cards and getting new ones reissued, but in this instance it didn't bother me because I had one less karmic debt to worry about. Several weeks later during a past life regression it was confirmed that a surrogate form of karmic payback had occurred."

"That's an excellent example, Scott."

"Oh—and there was another time—another personal karmic payback, this time it was good karma between a coworker and myself. For dinner one night when I was working late I slipped out to a nearby deli and purchased a sandwich and fruit salad. I returned to my desk, ate the sandwich and while eating the fruit salad, a large chunk of cantaloupe accidentally became lodged in my throat. I couldn't breathe and I was about to choke to death. I knew I wouldn't be able to talk if I called 9-1-1, and by the time they figured out something was wrong they would have trouble getting into the locked building and then would have had to search twelve floors to find me. I had two chances to survive, take the elevator to the ground floor to exit the building and find help on the street, or get lucky and find someone in the building to save me. I only had seconds to go. I started towards the elevator and suddenly spotted a light under another office door. I burst in, pointing to my throat and gesturing to the man inside to do a Heimlich maneuver on me. He jumped up instantly, performed the maneuver, forced the lodged food particle out and saved my life. Later when I checked for a karmic relationship, I was told that in a past life I had saved his life. My choking on a piece of cantaloupe in this lifetime allowed him to pay me back and balance the karmic ledger."

"Scott, those are wonderful real-life examples to include in your book. That leads to another key point about karma."

While refilling our tea cups, Connie continued. "Easterners, particularly the most downtrodden followers of Hinduism, have the fatalistic belief that there is nothing they can do about their poor lot in life. They accept the notion that they did bad things in a past life, and consequently must suffer for their entire lifetime. That is a major misunderstanding of the Law of Karma. There is nothing to prevent them from rising above their station in life through accelerated karmic payback.

"Once you have incurred some bad karma—and we all have—the question is how to pay it back? Accelerated karmic payback is similar to what happens when you get a new credit card and rush out and buy goodies until you have 'maxed' it out by reaching the limit on the card. Let's say you suddenly find yourself in debt to the tune of $5,000. You could make the minimum payment each month of $150, barely more than the interest incurred each month. It would take you forever to pay it off and you would have paid a small fortune in finance charges.

"Not a very smart solution. Instead you decide that you'll get a part-time job, evenings and weekends, which is not an easy or fun thing to do, but a rather effective solution. Then in six months time you would have paid off the debt and can quit your part-time job. Only now, you're older and wiser, so you only use your credit card for convenience and pay it off every month.

"The important thing to understand is that you can speed up your payback of karma by being extra kind, caring, and giving to those around you. Examine the records of almost any charity and you will discover that the most generous people are often those with the least resources. It's not uncommon to find poor women—and by the way women tend to be more giving than men—living on a small pension, or a social security check, who manage to mail off small checks to charities that they want to help. It isn't the amount of the check but the degree of sacrifice that earns them karmic credits. A small $5 donation from a poor person can be worth far more in the karmic record book than the $100,000 check given by a wealthy businessman motivated by the tax write-off and the media photo opportunity.

"Does that give you a better understanding of karma, Scott?"

"Yeah it sure does, thanks. You really helped me understand that reincarnation and karma work together. You can't have one without the other. I need to be going now but if you don't mind I might need to call or see you again as other questions come up."

Touching me lightly on my right forearm and flashing me a dazzling smile, Connie replied, "I'd be delighted to get together again. Just give me a call."

Twenty-eight minutes later, I pulled into our garage, located on the lower level of our three story townhouse, and went up the stairs to the main level of the house. Karen was in her fluffy white terry cloth robe pouring white wine into two glasses. She greeted me with a smile, "Hi, Honey, how did your meeting go?"

Walking over to her, I responded, "It was great. I learned a lot." Then as she turned her head toward me for the usual peck on the cheek, I put my left arm behind her and drew her toward me pressing our bodies tightly together. Our lips met, lightly at first, then increasing in pressure until our tongues were wildly dancing together. My body had come alive.

"Well, I don't know what got into you," Karen said, "but I think we should take our wine and finish this upstairs."

Even after being married for two of the four years we've known each other, Karen could get me as excited as when we first met. As long as I had her for my wife I didn't need to look elsewhere for happiness or pleasure.

We quietly put a CD in the downstairs audio system to distract the two dogs and two cats, so we could sneak upstairs without their noticing. Trying to make love in a bed with four animals watching and vying for space tended to detract from the romance.

Shutting the door, and standing in the dark beside our bed, our bodies came together, our souls joining and becoming one. In a matter of seconds after sliding between the cool sheets, we found ourselves slipping free from the bounds of Earth and entering the world of past lifetime lovemaking—a world where we could recall and reenact moments when we had made love to one another in different bodies in some far distant lifetime. The excitement and intensity of those memories propelled us to heights of ecstasy far beyond normal lovemaking. We raced from orgasm to orgasm, with torrents of emotions pouring through our bodies until at last our energies were balanced and we lay beside each other feeling our separate bodies united into one, floating gently in space.

Karen and I had been lovers over many lifetimes. Whenever we found each other in a new lifetime, our initial getting reacquainted period was marked by intense lovemaking, as we recalled the past and shared the emotional intensity of finding a long lost love. Past lifetime lovemaking is such a profound emotional experience that I wish everyone could break through the mental barriers that limit themselves from experiencing such heights of ecstasy. After experiencing the pleasure of this unusual form of lovemaking, I often ask myself if I should make my next book one called *The Joy of Past Lifetimes Lovemaking*. Then Mike's warning about getting the cart before the horse came to mind. No, first people have to be convinced reincarnation and karma are real before they can be exposed to more intense and delightfully ethereal sexual bliss.

Chapter 9

I spent the next couple of days working almost non-stop, keystroking, getting Mike's information about reincarnation, and Connie's knowledge of karma into my computer in an order that a reader could follow easily.

Checking the newspapers, I noticed that Connie had written a column about hate groups, specifically mentioning the Aryan Nations, the Defenders of God and a few other groups that all located in the Pacific Northwest. Her article didn't directly accuse DOG of the gay attack but one could draw the inference.

By the third day, I called Mike's beeper number. Within fifteen minutes he returned my call. "Hi, Scott, what's up?"

I quickly brought him up to date on my meeting with Connie Kamura. Then I asked Mike, "What's happening with the FBI and the gay attack case? The newspapers aren't giving out much new information?"

"They picked up Ernie Goddard and the maroon van but had to release him. According to the crime lab, the van did leave a tire print near the scene, but there's no direct evidence placing it at the scene at the time of the attack. The van had been scrubbed clean. If there had been any traces of blood they were gone. Ernie immediately clammed up and demanded his lawyer. Right now everyone is hoping the black victim, a guy by the name of Kenny Turner, lives and will be able to give a good description of the attackers. His remarks to the police shortly after the attack merely said it was five or six white skinhead type guys in militia garb—no more specific details.

"If Kenny lives, and can finger Drake's thugs, he'll need heavy around-the-clock protection. Witnesses against DOG have a habit of disappearing before the trial starts. The only good thing about this whole mess is DOG has pulled back into a defensive posture. Until the pressure from the SPD and the FBI lets up, Drake's boys will be keeping a real low profile—sticking tightly to their compound. That means it'll be a little safer to be out in the public."

"That's good to hear, Mike" I said. "What's next? I think you said something about how the Universe is structured."

"That's right, Scott. Only the version I'll share with you differs quite a bit from the conventional wisdom approach. And it certainly does not qualify as politically correct."

"Mike, I don't give a damn about politically correct—I care about understanding the truth. Do you want to meet at my place this coming Monday?"

"No, Scott. I have one very important rule. With the exception of Pudgy, I keep the identity of supporters' homes a secret. Just in case I'm spotted, I don't want to trigger an attack on someone's home and family. Likewise, you will never know where I live. That way, you won't have any information to give up if for any reason DOG grabs you. I want you to stay completely under their radar. How about a ferry ride?"

"Sounds, good to me, Mike, what do you have in mind?"

"I have an ulterior motive Scott. I want to visit a place in Port Townsend and I figured we could talk on the way over and back. Does that sound okay?"

"No problem," I replied. "I'll drop Karen off at school at 8:45 AM Monday. Where shall we meet?"

"Since you'll be in the Fremont area, pick me up at the Troll under the bridge."

I laughed, "The Troll it is. Tomorrow, around 8:45." As I hung up, I thought to myself, how does one explain the Troll to people who don't understand some of Seattle's quirks. Located in the Fremont district, home to some of Seattle's more eccentric free spirits, sits a gigantic concrete troll. Located under the North end of the Aurora Avenue bridge, the massive gray Troll, designed after the scary nursery story, actually has the crumpled, half-buried remains of a real Volkswagen Beetle automobile clutched in one of its giant concrete paws.

The next morning I dropped Karen off at NIAOM and drove north three blocks under the bridge and up to the Troll. There was Mike, playing Good Samaritan, holding a camera, and taking a picture of a family of four, standing in front of the Troll. I waited until he finished and gave a little beep of my horn. He returned the camera to the tourists and hopped in the Lexus.

Once I had us safely on I-5 headed North, I said to Mike, "I'll turn on the recorder and you can talk while I drive."

"Fair enough, Scott. Call this section: 'How the Universe Really Works,' or we could subtitle it, 'Everything Your Minister Never Told You.' The big question is how does one succinctly explain the Universe? It's not an easy task to say the least. It's occupied the minds of mankind over the centuries and has sparked an ongoing debate that has yet to be resolved. Throughout the ages, the relentless search for answers to the mysteries of the Universe has taken two different approaches, the scientific and the spiritual.

"For several hundred years astronomers have been looking upward toward the sky for clues that could explain the beginning of life and how life evolved down here on planet Earth. As science and technology progressed they went from primitive hand-held telescopes to gigantic telescopes built into observatories on mountain tops. Now telescopes are positioned in outer space beyond the distorting effects of Earth's atmosphere that can peer outward millions of light years. As each year passes, they make more discoveries and either alter pre-existing theories or discard them altogether in favor of a newer theory. Ultimately, when we overcome the speed-of-light barrier, and deep space travel becomes commonplace, even more of our existing astronomical theories will be dramatically altered.

"On the other hand, Scott, the spiritual quest to understand the Universe has focused on various beliefs in some form of higher being or beingness. Christians and Jews see the Universe as a creation of a Supreme Being they name *God*. Muslims call this Supreme Being *Allah* and they also have ninety-nine other names to describe Him or Her. All three religions, Christian,

Jewish, and Muslim, share the belief that there is only one God, regardless of what names they call the Supreme Being. Taking a different viewpoint, the Hindu religion teaches that there are several Gods, which is not unlike the beliefs of Native Americans who worship several Gods. Buddhism, Taoism, and other Eastern religions do not believe in a single Supreme Being or even the idea of multiple Supreme Beings. Rather they believe that there is a *Oneness* or a *Collective Unconscious*—a form of energy or Life Force that contains all beings and all matter."

Mike continued, "Two thousand years ago in the Western world it was much easier to explain this Oneness by personifying it. Everyone understood what a person was so it was much easier to explain the concept of a Oneness as a Special Person—a Supreme Being who was all powerful. Now that we're literate and have been exposed to more than two thousand years of philosophy and various teachings, both scientific and spiritual, we're in a position to re-examine our fundamental beliefs and update them. Not unlike when we discovered the earth was round and revolved around the Sun. Science is constantly updating existing theories as new information comes to light so it's only fair to apply the same rules to our spiritual leaders."

"Well, which is it," I asked Mike, "one God, multiple Gods or a collective Life Force?"

"Scott, here's the best part—whichever you or the readers believe doesn't really matter. The important thing to understand—regardless of whether you see the Universe and all that's in it as a creation of a single Supreme Being, multiple Supreme Beings, or just an all encompassing form of Energy—is that there is a force greater than our mortal human bodies. I think we can all agree on that."

"But, Mike, what do I say in the book? Do I just keep referring to every option, God, Allah, the Tao, the Universe, the Collective Unconscious, The Oneness, All That Is, the Supreme Being—then tell the reader to pick one?"

"Scott, here's the reality of the situation—most of the people who will read the book will have a Judeo-Christian upbringing, so they'll be more comfortable with the word 'God,' but the problem is too many people associate the word 'God' with an image of a person. An almighty, all powerful being like us only with great powers, sort of a super superman.

"This viewpoint creates a separation. Under the all powerful being approach, there is this one omnipotent powerful being telling us less powerful beings how to act. Remember, we used to think when thunder roared and lightening flashed 'He' was mad at us. We now know that's absurd, but the personalizing of this 'God-force' still dominates the thinking in our culture and promotes separation.

"As a result we debate whether God is cruel or kind? The reality is that God is neither. Energy in it's purest form does not have a morality. I'm sure you have heard someone say God is kind, all loving and all caring, but when a disaster happens they quickly claim 'God is testing us.' As I go through my explanation the answer to this statement will become apparent. You already have part of the answer in the information about reincarnation and karma. Tell the readers to analyze these statements in light of that knowledge. If they haven't been too brainwashed by their Judeo-Christian upbringing they will start to understand that life makes infinitely more sense when we introduce reincarnation and karma into the model.

"Instead of using the word 'God,' the Michael entity I'm channeling prefers to use the term *Tao*. It is spelled T-a-o, but pronounced *Dow*. Under this definition, you see not a person but an all encompassing energy that we all are a part of. It is the combined energy of all of us, not a single entity, that creates, controls, and guides us.

"Under this term we can say that each of us is God. Collectively, we all have created this Universe, and everything in it. It's a case of the whole being greater than its parts. But in answer to your question, you might want to use two words, the 'Tao/God.' While Tao is the better word to describe things, you won't be turning off readers who are so heavily imprinted with the word 'God' that they will reject the entire message. Remember the phrase, 'don't throw the baby out with the bath water.'

"Just be sure the reader understands that we are not talking about God as a person, or a Supreme Being. God in this sense represents the total energy of the Universe and every last bit

of matter and anti-matter make up God and we are not separate—we are one."

"Thanks Mike, that makes a heck of a lot more sense," I
replied.

Mike continued, "In time, science and spirituality will merge
back together. At that point we as a civilization will come to
universally embrace the long-held metaphysical understanding
that the Universe as astronomers see it, represents only one *plane*
or *dimension* of existence—the Physical Plane. The truth is there
are a lot more planes of existence and universes out there to be
discovered by the scientists some day."

"Mike" I said, "this is not revolutionary news to students of
metaphysics."

"You're right, Scott. Serious students of metaphysics have
known this for years, but in general they've taken a more relaxed
view about sharing their knowledge with others. I've observed
that most metaphysical students prefer a patient more passive
approach rather than rushing around the globe helter-skelter, like
Christian missionaries, aggressively attempting to convert people
of different beliefs to their belief. And, of course groups like DOG
go so far as to kill people who disagree with their viewpoint.
Most modern metaphysical teachers believe that when the time
is right the seeker of truth will come seeking and at that point
they will share their wisdom.

"So it is with this book, Scott. It definitely is not for everyone.
It's only those who feel the need for truth and knowledge that
goes beyond what they have been taught. It's a lot like being a
parent raising kids. You know a lot more about life than they
do, but you don't try to explain everything you know to them
too early in life. Until kids reach a certain age level there's just
no point in trying to explain things beyond their level of awareness and understanding. You know they simply can't handle it
so you wisely dole out your knowledge in digestible bits and
pieces as they grow.

"As you know, Scott, in ancient times very few people were
literate. Often only the priests or religious leaders had the ability to read and write. This gave them an enormous amount of
power since only they could interpret the written teachings

passed down from generation to generation. So, like the parents of small children, they often translated the more esoteric teachings into terminology that helped them explain quite complex issues in simple terms. They would say, 'the soul is the part of you that survives after you die' and 'if you're bad, your soul will go to Hell.' This rather simple approach worked quite well as a way to control the behavior of the people. Otherwise, if people believed that there was no soul and one was just born then died, they might not be as nice to each other. The strongest and meanest people would end up ruling everyone else and life would not be much fun."

"Not a very pleasant thought," I volunteered. "I'm going to turn off the recorder for a few minutes. We're at the Edmonds ferry terminal. Look, we lucked out. No long line and they've started boarding for the 9:25 crossing."

I stopped at the ticket booth, paid the fare, and swung in line behind a sporty black Honda Civic that had been lowered and over-customized by some kid with more money than taste. His blaring sound system was obnoxiously loud—as if he was trying to see how low his bass could go before he blew out a speaker. This was further proof that there was no personal God ready to fulfill our every prayer. Fortunately, with the windows up, the Lexus is about as soundproof as a car gets.

As all the vehicles boarded, I was forced to follow the Civic up the steep auto ramp on the right side of the ferry. After stopping and setting the parking brake, we quickly got out and headed up the stairwell to the passenger deck. Mike went to grab a couple of cups of coffee, while I motioned with hand signals that I was headed outside on the right side. There were hundreds of empty vinyl-covered seats inside but it was a nice day so I opted for fresh air—as far from the noisy young occupants of the Civic as possible. Standing at the railing on the outside walkway I breathed deeply, inhaling the invigorating salt air breeze wafting across the deep blue waters of Puget Sound.

Chapter 10

"Here's your coffee," Mike said, breaking up my day dreaming. "Now let me think—where did I leave off? Oh, yeah. Next I want to talk about the different planes of existence or what some people call different dimensions."

Pulling my recorder out of my pocket, and pushing the play button, I said, "So you mean like coffee—there are several different levels or grades?"

Chuckling, Mike responded, "Yeah, you got it. Ever had any free coffee at a freeway rest area? You know, where some church or civic group mans a booth and gives away coffee for a donation. They usually make the coffee in some old battered aluminum percolator and then let the stuff slowly bake into some gooey paste that tastes like hot rubber. You could correlate that with the lowest plane of existence—the Physical Plane here on earth. There are seven planes all together—so using the coffee analogy—a Starbucks mocha or latte would probably be way up at level seven—the highest."

Looking puzzled, I said, "Seven levels? I thought there were only a few?"

"No, Scott. Remember, I'm teaching you about an advanced spiritual system that goes beyond our comprehension at the more primitive level. The seven planes have always been there, we just weren't ready to understand them.

"Among the different religious faiths and various metaphysical teachings the subject of different planes of existence vary. In

Christianity, Judaism, and Islam, we recognize a few different planes of existence. They are commonly referred to as Heaven and Hell.

"Some Christians, Jews and Hindus believe in another place, sort of an in-between location between Heaven and Hell. Christians call it *purgatory*, Jews call it *gehinnon* and Hindus use the name *narakas*. Having an in-between place was one of the great inventions of all time, after all, the religious leaders set the standards to get into Heaven so high that few could get there."

"So, Mike are you saying purgatory is a lot like getting a five year jail sentence instead of life imprisonment?"

'That's correct Scott. After dying you could go to purgatory, accept your punishment for breaking your neighbor's plate-glass window, taking drugs, and stealing your kid brother's coin collection. After you finished your punishment you could then move on to Heaven.

Mike continued, "While scientists aren't quite ready to embrace the concept of a soul—after all it's still pretty hard to get a soul under a microscope—virtually every religion and metaphysical teaching agree that humans do have a soul that survives the body. These faiths believe that we have a soul that goes to either a plane of existence called Heaven, Hell, or somewhere in-between, after death.

"However, instead of just two or three other planes of existence, which were a lot simpler to explain to uneducated peasants, the metaphysical teachings in the book will be dealing with seven levels. But don't worry, all of this knowledge is already stored deep in your soul. You are merely getting re-acquainted with it.

"So Scott, let's call this section or chapter, *'The Seven Planes of Existence.'* I like to view the planes as steps on a ladder. We souls must climb each of the seven steps to get to the top, which is the Tao level or plane. Others may refer to plane seven as God, or Heaven. Each plane relates to a different form of energy and vibrates at a different speed:

"1. *Physical Plane* - You already know this plane Scott—it's the one you're living on Earth. For some people, living in this plane is Hell. It can be rough or easy depending upon what challenges you decided to take on during this lifetime and what karmas you chose to repay or create. I'll discuss this in greater detail later. This is the only plane where your body and soul are joined together. Once your body dies, your soul leaves your body and progresses through the higher levels as non-physical energy. This plane has the slowest speed of vibration, has the densest form of energy, and is the most negative. Next:

"2. *Astral Plane* - the first non-physical level. This is where you come to recover from the beating you took on Earth. You get to re-examine your entire life on the Physical Plane, the good and bad and prepare for your next life on the Physical Plane. This is similar to a halfway house between Earth lifetimes. You do not advance to higher planes until you complete your entire cycle of earth lifetimes, which can be from thirty-five to over four hundred lifetimes. Since you are not tied to a physical body, your soul can take any form you choose. Often what your body looked like at its prime in the previous life. Since the soul is gender-less you can experience sex with anyone on the Astral Plane, only the method is slightly different. Two souls merely embrace, creating an all-encompassing electrical spark as the two different energy fields merge together and become one."

"I don't know Mike—Astral Plane sex doesn't sound like as much fun as Physical Plane sex."

"Well, Scott, there's definitely a difference when you remove the human body from the equation. Since the human body is programmed to procreate to survive as a species, that adds an element of compulsive lust that's lacking on the Astral Plane where the sex act is more of spiritual reconnecting.

"3. *Causal Plane* - this is where you combine with other souls and learn intellectual lessons. Most of the information I'm sharing with you comes from this dimension.

"4. *Akashic Plane* - Edgar Cayce, the great American psychic tapped into this plane, also called the Akashic Records, to get much of his information. It has been called the repository of all knowledge, past, present and future. It can also be viewed as some sort of karmic ledger system, where the debit and credit entries are made— maybe that's the job accountants are given after they leave the Physical Plane.

"5. *Mental Plane* - at this plane you finally master the intellectual lessons you started on the Causal Plane, as well as learning universal principles such as truth, justice and awareness.

"6. *Messianic Plane* - This plane is all about emotional energy focused on love. Jesus was in contact with this plane for the wisdom he shared with us.

"7. *Buddhaic Plane* - This plane is where Buddha accessed the messages he shared with us on Earth. It's a level of pure energy and is the highest plane of creativity.

Beyond this plane, all that's left is for your soul to re-join with the Tao/God.

The Tao/God is the ultimate goal of your soul. The Tao/God could also relate to Heaven. Some people refer to it as the Collective Unconscious, or the Oneness. When some faiths say that God is everywhere at once and in everything, this is what they are talking about. It is the place all of us are striving to reach. At this level, we are all joined into one as pure energy or thought."

"So, Mike," I said, "when some people say that Hell is here on Earth, they might be right."

"That's right. Depending upon the type of challenges you pick for a given lifetime it could be Hell. Particularly if you agree to accept karmic paybacks for things you have done wrong in other lifetimes."

"Mike, a lot of people talk about angels or spirit guides that help them. Do you believe there are such things or is this just wishful thinking?"

"They are very real, Scott. From the time before recorded history, up to the present day, countless people have shared their stories of angels, ghosts, spirit guides or even little leprechauns. Add in the billions of people who have prayed to somebody or something for help or guidance, and you can see that the belief is quite common.

"We all have countless sources of non-physical information available to us. Only our Physical Plane amnesia and our individual density, or lack of awareness, prevents us from having a clearer more direct contact with the non-physical sources. Like the actor on the stage who is blinded by the footlights from clearly seeing the audience, so we, acting out our role in this lifetime, are also blinded from seeing our audience.

"The Astral Plane in particular is loaded with non-physical souls that could be your deceased Aunt Millie, or a whole host of your fellow souls. Some of them cycled off earth ahead of you and are available to help with your lessons on the Physical Plane. Like a school classmate, it isn't fair for them to do the lessons for you, but now and then they can slip you a clue or two.

"Remember when we talked about being one with everything? While in the Physical Plane we have the illusion of being alone, but it is only an illusion to make the game more real. You are always connected to All That Is.

"Picture a Nascar or Indianapolis race car driver. When the driver is in the race car, speeding around the track, he appears to be alone, not unlike your soul driving your body through the physical Universe. In reality, he is hearing information and getting helpful tips from his crew chief via a radio in his helmet. Your spirit guides do the same thing for you, but let's face it, race car radios are easier for most of us to hear than spirit guides. Following the analogy a bit further, after you crash, or leave your body, and go to the pits, called the Astral Plane in the spirit world, there's a crew there to repair your injuries, and help you assess what you did right or wrong in the race you just completed. In some cases, if you're in a rush to get back into the race to complete some unfinished agreements, they just clean you up, get you a new body, and shove you back into the Physical Plane race.

"The key point to remember is that your angels or spirit guides are not always going to give you advice, or if they do it might not always be good advice. Just like here on Earth, the quality of your source of knowledge is critical. Let's say your recently departed Uncle Louie, a compulsive gambler while on Earth, is acting as one of your spirit guides. All of a sudden you get a 'hunch' to go spend your paycheck on the lottery. Uncle Louie is still trying to hit it big only he's doing it with your money and he isn't any better at winning through you than he was on his own.

"If you ask an angel or spirit guide for help with a problem that is a lesson you are here to learn, they would not help as that is spiritual cheating. But they will always be ready to help you heal after the traumatic learning experience. Assume that one of your lessons is a karmic payback necessitating you break your leg balancing out the ledger from three lifetimes ago when you broke someone's leg. In this case, the angel or spirit guide is not allowed to tell you to duck when the car driven by the person whose leg you broke back then, is about to hit your leg.

"However, let's assume that you booked an airplane flight which was going to crash, and it was not your time to die. Then it would be permissible for your angels or spirit guides to maneuver things behind the scenes so you had to cancel the flight. While planes don't crash that often, when one does there are always stories of people that had to cancel out at the last minute, or got stuck in traffic and missed the doomed flight. It simply was not their time to go."

"Mike, how do I know when I'm getting a message from an angel or spirit guide?"

"For me, Scott, it works like this—I personally know it's a communication from a spirit guide when an idea or thought quite suddenly pops into my head and is unrelated directly to where my brain is focusing at that moment. Typically, although infrequently, I will get flash solutions to problems that have me stumped. These I consider to be from my spirit guides.

"However, I have one advantage as a channel of the Michael Teachings. I simply go into a light trance, ask Michael, who operates from the Causal Plane and has access to the Akashic Records, for confirmation. This helps to avoid bum tips from some deceased Uncle Louie."

Chapter 11

Mike's cell phone beeped, interrupting my thoughts. "It's Connie Kamura," he said. Just then the announcement came over the ferry's loudspeakers for all passengers to return to their vehicles and prepare for landing. The creosote-soaked wooden pilings of the ferry terminal at Kingston were looming up dead ahead of us.

"Hi, Connie, this is Mike, what's up?"

As he listened his face took on a somber look. This was not good news. "Was anyone hurt?"

Pause.

"Don't take a chance. Give Lee Chou a call. She and Pudgy have some extra room where you can stay until things cool down. No, they won't mind."

Pause.

"Scott and I are on the Edmonds/Kingston ferry and we're about to dock at Kingston. I'm meeting with a group in Port Townsend at noon. I'll call you when I get back to Seattle. Bye."

We rushed down the stairwell steps to the auto deck, found the Lexus, hopped in just as the ferry engines reversed, slowing the ferry for it's approach to the dock.

Mike said, "Things are getting serious. A package bomb was delivered to Connie this morning at the Seattle Times. It was placed on her desk while she had gone to the rest room and it exploded before she got back. Six people sitting at nearby desks were injured. Fortunately, no one was seriously injured. She was pretty shaken up. Just in case the people responsible for the bombing have her home address, I told her not to go home. She's going to be staying with Pudgy and Lee Chou."

Once the ferry docked, we exited following the loud crowd in the black Civic, which fortunately turned off the main road after a few blocks. In a matter of minutes we were out of Kingston cruising along Highway 104. Mike was deep in thought and didn't say a word until I turned North onto Highway 19. Then he spoke, "The violence and hatred has got to stop. Scott, we have to get our message out there—and fast!"

"Did Connie say who sent the bomb?" I asked.

"No, but I'm sure the FBI and the crime lab guys are all over this one. It had to be one of the hate groups she discussed in her article. The trick will be proving which one."

"Mike, let me ask you something on a different topic—when I first saw you in Starbucks you looked, acted, and spoke, like an old homeless person living on the streets. Now that I've gotten to know you better I see a totally different, and quite articulate person. Why the change?"

"You treated me differently then didn't you—when you thought I was a bum?"

"Yeah, I did."

"Why?"

"I'm not sure," I said. "I guess you fell into some stereotypical image that I don't like. I think of street people as mostly drunks too lazy to work, and always trying to make people feel sorry for them and give them hand-outs."

"You're not alone with that viewpoint. We're all guilty of applying our standards to others, and if they don't conform to some pre-determined ideal we think less of the person or even go so far as to harm them. Homeless people, blacks and other minorities, are often the target of suspicion and hatred solely because they are different in color, belief, or appearance. Even honest, hard-working middle class blacks are far more likely to be randomly stopped by the police than middle class whites. We tend to treat people who occupy the lower rungs on the socio-economic ladder differently than those higher up the ladder. All too often a person's worth is measured strictly in terms of his or her financial wealth."

"You're right Mike, I remember one day when I was a stockbroker—two people walked into the office to open an account—one guy was in a sharp three-piece suit and was carrying an expensive leather attaché case. The other guy was dressed about like you. One of the other brokers immediately rushed up and introduced himself to the guy in the suit. I got the other guy as a client. It turned out the guy in the suit was a Vice President in some company, making a great salary, but spending more than he made. Expensive clothes, fancy cars, big home, country club dues—the whole nine yards. He had almost nothing left to invest. The poorly dressed guy, on the other hand, was worth a bundle. He had worked hard all his life and saved almost everything he made. He turned out to be a great client."

"You apparently forgot that valuable lesson when you saw me."

"I'm sorry, Mike, you're right. I let your appearance deceive me."

"Well, Scott, you're about to get a second chance. When we get to Port Townsend, we're going to a bookstore where I'll be speaking to a small group of people. I can guarantee you that not a single person in attendance will be wearing a three-piece suit. But almost everyone of them will be a very kind and loving old soul. Judge them not by what's on their backs but by what you can feel coming from their hearts."

"Okay, I promise," I said.

After a few more miles I turned right onto Highway 20 and soon was in downtown Port Townsend. Strategically located at the entrance to Puget Sound, Port Townsend was a key port in the Northwest in the late 19th century. Now, it's a sleepy laid-back town of seven thousand or so people.

Following Mike's directions I soon found Water Street, the main drag, then spotted our destination—The Phoenix Rising Bookstore. Smaller than a modern Barnes & Noble bookstore, the Phoenix Rising was quite typical of most metaphysical bookstores. The selection of books was skewed heavily towards subjects like astrology, tarot, yoga, meditation, self-help, and all the far eastern philosophies. Near the front of the store were pendulums, hand-crafted jewelry, crystals, and scarves.

Spotting Mike, a middle-aged woman draped in a flowing gown with a vibrant purple and rose scarf around her shoulders, rushed out from behind the check-out counter, and gave Mike a big hug. Turning to me, Mike said, "Camille, I'd like you to meet Scott Hunter. Scott's a writer who's going to write a book about the things I'm going to talk about today. Scott, I'd like you to meet Camille Perry, a very spiritual lady who is the owner of this fine establishment."

After exchanging greetings, Camille lead us into a back room that was set up for a presentation, with a small portable podium resting on a walnut veneered folding table. Behind the table was an eight foot long white marker board with a collection of different colored markers resting in the tray at the bottom of the board. About a dozen tan metal folding chairs faced the podium, with four stuffed cushions on the floor in front of the chairs, for people who preferred sitting cross-legged on the floor.

Mike looked around, nodded and said, "This is perfect, Camille. When do we start?"

Camille looked at a small delicate watch hanging from a beaded strap around her neck and said, "In about thirty minutes. Can I get you anything?"

"Nope. It looks great. Scott, if you want to look at books for awhile, I want to meditate alone for about fifteen minutes before people arrive."

"No problem, Mike." I said as I turned and walked back into the bookstore area.

People were starting to arrive and milling around, looking at books and merchandise. Camille had a teapot set up with a nice assortment of herbal teas. I fixed myself a cup of Ginger Citrus caffeine-free herbal tea and wandered around the store. Having operated my own astrology bookstore decades earlier I knew running a store like this was not a huge money maker. Rather it was a labor of love, run by people who cared more about communicating spiritual wisdom than racking up big profits.

After about 15 minutes Mike emerged, looking relaxed and rested. He fixed himself a cup of tea and sauntered around the store introducing himself to people until Camille rang a small brass bell and started herding the people into the back room. I grabbed a chair off to the left side, near the front, where I could get a good look at the audience. There were nine women and five men present other than Mike, Camille and myself, ranging in age from early twenties to mid-sixties. Everyone appeared more laid-back and casual than audiences at all the business presentations I have facilitated over the years. There was an eerie similarity to the clientele who came to my astrology bookstore during the hippie era. I could have been in a time-warp back to the seventies. Most of the older people in the audience appeared to be aging hippies with the same long hair styles, only now turning gray. Three of the men had ponytails.

After everyone was seated, Camille walked to the podium, welcomed the audience, then pointed to me and made mention that I was a writer working on a book with Mike. I smiled and nodded politely.

She turned to Mike, then back to the audience and said, "Many of you have already met Mike our speaker today. Some of what he will say today you already know, in fact, in your hearts you already know everything he is about to say. His message has been said in a dozen different ways over thousands of years. However Mike approaches Karma and Reincarnation with a more concrete structure for understanding than most spiritual teachers. If the message resonates with you, I urge you to share it with your friends as his message is very special. Several attempts have been made on Mike's life in the past few years by right-wing fanatics who fear what he has to say. They perceive the truth he teaches as a threat to their out-dated belief system. So, while there are people who are afraid of what he has to say, I know all of you will welcome the truth. With that said I turn the meeting over to Mike for his talk called 'The Clash of Souls.' "

"I appreciate all of you being here today. If any of you are carrying concealed weapons now would be a good time for you to turn them over to Camille."

The audience broke out into laughter.

"Now why would anyone want to kill an old worn out codger like me? The answer is simple. I have a simple message. A message of truth that by the mere act of updating or modernizing ancient teachings, becomes a threat to old established orders

wanting to remain static. Call them vested interests, special interests, whatever, there are many groups of people who would
rather kill than consider modifying old beliefs. Because all of you
are most likely students of metaphysics, you might not think what
I have to say as that astounding, but believe me, in many parts of
this country, you would be beaten or killed for even discussing
the seven things I will share with you today."

He turned, picked up a red marker and while speaking wrote
each item on the board:

(1) Where do we come from?

(2) What is our purpose?

(3) Where do we go when we die?

(4) Why do we come back and how many times?

(5) What are the lessons of each soul age?

(6) Understanding the seven levels within each soul age,
and last

(7) Why souls clash?"

Mike put down the marker, walked out from behind the
podium and sat on the front edge of the table closer to the audience, looking very relaxed.

"First, where do we come from?

"The origin of all life, whether human or non-human, comes
from Tao, or God if you are more comfortable with that term, you
can call it the Oneness, or All That Is. I prefer to use the word Tao
to get away from the confusing Judeo-Christian personification
of the word God, but since the word Tao bothers some people I'll
simply refer to the Supreme Power as Tao/God. Then there's no
need for any of us to get mad and kill each other."

The audience, obviously more enlightened than people in
general, laughed.

Mike continued. "In the beginning, we were pure energy or
thought, all knowing, all powerful, all creative and all that existed. Being pure thought can be nice but it could be a little boring.
At least that was always what Star Trek's intrepid Captain Kirk
thought whenever he encountered aliens that were by-and-large
emotionless thought forms. In any case, whether from boredom
or playfulness, the all creative Tao/God decided to create a game
with itself that would expand the Tao/God infinitely.

"To make the game interesting, certain rules were set up:

(1) Tao/God would forget that they are part of All That Is. After all, when you are All That Is, there is only one of you, so to play a game you have to create another playmate. While it might seem a bit strange at first, remember that virtually every little kid does the same thing when they are the only kid in the family, and the neighborhood. They simply create an imaginary playmate.

(2) Those parts of energy, called sparks or fragments, which each of us are, will be led through a complex matrix of challenges until they are able to master them and discover who they are spiritually and then reunite with the Tao/God.

"Simply put, it's a lot like when you were a kid playing hide-and-seek. You were blindfolded, or covered your eyes, while your friends ran and hid. Then it was your job to try and find them. Only to make the game more interesting, just suppose that when you uncovered your eyes you had no memory of what or who you were looking for, or even the fact that you were playing a game. You would be faced with the same challenge as someone with amnesia, only you wouldn't even have a doctor or family members to tell you that you have amnesia. You would have to spot tiny clues in books, movies, television, or virtually anywhere. Even things like the pounding ocean surf could trigger an awareness deep inside you. Your fellow fragments, equally confused, might provide clues in a blind-leading-the-blind sort of way.

"Clues are everywhere, but if you don't even know you're looking for something, that you cannot explain, you could easily squash a clue by carelessly stepping on it, or eat a clue and not even know it. You have to admit it's one heck of a super challenging game. Parker Brother's Monopoly, one of the greatest board games of all time, can't even come close to the game the Tao/God created—the Universe and all the little pieces that dance around the board we call Life.

"The Tao/God is made up of billions, trillions or even quadrillions of sparks, also called fragments. Each spark or fragment is a soul containing a consciousness that is both independent while also a part of the whole. These souls are organized in groups of approximately one thousand, called an entity. Each seven entities form a group called a cadre.

"To start the game the Tao/God cast out millions of cadres. Then each cadre in turn threw out the seven entities. The entities, in turn, cast out the one thousand fragments to become individual human beings."

One of the men with a ponytail interrupted, "Excuse me, Mike, I'm not sure I understand."

Mike got up and walked over to the marker board, picked up a blue marker, and put the following on the board. "This would be how a single cadre would look.

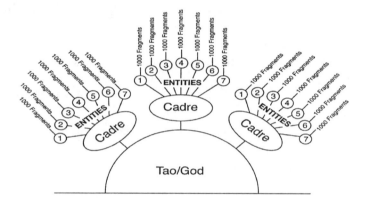

"If this concept is a bit hard to grasp, think of it like a giant fireworks display. The guy running the display—the Tao/God—ignites the main rocket—the cadre—which shoots upward, that explodes, sending out seven smaller rockets—the entities—that shoot up further then explode shooting out one thousand individual sparks—the fragments. Only instead of just igniting one main rocket, millions are ignited.

"This could be viewed as a parallel to astronomer's Big Bang theory for the creation of the Universe. Only in this case we are talking about the creation of individual souls that take on human form, rather than planets, galaxies, quasars, and all the other phenomenon that comprise the physical Universe.

"Or, if you're into sci-fi, you could compare it to an invasion of Earth. The mother spaceship—the Tao/God—sends out hoards of orbiting space crafts—the cadres. Each cadre takes up a position orbiting Earth, then sends to the planet's surface seven landing craft each—the entities. Then when the landing crafts reaches Earth, one thousand invaders—the individual fragments—pop out of each landing craft.

"We all tend to think of ourselves as unique separate individuals, but the reality is each of us is a part of an entity made up of one thousand fragments each. Each one of us is an individual fragment, not the whole entity.

"The individual fragments/sparks can also be called essences, or souls. Each soul, in turn, creates a personality that allows it to express itself in the physical world. Think of it as a car and a driver on a long and difficult trip. The car is the personality and human body, the driver is the soul, and the trip is the journey from the Tao/God through the scary and oftentimes difficult physical Universe. The soul needs the personality—and the human body—like the driver needs the car, to complete the journey.

"Picking a human personality is a lot more fun than picking out a car. There are no car salesmen to hassle you and sell you a lemon. You might end up with a personality that seems like a lemon at times but usually there is a very important reason why you picked your personality. Later, I'll delve in more detail into all the nuances of building a personality and why we pick certain characteristics."

An attractive thirtysomething woman with long flowing brown hair raised her hand. "Mike, let me see if I understand this completely by working backward. I have a body and a personality that I, as a soul, need in order to function on Earth. But my soul, or fragment as you called it, is joined together with approximately one thousand other souls to form a single entity. The entity I belong to is joined with six other entities to form a cadre, which is a group of approximately seven thousand souls. And there are billions and billions of cadres that make up the Tao/God. Is that right?"

"Perfect explanation," said Mike.

Chapter 12

"The next big question is what is our purpose?

"There has to be a reason to play the game set up by the Tao/God, and there is one. However, it's important to realize that first and foremost, you are a soul with a body. Not the opposite. Many religions get this point reversed and refer to you as a human with a soul, like it's something you carry around in your wallet or purse. Remember the driver and auto analogy? The driver is in charge, not the car, or at least that's the way it's supposed to be. Once the driver gets out the car is ineffective. With few exceptions, when the soul leaves the body, the body is either dead, asleep, in a trance, or in a coma. When the body is dead the soul leaves the body permanently and is ready to move on to the next plane, or dimension of existence.

"The physical body, the personality, this dense glob of cells we call a human, has a very simple goal—survival. The human has been programmed on a cellular level to survive as long as possible. Part of its programming includes an autonomic nervous system that keeps the basic organs running without much intervention required from the soul. It could be compared to the cruise control found in most automobiles, or autopilot used by airplane pilots.

"The physical body does a pretty good job of surviving. In fact, for some souls who are ready to cycle off planet Earth, they discover their body has a mind of it's own and stubbornly hangs on for years, crippled up in pain, refusing to let go.

"On the other hand, the goal of the soul is not survival. It can't die so survival is not an issue. It's goal is the acquiring of knowledge through experiences in the Physical Plane and the non-physical planes. Through an infinite variety of experiences, the soul gains new knowledge that it takes back to the Tao/God. The process is similar to a General sending out lots of scouting parties in different directions to discover as much information as possible and then to come back and report what they learned. As each fragment reports back with it's new experiences and knowledge, the Tao/God expands.

"To facilitate this process, life as we know it, constantly changes through a series of cycles that repeat, with slight variations in each new cycle. You can use the fashion industry as an analogy to understand this process. Fashion runs in cycles but each time it cycles back it doesn't repeat itself 100%. As hemlines go up or down the other parts of the dress will vary from an exact duplication the last time the hemline was at the same point. Color used in fashion also follows cycles but again when we cycle back to mauves for example, the hue might be different, or the accessory colors may change, again creating slight variations that create a new experience for us. If we didn't have a built-in evolutionary opportunity, life on the Physical Plane would become very boring and the Tao/God would not expand.

"While creating new colors and dresses can be challenging, the ultimate experience we're here to learn is love. The Tao/God is pure love, so by going forth from the Tao/God we're supposed to master love and expand love. At this level love means more than person-to-person love, it means having an incredible pure, unconditional love for everything in the Universe.

"That's not an easy thing to do. Look at couples who get divorces and describe their ex-spouse, the person they once professed to love forever, as the worst, most despicable person on the planet. Or the animosity you feel for the street thug who sticks a gun in your face and takes your money. It's not easy to love a cockroach that startles you when you open your cupboard door, or the fly that keeps buzzing around your face. Those are some of the challenges the Tao/God has created for us to get through. The good news is we don't have to accomplish everything in one lifetime. It takes a lot of lifetimes to get back to the Tao/God as you'll learn later."

Hearing Mike say that made me feel better. I don't like insects. Spiders give me the creeps and I usually kill ones I find crawling around my house. Karen on the other hand, is more loving and gently picks them up and takes them outside. I'll save learning to love insects for another lifetime.

Mike continued, "When people say that life is not fair they are 100% correct. It is not supposed to be fair. We are all here for different learning experiences and karmas. Not everyone can have the lead role in a play, or be the hero. Often times the greatest experiences we have are not as the hero but as the bad guy. Anthony Hopkins, the brilliant actor who played the evil Hannibal Lector in 'Silence of the Lambs' has often taken the role of the villain—it's usually more demanding and challenging and while he doesn't get to kiss the leading lady he ends up with awards and acclaim for his performances. Some of us play roles that are extremely demanding. We might have to suffer the horrors of imprisonment, physical violence, or a deformed, crippled body. The challenge is not to evoke pity from our fellow souls but to give the best performance possible with the challenges we face. The brilliant astrophysicist, Stephen Hawking, a quadriplegic who can only communicate by touching a keyboard with a pencil held in his mouth, has played his role about as well as anyone could.

"It's fascinating to hear people discuss their lives. Most people, when looking back over their lives, no matter how hard, will say that if they had it to do all over again, wouldn't change a thing. Think about that. Why would a person who had been through a bitterly hard life, full of difficulties and pain, not want to change a thing? The answer is simple—on a deep soul level we know that we picked our life, with all its many trials and tribulations. We wanted the hard experiences...and the satisfaction of having accomplished our goals no matter how tragic it appears to those not privy to the innermost soul strategy."

A middle-aged woman with wild frizzy hair in the front row spoke. "That's so true. I've had three marriages break up and suffered major emotional traumas as a result, but now, looking back, I know I grew a lot from each experience, and if I had it to do over, I know I'd do the same things."

The crowd murmured agreement with her and each other and I thought about the harder parts of my life. While I didn't enjoy the pain I suffered at the time, those experiences are a part of me, and I'm a better and stronger person for having survived them.

Mike asked the audience, "So, is anyone curious to know where we go when we die?"

A voice in the back said, "I know—we go to Ben & Jerry's!"

The crowd, as well as Mike and I, broke out laughing. Others added things like, Godiva Chocolate factory, the Playboy Mansion, and Tahiti.

After the audience calmed down, Mike chuckled and said, "Those are great answers. Of course you know what some religions would say. They would say you go to Heaven or Hell. While ultimately we all will end up in what could be called Heaven when we return to oneness with the Tao/God, the actual process is a bit more complex and Heaven is quite different from the place described in Sunday School.

"When you first go to school you start in kindergarten, graduate to the first grade, and work your way through twelfth grade. Then you have a decision to make. Do you go on to junior college? Or a four year college? If you chose the four year college once you graduate you might consider getting your master's degree. You might decide to come back and get another master's degree, or you might come back and get a Ph.D. degree. It's up to you.

"That's similar to how it happens when you die. You don't get out of elementary school—the Physical Plane—after just one grade level. You have to come back until you have completed all the levels. As I mentioned before, it can take anywhere from thirty-five to over four hundred lifetimes in the Physical Plane before you are ready to permanently graduate to the next level. Between lifetimes on the Physical Plane you spend time on the Astral Plane reviewing the life you just completed, learning what you did right and what you did wrong.

"If you did mean or evil things to other people you incurred bad karma, a form of debt that you'll have to pay back sometime before you graduate. If you did good things you earned some good karma. Think of good karma as an IOU from someone. At some point in a future lifetime when you need help, something unexpectedly good may happen. The magnitude of the good karma usually is related to the degree of the good you originally did in the particular lifetime.

"For example, let's say you found a young boy drowning in a river and you jumped in and pulled him to safety and performed mouth-to-mouth resuscitation and revived him. You saved his life. In some future lifetime you might be about to step off a curb directly into the path of a bus you didn't see approaching. Suddenly a 'stranger' reaches out and pulls you back, saving your life. He has repaid his karmic debt to you. So you can see that the more good you do, the more good karma you build up for future lifetimes. That's one of the ways people end up with so-called lucky or charmed lifetimes. They earned them by being good to others.

"It has been said that karma is a law, the Universal Law of Harmony, which unerringly restores energy disturbances to equilibrium. When we were cast out of the Tao/God a disturbance to the equilibrium of the Tao/God was created that will only be completely corrected when we all return to the Tao/God. When we enter into the physical realm to seek knowledge through experiences, the mere act of seeking triggers the Law of Karma. In order to know good we have to know its polarity, evil. This is part of the game the Tao/God created. Good and evil, in and of themselves, are nothing but polarities, like night and day, or black and white. For there to be a game there must be two opposing forces whether we are talking about chess, sex, war, or even the children's games of cowboys and Indians.

"The Old Testament story of Adam and Eve could well be a metaphor to explain the Tao/God to uneducated people. It's not too difficult to accept the Tao/God as representing both the biblical God and the Garden of Eden from which Adam and Eve were cast out. Even the casting out can be viewed as the Tao/God sending out the cadres and entities to seek knowledge. The forbidden fruit, the apple, is symbolic of the temptations we face in human form. The serpent is necessary to create the polarity of good and evil to play the game of life set up by the Tao/God. The process of experiencing good, and conversely, evil that life has to offer, creates a deeper and richer emotional experience which simply cannot be obtained in the Tao/God itself. Without the 'agony of defeat' there would be no 'thrill of victory.'

"Being a parent to a child is akin to the relationship between the Tao/God and a soul in human form. The parent knows much but cannot tell the child everything or save the child from everything. Only by getting a flu or cold virus can the child build the immunities for future attacks. Only until the child experiences the pain of a burn will they completely understand the parent's warning about touching the hot burner. That is the painful process we call life. We have governments that try to stop all pain and suffering in life but the effort, while motivated by caring concern, is often as futile as the parent who keeps sheltering the child from life's ups and downs. Intervening too much just leads to more dependency.

"Unwittingly, governments often overstep their role and get in the way of people fulfilling their karmic debts. All people are not, karmically speaking, created equal. Some people have chosen heavier burdens for this lifetime than others. Which doesn't mean they are better or worse than those with a lighter challenge, only that they have chosen to work through a heavier karmic load this time around. Last lifetime we may have had the heavy burden, and while we still might have karmic debt to pay maybe we decided to coast for a lifetime. Or, some karmic paybacks might require a particular situation that doesn't coincide with the plans for this lifetime."

After checking to see that the audience understood the purpose of life here on Earth, Mike went on to his third point—where do we go when we die? He basically repeated what he had told me on the ferry, only adding an analogy relating the different planes or dimensions as comparable to attending school.

"You simply graduate to the next grade or level, called the Astral Plane. After you have learned the lessons of the Astral Plane you move on to the Causal Plane where you have different lessons to learn. From there you go to the Akashic Plane, the Mental Plane, the Messianic Plane, and finally the Buddhaic Plane. From there it's back to the Tao/God or Heaven. You will have completed the journey and will have merged back in with

All That Is. You are no longer separate, you are now part of the Oneness."

The audience was nodding in agreement and I could see that they were understanding Mike's message. I just hoped that people in general, less enlightened than this group would understand how this information could help them in their day-to-day existence.

Chapter 13

After pausing for a sip of tea, Mike asked, "Ready for the next point—Why Do We Come Back And How Many Times?"

The audience responded enthusiastically, "Yeah, Okay, and You bet!"

Mike continued, "Since the whole purpose of life is to experience things and expand our understanding, this in and of itself implies that it can't possibly be done all in one lifetime. When we are cast out from the Tao/God our essence, or soul, goes through a fairly well organized cycle of lifetimes with specific things to learn at each step along the way. There are seven different soul ages."

He walked over to the marker board, took a black marker, and wrote:

1. Infant Soul
2. Baby Soul
3. Young Soul
4. Mature Soul
5. Old Soul
6. Transcendental Soul
7. Infinite Soul

"The first five levels, infant through old soul, occur when your soul is occupying a physical body. The last two are usually done on a higher plane of existence than the physical Universe. In the case of the first five soul ages, there is one fragment, or soul, occupying one physical body. In the case of the transcendental soul, instead of one fragment per body, the entire entity of approximately 1,000 fragments, or souls, can occupy the same physical body. While it is rare for a transcendental soul to take a physical body it does happen. In which case the soul can tap into the experiential knowledge of all 1,000 fragments. As you might have guessed transcendental souls are not your average Joe walking around on Main Street. They tend to stand out in a crowd and usually have a group of devoted followers. A few examples include:

> Mother Cabrini
> Mahatma Gandhi
> John the Baptist
> Mohammed
> Socrates

"Even rarer on earth is the last category, the infinite soul, who unlike the transcendental soul, is not a reunited entity but instead is a direct link to the Tao/God operating through the body of a seventh-level old soul. This rare class of individuals include:

> Buddha
> Confucius
> Jesus Christ
> Krishna
> Lao Tsu

"An infinite soul only appears every two thousand years or so in the same region of the world, at least that has been the past experience. Now that we are in an era of instant global communications it more than likely will be done differently in the future. Usually the reason for the appearance of the infinite soul is to update the spiritual teachings which, through the passage of time, and alteration by mankind, need to be straightened out. Each time a piece of information is translated into another language, or the original language itself evolves, with words taking on different meanings, the interpretation gets twisted.

"If you've ever read an instruction manual written in another country, for a product produced in that country and sold in our country, you know what I mean. One example is the manual for one of the first models of a Japanese automobile being sold in the

United States. The manual said to 'earth the battery,' which could be interpreted to mean put the battery in the earth, or bury it. However, after a few minutes of scratching my head, I deduced that it should have been translated to say, 'ground the battery.'

"In conventional Spanish the word coger means 'to catch' yet in Spanish spoken in Argentine it means 'to fornicate.' Same language, just different colloquial usage. The problem of language is ever present when dealing with communications between people. Throw in the vast changes that can occur over two thousand years and you can see how easy it is to twist the true meanings of our earlier spiritual teachers.

"Earlier I spoke about the different planes or dimensions of awareness. Each plane is unique and therefore the spiritual message that comes from that plane will be different than that from another plane. No plane is better than the other, just a different message.

"In the case of the great spiritual leader Lao Tsu, his teachings were from the fifth plane, the Mental Plane, where the message is about Truth.

"Christ chose to teach us about Love, the message to be learned from the sixth plane, the Messianic level.

"Buddha, in turn, taught us about Oneness, the lesson of the seventh plane, called the Buddhaic Plane.

"Understanding this, it is realistic to say that since Christ was a direct link to the Tao/God, All That Is, The Oneness, that he was in the truest spiritual sense, the Son of God. It would likewise be fair to say that the handful of other infinite souls were also in the same sense, Sons of God."

A small, delicate looking fifty-something man in the second row asked, "So, Mike, do your channeled messages say when the next infinite soul will appear?"

"According to some channels, the next appearance of an infinite soul comparable to Christ or Buddha, will be around the year 2040."

A voice in the back said, "Most of us feel that wouldn't be a bit too soon, judging how much we have distorted the original teachings of these great masters to justify all sorts of ridiculous beliefs as well as to condone wars, violence and persecution of innocent people with differing views."

Mike nodded in agreement, "You're 100% correct. But I'm not convinced we have to wait another forty years. That's why I'm here today. We need to spread this message throughout society now—while there's still a planet for infinite souls to come back to."

Heads around the room nodded and murmured agreement.

Mike pointed to the next point on the board. "Okay, How many times do we come back to Earth? There isn't an easy canned answer to this one. It varies considerably, depending upon one's soul age, soul level, your soul's role in life, and the number of karmas and agreements you need to complete. However, I can give you approximate averages for the five Earth plane soul ages."

Mike walked over to the marker board, and began to write the next important information:

First stage - Infant Soul ....5 - 70 lifetimes
Second stage - Baby Soul ....5 - 43 lifetimes
Third stage - Young Soul ....5 - 22 lifetimes
Fourth stage - Mature Soul ....24 - 26 lifetimes
Fifth stage - Old Soul .... 4 - 40 lifetimes

Average range of lifetimes.............. 113-201

"Now let's talk a little about these five soul ages correlating them to our growth as humans.

1. We start out as a newborn child.
2. We progress to the toddler stage.
3. We move on to becoming a child.
4. We turn into an adolescent.
5. We finally become an adult.

"Within each of the five life stages there are seven different levels to master—a total of thirty-five separate parts. Just think, when you went to school, typically you had thirteen years, kindergarten through twelfth grade, then four more years of college, and maybe two or four years of postgraduate study. A total of seventeen to twenty-one years—a breeze when compared to the game of life where it can take a minimum of thirty-five lifetimes—which is very rare—upwards to five hundred life times, with an average somewhere between one hundred thirteen to two hundred one. Buddha apparently liked it here on Earth, or he had a lot of karmas to work off because he went through a whopping five hundred fifty lives before he finally cycled off."

One of the men with a graying ponytail, who had spoken earlier, said, "Oh man, this life is tough enough. Are you sure I'm not done yet?"

"The good news," said Mike, "is that everyone in this room is either in the mature soul or old soul stage of your cycle of lives on Earth. You've already learned the lessons of the earlier soul ages. Which leads into the next point on the board:

What are the lessons of each soul age?

"Each soul age has different lessons to learn and master on the Physical Plane. There is no right or wrong, better or worse, just differences. Each soul age has it's positive and negative points.

"Infant Soul - this is the starting point when you take a human form on Earth. At this point, it's just like you fell off the turnip truck. You're pretty green. You don't know much about living on the Physical Plane, and your biggest lesson to learn is how to survive in a strange new body in a strange world you are unaccustomed to. You will tend to be quite simple, primitive and find yourself happiest in simple, uncomplicated environments. Often Infant Souls live in the woods or jungles as natives in small tribes where they only have to focus on honing their survival skills within nature. On a positive level Infant Souls have a highly developed instinctive side and are very much in tune with nature. On the negative side, if integrated into a more complex society they would have difficulty coping and may become psychopaths or mass murderers. Ted Bundy, serial killer, David Carpenter, serial rapist/killer, and Richard Ramirez, the Hillside Strangler were Infant Souls.[2] After thirty-five to seventy lifetimes learning the ropes and creating a lot of karma, you are ready to move on to Baby Soul.

"Baby Soul - the lesson here is how to live with people. Learning about rules, laws, and what is good and what is evil. At this level you will tend to see life in black and white terms. You might be an active member of a political party, a PTA member, and be a part of the Boy and Girl Scouts. You learn to follow society's moral code, or as in the case of Jimmy Swaggart, a Baby Soul, face an

2. See Author's notes in the back of the book

agonizing personal emotional struggle when you fail to adhere to the moral code you preach. The positive side of being a Baby Soul is mastering good citizenship. The negative is being dogmatic and inflexible. Again, this is a soul age where you would probably create more karmic debt than pay off your debt.

"Famous Baby Souls include: Jerry Falwell, Louis Farrakhan, Adolph Hitler, Mohammar Khadafy, and Oral Roberts."

"Excuse me Mike," said the woman sitting on a floor cushion directly in front of him. Is it fair to say that conservative religious groups are all Baby Souls?"

"That's a good question. You can have all soul ages represented in any group, depending upon what issues the individual soul is working on. But in general you will find Baby Souls drawn to groups that have strict black and white rules. Military organizations, right-wing militia, police departments, and even fanatical terrorist organizations, and yes, even conservative religious groups. Members of these groups rigidly follow and believe what their leaders say. Many are so devoted they will kill others that don't share their black and white beliefs. In fact, some of the groups that are trying to stop this message from getting out, and have attacked me on numerous occasions, are made up of predominantly Baby Souls."

Mike paused for a minute, took a sip of tea, and moved back to sitting on the edge of the table. "Once you master the lessons of the Baby Soul age, in an average of thirty-five to forty-three lifetimes, you will move on to become a Young Soul.

"*Young Soul* - this soul age is all about power. Learning how to master it by winning and acquiring things. It's the attitude of 'he who has the most toys at the end of the game wins.' Achieving fame, wealth and power are the dominant goals. This is the most competitive soul age and the place where you will be most interested in status symbols. Your body is important. You will want it to look as good as possible for as long as possible. The majority of the people in the United States are presently going through their Young Soul lifetime. Donald Trump, Imelda Marcos, Jacqueline Onassis, Garth Brooks, and Elizabeth Dole are all young souls. Typically, you can get through your Young Soul age in fifteen to twenty-two lifetimes. The positive aspect of young soulhood is your ability to accomplish things, and make progress replacing the old and obsolete parts of society with the new. The negative polarity of Young Soul is being too materialistic and a win-at-all-cost mentality that can condone breaking laws to achieve the goal.

"*Mature Soul* - at this soul age you are primarily learning the lessons of relationships and the emotional intensity that usually accompanies them. You might still be competitive and successful out in the world, but your real focus is directed inward as you search for more meaning to life. This can be a rough soul age because of all the inner turmoil. It's the time when you start to pay back all the karmas you have built up over all the preceding soul ages.

"The positive aspect of the Mature Soul age is their openness to spiritual growth and developing emotionally deep and meaningful relationships. The negative side shows up in the overly emotional, intense soap opera dramas that can and frequently do occur. It takes about twenty-four to twenty-six lifetimes to get through all seven levels of this soul age. Some famous Mature Souls include: Kevin Costner, Jay Leno, Marilyn Monroe, Elizabeth Taylor and Oprah Winfrey—and of course, many of you. The rest are at the old soul age.

"*Old Soul* - spirituality is the lesson to learn at this final level in the Physical Plane. Old Souls tend to be individualistic, with a live and let live attitude. While nothing stops them from being wealthy, it is not the prime driving force, nor is status. An Old Soul could be perfectly happy being a gardener for a Young Soul like Donald Trump. Some Old Souls are so laid back that they chose a simple life living on the street as a homeless person without all the societally imposed responsibilities that the rest of us have to deal with—such as paying the IRS. Old Souls are busy paying off any last karmic debts, and tackling any self-karmas they may have decided to master this lifetime. Some famous Old Souls include: Joan Baez, George Carlin, Jerry Garcia, Whoopi Goldberg, and Mother Theresa. Wrapping up the seven levels of Old Soulhood takes four to forty lifetimes. The positive side is a caring, easy-going, accepting nature and a willingness to teach others deeper spiritual lessons. The negative side can be a person too lazy and too weird to fit into society."

"Wow, that sure fits us," said a man with a ponytail and his arm around the shoulder of a woman with long straight hair. "All we wanta do is kick back, relax, tend our vegetable garden, and sell our arts and crafts at flea markets."

Camille stood up, motioned to Mike, and said, "Everyone, it's time for a break. Let's give Mike about fifteen minutes to rest before we continue."

Chapter 14

I grabbed Mike's mug and went off to refill it with some fresh hot tea. At the small table with the teas I quickly selected a couple of nice herbal teas for Mike and myself. As I filled our mugs, one of the women from the audience, a very attractive forty something, came over for a refill also. She spoke, "Hi, my name is Michelle. Camille said you're writing a book about what Mike is teaching. Do you know yet when it will be published?"

This is a common question authors are asked. Unfortunately, unless one self-publishes, the answer is always a big unknown. Often the author has to find an agent who in turn has to find a publisher. The big publishers frequently schedule books out more than a year into the future. It can be a long laborious process.

So, lacking a precise answer, I just smiled and gave a nice sounding, positive, but evasive answer, that contained a measure of hope. One can learn a lot listening to politicians who say nothing, very convincingly. "Good question. I'm hoping to have the first draft of the book complete by late summer, then Mike and I will have to decide what's the fastest way to get it edited and published. I'm sure once it's published Camille will have it for sale and a book signing as well."

Michelle replied, "Wonderful. I'd love to have an autographed copy. Judging by what Mike was saying, I must be a Mature Soul. My life at times has been like a soap opera. I've been married and divorced twice and always seem to get drawn to men who turn out to be wrong for me. My first husband was mean and abusive and the last one had affairs with other women. What about you? What soul age are you?"

For a split second, I wanted to laugh. Could it be possible that in a few years 'What's your soul age?' would replace 'What's your astrology sign?' as the hot new pickup line in singles' bars?

"Well," I replied, "your life certainly does sound like a Mature Soul's. Mike said I'm an Old Soul and Old Souls can have relationship issues also. Particularly if, between lifetimes, they have made multiple mate or sex agreements for this lifetime. Often we end up making agreements on the Astral Plane then get down here on the Physical Plane and discover we've over-committed."

Michelle pondered what I had said for a moment and said, "What if I find I'm strongly attracted to you. Does that mean we have a mate or sex agreement for this lifetime?"

Sensing the discussion was headed in the wrong direction, I quickly stammered a response, "Well ahh...well...it could...but one doesn't have to go through with all their Astral Plane agreements if circumstances on Earth are different than envisioned. For example, let's say while I was on the Astral Plane I made two mate agreements and ten sex agreements for this lifetime. In my younger years let's say I completed eight of the sex agreements then got married for a few years, then divorced and remarried. I can decide to postpone the two sex agreements until another lifetime because fulfilling those sex agreement could disrupt my mate agreement."

Sounding disappointed, Michelle said, "Okay, I think I understand. What you're saying is nothing is carved in stone."

"That's right. Like when two people eye each other across a crowded room and both feel an unusually strong attraction. Perhaps they had an agreement to meet in this lifetime but, for a multitude of reasons one or the other decides to do nothing and turns away."

"That sounds sad," said Michelle.

"In terms of life in the Physical Plane it is sad, but in the bigger picture perhaps the two people will have an even better and longer relationship in a future lifetime."

"What if the two people are so strongly attracted to one another they decide to complete their mate or sex agreement this lifetime?"

"According to what Mike told me there are a couple of possibilities. It could be the existing mate agreement one person had is coming to an end and the new person pushes the breakup along. Often, when an agreement is about over, circumstances occur that will facilitate the breakup. In this example it's the arrival of the new person.

"On the other hand, if the man's existing mate agreement is for a lifetime, and he breaks it to run off with somebody new, he could be incurring a heavy karmic debt to the mate he dumped as well as to their children if there are any."

"How do you know which it is?" asked Michelle.

"The best way is to have someone like Mike, who can tap into and channel the Michael energy, look at both of you and tell you what your agreements are with the parties involved."

"What about my first marriage?" Michelle asked. "Ted was always getting drunk and beating me."

"I'm not a Michael channel," I said, "so I can't say for sure, but based on what I've learned from Mike, it could be a couple of possibilities. First it could be a karmic payback from another lifetime. Perhaps you were the man and Ted was the woman, and you beat him/her in that lifetime. Now the karma ledger has been balanced. The other possibility is Ted is creating new karma and will owe you in a future life.

"The key thing to remember is that you can't escape karma. If bad things happen to you, chances are you're either getting a karmic payback for some past misdeed or someone is creating new karma and will owe you. Either way you win. The sooner you can clean up your bad karma the sooner you will evolve as a soul. If you have good karma coming to you it can make a future lifetime easier."

"Okay, Scott, that makes sense, but what about my second husband who had all the affairs?"

"How long were you married?"

"When did he start going out with other women?"

"After about three years, why do you ask?"

"Because it's possible," I said, "that you had a short mate agreement with him. Maybe it was for two and a half to three years, then when it was over, on a soul level, he knew it was time to move on to complete other mate or sex agreements he had.

"If he had started fooling around just after you were married I think the odds would be much higher that he was breaking his mate agreement with you and creating bad karma for himself. But remember, I'm only speculating. Mike or another Michael channel could confirm which possibility is correct."

"Thank you, Scott. It's amazing how that puts such a totally different perspective on my relationships. I had never considered that marriages, or mate agreements as you call them, could be for different, pre-arranged, lengths of time."

"Remember when Mike was talking about Baby Souls a short while ago? Well it wasn't that long ago that most of America was made up of Baby Souls, so of course the ruling philosophy was a very moralistic black and white one. That meant divorce was a sin in the eyes of the religious leaders. It was a time period when we were all learning Baby Soul lessons. But just like the rules you followed in the first grade are different in high school, so it is with soul evolution. There's a time and a place for different rules and beliefs. Those people, such as yourself, who are at the Mature Souls stage of evolution need more freedom from the Baby Soul rules in order to complete all your relationship lessons. Multiple mates and sex partners can be one way of completing more lessons in a shorter period of time.

"Tolerance of others is the key message of my book. It's okay for the Baby Souls to follow one set of rules and it is equally okay for the other soul ages to follow different rules. Earth is nothing more than a school with different grade levels and different classrooms."

Behind me I heard a pair of hands clapping, I turned and saw Mike standing there with a big grin on his face. "Well done, Scott. I caught the last bit of what you're saying. You're picking up the Michael Soul Teachings quite well. In no time at all you can be the one giving the talk."

Slightly embarrassed, I thanked him and introduced him formally to Michelle, just as Camille was ringing her bell to get everyone back into the classroom.

Mike walked over to the table and sat on the front edge. Then he closed his eyes and took a couple of deep breaths. I realized he was about to do some channeling. He opened his eyes and spoke, "Hello everyone. I thought this would be a good time to bring the Michael energy in and do a little channeling to determine your soul ages and soul levels. I think it will help you better understand them."

His piercing eyes slowly scanned the room, stopping at each person, until he had made contact with everyone, including Camille and myself. Then, starting with me at the far left, he went from person to person telling them what their soul age and soul level were:

"Old soul, sixth level;
Mature soul, seventh level;
Mature, fourth level;
Old, first level;
Mature, third level;
Old, seventh level;
Old, fifth level;
Old, fourth level;
Mature, first level;
Old, third level;
Mature, fifth level;
Mature, second level;
Old, second level;
Old, third level;
Old, first level;
Mature, sixth level;

and lastly, I'm an Old soul, seventh level. Now what does all that mean? You already know what the primary lessons Mature and Old souls are learning, now I want to share with you the seven different levels within each soul age. Please remember these levels apply to all soul ages.

"*First level* - this is a time for cautious exploration of a new soul age level. Somewhat like sticking your toe into a bathtub of hot water. You want to get the feel of it before you plunge in 100%.

"*Second level* - still a time of questioning, but you start to move into the purpose of the soul age you're in. The transition becomes more complete.

"Third level - at this level you start to introvert. You have trouble integrating your awareness in your everyday life and spend a great deal of time intellectualizing about it.

"Fourth level - a time when it all comes together and you become confident that you understand the soul age. It is a time for doing things.

"Fifth level - this is the time you start to become a bit eccentric as you stretch the limits of the soul age.

"Sixth level - a period of heavy karma. The infant, baby and young souls are off creating karmas while the mature and old souls are paying it back.

"Seventh level - a time to rest from the strain and stress of the cycle and start teaching others some of the lessons you've learned along the path.

"This pattern repeats itself each time you complete one soul age and start a new one, with the only main difference being the flavor of the different soul ages. Each is a higher octave of the previous one."

Mike pointed to Michelle, whom he had earlier identified as a sixth level Mature Soul and said, "So Michelle, do you see how the soul age and level are working for you?"

"Do you mean that I'm paying back karma this lifetime?"

"Yes, and since you're in the Mature Soul phase your karmic paybacks are often related to relationships."

"Okay," said Michelle, "I think I get it. Was Scott correct when he guessed that my abusive ex-husband in this lifetime was a payback from a past lifetime?"

"Yes. Five lifetimes ago you were the man and he was the woman. You were abusive to him in that lifetime. The good news is the ledger is now balanced and neither you nor he will have to endure any future abusive relationships."

"But, Mike, does it always have to be a blow-for-blow payback? People could twist what you're saying to always justify their abusiveness and that doesn't seem fair."

"I see what you're driving at. Karma is karma and it must be paid back at some point. However, if a person is just using it as a cop-out and there were no prior lifetime abuse that they received, then they are creating brand-new karma and will have to pay for it.

"Also, keep in mind that there often are alternative ways of paying back karma. Let's say you were the abusive person in ten different lifetimes or relationships. Rather than you being beaten in your next ten relationships, you might, with the agreement of the other souls involved, devote a portion of one or more lifetimes helping abused people deal with an abusive relationship. The key point is you need to emotionally feel the same pain you inflicted originally. If you can do this through working with others, then you are paying off your karma."

An older man with a white ponytail raised his hand. "Mike, you said I was a third level Old Soul. What main thing am I dealing with?"

"In your case you're mostly working on self-karmas where your soul has given you a challenge without someone else being involved. Health is the key issue and since you're at the third level you have spent a lot of time introverting and thinking about it. Am I right?"

"I'll say," the man replied. "I read dozens of different health magazines and alternative medicine newsletters and I spend hours every day on the Internet looking up health related information. Now I see why."

The young twenty something woman whom Mike had identified as a seventh level Old Soul spoke, "Mike, since you and I are both seventh level Old Souls does that mean we don't have to come back to Earth?"

"Good question. The answer is, it's up to you to decide.

"One would think that by the time we got all the way through the five soul ages and seven levels of each soul age, and had cycled off planet Earth, then went through the six other planes, we wouldn't want to come back and go through the whole process all over again. Yet surprisingly, most of us decide to play the game all over again, and then again, and again. Either things must be pretty boring back in the Tao/Heaven or we quickly forget how rough life can be at times down here on planet Earth.

"Apparently the reason we do it is by the time we have worked our way up through some of the other planes, life here on Earth doesn't seem that rough. Thanks to a 'spiritual' amnesia the bad moments we struggled through simply become the 'good old days' that we laugh about. Not unlike how we often view the bad moments of our childhood when we look back from an adult perspective."

Looking directly at the young woman, Mike said, "In your case, you have already cycled back two other times. This is your third cycle, so deep inside your soul you must like the game. Myself, this is my tenth cycle, so I either have a few screws loose or I enjoy the Earth plane challenges."

Most of the crowd looked at Mike as if he must have a few screws loose. The general consensus appeared to be that one time through the Grand Cycle would be enough. I made a mental note to ask Mike later whether I had done more than one Grand Cycle.

"Camille said I was going to talk about the 'Clash of Different Soul Ages.' This to me is the most important thing to understand about the Michael Soul Teachings because of the problems caused.

"As you might guess there can be problems between the different soul ages not unlike the inherent clash between different generations. Since each soul age group has different lessons to learn, and has amnesia concerning their previous existences at the other soul ages, there is a tendency to take the ever popular 'I'm right and you're wrong' attitude.

"*Infant Souls* in particular, have a tough time dealing with the other soul ages. Their inherent survival instincts clash with a society made up of confusing laws, sophisticated power control games, and complex personal relationship issues. When pushed too hard they can crack, becoming psychopaths and mass murderers. Fortunately, few of the other soul ages have much contact or interaction with infant souls.

"*Baby Souls* are the backbone of society. They support and enforce the rules, laws and moral codes we all live by. They can be outstanding when serving in roles in the military, law enforcement, and the government. They are typically solid citizens who are both church going and law abiding. They often have conflicts with other soul ages that either try to skirt the law for personal gain, or simply view the laws as outdated. They can, at times, be a bit oppressive to others, when they see the world as black and white with no shades of gray. Of all the soul ages they most need to work on being tolerant of others and understanding that laws must evolve with society rather than remain the same forever.

"*Young Souls* can't stand Baby Souls. They view them as stodgy, hung up on rules, and prone to throw cold water on all the great progressive ideas Young Souls come up with. Young Souls regard Mature Souls as too introspective, too busy wasting all their time getting in touch with their deeper feelings. Old Souls, from the perspective of Young Souls, are simply too lazy, or eccentric to be of much value. Young Souls need to slow down enough to understand that in their quest for power and success at all cost that they should follow the Baby Souls lead and play by the rules. That makes winning more challenging and more satisfying without the problem of creating more negative karma by cheating. They too need to recognize that people are different and it's okay to be different. Tolerance for other people's feelings, beliefs and attitudes will benefit Young Souls a great deal.

"*Mature Souls* tend to be the most balanced. They can be as family-oriented as a Baby Soul, and while not driven to success like a Young Soul, they can achieve it. They also relate to many of the environmental concerns of Old Souls. They just need to keep from becoming so introspective—Woody Allen, a fifth level Mature Soul, is a good example—that they fail to understand the needs or even the existence of the other soul ages.

"*Old Souls* are usually the most laid back. They have an easy going, live-and-let-live attitude that lets them get along with all the other soul ages to a great degree as long as they are not hassled too much. Their challenge is not so much a matter of being tolerant of the others, but of learning to take the time to teach the others the value of tolerance.

"One of the goals of the book Scott is writing is to make people aware that there are differences in people that extend beyond what we had known before this time. Simply by knowing how this complicated spiritual game is actually played should give all souls a greater degree of tolerance for each other. For example, say a Young Soul parent has an Old Soul child. In this case, the parent can be less demanding and not insist that little Jason or Jessica achieve all the status marks of success that the parent wants for them. Instead the parent can help the Old Soul child develop his or her own uniqueness even if it does not include attending a prestigious school. Similarly, a Baby Soul judge might learn to be more tolerant of the laid back Old Soul couple living peacefully up in the hills, growing, for their own use, plants that have mild hallucinogenic effects."

The here-to-fore quiet and attentive audience suddenly burst into laughter and cheers. Mike had obviously touched on a topic of great interest to his audience. After the excitement died down, a woman in the back of the room said, "Mike it sounds like Old Souls are better. Is this true?"

"No, I'm sorry if I gave that impression," said Mike. "When first exposed to this knowledge, almost everyone wants to be an Old Soul. Somehow they are perceived to be more with it, or ahead of the rest of us, but nothing could be further from the truth. Old souls can be lazy, irresponsible people who give nothing to society and take as much as they can. No soul age has it better than another. Each soul age brings with it different challenges. No one has an easy go of it. If they did there would be no experiences to grow from and no reason to return numerous times.

"Instead of viewing the entire process sequentially—where each succeeding level is higher than the last—you should view it as a spiral, like the coiled circular springs in a mattress. No spot on the coil is better than any other. You can readily see that a Baby Soul that had completed six Grand Cycles, all the way back to the Tao/God, could be viewed as ahead of, or more experienced, than an Old Soul on only their second Grand Cycle. So, resist the urge to rush out, discover your soul age, and start being critical of younger soul ages. We're all in this together, just learning different lessons. It is not unlike seven people being sent out to find food and survive in the wilds. One might be better at knowing where to look for game. Another better at killing the game the first one discovered. A third might be the best fisherman. The fourth skilled at finding edible plant life. The fifth most skilled in building a cooking fire. The sixth could be the best cook, and the seventh could know how to preserve the leftover or excess food.

"If it turns out your friends or even your children are 'older' souls than you, don't despair. Each soul age and soul level is but a different animal on a merry-go-round. You get to ride thirty-five different animals each Grand Cycle. Each one looks a little different but they all go up and down and around and around. Welcome to planet Earth!

"That completes my remarks for today. I hope what I had to say was informative and when Scott gets the book done we'll come back for a book signing party. Thank you for being so attentive."

The group, myself included, rose and gave Mike a well-deserved round of applause. I had a much better understanding of the Michael Soul Teachings and how they could, if understood on a broader basis, bring about more understanding and tolerance among all the people existing on planet Earth.

After a few more minutes chatting with the attendees, Mike and I made our way out to the front of the store where Camille gave both of us a warm good-bye hug. Minutes later we were on our way back to Seattle.

Chapter 15

I pulled into a fast food drive-thru and ordered two cheeseburgers, fries and water. I could hear my arteries pleading and screaming at me to say no to the fat hit they were about to face, but my stomach won. Sorry arteries. Next time, I'll pack one of Karen's healthy sandwiches.

While Mike and I inhaled the junk food, I switched on the car radio. The Seattle Times bombing was all over the news. Connie was mentioned as the intended target and the most common speculation centered around her recent article on hate groups as the reason for the bombing. Reporters were everywhere trying to get background information on the possible perpetrators. The politicians were making their usual tough-sounding, but meaningless statements about catching the people responsible. One politician claimed over-crowded schools were the cause, while another called for tougher drug laws. The Asian community claimed it was a hate crime against one of their more high-profile members. The police and FBI weren't saying much—just the usual bland remark about following up on several promising leads.

We caught the tail end of the Mayor's press conference. A reporter asked if the attack on gays and now the attack on an Asian would seriously hurt tourism and the economic development of the Greater Seattle area. Of course the Mayor did his best to play down the two violent events as random isolated occurrences that did not, in the least, detract from Seattle's image as a highly desirable place to live, work, or visit. One has to admire the ability of politicians to put a good spin on almost any situation.

A flood to them is an opportunity to fill reservoirs and the water shed which will keep us safe from a devastating drought the following summer.

Mike's cell phone beeped. It was Pudgy.

"Hi Pudge, what's up?" He listened for a minute then said, "Look, we're about 20 minutes away from Kingston. We'll meet you at the Ferry toll-booth." He disconnected the call and said to me, "Scott, Pudgy spotted the maroon van near Green Lake and he followed it. They got on the Seattle-Bremerton Ferry in downtown Seattle, got off in Bremerton and headed southwest on Highway 3. That's where he lost them. They could be going to the Bremerton National Airport or around Sinclair Inlet to Port Orchard or a thousand other places. Since the attack on the gays, DOG has all but disappeared. Pudgy has been unofficially helping the FBI try to locate their hideout. Pudgy is heading up from Bremerton right now. He'll catch up with us at the Ferry Terminal."

"I thought the FBI was on top of DOG—knew their location and everything? They didn't have any trouble finding them for questioning after the attack on the gays."

"According to Pudgy, the FBI raided their headquarters right after the bomb went off at the Times and the place was deserted. Apparently DOG got nervous and switched their headquarters to another location. They were located up in Snohomish County, in the woods near Monroe. Since some of their younger thugs are serving time at the Monroe State Reformatory, I guess Wolfe Drake wanted to be nearby to show support and keep anyone from going soft."

"Well, Mike, at least they'll be too busy hiding to bother us." I said.

"Don't be too sure. The big leader, McCallum, back in Mississippi, is an expert on guerrilla warfare and terrorism. They might be in hiding but they could still be planning a series of small hit-and-run attacks. Don't let down your vigilance for a minute. In fact the more you can lock yourself in your house and write, the better. Leave the cops and robbers stuff to the FBI."

"You're right, Mike. These creeps are scary. I'll keep my guard up."

"Good. Now, Scott, did you understand everything I said at the bookstore?"

"Ahh—I do have a question—about mate agreements. It seems like in my parents and grandparents generations divorce was rare, now it's too common—almost like it's inevitable. Can you explain that to me again?"

"Sure thing. back then, the U.S. was predominantly made up of Baby and Young Souls, with smaller numbers of Mature and Old Souls. As more people evolved up the soul age ladder we shifted into a society currently made up of more Young and Mature Souls. In your grandparents time you had clashes between the Baby Souls trying to enforce a strict adherence to law and order, and the moral codes of the Judeo-Christian world, on everyone, even Young Souls. Prohibition was an example. The Young Souls figured it was a stupid law so they were busy breaking the law and making a bloody fortune. Finally, society in general, took the side of the Young Souls and repealed the Prohibition laws. The Young Souls have been in control ever since then. But now, with a significant shift in the numbers of Mature Souls, the agenda for society is once again shifting. Making money is still popular, but relationships, the key lesson to learn for the Mature Souls has become more important. The way this works in the big spiritual picture is souls on the Astral Plane, getting ready to incarnate, start changing the agreements they are making with other souls, from money-related issues to relationship ones.

"Let's say in the last lifetime you were a seventh level Young Soul and you had mastered all the lessons of acquiring money, power and possessions. You're now interested in shifting your emphasis. You might still want to have a nice home and a good-paying job, but your focus and the key dramas in your life will now be about relationships. So, while still on the Astral Plane, you make a series of agreements that will help you learn the lessons of a First Level Mature Soul. Since it's just the first level you might limit yourself to a few teenage romances and one divorce. Or you might decide to live with someone instead of getting married. You might decide to go into business only this time you choose to have a partner so you can work on that type relationship. There are lots of variables that are considered but that gives you a general idea.

"But, if I remember correctly, Scott, you asked specifically about mate agreements. In your case you've been married three times. The first time you had a mate agreement for eight years, the second for fourteen years, and your last one is for thirty years."

"That Mike, is rather amazing. My first marriage went on the rocks after seven and a half years and ended officially after eight years. But I didn't want the divorce. If I had made an agreement shouldn't I have welcomed it?"

"Scott, you the spirit, or soul knew about the agreement and wanted it, but your ego, your personality—all the parts tied to your physical body didn't. They aren't privy to all the agreements made on the Astral Plane by the true you, the soul. Remember the car analogy. The car never knows where the driver is going until the car arrives at the destination. Left to itself the car might have preferred spending the day in a comfortable garage rather than being pelted by rain or baked in the sun."

"Now tell me about your second divorce."

"Well, it ended just as suddenly. I was caught completely off guard. The marriage started going bad around the fourteen year mark and the actual divorce occurred two years later, when finances were better. The big difference this time was I immediately consulted the regression therapist I was seeing at the time and what came out was rather startling. Even though my second wife wanted the divorce, it turned out that on a subconscious level I had wanted it. It sounds kinda weird but that's what I uncovered."

"Not weird at all, Scott. What you refer to as your subconscious, actually was your soul. Unbeknown to you the personality, your soul was quietly doing things and creating situations that would ultimately lead to your wife asking for a divorce. What's your current relationship with the two ex-wives?"

"Quite good. I know it's a little unusual, but I communicate with both of them and have a very good relationship. Karen also gets along well with both of them."

"That's probably because you're an Old Soul. You're no longer at the early stages of Mature Soul where it's common to despise an ex. You've polished off all your karmas and you can view the relationships from the positive viewpoint of the soul and not from the physical. Soul-wise you're able to understand the intent behind the mate agreement. In both of these mate agreements, your purpose was to become parents to the two souls who are your daughters in this lifetime, plus you were working out a gender swap. You had been married to both women in another lifetime, but you were a female playing the role of the wife. This time around you balanced out the relationships by taking the role of the husband."

"How common is it to switch gender?" I asked.

"Very common. In fact we call them Monads. Basically a monad is an agreement between two souls to experience both sides of a relationship, whether it be husband/wife, father/son, father/daughter, mother/son, mother/daughter, teacher/student, boss/worker. The possible combinations are enormous. Your daughter Joni was your mother in another lifetime and now the two of you are trying out a parent/child reversal with you the parent this time around."

"It's uncanny, Mike. At times she seems more like a mother than a daughter. There's a part of her that is bossy—like a mother.

"Mike, I also wanted to ask you about Grand Cycles. You said at the meeting that this is your tenth time cycling through all the soul ages and returning to the Tao. What about me?"

"You're just as crazy as me, Scott. This is your ninth cycle and your soul is planning on several more cycles. You must like struggling through the morass we call life in a human body on planet Earth."

"To be honest with you, Mike, there are plenty of times I want this to be my last lifetime on Earth."

"I know the feeling Scott, but by the time we work our way through all the other planes of existence, life here on Earth starts to look okay. The best thing is each time you complete one cycle and start over, it's not like going back to square one. It's more like an upward spiral. You still have to become an Infant Soul, but you work on higher octave issues of that soul age. You create much less bad karma so in later soul ages you have less karma to pay back, so it actually does get easier."

As we hit the outskirts of Kingston my mind flashed back to Connie and the bomb. What if she had been at her desk when the bomb exploded? What if she would've been killed or badly injured?

I heard the roar of a Harley and looked in my rearview mirror in time to see Pudgy deftly cutting in between my Lexus and the car behind us. I gave him a quick wave of the hand letting him know we had spotted him. We paid our fare at the tollbooth and pulled ahead to our spot in line for boarding the ferry. We had about fifteen minutes to go. Pudgy dismounted and roughly plopped his massive frame in the back seat of the Lexus. I could feel the shock absorbers groan.

"Damn it. I let the sons-of-bitches get away from me," he blurted out. "I had them weasels cold. I was on their tail all the way from Green Lake, through crowded downtown Seattle and I lose them of all places out in the friggin' wide open country. I got stuck behind some asshole trucker pulling around another truck and by the time I could get around him they were gone. Damn. They gotta have their friggin' hideout somewhere around Bremerton."

"Did Connie get to your place okay?" asked Mike.

"Yeah. No problem. Lee Chou has her staying in our guest bedroom. Man, she is shook up big time—scared shitless. She musta pulled in some damn good karma to miss getting blown up. Wes said the bomb turned her desk into a pile of kindling."

"I think I'll give her a call," said Mike as he punched Pudgy's home number into his cell phone.

"Hi, Lee Chou, this is Mike. Everything okay?"

Pause.

"That's good to hear. Is she up to taking any calls?"

Pause.

"Okay thanks. Hi, Connie. I'm with Scott and Pudgy. We're waiting for the Kingston-Edmonds ferry. Anything new developing?"

After a long pause, Mike finished the conversation and ended the call. Turning so he could face both Pudgy and me he said, "The guy who delivered the bomb was wearing a UPS outfit and carried a clipboard so no one suspected him. When he left some people outside the building saw him hop on a bike and pedal away which seemed odd for a UPS delivery man. He headed down Fairview going north and disappeared down some side street going west."

"Witnesses say he was wearing sunglasses but they said he was five ten to five eleven, about one seventy five to one eighty five pounds and had a prominent red mustache."

"That matches the description of Reamer," I said. "The guy is pretty busy. First he tries to knife you, Mike, and now he's trying to blow up Connie."

"Sounds like the asshole is bucking for a promotion," said Pudgy. "The meaner and sicker they are the more Drake likes them. I wanta catch up to the sick prick before the FBI does and give him a big dose of street justice—like reamin' his ass out with a friggin' blow torch. You know damn well if the Feds get him he'll end up in some cushy federal pen with friggin' lawyers and kissy-assed social workers claiming he's really a nice boy with low self esteem. You know what I mean. They'll say he was socially deprived and driven to do bad things because he was spanked as a kid for wetting the bed or some such stupid bullshit."

"From a soul standpoint," said Mike, "Reamer is a Baby Soul acting out the negative side of the soul age. He's creating a lot of bad karma for future lifetimes."

The approaching ferry started to slow as it neared the dock. It was about time to board so Pudgy hopped out of the Lexus and mounted his Harley. Two teen-aged girls in a nearby BMW Z3 sports convertible were eyeing Pudgy and giggling. As he swung one leg over the Harley and eased his massive torso down onto the seat, he turned towards the girls, gave them a wink and a thumb's up. Embarrassed at being caught staring they tried stifling their giggles by covering their mouths with their hands. One of the girls gave a timid thumb's up back to Pudgy.

A bored state ferry worker removed the fluorescent orange traffic cone in front of us and signaled our row to drive onto the ferry. Once on board we parked, and with Pudgy following, went up the stairs to the passenger lounge. I headed over to the food counter, grabbed a ratty looking warped orange-brown serving tray, still half-wet from going through the dishwasher, and picked up the three remaining donuts. Apparently they were fresh earlier in the day, but by now they were hard enough to cause serious injury if dropped on one's toes.

I spotted a couple of large Starbucks carafes and poured out three cups of coffee. No decisions to make. Someone had already decided what blend so I wasn't torn between trying to decide if I'd like Sumatra coffee better than Ethiopian, Arabian mocha, Colombian, or any of the zillion other choices Starbucks offers. All I had to do was fill up the cups. No waiting—no complex decisions. I was in Heaven.

Chapter 16

Pudgy and Mike had taken a table booth by a window. I chose to set on Mike's side, giving Pudgy's body as much room as possible.

Looking quite serious, Mike said, "Look guys, I'm worried. DOG is starting to stir up a lot of trouble on the West Coast. I haven't heard about much happening back in Mississippi, so I have a feeling old Calvin McCallum is targeting our area for his expansion. He's got Wolfe Drake out here—probably his best regional leader—and a flock of really nasty goons. What have you been picking up around the bars, Pudgy?"

The same kinda shit. The gay attack gave DOG a lot of free publicity. When the cops had to release the DOG thugs a lot of the losers hanging around the bars started to pay attention. There's a lot more hate shit goin' around. Assholes mouthin' off about gays, Jews, Blacks, Asians, Hispanics. Even Catholics and Arabs are gettin' trashed.

"At times I wanta smash some shithead's mouth but I know I gotta stay undercover so I have to play along with this shit. But I'm tellin' ya man, there's gonna be a time comin' when I friggin' lose it and start tearin' these stupid assholes apart."

"Pudgy, I know how you feel but you gotta keep focused on the big picture. We've got Scott on board. The book is being written. We just have to make sure it gets done and published. The spiritual truths we're disseminating can have a profound effect on people, and the more people that know the truth, the less power groups like DOG will have."

"Yeah. I know you're right Mike. But when these scumbags try to kill someone as sweet and loving as Connie, man I wanna go ballistic."

"We've got to stay focused and alert." Mike said. "DOG is capable of anything—and if Drake is able to start recruiting more people in our area that could make our job a lot tougher and could put us all in more danger. Pudge, keep your eyes extra open to spotting any DOG recruiters you see and any potential prospects. The more information, including descriptions, that we can funnel to Wes and Ty at the FBI the better the odds we can stop them before someone else gets hurt."

"I hear ya, Mike. Ya know—I was just thinkin'—we got surveillance cameras at the bar. They just re-loop every twenty-four hours unless we pull the tapes. We got one covering the front door. Another covers the people at the bar and the cash register, and one covers the back door. The back door one also picks up people using the phone or goin' into the head. I think I'll start pullin' tapes for a while. I think I still got a couple a bugs layin' around that could be put in the john and the phone. Just might pick up some shit goin' down."

"Pudge, the surveillance cameras seem like a good idea. However, Scott and I didn't hear anything about bugs, got it?"

"Gotcha man. I was talkin' about cockroaches at the bar—that kinda bug," Pudgy replied with a wink of his left eye.

I thought Pudgy's idea sounded great. Capture the bad guys on tape. See who the new recruits are and listen in on their plans. The only question I had was how do we know they'll come into the particular bar Pudgy works at as a bouncer?

Reading my mind, Pudgy turned to me and said, "The bar I work at in the Fremont area draws a lot of guys working for the ship repair places on Lake Union. A lot of these guys are young drifters, ex-military. They can get work in the nearby dry-docks without many questions asked about their pasts. It's a closed group. They can smell a cop a mile off. I've seen DOG members in there at least once a week. It's a perfect place for them to recruit new members."

Mike interrupted. "Gentlemen, we are pulling into the Edmonds ferry landing. I'd like to go see Connie. Scott, can you absorb more info today or do you want to spend your time writing what we've already covered today?"

"No, I'd rather hear more stuff then spend the next several days just writing. I'd like to see Connie too."

"Okay, it's off to Pudgy's place. Are you sure it'll be okay with Lee Chou?"

"Yeah. No problem. She's lookin' forward to meetin' Scott."

I tossed our empty coffee cups in the trash and returned the ratty tray to a stack of similar looking trays atop the trash bin. We descended the stairs, and while Mike and I got in the Lexus, Pudgy threw a leg over the Harley and softly dropped his frame down onto the leather seat, showing more respect for the Harley's shocks than the shocks on the Lexus.

Once we cleared the ferry, following Mike's directions, I headed straight for Pudgy's place. It turned out he lived on 17th near NE 80th. Pudgy was just coming out of a garage located under the house at street level. The house, a pastel yellow two stories with basement, probably was built in the forties, looked well maintained. As Pudgy led us up the brick red stairs, I noticed the flower beds on either side. They were alive with color, even this early in the spring. I was seeing the other, more gentle, side to Pudgy, the bad-ass bouncer. Looks can indeed be deceiving.

Inside, Pudgy slipped off his boots. Mike and I followed suit. Probably the Asian influence of his wife. We found Lee Chou and Connie sitting in the kitchen drinking tea. Connie immediately jumped up and hugged Mike, Pudgy and me in that order. She was still scared from her near-death ordeal. I could feel it in her trembling body as she pressed against me. After a long hug, she pulled away, turned to Lee Chou and introduced me to her. Lee Chou was about five two, medium build and in her early forties. Her face projected a calm demeanor but I noticed her eyes were wary as she sized me up, withholding her final judgment until she got to know me better.

After a brief rehashing of all the events, Mike said he wanted to go over more of the Michael Soul Teachings with me and asked the others if they wanted to join him. Everyone agreed and Lee Chou shooed everyone into the more spacious living room while she prepared more tea. Mike and I grabbed the sofa, Connie chose a large stuffed cushion. Pudgy took a seat in a huge black leather La-Z-Boy chair that he promptly tilted back and flipped up the foot rest bringing his big smelly feet up closer to the level of our noses. Lee Chou must have a poor sense of smell.

Mike stared off into space apparently contemplating how he was going to structure the next batch of knowledge he was about to share. First he rubbed his scruffy beard a bit then clasped his hands together under his chin.

"Scott, the others already know what I'm going to share, so they're here to add to what I have to say as well as give you a visual reference point to some of the information."

Chapter 17

"Scott, you already know how we as souls evolve through the different soul ages, next I want to explain the various *Roles* we act out as we go through the grand cycle of lifetimes. Then if time permits, I want to cover more of the intricacies of how we construct our human personalities. It's quite different from what you were taught in school. But first let's discuss the process of picking your Role for a series of lives. To make it easier to understand I want to relate it to shopping at a mall. In this case let's pretend there's a spiritual mall that's part of the Tao/God.

"As you already know, you're an old soul, but pretend you're just starting out. Assume for a moment that you have been recruited by the Tao/God to go out and gain experiences to help the Tao/God expand and grow.

"It's a lot like when a parent tells the non-working, nineteen-year-old couch potato to get up off his butt and go out and get a job to help out with the bills, or move out. Only instead of having the nineteen-year-old's option of moving in with a friend who has a job and mooching off him, fragments, which we are, have to go to work in the Physical Plane. It's a lot like going into the Army, only tougher. It's where you really learn how to 'be all that you can be,' and it starts more or less like this:

"There you are, when you get your marching orders, just a naive little pulsating ball of energy. You have nothing to wear and the whole gang is waiting to board the launch ship headed to the Physical Plane. What do you do first? Don't panic. One of the old pros who has been to Earth hundreds of times will take you by the hand and lead you off to the Spiritual Mall where you will get to shop at several different stores for your new spiritual wardrobe as well as your human outfits.

"Your guide, let's call him Rahji—it sounds more spiritual than Uncle Al—leads you into the first shop. Rahji explains this is where you pick a Role. It is also called your *Essence Role*—the role your soul will have regardless what role your human personality has. Essence refers to the fact that your role is your core beingness—your true essence, or inner spirit.

"Once inside the Role Shoppe you notice that the display shows seven quite different-looking models. According to their name tags, they are called:

1. Server
2. Priest
3. Artisan
4. Sage
5. Warrior
6. King
7. Scholar

"When you ask Rahji why there are not any roles like banker, cook, shoe salesman, lawyer, or manicurist, he explains that those are roles for your human personality. Your soul needs a broader type of role. One that explains it's dominant way of being. Rahji explains further that the names used for the different roles do not necessarily refer to a specific occupation, but instead are just convenient terms to describe a fragment's basic way of existing in life. For example a woman with a warrior role might be working in a corporate marketing department. Her warrior nature would drive her to be focused on details and driven to accomplish her tasks efficiently, thus exhibiting warrior traits.

"Rahji adds that whichever role you pick, you will have to keep it for an entire grand cycle of lifetimes, anywhere from thirty-five to four hundred lifetimes. How's that for pressure! Imagine wearing the same underwear for four hundred lifetimes. But as your guide Rahji suggests, you should think of it more like picking a career for your soul, which you don't want to change every season, not if you want to truly master something. And it's not for eternity. You can try out another role every time you complete each grand cycle of lifetimes. And of course, once you're on planet Earth you can have a variety of careers regardless of what your soul's particular role might be.

"Since, as a beginner, you are still unsure about which role to pick, your wise guide Rahji suggests that you talk to each role model and ask them more specific details about their role. You agree.

Server

"The server model appears to be a kindly soul, not too flashy, with a warm caring feeling emanating from him. While this particular model is a male, Rahji had told you that each role can be male or female. When you ask him to describe what it's like to be a server, he responds: 'First, you have to love being of service to others. You have to like to help others and want to get things done. If you like to be behind the scenes, quietly and effectively accomplishing things this is the role for you. Some are nurses, doctors, waitresses, masseuses, or the loving mother nurturing an upset child. We are always there to help out when people need us.

'While our role is not flashy, we can have famous human roles. Humans such as Jimmy Carter, Prince Charles, Tipper Gore, Martin Luther King, and Mother Teresa are all servers.

'Approximately 25% of the souls leaving the Tao/God pick server as their role, although if you are headed for the United States, only about 10% of the population there are currently picking server. The reason we are picked more than any other role is because we usually can complete our grand cycle of lifetimes faster than the others. Since we are so busy being of service to others we aren't out creating as much karma that has to be paid back. That can eliminate a lot of extra lifetimes.

'The negative side of being a server, if we choose to be negative, is becoming someone's doormat or letting ourselves become a victim, exploited by someone else. From the positive we are masters at learning how to let go of the ego, which really speeds up soul evolution.'

"Rahji introduces you to the next one.

Priest

"The first things you notice about the priest are her intense eyes and energy. Like the server, she exudes inspirational energy but not as tightly focused as the server. When you ask her about being a priest, she energetically says: 'Follow me.' Without hesitating you follow her command, going over to a table to sit down. While you sit, the priest, who prefers to stand, paces back and forth in front of you, acting very priest-like."

'First of all, being a priest is not an easy role. Only about 8% of all the souls can cut it. The phrase used by a military group on Earth, 'the Marines only want a few good men' describes us quite nicely. We see the big picture and avoid getting too caught up in the details. We inspire others to be better and accomplish more. When we spot a problem in life we urge people to correct it. While we can show great compassion for the individual, we can project it out to a large group as well. We are visionaries with a mission or a sense of purpose.

'We do have a negative polarity. If we chose to follow it we can, at times, become fanatical and inspire the masses to follow the wrong path or commit harmful acts. When we chose our positive path we are compassionate humanitarians helping to make the world a better place for people to live.

'As you might expect, throughout history there have been many famous priests, most following a positive inspiring path. They include Buddha, Princess Diana, Gandhi, Mohammed, and Oprah Winfrey.

'If you decide to pick priest for your role, you will be in for a dramatic series of fascinating and exciting lifetimes.'

"You feel so pumped up from the high-frequency energy radiating out from the priest model that you are ready to sign up on the spot. Rahji gently pulls you away saying it would be wiser to first understand the other roles before deciding.

Artisan

"As you approach the artisan role model, you notice that he is deep in thought and oblivious to your presence. Rahji taps him on the shoulder and he quickly turns and greets you."

'Excuse me. I was just looking at this shop. It's a disgrace. I've got to change the decor before it drives me insane. Just look at it. That green wall is hideous. You want to know what it's like to be an artisan? Well, we are the most creative ones. We go where others fear to tread. We see things that can be done that others are not even vaguely aware of. We see multiple variables where others see only one. We have rich imaginations that help us become inventors. When we play sports we do it with grace and style rather than relying solely on brute force. We can design clothes, skyscrapers, or even design the political structure for an entire society. We make up about 20% of Earth's population, except in the United States where 30% are artisans.

'There's a plethora of famous artisans, including: Drew Barrymore, Walt Disney, Alfred Hitchcock, Michelangelo, and Steven Spielberg.

'Like all the roles, there is a negative and positive side to artisans. If we decide to play out our negative qualities we can be spineless, tricky, act bizarre and ride an emotional roller coaster, often times bottoming out in deep depression or insanity. We can often leave projects incomplete while we chase a new dream. We can deceive ourselves as well as others. From the positive perspective, we bring creativity and innovation to the world. With our originality and creativeness we can breathe new life into the old or obsolete.

'I can see you as an artisan. Here, let me help pick out some personality traits to make you into a smashing standout.'

"Rahji, spotting your enchanted, longing look, quickly thanks the artisan model and leads you over to the sage role model.

Sage

"The sage is dramatically strolling back and forth in front of a group of curious fragments, engaging them in what appears to be more monologue than dialogue. When Rahji interrupts the fragments quickly slip away before the sage notices her audience is gone. But she appears delighted to have a new audience, albeit only one fragment.

'What's it like to be a sage? It's fun. We love to perform and inform, whether in a theater, an amphitheater or in front of a group of anteaters. We have much knowledge to share, our wit can entertain you, our optimism can delight you, and our spontaneousness can ignite you. Join us and you will stay young all your life.

'Like artisans, we like to express ourselves with broad energy rather than narrow-focused energy. At the same time, we are able to see the big picture like priests and kings. Yes, it is true—we have a few negative traits. At times, we can be too verbose, too irresponsible, slippery, prone to stretch the truth, and too focused on grabbing all the attention, but let's not forget the positive. We can be quite good in front of large crowds, entertaining, teaching, and sharing knowledge.

'Famous sages range from standup comedians to politicians. The list includes Bill Clinton, Jay Leno, Dolly Parton, Ronald Reagan, and Tina Turner.

'If you want the applause, come join the exclusive club of sages. Only 10% of Earth's population can qualify for this most challenging role.'

"Rahji, sensing you are a little overwhelmed by the sage's energy, wisely leads you over to the more grounded warrior role model.

Warrior

"The warrior role model is calmly bustling around the shop organizing things. After Rahji takes care of the introductions, the strong, solidly built male stopped working.

'I can finish later. I was just straightening out a mess the sage had made. I always know what needs to be done and I am the best qualified to do it. I can stay focused on the details and get the job done. Don't let the name warrior scare you. Sometimes warriors go through hundreds of lifetimes and never get into combat. We do however, love to compete and win, whether playing a spirited game of Ping-Pong or, if we happen to be in a female body, even a beauty pageant.

'Of all the roles we are the most physical and tuned into our five senses. We can savor the smell of a thick steak sizzling on a grill, stay up all night having sex, and still be at work on time in the morning, raring to meet the day's challenges whether operating a jack hammer or running a business. Give us a goal and get out of the way—we'll take it from there.

'Some say that our most negative trait is coercion. It's true. At times we can be too pushy and too domineering. When the action gets hot and heavy we sometimes can be intimidating to weaker roles. On the positive, we get things done, on time and on budget. We make great soldiers, athletes, police, organizers, teachers and administrators.

'Famous warriors include: Hillary Clinton, Clint Eastwood, Saddam Hussein, Janet Reno, and Mike Tyson.

'About 17-18% of Earth are warriors, but in the United States, the number is closer to 30%, probably because there are a disproportionate number of artisans. As you know too many artisans creating things mean there will be a lot of half done projects that need warriors to clean up and organize properly. If you want to be a warrior, I expect you to be here at 0700 hours ready to go to work.'

"Smiling, Rahji said good-bye to the warrior and pointed out the King, a woman sitting on a raised platform studying some documents. Before you could say a word, Rahji read your mind and said, King is a generic gender-less term for this role. To simplify matters, we use it for either a male or a female.

King

"The king turned and with a sweeping motion of her arm directs you to sit in a chair below the platform."

'Welcome. No doubt, by now you have had several models doing their best to convince you to select their role. I will not do that. King is too demanding and sophisticated a role to jump into your first time around. After you have completed a few grand cycles I might recommend you. You see, only 1-2 % of Earth's people are kings. Our ability to master life and lead people is our strong point. We are the visionaries who can run vast corporations, countries, armies, or even something as small as homeless shelter. We have the leadership qualities that people respond to, while at the same time we care very deeply for our followers and supporters. We assume responsibility for their well-being.

'We can be famous or not famous as we choose. It depends entirely on what we decide to master for a particular lifetime. Those kings who have chosen fame include: Katherine Hepburn, Jacqueline Kennedy, John F. Kennedy, Madonna, and Donald Trump.

'When kings slip into a negative polarity, they can be brutal, ruthless tyrants, both cruel and arrogant. When operating from a positive polarity they are charming, kind, gentle leaders assuming a burden of responsibility for those around them. Someday, when you are ready, you can experience this most challenging role. Now I have work to do. Good day.'

"The king turned away and Rahji gestured to follow him over to the last role, the one labeled scholar.

Scholar

"The scholar was behind a desk, buried in papers, file folders and books, intently examining a book on ancient cooking utensils. Upon spotting Rahji he looked up."

'So, Rahji, I see you have taken another fragment under your wing. Headed to Earth I'd guess. It's a great time to be a scholar on Earth. They have computers that link people together into a global information network. They call it the Internet. It's a scholar's dream. Information, facts, knowledge—it can now be instantly accessed from anywhere in the world. Their cars even have electronic maps linked to global positioning satellites, a far cry from the old days when I had to carry old faded buffalo hide maps in my leather saddle bags.'

'I'm assuming you want to be a scholar. It's the most interesting role because we know a lot about all kinds of things and what we don't know we can learn. That's what we do best, we learn new and interesting things, that way we can help all the other roles accomplish their goals. We can be anything we want to be, whether a historian, explorer, president, or a contestant on Jeopardy, a game show on Earth.

'Famous scholars include: Dianne Feinstein, Alan Greenspan, Henry Kissinger, Gloria Steinem, and Margaret Thatcher.

'When the negative side of a scholar comes out they can be boring, too abstract, too wrapped up in theory and not down to earth. From the positive perspective, they have a lot of knowledge from the past. They can help guide us and keep us from making the same mistakes over again. Plus, they can be fair and unbiased.'

"By now you might have an inkling of what role you want to tackle first. For the sake of discussion let's say you are vacillating back and forth between artisan and warrior, the two most popular roles at your future destination, the United States on planet Earth. Both roles are quite different, but you are leaning slightly towards warrior, however you like many of the characteristics of artisan.

Your Essence Twin (or Soul Mate)

"Rahji, sensing your inability to make a decision, suggests you head over to the launch ship preparing for liftoff to Earth. Once at the ship, you see a beehive of activity as seven different entities, comprised of 1,000 fragments each, scurry about, making last minute preparations.

"He points out that you are scheduled to be one of the one thousand fragments that will make up the fifth entity. He urges you to look over the six other entities and see if another fragment catches your eye. As you scan about you spot a fragment in the first entity that you are suddenly drawn to. You find yourself strangely attracted to this fragment. Rahji explains that you have just met your essence twin, or soul-mate as they are often called.

"Sensing your confusion, Rahji explains that all fragments, or individuals as you're called on Earth, have a very close relationship with one other soul throughout their cycle of lifetimes. This person is called your essence twin. Like two police detectives that work together as partners, they know each others faults as well as good qualities better than anyone else—even better than their respective spouses. Over time, they can get on each others nerves and develop a strong love-hate relationship.

"Your essence twin can project some of their role onto you, giving you a sort of shadow role, or secondary role. Rahji adds that since you are already leaning towards a role of warrior but still like artisan, it would make sense to pick warrior since the essence twin you are drawn to is already an artisan. Then through your series of lifetimes you will have the primary energy of a warrior, but able to relate to, and draw upon artisan energy when you want to.

"One of the most famous essence twin pairings is Elizabeth Taylor and Richard Burton. Their stormy off-and-on relationship over the years is typical of essence twins. Only one does not always marry their essence twin. You can be siblings, parent/child, cousins, close lifelong buddies, or even have no physical relationship. Some essence twins only connect up during a few lifetimes. The important thing to remember is that you can tap into each other's energy. Winston Churchill, Richard Gere, Ernest Hemingway, Charlton Heston, and Georgia O'Keefe are all examples of warriors who have artisan essence twins.

"At last you have your role and even a secondary role, and someone to be your close companion throughout the lifetimes awaiting you. Now it's off to the next shop to pick up a goal."

"Wait, Mike, I've got a ton of questions."

"Okay, Scott, fire away."

"How about the people here in this room? What's my role and what are their roles?"

"Well, let's go around the room. First I'm a Priest with a Scholar Essence Twin. So I basically play a priest role with a strong scholar influence. You, Scott, are a Scholar with a King Essence Twin—in fact, your wife Karen, who is a King, is your Essence Twin. Connie is a Sage with a Scholar Essence Twin. Lee Chou is a Server with a Warrior Essence Twin, and Pudgy is a Warrior with an Artisan Essence Twin.

"Now what does this all mean? If one studies the seven roles you will dramatically increase your understanding of your fellow human beings. Instead of seeing them as black, white, brown, red or yellow, or rich or poor, you'll see how their basic role coupled with their Essence Twin influence directs them to act in life. Look at Pudgy. Does anyone doubt that he is a warrior? And look at the flower beds out front. That's how he shows the Artisan Essence Twin influence. He is a blend of two quite different influences. Connie loves her fame. Years ago she insisted that her photo run next to her column in the Times. Because she has a Scholar Essence Twin, she always does very thorough research for her articles. Lee Chou, as a Server, prefers to stay in the background. With her Warrior Essence Twin influence, she's organized and no-nonsense.

"Does that give you a better understanding of the different roles? Remember, all people are playing one of these seven roles. I'd like to continue tomorrow evening with a discussion of the various personality traits a person may pick. This includes the seven different Goals, and finally the seven Chief Obstacles we face."

"Whew! Mike that's a lot to digest," I said. "It makes sense when I start to analyze people on the basis of their Soul Profile. Knowing a person's Soul Age, Soul Level, and spiritual Role gives you a real insight into the person's makeup. One can start to predict how somebody will react in different situations."

"That's right, Scott. By the time I finish the rest of a person's Soul Profile, you'll have an enormous advantage in truly understanding people."

After the usual good-byes, I hopped in the Lexus and headed north to Lynnwood.

Chapter 18

When I got home Karen had just wrapped up her studying for the day and was cooking some frozen enchiladas. When they were done we grabbed a couple of cups of Chamomile tea, turned on the gas fireplace, and sat on cushions watching the flames while consuming our simple dinner. I brought her up-to-date on everything and shared with her all Mike's information including what I knew about her Soul Profile.

"So, Scott, let me summarize—I'm an Old Soul, at the 3rd Level, and my Role is King and we are Soul Mates or Essence Twins as you called it. That explains the instant attraction when we met for the first time this lifetime. From what you've explained, it makes sense. I'll be looking forward to hearing the rest of our Soul Profiles. But for now, I'm tired after a day of heavy classroom lectures and a ton of homework. Shall we go to bed?"

"Go ahead. I think I'm going to write for awhile. I'll see you in the morning."

I gave her a nice kiss on the lips and went to my office and started keystroking. It was exciting having new information that not only made sense but could improve understanding between people.

At two minutes after midnight, my phone rang. It was Mike.

"Sorry Scott if I woke you, but we appear to have another attack by DOG thugs."

"Oh no. Not again. What happened?"

"A middle-aged black couple, Dr. Roger Johnson and his wife Andrea, were at the Space Needle tonight having dinner. Afterwards, as they were waiting for the valet attendant to bring their car, two thugs in paramilitary garb jumped them. Knocked them to the ground and started kicking and clubbing them. The doctor's wife escaped with a few abrasions and lacerations, but the doctor, who's a leading cardiologist at the University of Washington Medical School, ended up with a concussion and some broken ribs.

"The thugs did this in front of at least a dozen witnesses who all stood by like zombies and didn't lift a finger to help. It happened so fast that the thugs were long gone by the time the security people arrived. The SPD and FBI are getting descriptions of the attackers from the witnesses, but they were wearing black hoods so it's unlikely they'll be able to make a good I. D."

"Damn it, Mike. Why aren't the cops and FBI doing a better job?"

"That, my friend, is the question the Mayor, the City Council, the Asian Community, the Black Community, and the downtown business leaders are asking as we speak. The tension around City Hall is about to boil over. Unless something is done soon, some heads are likely to roll. The Chief of Police will be the first to go."

The Space Needle is the symbol of Seattle. Built for the 1962 World's Fair it's a recognizable landmark around the world. Over six hundred feet high, it has a revolving restaurant at the top that provides a stunning three hundred sixty degree view of the city and makes the restaurant a popular place for both visitors and Seattlites. If word got out that even the Space Needle wasn't a safe place to go, Seattle could suffer economically. This wasn't another case of some gang-bangers beating up another gang-banger, this was now threatening the mostly white business community

The next evening the group reconvened at Pudgy's and Lee Chou's home. Without wasting any time Mike quickly got the group focused on the night's lesson.

"Okay everyone, tonight we discuss more of the Soul Profile we all have. First, I want to share with you the possible Goals we can pick for a lifetime. Unless someone objects, I'll continue to use the analogy of shopping in a Spiritual Mall."

Mike glanced around the room, saw no unhappiness so continued.

"Now that you have picked a role for your series of upcoming lifetimes, Rahji, your guide while you're shopping at the Spiritual Mall in the Tao, suggests you stop into the Goal Shoppe and pick your goal. There are seven different goals to choose from, however unlike the role, you can change your goal every lifetime.

"Your goal is what you will try to achieve in a lifetime. The possible goals you can choose from are all general in nature rather than specific. They are basic life motivators rather than specific goals such as building the world's largest collection of Elvis memorabilia, or climbing Mt. Everest.

"As Rahji leads you into the Goal Shoppe you are met by the manager who points out the seven different models, all wearing name tags. They are called:

1. Re-evaluation
2. Growth
3. Discrimination
4. Acceptance
5. Submission
6. Dominance
7. Relaxation

"The manager quickly adds, 'I see you're a little bewildered. It's common for first timers. Let's go through each goal one by one and see which one interests you the most.' He beckons the first goal model over.

Re-evaluation

"The first thing you notice is the re-evaluation model is a female in a wheel chair. Spotting your curious look, the model says: 'Yes, my goal is re-evaluation. That means I want a lifetime of simplicity, a lifetime where I can reflect back over my previous lifetimes, or to focus on only a few things in life. Some of us with a goal of re-evaluation choose to have a handicap, physical or mental, as a way of keeping us from intense karma creation or payback.

'We need the time to go inside ourselves and reflect on our pasts and prepare for another hectic lifetime in the near future. Since someone else usually provides for our survival needs we can do this. It would be similar to a race car leaving the track for an extended stay in the pits, getting some well-deserved repairs.

'This is the rarest of goals, only 1% of Earth's population choose it. Generally souls with a goal of re-evaluation do not achieve fame, but a few souls have used re-evaluation as a way to limit everything in their life to one main point of focus, such as astrophysics. Most notably: Buddha, Albert Einstein, Steven Hawking, Helen Keller, and Edgar Allan Poe.

'The positive side of re-evaluation is achieving pure simplicity in life. The negative is to completely withdraw and spend your life drugged-out. However, as a first timer, this is not the goal for you. Pick another, more active goal first, go out and play the game. Get some of life's dings and dents, then you'll be ready for a lifetime of re-evaluation.'

"The manager, leads us over to the next goal model, a young man excitedly talking away with a phone pressed to each ear and three more ringing on a desk piled high with stacks of files and papers. The manager swiftly unplugs the phones and says, 'Here's our Growth goal model. Growth, meet a first timer, and of course you already know Rahji.'

Growth

'Hi guys. I've got to make this quick. I've got ten people to call, a real estate deal to close, a racquetball game at lunch with a client, a dental cleaning, my daughter's violin recital, and a big proposal to work on for a presentation tomorrow.

'Let me guess, you want to know what it's like to have a goal of growth. Man, it's hectic. I try to squeeze as much into a day and a lifetime as I can. Wherever there's a new experience, I want to have it. I go as fast as I can for as long as I can, then I'll crash, slide over and play the re-evaluation gig for a few weeks then back into the fray, learning new things and wishing that a candle had more than two ends to burn. My positive side is my enthusiastic ability to take on challenges and evolve. Negative side is a tendency to get confused and ignore the needs of others.

'Are there any famous people with a goal of growth? You kidding? There are tons of them. The most famous are: Carol Burnett, Bill Gates, Jerry Seinfeld, Barbara Walters, and Oprah Winfrey.

'As far as popularity, growth is the winner. Forty percent of Earth's people have a goal of growth. It might be a little too intense for you first time out of the chute though. My advice, keep looking. Gotta run. See ya again before your next lifetime.'

"Well, two down and no goal yet, but don't get discouraged," Rahji said encouragingly, as we walked over to talk with the next goal model, this one a striking woman labeled discrimination.

Discrimination

"The manager introduced us, then the goal model spoke, 'I'm not sure I want to waste my time talking to a first-timer. They're usually pretty naive and stupid. They have no business picking a goal of discrimination anyway. They aren't ready to handle the heavy karma we have to endure from all the other souls.

'You know of course that only 2% of us are sophisticated enough to take on discrimination as a goal—and sophistication is our most positive quality. Negatively, we can be a bit snobbish and prejudiced. We excel at occupations requiring the ability to discern differences between good and bad—movie critic, wine connoisseur, or as a quality control inspector on an assembly line. Some of the most discriminating people in the world have achieved fame with the goal of discrimination. For example: Katie Couric, Larry King, Andy Rooney, Gene Siskel, and Martha Stewart. Quite an impressive list considering that only 2% of the people have this goal.

'Now I must go. I have a movie to review.'

"Rahji quickly spoke, 'Don't get discouraged. Discrimination is a tough goal. Much too tough for a first-timer. It takes a very experienced soul that has the skills required to handle all the intensity that goes with it, particularly in relationship dealings.

But you will get your chance to have it as a goal later, everyone does! Now let's go check out the next one.'

Acceptance

"The acceptance goal model is a pleasant appearing male, who smiles and introduces himself. 'I couldn't help but overhear your conversation with Discrimination. I know you're going to be disappointed, but my goal, Acceptance, is not a very good goal for a first-timer either. We are quite popular, but more so with the older soul ages. But I don't want to upset you so I'll be delighted to tell you all about my goal for one of your future lifetimes.

'We like people and it is very important to us to be liked by people. We're not the most assertive, but we can be very kind and capable of agape, unconditional love of others—that's our most positive characteristic. On the negative side, we can be a little insincere now and then, and our fear of not being liked can make us stoop to doing things we don't always want to do just to please others.

'Because we are a popular goal, over 30% pick us, you will find many famous people who have chosen Acceptance as their goal. Some you might recognize are: Jim Carrey, Bill Clinton, Danny De Vito, Whoopi Goldberg, and Vanna White.

'Please come back after you've gone through some of the earlier soul ages. Acceptance is a wonderful goal. I know you will enjoy it. Thanks for stopping by.'

"Well," said Rahji, "there are three goals left, I know one of them will fit a first-timer."

Submission

"The model representing the goal of submission turned out to be a kind, gentle woman who was busy straightening up the shop. She, put down her dust rag, pulled over a couple of chairs for us, and quickly poured some herbal tea.

'I know you're here to pick a goal and I understand this will be your first trip to Earth. Submission is a possible goal for you. It's not the most popular, only 10% of the souls pick it, but it can be tremendously rewarding. It's a chance to really help out, usually from behind the scenes. The negative part would be a possibility of becoming a slave to someone else's needs, or find yourself a victim enduring a lot of personal suffering. On the positive side you can find happiness in devoting yourself to a group or a cause that is doing something worthwhile for humanity. We are good at getting things done.

'Since we are usually a low-key goal, there aren't a lot of people with submission as a goal that become famous. However, we have a few, for example: Winston Churchill, Jane Fonda, Mahatma Gandhi, Christopher Reeve, and Mother Teresa.

'It could work out quite nicely with the warrior role, with an artisan essence twin secondary role, that you have already selected.'

"As we left her, Rahji spoke, 'I see you are pleased that you finally have a possible goal for your first lifetime, but before you decide, let's see what the last two have to say.'

Dominance

"Upon spotting us approaching, the model for the goal of Dominance, a tall imposing male wearing a cape, stood directly in our pathway and said, 'I'm in charge here. I don't recognize you. Have I given you permission to be in this shop? Oh, it's you, Rahji, and I suppose this is another fledgling you've taken under your wing.'

"After Rahji's greeting and acknowledgment of the purpose of our visit, the model leaped up onto a desk to speak."

'So, you think you want a goal of dominance. Well, are you ready to lead? Can you take charge of a disorganized motley crew of slackards and whip them into a well-oiled cohesive group? We see the big picture. We lead and we get things done. Those are our positive characteristics. From the negative perspective, we can at times be controlling and dictatorial.

'Because we lead, one way or another, fame comes easily to many of us. You might recognize these names that all have dominance as the primary goal in life: Hillary Clinton, Saddam Hussein, Madonna, Charles Manson, and Mike Tyson.

'The question is, should you, a mere first-timer to Earth, assume the goal of dominance? Quite frankly, I do not endorse it. Having a goal of dominance requires leadership qualities that few souls can acquire in one lifetime. I would recommend you choose Submission or Relaxation, the last goal.'

"He snapped his fingers, and in a strong authoritative voice bellowed, 'Relaxation, hurry up! Get over here. There's a first-timer who might be interested in you.' He turned crisply on his heels and strode away.

Relaxation

"As she approached, Relaxation stretched and let out a small yawn. 'Sorry, I was catching a nap. So, you are a first-timer, headed to Earth. I like it there. I spent a few of my lifetimes there resting under coconut trees in the South Pacific. Another lifetime I was the rich daughter of an oil baron. I spent my days playing tennis and my evenings partying. Some lifetimes I've had to work, but always at interesting jobs without much stress. If there are problems that come up in life our challenge is learning how to let go and just go with the flow of life, rather than tearing our hair out, or becoming a workaholic.

'The positive side of this goal is having fun and being as easy-going as possible. The negative side is going too far and slipping into complete inertia, or the opposite, struggling against life, unable to let go.

'Some of the famous people in Relaxation include: Cindy Crawford, Ella Fitzgerald, George Hamilton, Hugh Hefner, and Ringo Starr.

'Overall, only about 7% of the souls pick Relaxation as a goal on Earth. Some first-timers do, but usually it's chosen as a goal after several really rough, intense lifetimes full of heavy karmas. That's when you really need a lifetime to kick back and smell the flowers. As a first-timer, you can pick Relaxation as a goal, but you probably would do better to wait until you have a few intense lifetimes under your belt.'

"Rahji thanks the goal model, waves good-bye to the shop manager and grabs your hand. 'Let's duck into the coffee shop next door and sort things out.'

"Once you're seated, Rahji quickly goes over the goals, their pros and cons, and asks you for your decision. You pick a goal of Submission."

Chapter 19

"**B**y this time you feel like you've got quite an interesting wardrobe and are ready to board the ship to Earth. Only Rahji tells you there's one more Shoppe. The Chief Obstacle Shoppe. When you ask Rahji why you need a Chief Obstacle, he smiles at you and explains that God/Tao didn't want to make things too easy for us, so we are all given a Chief Obstacle in life. This negative side of our personality, ultimately has to be conquered in order for us to evolve. The seven choices are:

        1. Self-deprecation
        2. Arrogance
        3. Self-destruction
        4. Greed
        5. Martyrdom
        6. Impatience
        7. Stubbornness

"You might be thinking, 'But I don't want any of these choices!' Sorry, we're all stuck with one of them. However, each new lifetime you can change your Chief Obstacle. And, even during a lifetime you can overcome and eliminate your Chief Obstacle. Ultimately you will experience each one as part of your spiritual growth.

Rahji leads you over to meet the first model:

Self-deprecation

"As you meet the model she immediately says, 'I'm not too important, you might want to meet someone else that's more interesting. We're the shy ones with low self-esteem and make up about 10% of the population. People who have managed to become famous with Self-deprecation as a Chief Obstacle include: Woody Allen, George Carlin, Rodney Dangerfield, Phyllis Diller, and Vanna White.'

"Next you move on to the model representing Arrogance.

Arrogance

"The model gives you a haughty stare." 'Hello Rahji, I see you have a newcomer. Those of us with Arrogance project an image that we are very good at what we do. In reality we are covering up a feeling of shyness and low self-esteem. Famous people include: Cher, Rush Limbaugh, Madonna, O.J. Simpson, and Mike Wallace. However, since you're a total newcomer this Chief Obstacle might be too advanced for you.' "You say good-bye and move on to the next model."

Self-destruction

'Oh hi, Rahji, I see you're outfitting another newcomer. Here, would you like some pills? I have lots of both uppers and downers.'

"After Rahji politely refused the offer, the model continues:

'Well, if you pick this Chief Obstacle you'll find you have the challenge of overcoming a motivation to hurt yourself either physically or mentally. Famous people dealing with this Chief Obstacle include: Drew Barrymore, John Belushi, Jimi Hendrix, Janis Joplin, and Richard Pryor.'

"Rahji suggests you continue looking."

Greed

"The next model, Greed, is busy stacking gold coins on a table, and frantically looking around for more."

'Hello, Rahji, want my advice? Since no Chief Obstacle is fun, why not try Greed. You'll always want more and more, either physically or mentally. It's a feeling of not enough. Famous people include: Yasir Arafat, Hillary Clinton, Adolph Hitler, Imelda Marcos, and Martha Stewart.'

"You thank the model, telling him you'll seriously consider Greed."

Martyrdom

"The next model, Martyrdom, is a woman with tears pouring down her face."

'Why does everyone pick on me and hurt me? Life isn't fair. Sob, sob. You try and help people but they either ignore us or want to hurt us. There are some famous people who bear the cross of Martyrdom. They are: John F. Kennedy, Robert Kennedy, Martin Luther King, Nelson Mandela, and Mother Teresa.'

"You quickly thank the model and move on to the next one."

Impatience

"The Impatience model nervously looks at his watch while he greets you."

'Love to talk, Rahji, but I've got to be in a meeting in three minutes. My list of things to do is a mile long. Where is that book I ordered this morning? Damn. It should've been here two hours ago. I don't have all day to tell you all the famous people who pick this Chief Obstacle, but here are a few: Tim Allen, Katherine Hepburn, Holly Hunter, John McEnroe, and Robin Williams.'

"You feel Impatience is a possible choice, but Rahji wants you to meet the last model before deciding, so you bid farewell to the Impatience model."

Stubbornness

"As you approach the Stubbornness model, you observe that she and the Shoppe manager are in an argument."

'I will not wear that ugly piece of trash. I don't care what you think or do. I refuse to budge. If you try and force me I'll quit.'

'Oh hi, Rahji. I can't believe what the manager is trying to get me to do. Lots of famous people pick stubbornness for a Chief Obstacle, including: Bill Gates, Rosa Parks, Ross Perot, Barbra Streisand, and Margaret Thatcher.'

"You say good-bye to the model and hit the coffee shop to discuss your options.

None of the choices sound good but forced to start somewhere, you decide Greed might be a good one to start with for your first trip to Earth."

"So, let's review our selections for our first time on Earth. She'll be a:

> First Level Infant Soul
> Role of Warrior, with an Artisan Essence Twin
> Goal of Submission
> Chief Obstacle of Greed

"There are other parts of our human personality that are selected before we are born, but these are the main ones to focus on for now," said Mike.

"Thanks, Mike." I said. "That's a huge amount of knowledge to assimilate in a short time period, I only hope I can make it clear to the readers."

"Don't worry, Scott. Readers will pick up what they're ready to handle. Most people will be curious to know what their Soul Age and Soul Level are. Others will want to know their Role, Goal, and Chief Obstacle. For people who want even more, we can include a few resources where people can go to get even more information."

Connie spoke, "But, Mike, how do people find out their Soul Profile? You aren't available to channel the information for every reader."

"That's an excellent point, Connie. Fortunately, some of the other Michael channels offer individual Soul Profiles for a nominal fee. A few of the Michael channels have developed a simple self-scoring quiz you can take to determine the answers. I'll get information to Scott so he can include it in the appendix of the book.[3]

---

3. see Appendix A for Self-Scoring Quiz

"The dominant, over-riding importance of the book is to change your thoughts on the 'Big Lie' of the Judeo-Christian-Islamic world and get people to understand that we are all one. We incarnate, we grow spiritually through the experiences we have while in the Earth plane, and we continue to reincarnate until we have mastered the lessons of this plane. We all play all the different roles, including gender, race, religion, and sexual orientation. There is no reason anymore to hate people because they're different. In reality, there are no differences, just different souls playing different roles at different times. The lesson we all have to learn is tolerance, for next lifetime you might be playing the very role you scorn and spit on in this lifetime."

"Mike, I think I now fully understand your fearless devotion to the cause of getting this message out. Your message—actually the modern, updated message from the Universe—is powerful. If enough people will open their eyes and see for themselves that the Michael Soul Teachings actually work, then there will be a huge shift in consciousness."

"Scott, even if the book only stirs people to start a national dialogue and then an international dialogue, we will have won. Just imagine the impact of having talk show hosts exposing and debating the 'Big Lie' that stripped the concept of reincarnation from us. The more the public openly examines and debates our message the more we win."

I knew the rest was up to me. Mike had given me the information, now I had to finish the book and get it out to the world as soon as possible. We ended the meeting and I headed back to Lynnwood and my computer.

Chapter 20

It has been nearly a week since the meeting at Pudgy's. I had buried myself in my office, emerging long enough to refuel and make pit stops. Whenever I was too tired to continue I would nap for two or three hours. I was nearing the finish line and that gave me the incentive to push myself to my physical limits. I wasn't just writing a book—I was on a mission with Mike.

Karen, my darling wife understood and supported me fully—she even tolerated my infrequent showers and unshaven face and straggly uncombed hair. She kept me fed and handled outside distractions so I could concentrate 100% on my writing.

Finishing a book is always a milestone. It's like crossing the finish line in a marathon. It doesn't matter how long it took. It doesn't matter how many people crossed before you. It's an exhilarating feeling of accomplishment. It's like keeping a New Year's Day Resolution. It's doing something many people dream of but few actually do. As a professional writer I know the feeling well, yet over the years I have never lost the warm glow of inner satisfaction that comes with completion of the project.

In this case, because of the global implications of disseminating spiritual information that could alter human awareness, I felt even more alive. This was truly important.

All the drama that had taken place since I first met Mike at the Pike Place Market resurfaced. It had been an extraordinary journey and all in such a short span of time. All together, I had finished the 100,000 plus words in only three months...double my normal writing pace. Now, at 9:30 AM, on June 21st, the Summer Solstice, I was ready to celebrate.

Karen put in a call to Pudgy and Lee Chou and arranged for a celebration party at 8:00 PM at their home. I decided I had earned a little R & R time so I hopped in the Lexus and headed for Green Lake and a brisk three mile walk around the lake. Everything looked brighter. The flowers were more brilliant. The water was a shimmering dark green. The other people on the path looked happier. I felt great. Then as I reached the Bathhouse Theatre I looked up to the grassy knoll where I had met with Mike to get the initial information on the Michael Soul Teachings. It seemed like five years ago. So much had happened since that day in late March when we had sat on a bench together.

After my walk I decided an ice cream treat was in order. Near the Children's wading pool I crossed Green Lake Drive and went to my favorite ice cream shop, Mix Ice Cream. I have nothing against Baskin-Robbins but this place has more personality and truly custom-makes each order, as well as makes their own ice cream on the premises daily. Starting on their left-to-right 'assembly line' I first ordered two large scoops of Sweet Cream ice cream that the clerk plunked down on a huge marble slab, then pounded into two flat thick globs of ice cream. Next I ordered fresh Marion berries that were poured over the ice cream. I skipped ordering any of the optional candies and requested some Rum extract added to the pile, then topped off the concoction with three Oreo cookies. The clerk proceeded to whack, chop, blend and fold the exotic creation together, then crammed it into a freshly baked golden brown waffle dish.

Having trouble controlling the saliva being generated in my mouth, I quickly ducked outside and grabbed an empty outdoor table and chair. The first bite was close to an orgasm. I finished the whole thing in record-breaking time. Feeling completely satiated I waddled back across Green Lake Drive, got back on the walking path and walked the half mile back to where I had left the Lexus. I got in and headed north to Lynnwood.

Arriving back home I found Karen busily working out the celebration details on the phone with Lee Chou. I would have just called up a few friends, then gone to the store and bought some champagne, beer, wine and chips and called it a celebration. The ladies, bless their wonderful female multi-tasking skills, were adding all kinds of complexities, such as fancy hors d'oeuvres, and flower arrangements. Give them another hour and we probably would have lined up a professional bartender, valet parking, and a belly dancer.

Once Karen was off the phone, I discreetly pointed out to her that I had just finished writing the book—I hadn't found an agent or editor, let alone a publisher. I diplomatically suggested we wait until the book is published before we have a big celebration. She agreed to keep things simple.

I left for OfficeMax, proudly taking my finished manuscript with me. I decided to use their high speed copier to make ten copies to give to friends for an initial reading and reaction. Three thousand pages, and $97.74 later, I left carrying my heavy stack of ten collated manuscripts. Fortunately, I had caught OfficeMax when they were running a sale on copies—only 3¢ each. After the State of Washington took their onerous 8.6% I still had $2.26 left from my $100. In this day and age of big governments with their insatiable appetites for higher and higher taxes for fewer and fewer services, I felt lucky to escape with anything.

With a few hours to go before it was time to leave for the party, I decided to grab a short nap. No sooner had I fallen asleep than I started dreaming. I was in a large ornate ballroom, hundreds of people wearing masks and dressed in costumes were dancing. It had a feel of Mardi Gras. Things were spinning and spinning and the laughter was growing louder and louder. Faster and faster the dancing couples spun around until everything climaxed in a series of violent explosions. Then people started screaming—blood was running from holes in their costumes. As bodies tumbled around me, I realized that the fireworks were really bullets. The crowd was going berserk—falling, screaming and spinning around. The smiles, frozen in place on their masks, stood in stark contrast to the grotesque sounds of death. Then a wild pack of vicious dogs, with white foam drooling from their yellow, bared fangs, came leaping through the windows, attacking the screaming and dying partygoers.

I awoke with a start. My body was drenched in a cold sweat. It took me a minute to get my bearings—the dream had been that vivid. As a young child I had frequent nightmares, but as an adult most of my dreams were rather benign. I was aware that there were all kinds of books available that purport to interpret dreams but I didn't put much stock in them. I have more faith in my own intuition. What the dream told me was expect more attacks from DOG. They're vicious, they're mad at Mike and now me, and they would love to slaughter us and our supporters.

I made a mental note to never let down my guard. Just when we were the happiest and celebrating the most, they could attack. I knew that I would likely have to be looking over my shoulder for years to come.

Chapter 21

Arriving at Pudgy and Lee Chou's home, all the choice parking spots on the street were taken so I parked a block away and walked to their house, lugging the heavy box of manuscripts. As we approached, I was struck with the sheer beauty of the flowers growing everywhere on their property. Even the parking strip, normally covered with grass, was full of stunning roses of various colors. Pudgy was the most unlikely gardener I had ever met, but I had to admit he was very good at it.

Inside, we quickly removed our shoes, shoved the box of manuscripts in an out-of-the-way spot and started the round of greetings and introductions. My idea of a quiet get together with a few close friends had suddenly, under the co-leadership of Karen and Lee Chou, turned into a house full of people, with more than half of them complete strangers to me. I guessed there were at least forty people crammed into every nook and cranny of the modest sized house.

Judging by the noise level of the attendees, I speculated that quite a few were already on their second or third drink. A giggling Lee Chou spotted us and motioned for us to come into the kitchen. Slithering our way through the bodies we made it to the also over-crowded kitchen. Lee Chou handed us each a large glass of champagne—forget about delicate little champagne flutes that hold six ounces—ours were of the twelve ounce variety. What the heck I thought, this is a big occasion. If Karen and I drink too much, we can always take a cab home.

Behind me I heard a loud voice bellowing, "Hey Hunter!" I turn and spot Pudgy moving towards me holding a glass of champagne in each hand. He apparently had recently bathed and washed his hair. Gone are the greasy American flag scarf and ponytail. In it's place is a wild mane of hair going in every direction a la Einstein. He's wearing a black Grateful Dead T-shirt under a silk cream-colored jacket. Under the jacket, I can just barely spot a pair of red and yellow Tweety Bird suspenders holding up his matching cream-colored silk slacks. Spotting my stunned look—jaw hanging halfway to the floor—he let out a big roar of laughter and said, "Hey, Good Buddy, thought I'd get a little dolled up for the shindig. Hey your glass is still full, what the Hell ya waitin' for—drink up—this a Goddamn celebration party and you da Man!"

A crowd quickly form around us and the next thing I know everyone is lifting their glasses and yelling semi-slurred congratulations. Sensing the party is about to pass me up, I quickly chug down my glass of champagne and find another glass shoved into my hand. Connie appears out of nowhere and gives me a long loving hug. She introduces me to a few of her friends from the Times and tells me she has some other friends she will introduce me to later when I have more time to talk. I spot Wes Conners and Tyrone Willis, both with female companions. They saunter over, obviously in more control than the rest of the crowd. Wes introduces me to his wife Cindi, a small, cute, cuddly-looking woman with short curly brown hair who looks as if she could be the perfect mom. Probably mid-forties. It's pretty clear her Role in life is Server.

Tyrone's companion turns out to be his live-in girlfriend Karin, a tall slender white woman who has the looks of a fashion model. Late twenties, blond hair, with full red lips and pale blue eyes. I vaguely recall Ty having said she is from Sweden. They make a great looking couple, although I'm sure the thugs at DOG would disagree. As I shake Ty's hand he whispers that Wes and he would like to chat with me briefly, if possible, later in the evening. I agree.

The party is loud and lively. After the first two hours, I've had too much champagne, and have forgotten the names of half the people I've been introduced to. I decide it's time for some food. Karen and Lee Chou have done a masterful job. The hors d'oeuvres are smashingly delicious.

Suddenly I realize that I haven't seen Mike anywhere. As Pudgy comes within range I make eye contact with him and mouth the words, "Where's Mike?" Pudgy turns his head towards the back door gives his head a little flip. I ease myself through the crowd and upon exiting the back door I spot Mike relaxing on an old white and green chaise lounge situated under an apple tree. Beside him is a half empty glass of champagne and an empty hors d'oeuvres plate. I grab a nearby white plastic lawn chair and set down next to him. "Hey Mike, how's it going?"

He looks me in the eyes for several seconds, saying nothing, a small smile on his face, then he says, "Scott, Thank you. Thank you so very much. We're not done yet, but to paraphrase an astronaut, we have taken one giant step forward for mankind."

Not knowing what to say, I just nod my head and give his right forearm an understanding pat.

"The Universe is already preparing us for the next step. I can sense it. Do you think you'll be up for it?" he said.

"Mike, I honestly don't know. But I will give the battle everything I've got. I just hope that will be enough." I told Mike about my dream.

"Scott, trust your intuition. I'm also picking up warnings that there is still a lot of danger ahead. Writing the book is half the battle. The next half is getting it published and read. Once the hate groups hear about our message and read a copy they will attack. That I know for sure. Up until now we have had the luxury of being able to hide out and write, but now, to get our message broadly disseminated, we have to come out of hiding and take a high profile stance. That means doing lots of lectures, seminars and book signings. Not to mention scores of media interviews with newspapers, magazines, radio and TV stations.

"Scott, one of the reasons the Universe sent you to me was for this promotion phase—not just the writing. I'm just a pissy old man. I don't make that good an impression with the public. Hell, remember when we first met? You thought I was a homeless bum. Small groups of old souls are the ones I can best communicate with. You come from the business world. You've been in the advertising and PR fields. You're an excellent speaker and above all you project a sincere, honest, credible image. I got the ball to this point, but now you're the one who has to carry it over the goal line. I'll be in the wings supporting you as long as I can, but my friend you're the one who is about to step into the spotlight."

Mike and I had already decided weeks earlier that I would be listed as the primary author and he would be acknowledged as the primary source of information and major contributor. But now, the solemn way he talked about the future—and the potential dangers—made me question my abilities. The idea of constantly looking over my shoulder and worrying about some psychotic thug like Reamer was unsettling. Up until now I had been able to maintain a low profile. DOG didn't even know I existed.

I thought about Karen. Was I putting her at risk? After the bomb attack that nearly killed Connie, I realized that we weren't playing a kid's game of cops and robbers. This was for real. Yet, deep inside, I knew I had no choice. Destiny had brought me to this point and whatever was about to happen I had to go forward. It was too late to back out—even if death's ugly face was waiting for me in some dark alley. On a soul level, I had agreed to play out this drama. It seemed as everything I had done in my life, up to this moment, had groomed me for what lay ahead.

Deep inside, some past lifetime memories were stirring. I was getting faint images of strapping on armor, nervously contemplating the battle that was about to begin. In my memories there had been many battles, with much blood spilled, including my own. Deep, dark memories recall the enormous, almost euphoric, adrenaline rush that comes from surviving death by killing someone who is trying to kill you. The feel of life leaving a body as you plunge your sword deep into an opponent's chest, followed by the smell of death are not memories that fade away easily. I have done battle many times in many lifetimes as I evolved through the soul ages. Now, as an old soul, I do not relish the thought of once again entering the arena—but I know I must.

While I intellectually know the soul is immortal, the intense emotions generated by the mortal physical body usually dominate when the soul is in the body. Only after the death of the physical body can one see the illusion that we call life. The Holodeck, portrayed on the television series, *Star Trek: The Next Generation*, is an excellent way of viewing physical life versus spiritual life. When one of the Star Trek characters was in the Holodeck, everything seemed totally real and all the human emotions, including fear, were present.

Karen appeared by my side, glass in hand, relaxed both from the champagne and from seeing that the party was a success. Her efforts, as well as Lee Chou's had paid off. As she slipped her left arm into my right arm, she sensed the seriousness emanating from Mike and me.

"Hey you two. Lighten up. We're here celebrating the successful completion of a future best-selling book and you guys are acting like it's a funeral."

"Sorry Karen," Mike said, "Scott and I are already looking ahead at the job of finding an agent and a publisher, then all the promotional work."

"Then you can lighten up. Connie invited a literary agent who helped one of the staff writer's at the Times get his novel published. Let me go see if she's here yet."

As Karen walked away to go and find Connie's contact, I looked at Mike and smiled. "Well, the Universe seems to be helping. Let's just hope the bad guys prove to be more big talk and little action."

"Nothing would make me happier. But unfortunately, your title is accurate. We are dealing with a clash of souls that is very real. Do not be afraid to call upon the Universe for help and protection. Remember—in case something happens to me—you are never alone. Trust your intuition—that's the Universe trying to help you. And if this frail old body of mine dies off, I'll be there by your side—in spirit form. I promise I won't leave you until this project has been completed."

"Geez, Mike, you're getting too serious. You've got another twenty, thirty years at least to live."

"Look" Mike said as he got up off the chaise lounge. "Here comes Connie and Karen. That must be the agent with them."

I turned and saw an attractive strawberry blond woman walking between Karen and Connie. I guessed her to be five foot seven, maybe one hundred thirty pounds and mid-to-late thirties. She was wearing a silk floral-patterned dress accented with tasteful gold jewelry. Connie handled the introductions.

"Mike, Scott, I'd like you to meet Katherine Morgan. She runs the Morgan Literary Agency. Kathy, this is our spiritual guru Mike, and Scott Hunter, the writer."

I noticed Katherine had a firm professional handshake and made good eye contact. Her eyes were an interesting shade of pale green—quite striking.

"I'm delighted to meet both of you. Connie has briefed me on your book and I'm quite interested in reading the manuscript. From what I've gleaned about it, it should fit quite nicely into the areas I specialize in."

"We would be honored," I said. "Usually a writer has to spend months trying to find a good agent. I brought some copies with me today, I'll get you one before you leave."

"Thanks, but Karen already gave me one," said Katherine, pulling a copy out of the large purse slung over her shoulder. "I'm heading out now, and I'm planning on starting to read it this evening."

"Wow, that's fast," I said. "I thought agents took three months to get around to reading a manuscript?"

"Normally we do. But I have a break in my schedule right now and since I already have a very good idea of your subject matter, I've moved yours to the top of the stack. Can we get together a week from today? I'd like to tell you what I think and figure out what the next step should be."

"That's great. I hadn't expected things to be happening this fast but the sooner the better. I was going to start looking for an editor to help me polish it up before I started looking for an agent."

"Don't worry about an editor. I know of several good ones. After I've gone through your manuscript I'll know who to recommend.

"Have you thought about putting on some workshops or seminars? It will help me sell your book to a publisher if they know you're presenting the material to the public and that there is interest."

"No I haven't however Mike has, and I guess I could start."

Mike interrupted. "Scott, don't worry. You're ready. I'll help you with a few seminars until you feel comfortable. But it's time for you to come out from behind the keyboard and present this knowledge to the public."

"We don't want you to think we're ganging up on you Scott," said Connie, "but Katherine had already mentioned to me that the seminars would be important, so I invited Crystal Becker to the party. She's the event coordinator at the New LotusBookshop." Connie turned and pointed. "She's that tall brunette standing over there talking to Lee Chou."

"I don't know what to say. Everything is happening so fast." I said.

"Relax Scott, and just tune into the Universe. You'll have all the help you need," said Mike. "When you're on the right path the doors open. And yeah, there can be some setbacks but the Universe will never throw any challenge at you that you can't handle on a soul level."

Connie grabbed my arm and said, "C'mon, Scott, let's go meet Crystal."

As we approached her, Crystal spotted us and finished her conversation with Lee Chou. She was tall, probably five feet, ten inches, and had long straight brown hair, parted in the middle, that hung down her back. She appeared to be late twenties or early thirties. Very attractive with a minimum of makeup and dark brown eyes. Connie made the introductions and as our eyes made contact I felt an instant rapport.

"Congratulations on your book," Crystal said. "We'll be looking forward to selling it at New Lotus once it's published and if you'd like to do a book signing we would be delighted to have you."

"Thank you, Crystal. That sounds great. I love your store. You've got a great selection of books plus your crystal and gemstones selection is fabulous. My wife is always coming home from New Lotuswith more gemstones."

"Crystal," said Connie, "Scott's agent Katherine Morgan said it would be good for Scott to hold some workshops. It would improve the chances a major publisher would take Scott's book. Is that something New Lotus would be interested in?"

"Of course. We'd be delighted. When would you like to put one on?"

"Gee, I don't know." I said. "I hadn't even thought about it before today. Maybe I could pull together an outline in a week or so. Definitely in a couple of weeks."

"Well," said Crystal, "our Summer Schedule listing all the programs we put on has already come out. So it would be too late to be listed in it. However, we do have several days or nights open. We could promote it with signs in our store but it usually works better if we can list it in the Quarterly Schedule."

"Scott, don't worry about the promotion," said Connie. "Just jump in and do one as quick as you can. You can always do more later."

Connie was turning into an aggressive promoter for me...pushy, but pleasant about it and done with a high level of enthusiasm. She obviously was the cheerleader in our little group. Not being able to say no, I said, "Okay. Let's get things rolling as soon as possible."

"Great. I'll check the schedule," said Crystal. "Just give me a call at New Lotus and I'll give you a list of available time slots."

Chapter 22

Out of the corner of my eye I saw Pudgy waving for me to join him and a small group consisting of Mike, Wes and Ty. I politely excused myself from Crystal, Lee Chou and Connie. As I approached, I noticed a seriousness on their faces.

Mike spoke first. "Scott, Wes and Ty want to talk to us about the possibility of our helping them. Wes, do you want to give them the details?"

"Sure thing, Mike," said Wes Conners. "Scott, as you probably know we have not been able to locate DOG—nor get enough information on them for an arrest. Everything we know points to them as the perpetrators in the gay attack on Capitol Hill, the bomb attack at the Seattle Times, and probably the attack on the Johnson's, but for the time being our hands are tied. The Mayor is jumping all over our superiors demanding we do something and we keep running into dead ends. He's got the SPD throwing all sorts of man-hours at it, too. It's starting to turn into a real political mess. So, we've decided we have to flush them out of hiding, and we need your help to do that."

"Well sure, I guess I can help, but I don't know how—I'm just a writer."

"We want to set a trap and get DOG to walk into it," said Tyrone.

"It sounds like a good idea. I just don't see where I could be of any help."

"Scott," said Mike "they want us to be the *bait* for the trap."

Suddenly I remembered having seen on the Discovery Channel some little bleating lamb tied to a stake in the jungle near a trap designed to catch a tiger. As I recalled the tiger killed the lamb before it got caught in the trap. The idea of being bait to catch a bunch of vicious murderers was not very appealing. Lifting my eyebrows, and in a highly skeptical voice, I said, "Bait? What kind of bait?"

"There is an element of danger involved," said Wes. "We would never ask you and Mike if we had any other options at this time. We're looking at having you and Mike put on a seminar which we've heard you're already going to do. Connie would run an article mentioning the seminar. They don't know you, Scott, but they do know Mike and want to get to him pretty badly. We'd set a trap where you hold the seminar hoping they would show and quietly observe the two of you. Then we'd follow them back to their hideout bringing a search warrant so we could look for evidence of the three crimes.

"If they try to get violent and harm you, Mike, or anyone else, we would arrest them on the spot. Our goal would be to do this as quickly and discreetly as possible so no civilians are harmed."

Visions of government foul-ups raced through my mind. I must have watched too many *NYPD Blues* re-runs, because all I remember was whenever the Feds got involved in a local police situation something always seemed to go wrong.

"It seems like a lot could go wrong." I said. "If there are several people in the room with guns what's to keep one of them from getting off a few shots before your guys can react? Kevlar vests don't protect you from a close-range shot in the head. Mike and I could get killed before you could draw your weapons."

Lowering his voice, Ty said, "We're planning on setting up metal detectors at the entrance that will look just like the regular retail detectors that stop people from stealing store merchandise. Only the alarm will be silent, so we'll know who's carrying a weapon and who isn't. Then we'll position our people in the audience so we have two people—one on each side of those with weapons. And possibly a third person sitting right behind anyone with a weapon. Our people will all be armed with hand guns as well as stun guns and mace. Outside, we'll have as much artillery as needed. If we see any signs of a large scale attack—say more than six DOG members—we'll call off the meeting and get you guys out of there before the fireworks start."

I looked at Mike to try and discern what he was thinking. He looked back—directly into my eyes.

"Scott, there comes a time when running and hiding is no longer the best strategy. The trick is picking when and where to make a stand. If we go along with the FBI plan we will have better control of the situation than would be the case at some later time.

"Let's be totally honest—DOG will come after us. They don't give up easily. So it's up to us to dictate when and how we meet. If the FBI plan works, hopefully they will get enough evidence to put a lot of them away for a long time. Maybe even one of the members will rat on the others to save his ass. Then we can nail Wolf Drake and maybe even Calvin McCallum under some federal conspiracy law. Only then will we have some measure of peace. The world is full of wacko people but so far, DOG is the only group that has vowed to stop us from getting our message out. If we can seriously weaken DOG for a few years it will be too late for them to stop our message from being broadly disseminated. I can't speak for you, but I'm ready to take a stand now."

Reluctantly, I said, "Okay. I guess you can count me in too."

"Thanks fellows," said Wes. We'll get things rolling as soon as possible, and don't worry, we won't screw up."

Wes and Ty strolled away, leaving Mike, Pudgy and myself staring at each other. Pudgy broke the silence and spoke first. "Shit man, I'm ready to tear those assholes apart but the FBI won't let me."

"Scott, before you joined the discussion, Wes was saying Pudgy should not be at the seminar. He's too high profile. Working at the bar near the Fremont dry-docks he's already run into a lot of Drake's thugs. They know him by sight but think he's just a biker working as a bouncer and more likely to be on their side than ours. He would look totally out of place at the workshop and could jeopardize his undercover work."

Pudgy added, "Wes, did say I could be over in the Bremerton area—near the ferry dock—ready to pick up their tail if they're running back to their friggin' hideout. Only this time I'm not gonna lose 'em."

Gradually the party wound down. I accepted congratulations again from everyone as they left. I was smiling on the outside but inside I was in turmoil. A few days ago I was just wrapping up the book and now I was suddenly thrust head first into a whole new world where the risk and danger to me and my loved ones had taken a quantum leap forward. It appeared that we were like two huge locomotives, in the dark of the night, hurtling down the tracks toward each other into mutual self-destruction. I knew I still had the option to remove my name from the manuscript and hand it over to someone. I could walk away with Karen and let the others sort out the mess. They had been fighting with DOG before I came along. Was it fair to pull me into their battle? Was it fair to put Karen and me at risk? Damn it! I hated being put in this position.

Strolling back into the kitchen I spotted a half-empty bottle of champagne and poured myself a refill, then stepped out into the backyard where the core group of people were clustered in lawn chairs around a patio table. Everyone had left except Mike, Connie, Karen and me, and the hosts, Pudgy and Lee Chou. I slumped down into an empty chair and sipped my champagne, deep in thought.

"Scott," Mike said, "you look pretty serious. Having second thoughts? I can't blame you if you are."

"Yeah, I guess I am. One moment I'm ready to take on any-body then the next I'm ready to walk away. Like right now—this whole thing is starting to sound too dangerous. I had envisioned traveling around the country appearing on radio and television shows promoting the book. Now I feel like the little lamb staked out in the jungle to lure the tiger into the trap. And as I recall the tiger usually got caught but the lamb got killed in the process.

"We're not dealing with harmless kooks who stand on street corners waving bibles over their heads while noonday crowds swarm by ignoring them. From what I've seen of DOG these guys are mostly well-trained ex-military and know how to kill. They're well disciplined and fanatical. We all know the FBI has had their share of screwups. Who can guarantee that something won't go wrong at New Lotus Bookshop? The thought of some innocent person—or any one of us—getting killed is not a pretty picture. I mean—look at us—Mike you've been shot at and attacked several times. Connie almost got blown up. Now I'm about to walk out into the spotlight and introduce myself as the newest target. I picture some trembling rabbit being dumped into a room full of hungry pit bulls."

I could sense my negative talking was sobering up the group. They too were starting to weigh the risks versus the rewards.

"You're absolutely right, Scott," Mike said. "Our undertaking is full of danger. Most things that are worthwhile in the Physical Plane come with a risk. Before any of us were born this lifetime, we had all met on the Astral Plane and agreed that this would be one of our goals for this lifetime. From the perspective of the Astral Plane it didn't appear to be as dangerous as it now does from the Physical Plane perspective.

"But let me ask all of you a question. What's the worst thing that can happen?"

"We could all die." I said.

"And what's the best thing that could happen?"

"We succeed in getting the book published and our message disseminated broadly." I said.

"The message sinks in and the world starts becoming more tolerant. People suddenly have an awareness of why people are different. What soul ages and soul levels are, and how and why people have particular personalities," said Connie.

"People start bein' more tolerant of each other and stop fightin' and killin' each other," Pudgy added.

"Instead of treating people differently because they appear different, the world might start seeing people as the same," said Lee Chou.

"Okay—okay. I hear you. You're all saying that our ultimate goal outweighs the possible personal risk we face," I said.

"Not only that, Scott, but it's the reason for our existence on Earth at this point in history. If you could go back to the early days just before the colonists signed the Declaration of Independence, you'd hear the same concerns being expressed. As spiritual beings, as souls, the signers knew it was their destiny to sign. As mortal humans, their physical being, said no. Remember the body is programmed to survive and will act in ways it deems pro-survival. The soul can see the bigger picture. Many of the signers died or suffered a great deal, but what they accomplished has benefited billions of people around the world. Remember we keep reincarnating. The reality is we are not only making the world better for our children and grandchildren but for ourselves when we are re-born in a new body. How would you like to come back and live in a world run by DOG's ideology?

"No, for me this is the time and place to make a stand—not to go down in a hail of bullets—but to outlast the bastards and win. This means we go forward but we do it extremely carefully with our eyes wide open and all of our senses in a state of high alert."

Every eye turned to look at me. Violence repulsed me but I knew Mike was right. Good can only survive over evil when ordinary people become extraordinary. I slowly turned my head back and forth, pausing as I made eye contact with each person. I saw worry, some fear, but beneath it I saw determination. Their fear of not acting had won out over their fear of acting. It was time to step out of my comfort zone and become extraordinary.

I spoke, "I don't remember the military leader's name, but at a critical point in the civil war he said, 'Damn the torpedoes! Full speed ahead!' I just hope all of us will be present at the victory celebration."

"Here's to victory," said Pudgy, raising his glass skyward. "To victory" we all responded as we reached forward to click the others' glasses.

"Now" said Mike. "It's time to do a little analysis of our opponent. Wes dropped off a few mug shots of the known local DOG members. Let's go over them and I'll tell you what I can glean by channeling.

"First, here's Wolfe Drake, the local leader. In the Michael Soul Teachings system he is a 2nd Level Young Soul. His Role is

Warrior with a Priest Essence Twin. He has a Goal of Dominance and his Chief Obstacle is Arrogance."

"Mike, I thought almost all of the DOG members were Baby Souls?" asked Connie.

"Yes, most of them are, but not Drake. His prime underlying motive for being involved with DOG is power, a young soul objective. His Priest Essence Twin influence makes it easy for him to buy into the groups dogma and spew it out with the best of them, but deep inside he's marching to a slightly different drummer. Because he's in Dominance, this lifetime is about developing leadership skills. Now what does this tell us?

"First, he's a strong leader who will be ruthless in making his men follow. Any disobedience will be dealt with harshly. So his men will be in fear of his wrath if they disobey orders. Where he is vulnerable is his Arrogance. He can't stand being thought of as normal or mediocre. Also, since his inner allegiance to the cause is not as strong, he is more susceptible to being pulled away over issues of money and power."

"What's a good example?" asked Karen.

"Say he asked for more money and equipment and got turned down because McCallum favored another regional leader instead of Drake. That could drive a wedge between the two men. Or Drake might already be appropriating local funds for his personal use. He probably would not like to be audited by McCallum's people. Drake might also have another secret source of income that he isn't sharing with McCallum. Supposedly, a lot of DOG's funding comes from international credit card fraud. McCallum hates Jews and maintains they control the world's banking system so it's acceptable for him to rob from them. The FBI say that the DEA thinks Drake is doing some drug running on the side. McCallum stays away from drugs because he doesn't trust any of the minorities involved. He refuses to work with Mexicans, Colombians, Asians, or Blacks. As a Young Soul, Drake doesn't care where the money comes from. He will work with whoever can deliver the money."

"I know you want to cover just the local DOG members but can you fill us in a little on McCallum?" asked Lee Chou.

"Of course. Calvin McCallum is a 5th Level Baby Soul. His Role is King, with a Scholar Essence Twin. His Goal is also Dominance. His Chief Obstacle is Stubbornness.

"This means he sees things in a very black and white way. He reads a great deal but only dogma that supports his Baby Soul beliefs. He considers his viewpoint the correct one. Anyone who disagrees is either an idiot or an enemy. His men are expected to be 100% loyal to him. The slightest disloyalty, or even perceived disloyalty, will be dealt with brutally. The guy is like a brick wall surrounded by a concrete wall. He's a good military strategist and his hideout is probably well-designed and well-protected. If you're going to fight him it's better to get him out in the open where he's more vulnerable."

"Hey, I'd love to have a shot at the bastard. What are the chances he'll be coming out here?" asked Pudgy.

"Not very good—which is good for us." Mike said. "The FBI has been doing a fairly good job of tying him up with other problems down south. He's been in more of a defensive mode lately. Wolf Drake is the only one of his regional guys who is currently on the offensive and causing problems. Drake probably prefers that McCallum doesn't come out here, particularly if Drake is doing any skimming of money or drug dealing.

"Mitch Reddick is Drake's top Lieutenant. Like Drake, he's a Young Soul, probably First Level. His Role is Warrior. Goal of Growth, Chief Obstacle is Greed. His loyalty is to Drake. If Drake is doing any drug dealing, Mitch is most likely the guy in charge of it. His weakness is a fear of being left with nothing.

"Ernie Goddard is a Sixth Level Baby Soul, Sage/Warrior ET, Goal of Acceptance with a Chief Obstacle of Impatience. He's the showoff in the group. Likes to talk and be the center of attention. His weakness is a fear of missing out on what's happening.

"Reamer is a Fourth Level Baby Soul. Warrior Role. Goal of Submission, Chief Obstacle is Self-destruction. His greatest fear is of life and all the pain that comes with it. He is the most likely to abuse drugs.

"Ronald Farley, also known as 'Razor,' First Level Baby Soul Priest. Goal of Growth, Chief Obstacle of Martyrdom. Watch out for this guy—he will die for the cause. He's capable of strapping dynamite to his body and walking into a building and setting it off. His greatest fear is being taken advantage of by others.

"That covers the key people we have identified so far." Mike said. "Remember as much of it as you can. Someday this little bit of extra knowledge might save someone's life. I personally think it's better than the psychological profiles law enforcement uses to try and understand the really bad guys."

It was time to wrap things up and head home, so we all pitched in and helped pick up dishes and glasses. Once things were under control Karen and I headed home with an almost empty box containing only two manuscripts. One went to Katherine the agent, one each to Mike, Pudgy, Connie, Wes, Ty, Crystal, and one to someone Karen knows who would be a good critic. Those who received a manuscript were expected to read it and get their comments back to me in a week if possible, so I could make the obvious changes before I started working with the editor.

Chapter 23

The next morning I contacted Crystal at the New Lotus Bookshop and discovered that there was an opening in ten days on Wednesday evening, from 6:30 PM to 8:30 PM. I told her to reserve it for Mike and me, and we would get her an in-store promotional flyer tomorrow. I didn't inform Crystal of the FBI's plan to use the seminar as a trap. I figured Wes, and Ty were the best people to break that news to her.

After quickly designing a flyer on my Power Mac I faxed it to Crystal at New Lotus and to Connie at the Seattle Times. Since we knew Drake was likely to read Connie's column that seemed like the best place to advertise.

Two days later the story appeared. About halfway down her column it said:

"While hate groups flourish among us, there are also some bright lights of hope. The New Lotus Bookshop is holding a seminar titled 'Clash of Souls' July 10th from 6:30 to 8:30 PM featuring author Scott Hunter. Mr. Hunter, along with his spiritual teacher, a man who goes only by the name of Mike, will discuss the Michael Soul Teachings. A modern look at God, the Universe, reincarnation and how we as souls evolve through various lifetimes. The seminar is open to the public. Contact the New Lotus Bookshop at 206-555-4200 for details."

It was perfectly written to lure Drake's thugs. The only downside was I was mentioned by name so from this point on I too would be a hated and hunted target. I had to admit I was more than a little scared at making DOG's hit list. But I had made my decision and there was no turning back.

The day before the seminar I met with Mike and Pudgy at the FBI offices in downtown Seattle. In the briefing room, I grabbed a front row seat next to Mike. Tyrone was at the marker board, and approximately a dozen agents were also in the room. I didn't see Wes anywhere. Mike told me Wes had explained the situation to Crystal and the store manager, who while not pleased, calmed down after they understood the importance of stopping the Defenders of God before they attacked more people.

The plan was to have a female agent at the store entrance monitoring the metal detector. A surveillance camera would be covering it as well. Everyone who failed the metal detector would be identified quietly. When they entered the seminar room they would be seated between two agents. A third agent would be sitting right behind each identified person unless there were too many. The FBI would assume the identified people were DOG members. They planned on four to six plus a getaway driver.

Outside the building there would be a half dozen FBI agents and several SPD undercover cops in plain clothes. Their job would be to locate the getaway vehicle and, if unmanned, they would attach a transmitter so it could be followed easily. Photos of all known DOG members were passed out as well as photos of any of their girlfriends, since they might be carrying the guns for their thug boyfriends. Once everyone was seated for the seminar the sliding doors to the seminar room would be closed so any shoppers out in the main part of the store could be evacuated. The store personnel would be replaced by agents and SPD undercover cops.

The unknown was the number of people that would attend the seminar. The more innocent people in the audience the greater the risk something might go wrong. If more DOG members showed up than expected, our resources would be stretched thin, maybe too thin. The consensus was DOG would show up but do nothing inside. They would most likely strike after we exited the building. Agents with high powered rifles would be posted on two building roof tops facing the front entrance to the Bookshop. If any DOG member draws a weapon, orders were to shoot immediately and block or disable the getaway vehicle. If no guns appear they will be allowed to leave and the vehicle will be followed discreetly to their hiding place.

My cell phone beeped. I looked at the number, it was Connie. I slipped out of the room and punched in her number.

"Scott, thank God you called. There's been another death threat. This time to Katherine," said Connie.

"Katherine Morgan? My agent? You gotta be kidding" I said.

"No, it's true and it's scary. Someone broke into her home and trashed her condo and her Siamese cat is missing. She said there's blood everywhere. It was gruesome. A big chuck of raw, bloody cow liver was pinned on the wall in her office with a knife stuck through it. There was a note under the knife that said 'DEATH TO ALL WHO ALIGN WITH THE ENEMIES OF GOD.' She's called the police. She's terribly upset. You better give her a call."

"I will." I said, "But how did they know she was my agent?"

"Her name was listed in the promo for your seminar at East West."

"What? Why would they do that? It makes no sense," I said.

"Apparently New Lotus and Katherine thought it would add more prestige to the seminar since you're still unknown and she represents several popular authors. They thought they were helping you," said Connie.

"Okay. I suppose at the time it looked like a good idea. I'll give her a call right now," I said.

Hanging up the phone, I quickly dialed Katherine. She was obviously upset. Her voice was choked up from having done a great deal of crying. I wasn't sure what to say—I wasn't very good at dealing with this kind of grief. All I could think of was to say how sorry I was and ask if there was anything I could do.

She said, "Scott, Bookman was ten years old. I raised him from a kitten. He was everything in my life. I loved him like he was my child. I named him Bookman because when he was a little kitten he liked to sit on top of a stack of books on my desk.

Now he's gone," she sobbed.

"I'm so very sorry, Katherine. Maybe Bookman escaped when they broke into your place. I'm in a meeting with the FBI right now figuring out how to catch these sick people and put them where they can't harm anyone else."

"Scott, I can't take any more of this. Your manuscript was trashed. They had set several pages on fire, torn up others, and shoved some pages down the garbage disposal and the rest in the kitchen trash can. The cow liver blood was smeared over it and all over my walls. I'm sorry Scott but I have to resign as your agent. I never bargained for anything like this. My brother is staying with me now for protection, I can't stay here by myself. I've got to move right away. I'm sorry but I'm too scared."

"I understand, Katherine. We'll figure out a way to get the word out to everyone letting them know that you're no longer my agent. In the meantime, why not post a 'missing cat' flyer around the neighborhood. I'm sure he'll turn up."

"Thank you, Scott."

Feeling depressed, I disconnected and started to walk back into the meeting.

"Hunter!"

I turned at the sound of my name and spotted Wes coming toward me with some papers in his hand.

"Hey, Scott, I just got a report from the SPD—about your agent Katherine Morgan."

"I know, Wes, I just got off the phone with her. It looks like DOG struck again. She resigned as my agent, and frankly I can't say I blame her. These guys just keep intimidating people and we seem helpless to stop them. It pisses me off."

"Your seminar is tomorrow night. With any luck we'll nail them at that time. The sooner we can get these thugs off the street the better, but they've been pretty slippery. That's why your seminar is so important."

"I know you're right, Wes. I'm just frustrated as well as worried for the safety of my family and friends."

We walked back into the briefing room and Wes interrupted Ty to bring everyone up to date on the latest attack by DOG.

Mike just sat in a near stupor shaking his head back and forth as if to say, 'I'm tired, I'm an old man. I don't know how much more I can take.' Then he stood, turned towards me, and our eyes locked. I saw sadness yet an almost superhuman determination to keep going. I imagined the look would be similar to what you'd see in the eyes of a mountain climber 100 yards short of the top of Mt. Everest. All physical energy gone and only the internal power of the soul forcing the frail human body beyond its limits. Forcing one foot to move forward and then the other even though the muscles had long ago protested and told the brain they couldn't go forward. I knew I couldn't desert this old man and his determination to get the message out.

The room full of FBI agents started murmuring among themselves. I could feel their anger slowly surfacing, and with it their resolve to annihilate the members of DOG. I knew they would do anything legally possible to bring Drake's hoodlums to justice.

I turned to Wes and explained that Mike had done a personality profile on some of the DOG members using the Michael Soul Teachings. I asked if Mike could do the same for the FBI agents, explaining that any little tidbit of information could give us an edge that could possibly save a life. He agreed and whispered in Ty's ear. After a couple of minutes Ty turned to the agents and briefly explained what was going to happen.

"Is this a profile from our people?" asked one of the agents.

Mike spoke before Ty could answer and said, "No. The profiling I've done is based on information I have channeled and is based on the Michael Soul Teachings. It doesn't replace your profiling it just adds to it."

The agent persisted. "Why do we need two profiles? I'm a little confused when you say channeled and something called the Michael Soul Teachings. What does that mean?"

Wes stepped in and said, "Mike is a gifted psychic. How he does it we don't know. What we do know is that over a period of time he has been unusually accurate. The Michael Soul Teachings are a philosophy that has evolved over time. It's based on the philosophies of Gurdjieff, Ichazo, Taoism and Humanistic psychology. What makes it unique from other philosophies is it's structure. Based on dividing people into different categories it explains why we are the way we are." Then turning to Mike, he asked, "Mike, is that it in a nutshell?"

"Not bad Wes. You're starting to get the hang of it. Let me just add some of the details. First we determine the age of a soul—that part of you that actually operates your body—then we look at the Role the soul chose to operate from as well as the personality characteristics the soul chose for this lifetime. The Michael system explains the differences between people. To give you all an example, if Wes and Ty agree, I can explain their profiles to you. Okay Wes? Okay Ty?"

Both Wes and Ty nodded in agreement.

"Okay. Wes is a 7th Level Mature Soul. His Role is Scholar with a Goal of Growth. His Chief Obstacle of Self-deprecation.

"What this tells us is he's at a point in his soul evolution where understanding relationships and philosophies are more important than say making money. As a Scholar, he loves to read and learn things and is fond of research. His Self-deprecation can make him appear humble.

"Tyrone, on the other hand, is a 4th Level Young Soul. His Role is Warrior with a Goal of Discrimination. He operates with a Chief Obstacle of Impatience.

"Aside from the difference in age, Ty, as a Young Soul is more concerned with worldly success. Power, money, prestige and looking young are more important to him than to Wes. His Role of Warrior fits in perfectly with being in law enforcement. Under fire, you can always count on him to hold up his end of the battle. With a Goal of Discrimination, he's highly precise and analytical. As I understand it he's the handgun champion for the Western Region. His Impatience makes him frustrated when things appear to take too long. He hates red lights and cases that can't be solved quickly."

One of the agents who had been holding his chin with a skeptical look spoke, "Not bad. You actually got all that from these Michael Soul Teachings. I've know Wes for ten years and Ty for four, and you were right on. You sold me."

After handling a series of additional questions from the curious agents, and a promise to come back and do a profile for each one of them, Mike quickly ran through the profiles with photos of the DOG thugs.

Chapter 24

I arrived at the New Lotus Bookshop at 5:30 PM, an hour before the seminar was scheduled to start. Everything looked normal both inside and outside the store. I had already put on a Kevlar vest under a turtleneck sweater and a loose-fitting tweed sports jacket to hide it from the attendees. Mike and I had decided that I would do most of the talking and he would channel the Michael Soul profiles for some members of the audience.

In no time at all, the crowd started arriving. I spotted what appeared to be a couple of DOG members arrive. One had a shaved head and the other had a very close cropped haircut. Their clothing was nondescript and loose-fitting enough to be concealing handguns. Both were in their early twenties and had the usual assortment of body piercing. I could see parts of tattoos that extended under the sleeves of the jackets they were wearing.

The two appeared nervous and slowly worked their way around the store, pretending to be looking at books, but their eyes were casing the place—taking in the layout of the store, the clerks, book browsers, and the people attending the seminar.

One of the female FBI agents, disguised as a store clerk, approached the two and asked them if they needed any help. The one with the shaved head, shook his head and mumbled something about being there for the seminar.

Another agent, a male, who was pretending to be a book browser, positioned himself behind them keeping an eye on what they touched. As the two moved around they would occasionally pick up a book and pretend to be skimming it. As they replaced the book and shuffled on to the next row of books, the agent carefully removed the books they touched from the shelves and put them on a nearby book cart. At first I was confused, then I realized the agent was picking up the books to get the fingerprints of the two DOG thugs. Very clever, I thought to myself.

The moment of truth finally arrived—Crystal, looking worried, rang a little bell and announced that the seminar was about to start. My heart started racing. I had given hundreds of speeches and seminars before, but never with the prospect of an audience member pulling out a gun and shooting me.

Another agent, a young female posing as a clerk, approached me and whispered in my ear as she pointed towards the two suspects, "Mr. Hunter, the scanner indicates both of those guys are likely carrying something like a gun or a knife. They're the only ones who set off the scanner. Remember, if anyone pulls a weapon hit the floor immediately."

Taking a deep breath and exhaling the air to calm myself I said, "Okay. Just make sure none of the good guys get hurt."

As I entered the seminar room I noticed the two thugs were seated in the back row on the left end preventing the FBI agents from being on both sides and behind them. Great! Here's the first screw-up in the plans. One agent was seated just to the right of one of them but there was nobody on the left or behind them.

Then, as the room filled up, there was a shortage of seats. The agents, acting as store personnel quickly started grabbing chairs from a folded stack and setting them up. A row was quickly placed behind the suspects and agents took their place. An additional two chairs were added to the aisle to the left of the two. Agents quickly filled them. Now there were two agents on their left, one on the right and two behind them. Another agent took a position on a chair near, but slightly behind, the podium and turned so she could see both the podium and the two suspects. I was still nervous, but feeling a little better.

As I was about ready to walk up to the podium Mike grabbed my arm. "Scott, I know you're nervous but try to relax. The Universe will ensure that everything turns out okay. Just trust that you are on the correct path."

I nodded back and walked up to the podium. After Crystal introduced Mike and me to the audience, I started giving some background information to set the stage for the presentation.

One of the agents sitting behind the suspects raised his hand and asked when my book would be out. This question had been planted beforehand so I could take some of the pressure, and any future danger, off of Katherine Morgan. I answered, "I don't know for sure. We had a literary agent who was looking for a publisher but she had to quit for personal reasons. At this time, we're looking both for an agent and a publisher. So, if any of you know of someone please let us know."

As I gave my answer, I noticed the shaved headed thug jabbed his buddy in the side with an elbow and gave him a satisfied grin and nod of his head. It was obvious they knew the whole story of what had happened to the agent.

Normally when I speak, I try to balance my eye contact with the entire audience but tonight I felt myself more frequently checking up on the two suspects, anticipating one, or both of them, reaching for a weapon. I went through my material, following the format Mike had used over at the bookstore in Port Townsend. Then Mike did some channeling. While he was the focus of everyone's attention, I positioned myself behind him so that when I looked at him my eyes were also directly on the suspects. At the slightest hint of an attack, I could grab Mike and dive to the floor behind the podium.

As time started running out, my apprehension increased. Would they wait until the end, and then when the audience got up and was milling around, attack? I noticed the agents seemed to be coming to a similar conclusion. Tension was mounting. A crowd milling about could endanger a lot of people. I quickly concluded my remarks, then as I was taking some questions, several members of the audience stood up and started heading for the door. I could see an agent in the back quietly pulling people out the door as fast as possible, without tipping our hand.

The moment I concluded my remarks, the two suspects stood, looked at each other, and turned to leave. The one with the close cropped hair put his hand in his pocket and immediately I saw an agent right behind him quickly draw his weapon, holding it low and behind his back.

The two headed for the door then stopped just inside. The close-cropped one, mumbled something to his buddy, motioning with his head, towards one of the agents—an attractive woman in her twenties. Then he turned and approached her. Suddenly, I realized what was happening. He was hitting on her! I had to stifle a laugh. Here was our enemy, one of the DOG thugs trying to pick up an FBI agent!

He started talking to her and she played along with him. After about a minute, I saw her reach in her purse, take out a pen and, grabbing the seminar flyer from him, proceeded to write down her phone number and returned the flyer to him. I looked around the room and saw the looks on the faces of a few of the other agents. They were having a hard time controlling the urge to laugh.

The thug thanked her and turned to rejoin his buddy. Together they walked out of the room with the one boasting what a cool stud he was. They walked into the main part of the store then quickly went out the door, much to my relief. Whew! At last, the nerve-racking seminar was over. I was alive. Mike was alive—and no one got hurt.

Now it was just a simple matter of tracking the van back to their hideout, or so I thought. Murphy's Law was about to rear its predictable head.

Ty came into the store, talking on his cell phone. "Damn it. Don't lose them whatever you do. Keep me posted." Then he disconnected.

"Scott, Mike, apparently they were just here to observe you and get information about your book. That's the good part. No one got hurt. The bad news is we couldn't get a transmitter planted in their getaway vehicle. There were four of them all together. They parked across the street, right out in front on Roosevelt Way, and two of them stayed near the vehicle during the entire seminar while the other two went into the seminar. Most of the time they were standing on the sidewalk smoking so there was no way we could sneak up and plant the transmitter.

"Now we're going to have to follow them and hope we're not spotted. SPD is helping. We're running a six car rotating tail on them. We're ahead of them, behind them and on both parallel streets. They appear to be heading south, probably to the Bremerton Ferry dock at Pier 52. If they take the ferry, we'll try to install the transmitter if they leave their vehicle during the crossing."

"Why not use a helicopter?" I asked.

"It would work while we're in the city, but as we got closer to their hideout, out in the country, it would be too obvious, and we don't want to lose the element of surprise. We don't want to give them any time to get rid of evidence," said Ty.

"Do you mind if we tag along?" said Mike.

"No problem. We can monitor the chase in my car," said Ty.

Mike, Ty and I left New Lotus and hopped into Ty's dark blue four-door government issue Ford Taurus. Inside, Ty switched on the tactical channel being used by the chase cars. By listening closely, I could visualize the unfolding drama. Six vehicles following DOG—and the thugs totally unaware—or at least we hoped they were unaware.

Piecing together the snippets of dialogue I heard:

"Suspects turning right on 45th. Westbound on 45th."

"Suspects turning left onto I-5 South on-ramp, directly behind unit 158. Parallel units converge on I-5 temporarily."

Ty said, "158 is the unit we have in front of the suspects. We're assuming they're heading for pier 52, but if they take another route we have units close enough to replace them. Because there really aren't any easy streets paralleling I-5 as it passes over the ship canal from Lake Union to Portage Bay, our parallel vehicles are now on I-5, a block or two behind the suspects."

"880 requesting chase rotation."

"Roger 880. 970 moving up."

"880 dropping back."

"What's happening?" I asked.

"880 is the unit following directly behind the suspects. They feel it's time to switch places with another unit. They have been following for a while and are afraid the suspects might be getting suspicious," said Ty.

"Suspects taking Mercer Street exit. Unit 158 anticipate suspects will take Broad Street to Alaskan Way then left to Pier 52."

Ty continued translating. Since they took the Mercer Street exit, it's a good bet that they are headed to the ferry terminal, so that's the way the lead unit, 158, is planning on going."

"Suspects on Broad westbound."

"Unit 335 will parallel on Elliott Avenue southbound."

"Unit 420 will parallel on Second Avenue southbound."

"Unit 880 now in drop-back tail position."

"Unit 518 continuing drop-back position."

"Suspects turning left on Alaskan Way. Southbound."

"Perfect so far," said Ty. "They're heading for the ferry."

"Suspects slowing, signaling for a left turn. Not sure what's happening. Ferry terminal is about a half mile south of here."

"I spoke too soon, these guys aren't following our script," said Ty.

"Suspects turning into Market Parking Garage. Unit 970 to follow. All other units hold positions."

"Suspects parking and leaving vehicle."

"Suspects at elevator."

"Unit 970 parking. Following on foot. Elevator stopped at 7th level."

"Agents Ramon and Radcliff on elevator. Going to level 7."

"Entering the Market. Suspects not in sight. Units 335 and 420 cover entrance at Pike Street. We'll search on foot. Maintain distance if suspects spotted. Might just be a coffee break before boarding the ferry."

The cryptic messages continued. By now, we were approaching the parking garage. Unit 518 had set up a watch on the suspect's vehicle while the two agents from unit 970 were working their way through the shops in the market.

After ten minutes it was decided to plant the transmitter on the suspect's vehicle. With one agent keeping an eye on the elevator, the other quickly dropped to his knees, reached under the vehicle and attached the transmitter. Once it was in place both agents retreated to their vehicle, parked a discreet distance away.

Mike shook his head. "Something's wrong Ty."

Tyrone walked over to the cashier's booth at the entrance and spoke to the attendant. "Did you see a car with four white men, in their twenties or thirties leaving? A few of them had shaved heads."

"No. Things have been pretty slow for the last hour. Why don't you check with the cashier up on Western Avenue?"

"What do you mean? I thought this was the entrance and exit?"

It suddenly hit me—this parking garage is built right into the side of the steep hill from the waterfront up to the Pike Place Market. Cars can enter or leave at the bottom level or up at the top level. We jumped back into Ty's vehicle and he did his best imitation of a NASCAR pro, racing around the curves, squealing his tires, burning rubber, and spiraling up to the top level. At the upper booth, he pulled his badge and said to the cashier, "Hey, Buddy, have you seen a car leave here in the last half hour with four guys in it? Young white guys with shaved heads?"

"Yes sir," said the cashier. "I remember them. As they was leavin', one of them yelled some cuss words at me. Told me to go back to Africa. You know—that kinda stuff. Those dudes are scary. Are ya gonna catch 'em?"

"I hope so," said Ty. "What were they driving?"

"It think it was Jeep Cherokee. Pretty dirty. I think it was a tan or light gray."

"License plate number?"

"Sorry. They got me mad and I wasn't payin' much attention."

"You did fine. Thanks a lot," said Ty.

As we pulled out of the garage, Ty alerted the chase team to the latest developments. Two units went to the ferry terminal to see if they had boarded while the others called it a night. An all points bulletin went out in the hope that some patrol car would spot them. But unless we got real lucky, they had escaped our fool-proof plan. I was depressed and Mike didn't look any better. After dropping Mike off near the Seattle Center on lower Queen Anne Hill, Ty drove me back to my car at the New Lotus Bookshop.

Chapter 25

It was time to regroup and figure out our next steps. After speaking with Mike, we decided to have a meeting at Pudgy's home at 7:00 PM.

Karen and I arrived at 6:45 PM. Pudgy, Lee Chou, and Connie were already sipping tea and munching on some coffeecake. Five minutes later Mike arrived."Folks," said Mike, "we have hit a roadblock. Let's figure out how to get around it. DOG has done a pretty good job of slowing us down. Connie can't even stay at her own place for fear DOG will attack. DOG now knows about Scott and will probably soon figure out where he and Karen live. The FBI is trying to catch them but look what happened last night. A fool-proof plan failed. A rough draft of the book is done but it has to be edited and published. Our agent resigned and none of us can blame her—because of us her cat is missing and she's an emotional basket case. Does that pretty much sum it up?"

"Hey," said Pudgy, "I ain't quittin'. We knew there was risk. I say let's figure out how to win and focus on that. This is war man and in war there are gonna be casualties. We been losin' some battles but we ain't lost the war."

"You're right, Pudgy," I said, "there's an answer, let's find it. The biggest problem I see is finding a publisher. There's a danger in getting another agent—and I couldn't blame anybody for turning us down."

"Why don't we start brainstorming and see what we can come up with," said Connie.

"Good idea," said Mike. "Pudgy, you have a marker board don't you?"

"Yeah. Let me get it."

Pudgy went to the hall closet and brought out a small white twenty-four inches by thirty inches marker board and a few color markers. Connie was appointed in charge of writing down all the ideas, with the standard brainstorming rule of no evaluating until all ideas are out on the table.

Karen spoke, "What if we self-published the book?" Connie wrote it down.

"We publish on the Internet," said Pudgy.

"We move ahead with the editing," I said.

"We help the FBI find DOG," Lee Chou said.

"We go directly to publishers without getting an agent," said Connie.

"We do our own advertising and marketing. We could even do a direct mail campaign," I added.

"Why not get some national publicity about the problems we're having?" said Connie.

The brainstorming continued for an hour and after a stretch break we went back over the list and culled out the weaker ideas. What we were left with was:

(1) A need to start the editing process immediately. Everything would be done to keep the editor's identity secret from DOG.

(2) No attempt would be made to get another literary agent. There was too much risk of harm to the person and we couldn't easily keep his or her identity a secret.

(3) Once editing was complete, we would self-publish a small run of approximately twenty-five hundred books.

(4) We would distribute the books to selected bookstores on the West Coast.

(5) Seminars and book signings would be arranged in cities outside our local area where the likelihood of running into DOG was small.

(6) A direct response television commercial would be done and media time would be bought in selected markets. We would handle the fulfillment of the orders.

(7) National publicity would be sought.

The plan seemed good. Just going through the process helped snap the group out of our collective funk. We weren't completely stopped. Our strategy wasn't the ideal situation, but it was better than nothing.

My part of the process was to get the editing done. Connie gave me the name of a lady—Dorothy Kellerman—who had moved to Seattle from New York. She had spent several years working for a major publishing house so we were assured of a first class job of editing.

Mike put in a call to Wes and discovered that the car DOG left in the Market Parking Garage was stolen, so the transmitter placed under it was worthless. It was ditched and another vehicle in the garage, the Jeep Cherokee, was used for the getaway. However, prints were discovered in the stolen car. It had been wiped fairly clean, but with four people riding in it, a few prints had survived. The prints turned out to belong to two of the occupants—both recently discharged from the military. Neither had a criminal record, but their military records indicated some disciplinary action taken for being involved in a racial incident that had occurred at Ft. Bliss, Texas.

The meeting broke up and Karen and I left. On the way home, we stopped at Whole Foods, our favorite grocery store, located down the hill from Pudgy's house and a block from the New Lotus Bookshop. Karen loved the fact that Whole Foods carried such a broad line of organic foods. I loved their deli section. Not only did they have a huge section of the store devoted to lavish spreads of ready-to-eat food—soups, salad bar, pizza, casseroles, cheeses, fruits and desserts—they had a dining area with tables, chairs and counters to sit at and enjoy whatever delights one selected.

We were both hungry. I loaded two baked chicken breasts onto a paper plate and then filled a small white carton with a fabulous salad. Karen went for the white bean soup, one chicken breast, and a few slices of fresh, organically grown cantaloupe. While I staked out a table, Karen went to the bakery/coffee counter and ordered a couple of mochas and some carmelita treats for dessert.

After several moments of silence, while we scarfed down enough food to balance our blood sugar levels, Karen finally spoke, "So, Scott, what do you think? Do you think the plan will work?"

"To be 100% honest, I don't know. I'm a writer—a damn good one—but this is about a lot more than just writing. Self-publishing has a lot of drawbacks. It's normally better to go with a publisher. I would love to have an agent out there beating the bushes for us to find the best possible publisher for the type book I've written. For the book's message to reach enough people to matter it needs promotion and marketing, and that's what publishers are good at. But there have been other influential books that started out being self-published. It just took a lot longer. Word-of-mouth is a great form of promoting but it's not as fast as a professional marketing campaign with publicity appearances.

"The next step is editing and rewriting—maybe by the time I'm done with that the FBI will have neutralized DOG and they'll no longer be a threat. Then we could go back to the original game plan and get a good agent."

"I know, Scott, but in the meantime I'm afraid. These creeps are scary."

"I don't blame you for being scared. The DOG thugs are dangerous. We just have to be extra cautious. I'll pick you up from school every day and we'll stay in a highly alert state when out of the house. You know what a lot of the DOG thugs look like so if you spot one of them use your cell phone immediately. You've got Wes Conner's number as well as Ty's and Pudgy's. If something goes wrong, call any of them as fast as possible."

"Okay, Scott, I'll be careful and you too. When are you going to contact the book editor?"

"As soon as we get home. Are you ready to go?"

"Yeah, let's go."

On the drive home I kept checking the rearview mirror to verify no one was following. We were starting to feel like fugitives.

Once we got home, I called Dorothy Kellerman, the manuscript editor. Much to my delight she had, just two days earlier, finished a major editing job and was wide open to work with me. We scheduled a meeting for 10:00 AM the next morning.

With that done Karen and I decided to kick back and watch TV. We watched an old *NYPD Blues* re-run. At least on TV, the bad guys get caught and everyone lives happily ever after.

At 7:30 AM, the phone rang as I was waking. It was Pudgy. "Hey Man, I think we got a break. Thought you'd wanta know."

I snapped alert instantly. "Yeah, of course. What's up?"

"Last night, down at the Rusty Anchor—ya know the dive where I play bouncer—three DOG thugs showed up. One of them was a new recruit who got louder the more he drank and the other two were pretty tanked too. When two of them were in the head, one guy was braggin' about how they beat up the gays and killed one and maybe two. One guy, by the name of Tony, said that Ernie was the one who castrated the gay black guy, and Reamer was the guy who used the shotgun on the white guy that died. Then Tony, the loud mouth, starts braggin' that Drake had the idea to blow up Connie. Tony said he was supposed to deliver it but at the last minute Drake had Reamer do it. Tony was pissed, so Drake let him lead the attack on the black couple at the Space Needle. Apparently, he got some kinda promotion for doin' such a good job.

"I called Wes and told him what I heard, but because it was a bug we placed in the head the testimony would probably get tossed outa court. Now we know who the bad guys are and Tony might be the kinda jerk who'll squeal like a pig to the FBI. I know I sure as hell could get the friggin' shithole to talk. I was gonna follow them back to their hideout when they left, but I was in the kitchen takin' a food break when they up and split. But if they come back again, I'll make damn good and sure I follow them back to the hideout."

After we finished talking, I briefed Karen. The thought of anyone being so violent and cruel to another human being was totally beyond her, but she agreed, while she was still scared, that it sounded as if we were getting closer to nailing them.

"I just hope," said Karen, "that after they're caught some slippery-tongued lawyer doesn't find a stupid loophole to get them off."

"I don't think that'll happen. Wes and Ty are pretty savvy. They'll do everything possible to make sure the arrests are done by the book. It's getting late so I better shower, shave, and get to my 10:00 AM appointment with the editor, Dorothy Keller-man."

At 9:30 AM, I left the house and headed to Kirkland to meet Dorothy Kellerman at her home. Kirkland is on the east side of Lake Washington, a nice quaint little suburban town of forty thousand that happens to be the home of the Seattle Seahawks professional football team. Like most Seattle east side suburbs, Kirkland has attracted the affluent. Microsoft and scores of other high tech firms have created droves of millionaires who live in the area.

Dorothy's directions were good and I easily found her condo, a rather bland looking building with a row of tiny arbor vitae shrubs planted in front.

Her unit was in the back, accessible by a short walkway through the building. I glanced at my watch as I pushed the doorbell for unit twelve. It was 9:58 AM. Good. I'm a stickler for being on time.

I was greeted by a tall, elegant looking woman with white hair tucked into a bun. I'd guess she was mid-fifties. Dorothy looked trim and fit in her cream colored slacks and matching turtle neck sweater topped off by a multi-colored scarf. Everything about her reeked of competency and precision—nice qualities for a manuscript editor.

After the usual greetings, we settled in on her cream-colored sofa accented with soft rose throw pillows. She excused herself long enough to get a pot of herbal tea from the kitchen. A quick scan of her living room indicated that she was either divorced or widowed. There was a cluster of various framed photos on the fireplace mantle and the end tables. It looked like she had three kids, some of who now had their own kids, making her a grandmother.

Dorothy poured tea for both of us and while I sipped mine she picked up my manuscript and said, "Scott, Connie already told me what your book is about. It sounds fascinating and I'm looking forward to reading it. If you don't mind, I want to take just a few minutes right now skimming through it to try and get a feel for how much editing it might take."

"Sounds good to me," I said as I picked up a National Geographic from her coffee table with a cover shot of a huge shark with its mouth wide open, "it'll give me a chance to learn more about Great White Sharks."

The shark photos reminded me of the thugs from DOG—wild beasts with no hesitation to kill. Simple, but deadly, killing machines. The main difference was the sharks needed to kill to survive starvation. DOG on the other hand was trying to help their repressive dogma survive—a big difference.

I glanced occasionally at Dorothy. She would flip pages rapidly, then periodically stop, look serious, make a note in the margin, then continue flipping pages. As an author, I'm a word-smith. My job is to link words together in an appropriate manner to best tell my story. When writing for the advertising industry, the use, or not use, of a particular word could dramatically effect the results of an ad campaign, so I was used to arguing with anyone, including my clients, who wanted to change my words. I was hoping that Dorothy and I would see eye-to-eye on my choice of words, and most of her work would involve catching little glitches in tense or grammar.

Finally she lowered the manuscript to her lap, removed her gold-framed reading glasses, looked at me and spoke. "Not too bad. I see a lot of the usual mistakes, but overall your writing is very good. Obviously, I might've skipped past some major problem but I'm fairly confident that I didn't. Did Connie tell you what my fees are?"

"Ah yeah, she said you charge $50 an hour. That you're a real pro with great credentials from the major publishing houses you worked for back in New York, and you're fast so your price is a real bargain."

"Well. I think I should hire Connie as my promoter. I have had over twenty years experience in the trenches in New York so I know what's required and I do try to work as fast as possible. I'm keenly aware that most authors who have to pay for editing themselves do not have a lot of money. So, if you're comfortable with me, I'm ready to start."

"Okay, let's do it," I said.

Dorothy pulled out her standard contract form and I signed it and gave her a down payment check for $1,000. We agreed to work by phone as much as possible but she cautioned me that an occasional face-to-face meeting might be required.

I left Dorothy feeling much better—feeling that the manuscript was in very good hands.

Chapter 26

It had been nearly two weeks since I turned my manuscript over to Dorothy Kellerman. She was doing an excellent job, faxing me changes twice a day. I made the changes as fast as I got them and in most cases had no argument with her corrections. We had one face-to-face meeting to resolve a few technical issues, but in general, the editing was going smoothly.

In the meantime, I contacted several small publishers using new digital printing technology to produce small runs for authors going the self-publishing route. It looked like we could get our twenty-five hundred copies, 8.5 inches x 5.5 inches, soft cover, for approximately $5.00 per book, or $12,500 total. We had decided to retail the book at $16.95 in order to reach as broad a market as possible.

With the editing going smoothly and potential printers lined up, I had a little spare time to call Mike to see what was happening.

"Hi, Scott, what's up?"

"Things are going great on this end," I said. "The editing is moving along quite nicely and I think I've got us a printer who can handle our small press run."

"Great news."

"What's happening with the FBI and DOG? Any breakthroughs yet?" I asked.

"Not really. They seem to have vanished from the face of the earth. Pudgy hasn't seen any of them come into the Rusty Anchor either. They might have taken off and headed south to the Mexican border for a little human target practice—their disgusting initiation process for new members. The Border Patrol has been alerted for any signs of them."

"Wouldn't it be great if the Border Patrol could catch them in the act and arrest them?" I said. "It sure would," said Mike. "By the way, check today's issue of the Seattle Times. Connie wrote an article summarizing this struggle we've been going through to get this book out. It should be a real zinger. She's hoping it will be picked up nationally and stir up some interest for the book."

"Okay, I'll pick up a copy of the Times right away. Keep me posted on anything that breaks."

We disconnected and I went out to the nearby Seven-Eleven and picked up the Seattle Times. Once I got back home, I opened the paper and located her article.

Violence Threatens Freedom of Speech in Seattle

by Connie Kamura

Many residents of our fair city are too young to remember the wild and tumultuous sixties when hundreds of thousands of protesters, mostly young college-aged people, often called hippies, took to the streets and protested the Vietnam War. In many countries around the world, they would have been met with tanks and real bullets. Their protests would have been ruthlessly crushed. In some other countries, the facade of freedom of speech is presented to the world while behind the scenes so-called death squads are both tolerated and often encouraged by the ruling party to silence dissent.

All too often, we Americans take our freedoms for granted and fail to see how fragile democracy really is. We assume that what we have will always be there, but there's no guarantee. Under the right circumstances, our democracy could collapse. Our founding fathers had the wisdom to create a three-legged government with power divided between the executive, the legislative and the judicial branches. If over a period of time, one branch seizes more power than the other two, our democracy will be threatened. One only has to look back in history to Rome to see what happens when the executive branch has too much power. As the various Roman Emperors seized more power, the Roman Senate lost theirs, and ultimately became powerless.

Then, as now, the prime way of destroying democracy was to stifle dissent. If you can keep anyone from presenting differing viewpoints, soon there will only be one viewpoint and dissenters will be silenced and forced to live in fear.

In Seattle, several events have occurred recently that threaten our precious freedoms. Remember the recent attack on two gay men on Capitol Hill? A gang of marauding right-wing militia hoodlums decided they didn't like people with a different sexual orientation. The thugs could have paraded around on our streets with protest signs — that's legal and a part of our freedom of speech — but instead they decided to violently attack the gay men. One of the gays, a white male was killed on the spot. The other, a black male, is still in a coma in a Seattle hospital.

Then, in an article I wrote shortly thereafter, I wrote about several hate groups headquartered in the Pacific Northwest. My intent was to raise the awareness level of our community about groups among us that would like nothing better than to stifle all viewpoints except theirs. The response to my article was a nearly successful attempt to kill me with a package bomb. They certainly were within their right to write letters to the editor disagreeing with my article but instead they chose violence which has two benefits from their viewpoint. First, it can completely eliminate the person who disagrees with you and second, it can intimidate others from being critical in the future.

In another case, that heretofore has not received any publicity, a hate group, possibly the same one responsible for the attack on the gays and the bomb sent to the Seattle Times, is up to the same dirty tricks. For the past two years, a kind, gentle old man, a spiritual teacher who simply prefers to be known as Mike, has been quietly trying to disseminate his particular spiritual message.

Unfortunately for Mike, his spiritual message does not align with the religious interpretations of the hate group. Solely because he wants to present a different interpretation he has been shot at twice and survived a knife attack on another occasion. To stay alive, while struggling to get his message out, he has been living in fear for his life, constantly on the move, and hiding like a hunted fugitive. One particular hate group has a $100,000 bounty on his head — dead or alive.

Recently Mike found a writer, Scott Hunter, who was brave enough to help. Mike gave his information to Hunter who has just completed writing a book based on the material, called 'Clash of Souls.' Hunter found an agent who in turn was about to find a publisher for the book. The hate group, intent on stopping the book from getting published, threatened the agent's life, and smeared blood all over her home. The intimidation worked. The agent resigned immediately.

Yes, folks, our lovely Seattle, the home of Starbucks, Nordstrom, Microsoft, the Space Needle, and the site of the charming movie, 'Sleepless in Seattle,' has become the home for a deadly group of violent right-wingers who are out to destroy the very freedoms that created this wonderful city and country. I think it's time for the people of Seattle to awaken and take back their city from these forces of evil that have no respect for the law and for the democracy that we hold so dearly. As Edmund Burke said, "All that is necessary for evil to succeed is for good men to do nothing.'

If, and when, Scott Hunter and Mike, the spiritual teacher, get 'Clash of Souls' published, you, the public, will be in for a fascinating story that could dramatically alter the way you think about life, death, religion, reincarnation, and the meaning of life itself.

Wow! Excellent article I thought to myself. Connie really laid it all out. Once Wolfe Drake and his band of thugs read it, they are sure to go ballistic. Hopefully they would surface enough so the FBI could locate and arrest them. With Connie staying at Pudgy's home, I felt she would be fairly safe. While going and coming from the Seattle Times, she always entered a back door and had the security staff check the area before she left. By using different vehicles and varying disguises, she was able to work reasonably freely. For any public appearances, where risk was higher, she used a bodyguard provided by the Times.

I called Mike and we discussed the article. He told me that frequently Connie's articles got picked up by a syndicate and published nationally.

I responded, "Mike that would be absolutely sensational if that would happen. But realistically what are the odds, a hundred to one?"

"Not as long as you'd think. The Seattle Times is not in the same league as the New York or the Los Angeles Times, but it nevertheless produces some pretty darn good journalism that frequently gets noticed across the nation. We have some big name companies headquartered here, not to mention Microsoft's billionaire founders, Bill Gates and Paul Allen, who are of national interest. Plus, Connie has had dozens of her articles carried across the nation. That little lady is one heckuva journalist. Just check the paper everyday and hope that it happens.

"Now what if we go national? How close are we to being in print?" Mike asked.

"Well, Dorothy is a ball of fire. She's almost done. The first week she threw a ton of changes at me, but now we're down to minor stuff. Computers make editing so much easier than the old typewriter method. I would guess we could have the copy on a diskette to the printer in a week. They can turn around a small run like ours in no time, so if we need some copies for PR purposes, we'll have them soon."

"Super! Scott, I don't know if you realize how much this means to me. After years of struggling and being shot at, it's finally going to happen. My life's dream—and my major task for this lifetime—is finally coming to fruition. At last people will understand how the Universe works and the importance of understanding and respecting each other. Just knowing that we all have unique soul profiles will be enormously enlightening—but you know all that—I'm just rattling on like some old man. I'm sorry."

"Don't be sorry, Mike. You've brought a very special gift to people and a message of tolerance that the world desperately needs. I'm personally honored to be the person given the opportunity to author it."

We disconnected and I felt a warm glow of satisfaction. In spite of all my earlier fears, things had turned out okay. The book was done and soon to be published. If things went well, there was a good chance a major publisher would become interested and the book would get the broad national exposure necessary to become a bestseller.

Chapter 27

The following day, while driving Karen to school, the cell phone rang. It was Connie.

"Scott, guess what? Two things—first, Katherine Morgan's Siamese cat turned up at a neighbor's home. She is thrilled to have Bookman back. And get this—my article has been picked up by the Associated Press. It's appearing all over the country. Phone calls are starting to pour in."

"Connie, that's fabulous. You did a great job on the story."

"Thanks, Scott. The only downside is locally. The Mayor and the Chamber of Commerce are not too happy. They're worried about tourism and think I painted the situation in Seattle too negative."

"Huh? Too negative? Maybe the Mayor and the Chamber oughta have to dodge a few bullets and bombs from DOG, then come back and tell you that you're being too negative.

"The Mayor seems to have forgotten the PR disaster that occurred when Seattle hosted the World Trade Organization meeting last year. The whole nation saw rioters breaking windows and looting stores while cops in full riot gear tear gassed the crowd and shot at them with rubber bullets. As I recall, the Mayor's handling of the WTO fiasco left a lot to be desired—to put it mildly," I said.

"You're right, Scott. We won't solve the problem of DOG and hate groups like them if we try to hide their existence under a blanket of denial just so more tourists will visit Seattle. But now, with the national spotlight on us there's a pretty good chance something will finally be done."

We disconnected and I told Karen the other side of the phone conversation she had been listening to. I dropped her at school and headed to Green Lake. Swinging left, around the Green Lake par three golf course, I turned in by the Rowing Center and parked. The weather was pleasant and there were numerous people going around the lake on the popular path. After a brisk walk for two miles I took a rest at the Community Center on the east side of the lake. I sat in the same spot I had weeks earlier when I overheard the DOG thugs' conversation. It seemed like that was light years in the past but really was only a few months ago. Now the book was written, in the final stages of editing, and soon would be published.

After a ten minute break, I finished my walk, got in the Lexus and headed back to Lynnwood. While waiting for some more corrections from Dorothy, I went on the Internet and was amazed at the number of sites running Connie's story. It was not only picked up by the national media, it was being run internationally. Many of the articles were critical of the United States, saying that while we were busy running around the globe telling everyone how to behave, we were being hypocritical by condoning such despicable behavior in our own country.

The next day I called Connie for an update.

"Scott, the Times is being flooded with requests for more information about your book. You've gotta wrap it up and get some copies published right away. How close is Dorothy to finishing the editing?"

"We're on the last part. I'd say by late tomorrow. I've lined up a printer that does small runs for the self-publishing marketplace. They can turn things around on a dime. They can have a hundred books to us ten days after they get our manuscript on a diskette, then they'll have the balance of our twenty-five hundred book run done in another week."

"Good. Very good. If it's okay with you, I'd like to send out copies to a few VIPs as soon as possible. Can you set up a post office box and get a telemarketing phone that will take phone orders?"

"You bet. I'll do it right now Connie. Talk to you later."

I immediately made a few calls and located an available post office box at the main Lynnwood post office. Since time was of the essence, I quickly drove to the post office, and in less than twenty minutes I left with a key to a postal mail box.

Back home, I flipped through my old Rolodex from my advertising days and called Martha Kincaid, an old friend and owner of Kincaid Telemarketing. I told her what we needed and she said she would fax me the necessary papers to sign and we could start using 1-800-555-5050, one of her inbound phone lines for order processing as soon as she got the details.

To be on the up-and-up with Martha, I told her about the potential threats from DOG once they heard about the phone number.

She laughed with her rough, gravelly voice, abused by decades of chain smoking and drinking Cutty Sark on the rocks on a daily basis. "Scott, don't you worry. Let Ol' Martha take care of it. My operators never give out the address where we're located. And just in case some sorry-assed son of a bitch does find me, I got Bernie's old army .45 and his 12 gauge shotgun. Before he died, he made damn sure I knew how to use them. I read about those creeps in the paper and nothin' would make me happier than to splatter their sick little asses all over the street."

"Thanks, Martha, you're a true friend. I'll fax back your form and the details for the order processing this afternoon."

The call waiting on my phone beeped so I ended my call with Martha. It was Alison, my younger daughter. She was upset. "Dad, I just talked to Joni. She read in the paper where you're involved in writing about some bad guys that hurt people. We're scared that you'll get hurt."

I tried to calm her as best I could, and knowing her fondness for fame and celebrities I said, "Alison, don't worry. I'm okay, and the best part is there's a good chance I'll be invited onto some TV talk shows to discuss my book. If a television producer calls to book me on a show then you can come along and see what it's like to be on TV."

That seemed to calm her down, so we said our good-byes.

No sooner had I hung up than the phone rang. It was Connie again.

"Scott, things are going crazy. I've got a three inch stack of phone messages and e-mails—talk shows from all over the country are calling. They all want a copy of *Clash of Souls* and they want to interview you and Mike—even some big New York publishers are calling. Things are out of control. We better get everyone together quickly and figure out what to do."

"Good idea. How about at Lee Chou and Pudgy's place at six tonight?"

"See you then. I'll bring all these messages."

After hanging up, I got up and walked around the townhouse. Looking out the front window, in the far distance I could see the majestic Olympic Mountain range. One of the advantages of living in the Pacific Northwest is the spectacular outdoor scenery. Within minutes of where Karen and I lived one could get to the Pacific Ocean, or Puget Sound, as well as see spectacular mountains, clear streams, fresh water lakes, and forests full of evergreens. It always gave me a great sense of peace and lifted my spirit to soak up the beauty of this outdoor mecca.

As I stood gazing off into the distance, a feeling of great calm came over me. A voice inside whispered to me, *'the path that lies ahead has more curves but in the end all will be well.'* It was a reminder to me that there was still plenty to do and even more problems but not to worry—everything will turn out for the best.

At 5:00 PM, I drove into Seattle to pick up Karen and head over to Lee Chou and Pudgy's home. By the time we arrived everyone was there and buzzing excitedly about the sudden change in our fortunes.

Connie went through her stack of messages. It was mind-boggling. People were calling from every major city in the U.S. as well as the BBC from London. Suddenly she screamed. "Oh my God! Oprah called. I don't believe it!" She held up the phone message for everyone to see. Everyone was whooping it up excitedly. "And the Larry King Show—this is absolutely unreal. Oprah and Larry—the two biggest names in the world of talk shows."

Pudgy grabbed Lee Chou and lifted her up in the air like she was a twenty pound toddler and spun around in a circle, letting out some primal scream of joy that shook the windows in the house. Mike and I hugged each other and soon everyone was hugging everyone—deliriously happy. The living room resembled the locker room of the winning Super Bowl team. The euphoric

joy was etched in everyone's face. There were no words in the
English language to adequately describe how we felt. Connie and
the others kept saying "I don't believe it" for lack of anything else
that could communicate the emotional high we were all feeling.
Lee Chou and Karen rushed into the kitchen and grabbed three
bottles of champagne from Pudgy's well-stocked refrigerator.
Soon corks were popping and toasts were being made.

Gradually, the exuberance died down and when the crowd
was calm, Mike said, "I knew this day would come. I never
doubted it—not for a minute. The Universe told me to have
faith and I did. There were many times I felt like giving up but
the Universe gave me the strength to fight on. Then as each one
of you appeared the Universe was reassuring me that if I per-
severed all would be well. Now my friends, we are standing on
the threshold of achieving our dream—that of getting our message of understanding and tolerance out to millions—perhaps
billions—of people." Mike picked up Connie's stack of phone
messages and e-mails and held them up in the air. "And once
again the Universe has led us to the beautiful souls who will help
us take the final step. Many of these people, on a Physical Plane
level, think they are drawn to us only because we are another
story and they need stories. But on a deep spiritual soul level,
these people care about helping accelerate the evolution of souls
here on Earth. On a soul-to-soul level, they have made spiritual
agreements with us to help spread the message of tolerance."

"Mike, I know what you're saying," said Karen. "Years ago,
I was visiting a health spa in Arizona, unwinding from the pressures of my job at the time, and I had an opportunity to meet
Oprah. I had met various celebrities but there was a quality
about Oprah that was different from the others. She exudes a
genuine love for others that has to come from a higher level of
spirituality. She is one of the most genuinely beautiful souls you
will ever meet."

"Well it sure looks like we'll have a chance to meet her
soon," said Connie. "The only problem I see is how we're going
to handle the requests? We're being inundated. Does anybody
have any ideas?"

I spoke, "Based on some of my past experiences, I think we
need to hire a publicist to coordinate things and arrange a media

tour. And, if we do a media tour, the demands for books will quickly exceed our local short-run printing arrangement. We'll need a bigger, and more cost-effective publisher."

Grabbing her cell phone, Connie said, "let me call a friend at the Times. Marcy should know of a good one." As she quickly punched in the number, I headed for the bathroom.

By the time I returned, Connie handed me a small slip of paper with a name, number, and e-mail address listed, Debbie Windsor. Windsor Publicity, Chicago. (312-555-3883,) dwindsor@windsorpublicity.com. "Scott, Marcy said Debbie is a very good publicist. I'll e-mail all the PR requests to her tonight then tomorrow morning you can call her."

"Thanks, Connie, this is great. Also, after Debbie, I'm going to call a couple of editors I know at big publishing houses. Now that we have this phenomenal interest, one of them might want to take us on as a client."

"But," said Pudgy, "what about an agent?"

"If they like the book, and they should with all this media attention, they'll sign a contract with us directly, or they could refer us to a New York agent they're already used to working with. We don't need an agent, but it simplifies doing all the contract negotiating and things like that. DOG doesn't seem to operate in the New York City area—it's far too liberal for them. New York is loaded with Young Souls out to make a buck and not interested in right-wing religious views of Baby Souls. What would be ideal is finding a publisher willing to put this book on a fast track so we could tie it in to our media appearances. We can use our self-published copies for some early media exposure and come back and do a far broader exposure once the big publisher kicks in."

Chapter 28

The next morning I called Debbie Windsor. She greeted me enthusiastically and said she had received the e-mail from Connie listing the requests for information and interviews. Connie's e-mail had also briefed Debbie on the situation so all I had to do was discuss fees.

Debbie said she'd have a strategic marketing plan drawn up in a couple of days for me to review and then she would start drafting press releases to send out.

Having worked with publicists before, I know the good ones are worth every penny. Their contacts in the media are priceless, and their skill at scheduling, and coordinating events takes a ton of pressure off the author. Oftentimes they will provide over-worked and understaffed talk show hosts with questions to ask the author, making the process about as smooth and efficient as possible.

After Debbie, I called Angela Stuart, an editor at Warner Books, a division of Time Warner. Warner had published *The Celestine Prophecy*. I had met Angela a few years earlier at a Willamette Writer's Conference in Portland, Oregon. After I explained the saga behind *Clash of Souls* she said, "Scott, I can't speak for management, but I'm very interested and will discuss it with them later today. I'll also get back to you with the names and numbers of a few agents who I believe would love to handle this project."

After completing my call, I contacted Jill Lundborg who worked for the Fireside Books division at Simon & Shuster.

Fireside had published *The Seat of the Soul*, a bestseller by Gary Zukav. I had also met Jill through a Willamette Writer's Conference. She was equally interested. Her biggest concern was time. Could they get it approved and published fast enough to take advantage of the timeliness of the story, particularly, the struggle with the Defenders Of God. Jill said she'd get back to me after discussing the project with her approval team.

I worked on the last little bit of editing changes and called Mike for a lunch meeting. We agreed to meet at Dick's on lower Queen Anne at 11:30 AM, before the noontime crowd arrived. Since it was 11:00 AM, I hopped in the Lexus and headed into Seattle. Dick's cannot be called fine dining. It's a small local fast food joint that has been a Seattle landmark since the 1950's. They offer similar fare, only not as wide a selection as the giant chains like McDonalds and Burger King. What makes Dick's stand out and survive against the giant chains is their great tasting low cost burgers. Even Microsoft founder and billionaire Bill Gates still frequents Dick's, one of his hangouts while growing up.

As I pulled into the parking lot and got out, I spotted Mike standing at the entrance holding the door open for me, with a newspaper tucked under his arm.

"Hey, Mike, ready for some of Seattle's finest cuisine?" I joked.

"You bet, Scott. I grew up eating at Dick's. Back in the old days I only paid twenty-five cents for a burger, but back in those days a quarter would also buy you a gallon of gas. Whata ya pay now for a gallon for that Lexus?"

"Well, it's been running $1.79 lately, but with the six-cylinder ES300 I average between twenty-four and twenty-eight miles per gallon so I'm probably better off than back in the old days when we had those big eight-cylinder gas guzzlers with tail fins."

The line was short and in a matter of minutes we had ordered our cheeseburgers. We both picked Dick's Deluxe Burger—$1.80 for two beef patties, cheese, lettuce, tomato and bun—what a bargain. Mike went for the whole cholesterol hit—fries and milk shake. Karen had weaned me off fries and shakes so I settled for a glass of water.

As we grabbed a booth in the back, Mike whipped out the newspaper. More violence in the middle east, and in the U.S.

there was a story about three white cops shooting an unarmed black male somewhere back east.

"Same old crap, Scott. People killing each other just because they don't understand each other. They only see the differences, not the similarities, between people. In the middle east it's mostly Infant and Baby Souls killing each other. In the U.S. it's mostly Baby and Young Souls doing the killing. They just don't get it. The only real difference is where someone is on the evolutionary ladder. And we all have to climb the same ladder. And just because you're on a different rung this lifetime doesn't mean you deserve to be hated or killed."

I briefed Mike on my phone calls and he was delighted. "Scott, remember what I said before—I'll go on a few media interviews with you, particularly, if we'll be speaking to an Old Soul audience, but for the Young and Mature Souls, I want you to do those appearances by yourself. The Old Souls don't get uptight or challenge my credentials if I look a bit scruffy or unpressed, but the Young and Mature ones tend to judge a person by their appearance. That's where your conservative, business world look helps get the message across a lot easier."

"You're right, Mike. I learned years ago that one's appearance goes a long way in convincing some people to believe you. And solely because I've got a sincere businessman look I have been able to sell far-out metaphysical concepts to straight-laced types. It's sad that that's the way it is but since it is, we might as well play the game. What really counts is getting the message out, so one day, the newspaper will only have good things to write about."

Mike's cell phone abruptly interrupted our conversation.

"Hello?"

"Oh hi, Wes, what's up?"

As he listened to the phone, I watched Mike's face turned ash gray. This was not good news. He asked, "When did it happen?" Pause. "Any idea where they took her" Pause. Pause. "Yeah, we'll be down as soon as possible." Mike pushed the disconnect button and turned to me and said, "Connie Kamura has been kidnapped. Apparently, her latest article, the one on *Violence Threatens Freedom of Speech in Seattle*, got somebody very upset. Let's get down to the FBI offices and see what we can do to help."

I quickly scooped up our hamburger wrappers, empty cups and trays and put the wrappers and cups in a nearby trash receptacle and left the trays sitting on top. I found myself almost in a state of shock as I unlocked the car and hopped in. Mike wasn't handling it much better.

By the time I reached Denny Way and turned east Mike spoke, "I'm going to call Pudgy." Mike quickly punched in Pudgy's home number on his cell phone. "Hello, Pudge? Sorry to wake you. I know you worked late last night, but there's an emergency. Connie Kamura has been kidnapped." Pause. "Wes Conners just called me. I'm with Scott. We're on lower Queen Anne headed down to the FBI offices. Just be in standby mode. We'll keep you posted as soon as we get more information."

Mike disconnected and sat holding his phone in his lap, deep in thought.

"Did Conners say how it happened," I asked.

"It appears, Connie got a call from a woman who said she had more information on the hate groups. Connie agreed to meet her at a Wendy's in Ballard. Someplace on 15th Avenue NW. Witnesses saw a woman and two men grabbing her and shoving her into a van and taking off."

"Did they get a plate number?" I was wondering if it was the maroon van I had seen.

"I don't know. We'll find out when we get to the FBI offices."

"Mike, what do you think her chances are? You've been dealing with these wackos a lot longer than I have."

"Well...to be honest with you Scott, it's not good. Connie's articles have really pissed these guys off. In past similar situations, some hate groups have completely eliminated their most vocal opposition. They operate under the principle that if you knock off the people leading the parade everyone else will back down. They use fear as one of their weapons.

"And they have such a low level of respect for human life that it doesn't bother them to put a gun to someone's head and pull the trigger. In fact, some of the real psychopaths in these groups enjoy killing.

"It doesn't make much sense for them to call and demand the government release some of their men who are locked up at

Monroe or over at Walla Walla because then we would know for certain that it's DOG. Right now, we don't know for sure. Connie mentioned ten different groups in her articles. So this way, they can all claim ignorance and say maybe it was one of the others. Their highly paid lawyers can run us in circles.

"They might try ransom, to get some money, but my hunch is they won't because if Connie is released she might be able to identify some of them. Besides, Pudgy tells me that Wolfe Drake and his boys are pulling in plenty from their drug business. No, I think it's pretty clear. This is a message to the media to back off and quit writing negative stories about hate groups."

By the time Mike finished, I pulled into a parking garage near the FBI offices. Two minutes later we were in the lobby along with a crowd of television and news reporters. The place was bedlam. One of their own had been kidnapped and they were more frantic than normal and demanding action. We fought our way through the noisy crowd to the harried receptionist. I shouted at her, "Scott Hunter and Mike. Wes Conners is expecting us." The receptionist called Wes then motioned for us to squeeze past the crowd and go through a doorway with a guard standing in front. The receptionist made eye contact with the guard who nodded then opened the door to let us through. Once on the other side of the door, the sound level dropped back to normal. Wes appeared, looking frayed, and signaled us to follow him. We entered a large conference room that had been turned into a command post. Several maps of the Seattle metro area hung on the wall. A crowd of seven or eight special agents was buzzing about—two of them marking on the laminated maps while half of the others were on cell phones.

Wes directed us to one end of the table and pointed to a couple of chairs. "Sit there. We're about to have an update meeting," he said.

A senior agent spoke, "Listen up everybody. Update time. Wes, what do you have?"

"Okay, Larry, here's where we stand. We know where she was grabbed. The parking lot at Wendy's, 5300 block of 15th Avenue NW. Witnesses identified the maroon van that was probably the same vehicle used in the gay attack on Capitol Hill. No good

ID on the perpetrators. They wore paramilitary clothing with boots and black ski masks pulled down over their faces. One guy grabbed her from behind while the other had an Uzi covering them. She was struggling and kicking but couldn't break loose. Two or three other guys were in the van. All holding weapons. As the van took off a guy in the front passenger seat fired off a half dozen rounds at the building, apparently to scare off any witnesses. It was a well-timed and coordinated attack. These guys knew what they were doing and had been well-drilled.

"We've recovered the rounds and a few of the casings that were fired off. The van left some nice prints on the pavement. We're in the process of running them against the tire tread prints we got up on Capitol Hill.

"It's about a 90% probability that this is the work of the Defenders of God. Special Agent Tyrone Willis and three other agents are at the crime scene showing photos of the DOG hoodlums we know about. We know no one got a good look today, but there's a pretty good chance this was well planned and they had cased the place thoroughly in the past week. Hopefully some employee remembers them.

"According to the Times, Connie has caller ID and made a note of the phone number when she was called. It was a pay phone two blocks from Wendy's."

"Excuse me, Wes." I turned to see one of the other agents holding a phone in one hand and waving his other hand at Wes to get his attention. "They just found the van. It was left in the parking lot at the south end of Golden Gardens Park. An SPD unit spotted it. No witnesses found yet."

Wes went to the blown up map of the Ballard district of Seattle. "Okay, we know they left Wendy's headed south on 15th—apparently headed towards downtown Seattle. They must've turned off on Leary and doubled back heading north and west. For all we know they're headed north up near their old hideout in Snohomish County."

Mike raised his hand, "Wes. Do you see what's just south of Golden Gardens Park? The Shilshole Bay Marina. They escaped by boat. I'm convinced of it."

Another agent spoke, "But why up at Shilshole? They were much closer to Fisherman's Terminal."

"Remember," said Mike, These thugs were all trained in the military. If they would've switched to a boat at Fisherman's Terminal, they would have had to go through the Government Locks to get into Puget Sound. If there was any delay at the locks, we might have trapped them. Just like the old westerns. Remember when the cavalry would have to go single file through some narrow canyon? The Indians would be waiting up on the top ready to wipe out the soldiers. We're dealing with sick people, but very smart military minds."

"Mike's probably right," said Wes. "I've seen his hunches pan out in the past and he knows these low-lifes better than any of us. Let's get some people out to Shilshole Bay Marina right away. Terry, alert the Coast Guard. If they went by water, they would've had a big enough boat to hold at least six or seven people."

Mike raised his hand again. "That's assuming only one boat. Remember military minds like redundancy. If one system fails, you need a backup. My guess is they used two or three boats. Small, but fast and highly maneuverable. The backup boats could also be used as decoys or escorts if something went wrong. Tell the Coast Guard to look for a grouping—two or three boats all headed together in the same direction—and at high speed."

Remembering Pudgy's encounter with DOG near Bremerton, I said, "Once they get into Puget Sound they could go almost anywhere. Since one of them was spotted near Bremerton a few weeks ago, there's a chance they may be headed to a hideout in that area, or, maybe even along Hood Canal."

"Terry, tell the Coast Guard to pay particular attention to the Bremerton area and let's stake out all the Ferry Terminals west of Seattle—just in case any of them will be going back and forth to Seattle." Wes said.

"But wait," said another agent. "Remember these guys had a place up near Monroe. What's to keep them from boating north up to Everett or Marysville and coming ashore there? Hell, for all we know they could be halfway to the San Juan Islands. We can't afford to concentrate all our resources in the Bremerton area."

Wes let out a long sign of frustration. "Russ is right. They could be anywhere. We're going to have to spread out over a wider area and coordinate tightly with all the Sheriff's departments in the various counties. And I suppose we had better let the Canadians in on this just in case Drake decides to cross the border and hide out up there."

"Excuse me Wes," said a female agent just entering the room, "SPD just reported that a late model Honda Accord, dark blue, was stolen near Golden Gardens Park sometime early this morning. They found it about fifteen minutes ago in the Boeing Employees Credit Union parking lot up on highway 99 in south Everett. A white Dodge Caravan was reported stolen from the same lot. It looks like they're moving north and switching vehicles as they go. I told them to get out an APB on the white van and mention that it might be related to our kidnapping case."

"Okay, thanks, agent Shelly."

Wes stood staring at the map, hands on his hips, saying nothing. Then finally he spoke. "Jesus! I never realized how many damn waterways, lakes, passages, inlets, bays, harbors and canals there are within fifty miles of us—and we don't even know for sure they're going by water. We damned well better get a lucky break, and quick, or the Director will have all of us back working outa some field office in North Dakota."

Chapter 29

Mike raised his hand and spoke, "Wes, maybe I can provide that lucky break. I have a friend named Temera who's a psychic. I can give her a call and see if she can help. Also, I can contact Dr. Wayne Carr. He's the head of the Western Institute of Remote Viewing. He and some of his best remote viewers might be able to turn up some clues."

While a few agents snickered at the mention of psychics, an agent on the right side of the room spoke, "What's remote viewing?"

Wes rolled his eyes, and said, "Tim, don't you read any of our publications? Your U.S. Government has spent millions of the taxpayer's dollars experimenting with it. Trained remote viewers—supposedly—can go to remote locations and view the area. And, it's all done with their minds.

"In theory they can mentally go to where Connie Kamura is being held and see what's going on. Does it work? I don't know. Mike here claims it does. He also has a lot of faith in psychics. I, personally, have worked on a couple of cases where we were able to close them because of the help we got from a psychic.

"So, Mike, back to your psychic and remote viewers. Whatever information they give us we'll be grateful for, but until we start getting some clear leads, we have to keep all options open and throw a very broad net over the entire Puget Sound region. Is that understood?"

"Yeah, Wes. The moment I get anything I'll get it to you."

"Okay everyone, the briefing is over. Let's get going," said Wes.

As Mike and I left, I turned to Mike and said, "No one seemed overly impressed with the idea of a psychic and remote viewers being of much help."

"I know. I'm used to it. Don't get discouraged though. It's not what people think that matters but what gets accomplished. The important thing is getting Connie back alive. Eventually, the public's level of spiritual awareness will rise to a level where these methods will be understood. That's one of the reasons for writing the book."

After fighting our way through the noisy media crowd, we got the Lexus out of the parking garage and headed north up Aurora Avenue.

"Scott let's head up to the Wendy's where she was kidnapped. On the way, I'm going to call a few friends and see if they can help."

Mike punched in a number and put the phone to his ear. "Temera? Mike here. We've got an emergency. You know Connie Kamura, the writer at the Seattle Times?" Pause. "Yeah, well she just wrote some articles on hate groups in the Pacific Northwest and now she's been kidnapped. Can you pick up anything on her?" Pause. "It happened about two hours ago in the Ballard district. At a Wendy's located in the 5300 block of 15th Avenue NW—just south of Market Street." Pause. "We'll meet you there. I assume you want some of her personal articles?" Pause. "Yeah, personal stuff like jewelry. Gotcha. I'll call Pudgy Walters right now. She's been staying at his place. I'll have him meet us at Wendy's. We need to know if she's alive and where they've taken her." Pause. "Yeah, any lead possible. See you shortly. Thanks, Temera."

Mike disconnected, turned to me and said, "Temera is one of the best psychics around. I'm hoping she'll be able to tune into Connie. Temera is good at what is known as psychometry."

"What's psychometry?" I asked.

"Temera is one of those people gifted with the ability to tell things about a person just by holding an article of their clothing or jewelry. Now in the case of Connie, Temera has already done readings for her in the past so that'll also help her pick up Connie's energy pattern. But to be on the safe side, I'm gonna have Pudge get her some of Connie's personal belongings."

As I headed up Aurora Avenue, towards Ballard, Mike punched in Pudgy's number.

"Pudge. Mike here. You know Temera. Yeah. Yeah. The psychic located up in Mukilteo. She needs some of Connie's personal stuff. Stuff that she's worn often, like jewelry, watches—anything that would have a lot of her energy. Grab a bunch of her stuff so we can get it to Temera as fast as possible. We're gonna meet her shortly at the place where Connie was kidnapped—the Wendy's just south of Market Street in Ballard on 15th. Speed is of the essence my man. See if you can kick that Harley in the butt and get there in ten minutes. Thanks, Pudge. Bye."

Mike disconnected and turned to face me.

"There's another person who might help. Scott, had you ever heard of remote viewing before I mentioned it at the FBI meeting?" I shook my head no. "Well, the U.S. Government has. A few years ago they had a secret research project that used trained 'viewers' to locate people or things anywhere in the world. Sometimes the results were excellent and sometimes not so good. I'm going to call the guy who trains people to be remote viewers. His name is Dr. Wayne Carr, and he's located in Kirkland."

Mike turned on his cell phone and called the number. "Dr. Carr, this is Mike." Pause. "Yeah that's right. The Mike that's into all the past life stuff. Look Dr. Carr I've got a life or death emergency. Can you and some of your prize students try to locate a missing person?" Pause. "It's Connie Kamura. She wrote an article for the Seattle Times about hate groups and has just been kidnapped, probably by one of the groups mentioned in the article." Pause. "Great. Call me the moment you get something."

When I stopped for a red light at the intersection of Market and 15th, we could see the flashing lights of a half dozen SPD vehicles. The whole area around Wendy's was wrapped with police yellow crime scene tape. Traffic was being diverted into one lane southbound lane on 15th. In addition to a large crowd of curious bystanders, there were a half dozen remote crews from television stations, complete with their backup satellite trucks, busy broadcasting live from the scene. The on-camera personalities, with microphones in hand, were standing so Wendy's would be in the background for their news segment. A half dozen kids were vying for space behind the reporters, pushing each other so they could wave to the world and tell their friends they were on TV.

We parked about a block away and worked our way toward Wendy's. When we hit the first barrier, Mike asked the SPD officer if any FBI agents were present. The officer said "Yeah. See those two over there. They're Fibbies. Ya wanna talk to 'em?"

"Yes, please," said Mike.

The police officer yelled at the special agents, while gesturing with his right index finger for the agents to come over to us. As the agents turned, I could see that one was Tyrone Willis. He brightened up when he spotted us.

"Hey, Mike, Scott, glad to see you could make it here so fast. Wes called and said you were downtown and sat in on a briefing."

"Yeah, we did. It sounds like DOG is up to their usual evil tricks. We've got a psychic on her way here to help out. Wes said it would be okay."

"Well, Mike, you know I'm not a real strong believer in that kind of stuff, but as Wes said 'It can't do any harm.' So where's the fat lady with the crystal ball?"

"Ty," Mike said jokingly, "someday you'll become a believer. Maybe this case will be your awakening point to understanding that there are higher dimensions of consciousness beyond the five senses."

"Find Connie and I'll be a believer!"

"Hey there's Temera," said Mike, pointing up the street. "And Ty, please note she's not fat and isn't carrying a crystal ball."

I turned and looked. I didn't see anyone who fit the stereotypical image of a fat psychic in a floral colored muumuu. Then an attractive, young looking woman waved at us. That must be Temera I thought. Wow. As she approached, I quickly scanned her top to bottom. Lightweight tan colored jacket, white turtleneck sweater, blue jeans and white sneakers. Nice figure, probably five foot six or five seven with long straight auburn hair hanging at least six inches below her shoulder. She wore bangs that highlighted a beautiful heart shaped face with high cheekbones and a pointed chin. As she got closer, I guessed her age as between late twenties and early thirties.

Temera went up to Mike and gave him a big hug, then as she turned to be introduced to me I could see her eyes were a cross between hazel and green. Quite striking.

"Temera, allow me to introduce Scott Hunter. Scott's the person I told you about," said Mike.

Temera looked me directly in the eyes and I felt the surge of energy coming from her connecting with my soul. Our eyes held contact for several seconds than she spoke, "We've met before, but not this lifetime."

"Temera, allow me to also introduce special agent Tyrone Willis from the FBI. Ty was curious where your crystal ball was," said Mike with a twinkle in his eye.

Temera burst out in laughter, then as she shook hands she said, "Hi, Ty. I'm sorry to disappoint you but I don't own one. On a more serious note, I notice from your aura that you're still feeling some grief from your father's death. He's here with you and says for you not to worry. He's very happy where he is."

Ty took a step backwards. "Who told you my father died?" Ty looked at me and then at Mike. We just shrugged to indicate that it wasn't us.

"Ty, your father wants you to know reincarnation is real. He wants you to quit thinking it's not. He says 'he's living proof...no pun intended.' Right now he's wearing a white Ben Hogan golf cap, a yellow cardigan and red/blue checkered golf slacks."

I looked at Ty. His eyes had a stunned look and his jaw was hanging slack. He stammered as he spoke. "I, ah, ah, who, ah, this can't be true. Who told you? This is a joke right? My mother? My wife? My partner, Wes? Someone told you. That was what my dad was wearing the day he died. He had a heart attack on the golf course."

"I know, Ty. Your father says it was his time to go."

"I mean, ah, ah, then you really can see him? Just like we can see each other?"

"It's not quite the same. I see him in color, but more like what you would see if you copied a color photo onto a sheet of clear plastic, where you can see through the image," said Temera.

"And, you'll swear you're not bullshitting me and that this isn't some sick joke some of the guys are playing on me?"

"I swear this is for real. But why not ask your father a question that no one but he knows the answer to?"

"Okay. Ask him what happened to grandpa's pocket watch the railroad gave him when he retired. Dad said he was going to give it to me when he died."

"I don't have to ask him. He heard you. He said to go over to your mother's house and go down into the basement. Up on the shelves where the old left over paint is stored, you'll find an old yellow enamel paint can. The can is empty except for the watch and a few other trinkets. He's sorry he forgot to give it to you before he died. He wants you to tell your mother that he loves her and misses her also. He has to go now."

"Tell him I love him too."

"He heard you."

Ty turned away, wiping the tears from his cheeks. Then, once he had regained his composure, he said, "Well, the kidnapping took place next to that red Mazda Miata. That's Connie's car. Apparently, when she parked and got out of her car, a white female approached her. The female was identified as age thirty to forty, medium height and build, short dark hair wearing sunglasses, blue jeans with a short denim jacket. A maroon van suddenly swung along side them, two guys in military garb and black ski masks jumped out and grabbed her. They were all gone in a matter of seconds. They went south on 15th. Hey, that looks like Pudgy. What's he doing here?"

"Pudgy is bringing Temera some personal things of Connie's to help tune into her energy. Connie's been staying at Pudgy's place since the bomb attack at the Times," said Mike.

"That's right. Sorry, I forgot," replied Ty.

As Pudgy approached I could see he was carrying a large brown paper bag.

"Hey guys. Here's some of Connie's stuff. I hope I got the right things. Lee Chou picked out the things she knows Connie likes best."

Temera took the bag, looked in it and said, "This will be fine. Thank you." She turned and walked over to Connie's car and set the bag down on the hood and started taking items out and holding them in her hands. Then she took out a notebook and started writing swiftly.

"Okay, here's what I'm getting right now. I'm picking up Robin Hood, Maid Marion and Sherwood Forest."

"That sounds like a fairy tale," said Ty. "How can that help us find Connie?"

"I pick up images that often are symbolic for something else. In this case, I'm assuming Robin Hood is the kidnapper and Maid Marion is Connie," said Temera. "Look for something that is called Sherwood. It should be in or near a forest. I see Robin Hood on a boat. It's cold. It's real water. I can hear ferries. I can smell salt water. We are on the water for a very long time—between a half hour and two hours. I see two bridges. I see Ostriches—Mud—Bass. I see two, maybe three points—military ships off the points of land. They're parked—surrounded by military— protected area—they're protected in an inlet with only one outlet. Oak trees—could be a forest or a street. I'm facing north—white mountain peaks off to my left—water in front of me—old farm—barn—outbuildings. That's all I'm getting right now but that should help tremendously. The important thing I'm picking up is Connie is still alive."

"Thank you, Temera" said Mike.

"Yes. Thank you very much," said Ty. I'm going to head back down to my office and start going over maps, phone books and directories to see if I can crack these clues and narrow down the search. We have teams canvassing the area over at Golden Gardens and Shilshole Bay Marina. Wes is leading teams up in Snohomish, around Monroe. I'll tell him about Temera's clues. Since it sounds like they went by water, he'll probably want to canvass the area up by Everett and Marysville. There are a lot of inlets and some bridges up there. If you get anything more please call me immediately."

We said our good-byes to Ty. Then our caravan, led by Pudgy on his Harley, followed by Temera in her Ford SUV, then the Lexus holding Mike and myself, headed up 15th to 85th where we turned east. Twelve minutes later our strange team made up of a burly Harley biker, his Asian wife, a psychic, a spiritual teacher, and a writer, were huddled around the dining room table poreing over maps. While I put each clue on a separate three by five index card, Lee Chou was busy looking for anything called 'Sherwood' in phone books. Mike was looking for 'Sherwood' on various regional maps. Temera excused herself and went into Connie's room to spend some time alone feeling Connie's energy.

We were all so intent searching for answers that we all jumped when Mike's cell phone rang. "Hello? Oh, hi Wayne. You got something! Great. What is it? All three remote viewers picked up strong images of submarines and two viewers picked up the image of an anvil. What do you think it means? Huh, Yeah. That's a possibility. Yeah. Okay. Yeah, water of course if you picked up subs. Yeah. Okay we'll add that into what we're already working on. Let me know if you get anything else. Thanks a ton for these clues. Bye.

"Okay team, listen up. The remote viewers all picked up submarines and two of them picked up the image of an anvil. I think for a starting point we have to consider the area around the Bangor Naval Submarine Base over in Kipsap County. It's north of Bremerton and west of Poulsbo. I don't know what to make of the anvil image."

I added the two new clues to index cards and shuffled them for a few seconds then said, "Ya know, it's going to take hours to work through all these clues. I think I should head over to Bangor and start looking around."

"Scott, let me join you," said Mike. "We can do an aerial fly-over. I know the guy who runs Seattle Seaplanes over on Lake Union. We can be over there in no time and can cover a pretty good sized area from up in the air. Is that going to be okay with the rest of you?"

"Go for it, man," said Pudgy. "If we narrow the clues down, we'll call you. But if you spot them, I wanta be there when we take 'em down. I gotta few special little presents I wanna give those scumballs. You understand what I'm sayin', man?"

"Don't worry, Scott and I would never consider taking on Drake and his thugs without backup. He's got to have a damn arsenal at the hideout."

Lee Chou interrupted, "I haven't found any Sherwood Forests, but I've found six different streets named Sherwood. One in Tacoma. Four are in Pierce County. One in Seattle. And, I found one elementary school named Sherwood. It's in Edmonds not too far from their marina.

"The Sherwood street in Seattle is close to Puget Sound, just south of North 145th."

"Any Sherwood streets in Kitsap County?" asked Pudgy.

"I don't know. I don't think we have a Kitsap County map," said Lee Chou.

"I'll run down to the Texaco and get one," said Pudgy as he lifted his beefy frame from the chair, tugged up his sagging blue jeans and headed for the door.

Chapter 30

As I drove to Lake Union, Mike called ahead and got a hold of his buddy Jim Chrysler at Seattle Seaplanes and was assured that both Jim and a four passenger seaplane were available. Then Mike put in a call to Wes and briefed him on the remote viewers' clues. He told Mike that at their briefing tomorrow they would put more men in the Bremerton area if the Snohomish leads didn't pan out.

Located just off Eastlake Avenue on Lake Union, Seattle Seaplanes was easy to find. We parked on a bluff overlooking their dock and walked down a flight of stairs. Mike spotted his old buddy, Jim Chrysler, by one of the seaplanes. After they exchanged their greetings, Mike introduced me to Jim. Jim had a wiry build and a weathered face that was used to being outdoors. He projected an aura of no nonsense and complete competency.

We hopped into the seaplane and fastened our seat belts. Jim cranked up the engine and quickly checked the instrument gauges. Satisfied, he gave the seaplane some gas and pulled away from the dock heading out to the middle of Lake Union.

Having never flown in a seaplane I immediately noticed that the runway—the lake—was a lot choppier and rougher than a standard runway. After bouncing along for what seemed like an eternity, Jim pulled back on the stick and we lifted off the water.

The seaplane quickly reached cruising altitude of one thousand feet and turned west. As we passed over Bainbridge Island,

Jim turned to a new course heading northwest that took us over Silverdale. To my right, I could see the Bangor Naval Submarine Base. A mile further west and we were over the eastern edge of Hood Canal. Jim started a wide counter clockwise circle that ended up over Warrenville, the southern boundary of our pre-determined search area.

From Warrenville, he headed north following the coast line. About fifty yards out from the edge, Mike and I locked our binoculars on the shore hoping to spot something out of the ordinary. No luck. I had spotted a SUV that had been painted in camouflage colors but it turned out to be a couple of fishermen heading down a dirt road towing their fishing boat to a small boat launch.

When we reached the coastline where the submarine base touched the Canal, we quit looking. We figured there was no way their hideout would be on the base.

Once Jim reached the northern end of the base at Vinland, we started looking again. Still nothing. Finally at the Kitsap Memorial State Park, our predetermined northern search boundary, Jim made another circle and we headed back down the coast. Only this time, we moved inland about fifty yards just in case their hideout wasn't right on the water. By the time we had reached the two fishermen with the camouflage SUV, they had completed their boat launch and were out in the Canal with their fishing lines in the water.

"Scott, I know we're near. I can feel it," said Mike.

"Well," said Jim, "do you want to take another pass over the area?"

"One of the clues said to look for a pattern in the shape of an anvil," I said. "Did anyone see anything that remotely resembled an anvil?"

"No, I was concentrating on spotting some signs of a para-military camp or a grouping of boats," said Mike. "Maybe we should make one more pass looking for some anvil shape."

Without saying a word, Jim circled the seaplane back into a north heading. We looked for rock formations, jetties, little peninsulas, virtually anything that looked like an anvil. Every time we spotted something that might qualify it was quickly eliminated when Jim went in for a closer look.

By the time we reached the northern boundary at Lofall, Jim turned and looked at me with a questioning look in his eyes. I finally shook my head and said "Let's head back."

For most of the way back we all sat in silence, feeling frustrated and depressed. Was Connie still alive? Temera said she was but that was over an hour ago. Was she hurt? Would we find her in time? My mind flashed back to how brutal they had been to the two gays on Capitol Hill and their low regard for human life.

Mike had both hands pressed against the sides of his head, as if trying to squeeze the answer out of his brain. "I know she's not up in Snohomish County. She's somewhere near here. I can feel it. Wait. Let's try the other coastline—on the other side of the Hood Canal."

Without a word Jim swung around and headed west. At Thorndike Bay, he turned south heading down the western coastline of Hood Canal. This time we looked for anvils, boats, military equipment, people milling around or anything that looked even remotely suspicious. The side of the Canal was even more deserted than the other side. There was nothing. We had struck out again.

Mike kept insisting that we were close but finally told Jim to head back. Jim put the plane in a wide turn on a path that would take us just north of Bremerton. Feeling depressed at failing once again, I looked out the left side of the plane, watching the street lights below us start flickering on as twilight descended on the area. Suddenly I blinked my eyes and stared at the ground below. "Wait!" I shouted at Jim. "Look down there, off the left side—just east of the water. There's the anvil. Don't you see it? Look at the street lights. See how the streets form a rectangular shape with a bend in the road on the southeast corner forms a point that looks like an anvil. Do you see it now?"

"Yeah, I think I do. I guess that does look kinda like an anvil," said Jim. "Let's swing around and take a closer look."

"Good work Scott. That's it all right," said Mike.

I grabbed the map and quickly located the spot—just south of Silverdale and east of Dyes Inlet—a few hundred feet east of Windy Point. Fairgrounds Road formed the left edge of the anvil. Stampede Boulevard NW defined the top edge, Tracyton Boulevard formed the bottom side, and curved around to form the right side. Where Tracyton met Stampede was the point of the anvil.

While Jim circled the area, Mike and I focused the binoculars on the area—both inside and outside the boundary of the anvil. It was getting too dark to see much. The area was heavily wooded with a few homes scattered throughout the area. The hideout could be there only we would have to come back in daylight to improve our odds of spotting anything. I grabbed my 35mm camera and took several shots of the general area around the anvil. When I was done I told, Jim to head back home.

Back at Lake Union, Jim brought the seaplane in for a smooth landing and up to the dock as easily as if he was driving a car. When we deplaned, he shook his head and apologized for not being able to spot the hideout.

Patting him on the arm, Mike said, "Jim, you did fine. The street lights are what saved the day. We now know the general area where Connie's being held—we just have to get her location narrowed down."

Turning to me, Mike said, "How about you and Jim doing an early morning reconnaissance from the air while I canvass the area on bike? We can keep in touch by cell phone."

"Sounds good to me," I said, "how about you, Jim?"

"You bet. Boys, we're gonna find that girl. Scott, you have your ass down here at 5:00 AM cuz that's when I'm takin' off."

"I'll be here," I said.

As Mike and I left the seaplane dock and hopped in my car, he said, "Let's head back to Pudgy's."

Getting from Lake Union to Pudgy's home took only ten minutes. Spotting the grins on our faces, Pudgy and Lee Chow both spoke at the same time. "What's up?"

"We found the anvil. It's over between Silverdale and Bremerton. Here look at the map," I said as I spread it out on the table.

"Son of a bitch." Pudgy shouted. "You remember when I was trailing that asshole? I thought he was going south of Bremerton. He musta turned off somewhere and headed north. Damn. He sure faked me out."

"Remember everyone, these thugs are very good at misdirection. They've had us going the wrong way several times. In fact, I'd better check in with Wes. I think they're still concentrating on the Snohomish County area."

Mike punched a number into his cell phone and spoke, "Hi, Wes. Anything?"

Pause.

"Well, I know you think they're up there but we found one of the clues the remote viewers gave us. Remember they said to look for an anvil shape as a landmark? Yeah, that's the one. We were doing an aerial search in a seaplane today and Scott spotted it north of Bremerton just east of Dyes Inlet. We figure after they kidnapped her they switched to a boat, crossed Puget Sound, circled around Bainbridge Island and cruised right through the middle of Bremerton, up the Port Washington Narrows into Dyes Inlet. We're gonna check out the area tomorrow morning early. Scott's gonna take a seaplane and I'm gonna be on a bike on the ground. If Pudgy's available I'll ask him to back me up."

Pause.

"No, I'm really convinced you're lookin' in the wrong area. Well, I know you got a lotta sightings up there but these guys are masters at misdirecting us. Can you spare any agents for our area?"

Pause.

"Well, that's better than nothing. Thanks, Wes."

Mike disconnected and shrugged his head. "They're convinced they're closing in on them up near Monroe. In fact there have been several visits to the DOG members serving time at Monroe. No one we're after, just women, probably girlfriends, have been visiting the inmates on a heavier schedule than normal. Probably briefing them on what's goin' down to keep their morale high. Wes is trying to get some news from snitches inside the prison but all the DOG inmates stick real close to each other. No one's talking. A well-disciplined bunch.

"Wes was interested that we found the anvil but he doesn't think the psychic and remote viewers are right this time. But, I think to humor me, he's gonna send a few agents down to the area to check it out.

"Now let's plan tomorrow. We will need a backup plan in case we find them. Pudgy, what are your plans?"

"Hey, man, if things work out right there's a chance I'm going to get taken to the DOG hideout soon."

Mike looked at me. We both had startled looks on our faces.

Pudgy spoke, "While you dudes were off on your fancy little seaplane safari I was working my own angle. One of the DOG regulars that comes to the bar down in Fremont stopped in last night. This one nitwit, called Nick, thinks I'm in sympathy with DOG's causes and that I'm a racist asshole like them.

"Last night, after he had tossed down a few pints, I invited him outside for a chat and told him I needed some weed. Told him my supplier got in a beef with someone down in Chinatown and took a couple of slugs in the brain. I gave him the impression that I moved a lot of weed to patrons of the bar. Said I could use one to two hundred pounds a month if the price is right and the quality good.

"Nick fell for it hook, line and sinker. He got excited at the chance to land a big-time buyer. Claims the shit they sell is super premium. Called it Mendocino Triple Astro Gold, also known as Mendo TAG, which is a special hybrid some smart-ass Berkeley dude came up with after five years workin' in the lab. One good toke can knock you on your ass. Said the first time he took a hit of Mendo TAG he was circling Jupiter for two hours. He said it goes for $500 an ounce on the street. I told him it's a little steep for my blue collar crowd at the bar. Nick said he should be able to wholesale it to me for $300, and if the crowd can't handle the higher tariff, I should sell it by the half ounce or smaller. Once they try it—man they won't want anything else. I said okay. If it checks out I'll be in the market for $40,000 to $50,000 a month. Set up a meeting with the Man. I'll bring cash for the first week and check out this super weed. But I said I don't carry away more than an ounce, just in case I'm nailed. You guys have to deliver to a place I use near the bar.

"Then the stupid dipshit asks if I need any guns. I tell 'em now and then someone makes an inquiry but currently I don't have a regular supplier. So I ask him what does he have? He sez 'you name it.' Nick claims he can deliver anything up to a rocket launcher. 45's, nine millimeter Glocks, AK47's, UZI's, grenades, even some nasty bad-ass explosives. I said right now I don't know anyone planning on starting a war, but occasionally I might be able to move a handgun or two—maybe an AK47 or UZI.

"Anyway, this asshole Nick said he'd set up a get-acquainted meeting with his top man so we could work out the money details. I said the sooner the better because if I can't work out something with them I gotta find somebody else fast. I got customers who are gettin' low and I sure as hell don't want 'em goin' somewhere else. I need the bread.

"I'm thinkin' I might get to meet Wolfe Drake himself and maybe get inside their hideout. If I can get inside, I can scope things out cuz when the time comes for the Fibbies to go in with guns a blazin' any information I get could save Connie's life."

"Great job, Pudgy. You're right," I said. "Their hideout has to be a damned arsenal. Hell for all we know they could hold off several SWAT teams. And by the way—Mike—when you call Wes again—he might want to alert the DEA and ATF. Now that we know DOG is dealing dope and guns they'll wanta get involved.

"Okay, now let's review our plans," I said. "I'll take off with Jim at dawn in the seaplane. We'll cover the area around the anvil. Mike, you're gonna be on a bike working the same area. If Wes sends some men, Mike will coordinate the search efforts with them. Lee Chou and Temera will keep working on the clues to narrow down the area. Pudgy will be on standby for the drug meeting. Does that sound okay to everyone?"

"Naw," said Pudgy. "My deal won't happen until later tomorrow. I can go along on the seaplane recon and back up Scott. We're starting to get close and remember shit happens. We're all going to be at risk. Something goes wrong and they got two or three more hostages. So remember the Kevlar vests—wear 'em if you can—and both of you should at least carry a razor blade and mace."

"What for? If we got captured, they'd find them when they searched us," I said.

"No. Not always. Here take this single-edged razor blade and a piece of duct tape and tape it inside your sneaker. They'll frisk you around the ankles for a knife but chances are they'll never take off sneakers."

Mike and I quickly did as Pudgy suggested and nodded in agreement. No one, except someone doing a very thorough search would find the razor blade.

"Okay, Pudge, that worked. What about the mace?" I asked. "Isn't it too big to fit in a sneaker?"

"I got some special stuff from an ex-Nam buddy of mine who's CIA now. Highly concentrated mace that comes in a tiny capsule. Half inch wide, only two inches long. 'Bout the size of a cap on a ball-point pen. Now, it won't fit in your sneakers but it will between your legs."

"Whata ya mean, between our legs? When guys are searched they always check up around the crotch." I said.

"Scott, you're *partially* right. Go ahead and show me how you would frisk Mike."

"What?"

"Go ahead and show me how you'd frisk Mike."

"Well, I'd have him put his arms up, and I'd...ah"

"Don't tell me. Show me."

I stood up and had Mike stand. Feeling a little awkward and embarrassed, I lightly brushed my hands under his arms, then crouched down on one knee and ran my hands around his ankles and up to his crotch on the inside of his trousers.

Everyone started laughing.

"What's so funny?" I said.

"You didn't even touch his genitals, let alone feel behind his balls," said Pudgy.

"Of course not," I replied, "that's a very sensitive area. All men know that. It's embarrassing to touch another man's genitals."

"Exactly, Scott" said Mike, "that's Pudgy's point. When most men search each other, unless they are extremely well trained in how to search they usually barely touch the groin area. Just enough to detect a hidden gun or knife."

"So now you know it's a safe spot, so just stick the mace up behind your balls, in the crack between your butt cheeks, right by your asshole. Got it?"

"Okay Pudge," I replied, "but I sure as hell ain't gonna use duct tape. In case you forgot your basic anatomy I happen to have something called short hairs located down there."

"I figured you little sissies would whine about that so I got you some Poligrip."

"What? Did you say Poligrip?" I said with a confused look on my face. "Isn't that what old people use to hold their false teeth in their mouths?"

"Well, yeah, it can be young people too. But the thing to remember is it sticks to skin temporarily and can easily hold the mace in place for at least a half a day or maybe even a full day. The stuff eventually dissolves and sure beats the hell outta duct tape. You'll be able to pull the mace out without pullin' the ol' short hairs. In a life or death situation, the mace might save your life."

"You're right, Pudgy," said Mike. "Scott and I will accept your kind gift. However, let me remind you, while Scott and you are going to be sitting in a comfortable padded seat in a seaplane I'm going to be riding a bike. I think I'd better tape some extra foam rubber on the bike seat."

Mike added, "I think it's also important to remember the Soul Profile on any of the DOG members we know. Knowledge is power and just that slight extra bit of knowledge could save one or more of our lives some day. We aren't dealing with any Old or Mature Souls—only Baby Souls and a few Young Souls. Don't challenge the beliefs of the Baby Souls—they won't budge. The Young Souls will listen to your arguments if they can see where they will personally benefit them. Greed and power motivate them. It's possible to drive a wedge between the two different factions. But it's got to be done very carefully."

Chapter 31

Knowing that I wasn't going to be riding a bike with a can of mace jammed behind my scrotum made the drive back to Lynnwood a bit more pleasant. In fact, it gave me a chance to think about Karen. I had been so caught up in Connie's kidnapping that I had hardly seen her. She, in turn, had been so busy studying and taking tests that we hadn't had much time for each other. I hoped that tonight she would be able to take a break and we could spend a little time with each other.

Apparently, she had come to the same conclusion. It's nice being tuned in on the same wavelength. Karen was in the kitchen busy preparing a nice steak dinner, and had two glasses of Chateau Sainte Michelle's delightful Johannisberg Riesling resting on the counter.

Taking the hint from Karen, I set the table, lit some candles, and turned off the lights in the dining room and the adjoining front room.

As we savored the wine I noticed the flickering candlelight created a shimmering effect on Karen's silk blouse. The shifting shadows highlighted her now erect nipples. After we finished eating she gently laid her left hand on my right hand then picked it up. She stood up, slowly pulling me up by the hand, drawing our bodies close together until they softly touched. My arms moved around her back and slid down to her hips as we kissed. First lightly then more aggressively until we were both aroused. She led me into the living room to the white sheepskin rug in front of the gas fireplace. I reached out and flipped on the fireplace as she started undressing me.

Hours later, we wandered upstairs to bed feeling a blissful afterglow.

At 4:00 AM, still groggy from my lusty evening with Karen, I crawled out of bed and staggered down the stairs to the kitchen. I popped a couple of frozen waffles in the toaster and poured myself a cup of Karen's favorite Starbuck's blend—Mild Colombian.

When the waffles popped up, I quickly slathered on some butter and then proceeded to drown them in organic maple syrup. By the time I had finished off the coffee and waffles, I was starting to feel as if I was ready to take on whatever the day had to offer. I showered, shaved, and slipped into my Kevlar vest, pulled a black polo shirt over it, slipped into a pair of olive green twill trousers, and black sneakers with a razor blade duct-taped in place, and grabbed my navy windbreaker.

I spotted the miniature can of mace and tube of Poligrip. I spent a few seconds trying to rationalize not taking it but quickly reasoned that if something happened and I didn't have it the consequences could be a lot worse than the discomfort of stashing it on my body. I quickly squeezed some Poligrip from the tube and spread it all over the mace cylinder, then gingerly placed it behind my scrotum. After a few adjustments, I found a spot that wasn't too uncomfortable when I walked. As I pulled up my briefs and trousers, I rejoiced that Mike was on the bike and I was going to be sitting in a plane—reasonably comfortable.

I went back to say good-bye to Karen but she was sleeping soundly with a smile on her face. I bent over and gave her a kiss on the cheek. She awoke and put her arms around my neck and pulled me closer for a long passionate kiss. For a minute, I thought she was going to reach for my trousers and unzip them, but she settled for one more long tantalizing kiss that triggered a sudden swelling in my groin. It took every bit of willpower I could muster to pull away.

I backed out of the garage at 4:35 AM and soon was heading south on I-5. Traffic was still light so, with my eyes scanning for the State Highway Patrol, I pushed my speed up to seventy miles per hour, a mere ten miles over the limit.

At 4:55 AM, I pulled into the lot at Seattle Seaplanes. Jim was already fussing around a plane and waved for me to join him. Looking at the plane's pontoons, I asked, "Hey Jim, what happens if the pontoons spring a leak? How do you land on water then?"

"Well," he said, chuckling, "ya just gotta do it then get out damn fast."

"So, if we happen to spot the bad guys and they shoot at us, and hit a pontoon, we might have to swim to shore? I hope you've got a lifejacket I can use. I can't swim."

"Relax, Scott. I got plenty of lifejackets but don't worry about the pontoons. See these here plugs on the top?"

I looked to where he was pointing. Along the top of each pontoon I saw five different plugs spaced equal distance apart.

"The inside of these pontoons are divided into sections that are sealed off from each other. Shoot a hole in one and the others will still keep us afloat. We'd probably stay afloat with just half the sections workin' but what's this talk about getting shot at? I thought we were just doin' a reconnaissance flight lookin' for possible hideout spots?"

"Yeah, that's right but I just try to anticipate every possible scenario. I don't like surprises. All we have to do is locate possible hiding places. The FBI and the cops will do the rest. If anything even looks remotely like it's going to be dangerous, we'll get out of the area fast."

"You got that right."

At that moment, the roar of a Harley broke the quiet morning air. Jim glanced at his watch and said, "this must be the Walter's guy you said would be flying with us. He's a big fellow ain't he? Well, it's a good thing we're taking a ten passenger plane this time. The smaller one's off on a Charter."

I made the introductions and then Jim told us to get on board. In a matter of seconds, Jim revved up the engines and pulled away from the dock. Another choppy trip down the liquid runway and then airborne. Jim banked the plane to the west while I studied the map. I did a double take. "I'll be damned. There it is. Right in front of me."

"What's that, Scott?" said Pudgy.

"Temera's clue. Sherwood Forest. It's not a forest or a dry cleaners—it's a damn street. Look—it touches the bottom of the anvil. It runs west from the anvil to close to the water." My eye's were jumping all over the map like a kid in a candy store.

"Look! Down here. See these points of land? Look at the names. Ostrich Bay, Mud Bay, Bass Point. Temera said she saw ostriches, mud and bass. There are the two bridges she saw. The ferries—it's all here. They must've crossed Puget Sound and came through Bremerton, going under both these bridges, up into Dyes Inlet. She said there was only one outlet. This has got to be the place."

As we approached the general area, I told Jim to circle south then turn north and follow the route they likely took. I remembered Temera's words, 'Oak trees—could be a forest or a street— I'm facing north—white mountain peaks off to my left—water in front of me—old farm—barn—outbuildings.' I looked off to my left and there were the Olympic mountains she'd seen. I asked Jim to line up on a northerly heading over Rocky Point, which pointed us directly at the anvil. Another look at the map showed a Red Oaks Court branching off the anvil near Sherwood Street. We were close.

Below us, there were the signs of life as people and vehicles started appearing ready for another day of work or play. Street lights started to flicker off. There was a light mist, or fog hanging over the water in Dyes Inlet. Now our task was narrowing things down. We needed to find the exact building, but first I thought it would be smart to touch base with Mike. He answered his cell phone on the first ring.

"Mike, I've found Temera's clues. Almost all of them." I went on filling him in on everything. He said he'd give Wes a call. The evidence was getting too strong that Temera and the remote viewers were right. He reported that he could see our plane and he was at the north end of the anvil area, by a small park. Just then we passed over him, circling west and heading back south for another pass over the area. Before disconnecting, I told him we were going to concentrate on spotting any old farms in the area.

As Jim circled over the area, I spotted three possibilities—all within the target area. All had piers. Two of the piers had motor boats moored to them. There was one motor boat about fifty yards offshore with two fishermen in it. I pointed them out to Jim and asked him if we could go in for a landing. I thought if the fishermen lived around that general area they might help us narrow the search.

Jim made a small circle, checking to make sure he wasn't going to hit any boats, then started his approach. The landing was smooth and he started taxiing slowly toward the fishing boat. As we approached the fishermen, both reeled in their lines. I hoped we weren't screwing up their favorite fishing spot by churning up the water. Jim cut the engines and let our momentum carry us forward the last twenty yards. I opened the door on my side and waved to the two men. Both were bundled up pretty well against the early morning chill. I have never been able to understand fishing. I simply don't have the patience to sit still for hours on end.

One of the men cranked up their engine and slowly started toward us so they could come in along side the pontoon on my side and talk. Once along side, they tossed a rope to me so I could tie them up to the plane.

The one who tossed me the rope spoke first, "If you fellows are lookin' for a good fishing spot, ya sure as hell didn't pick a very good one. We been trying this here inlet for three days and ain't got shit ta show for it. We're thinkin' a headin' over to Hood Canal tomorrow."

"Sorry you're not catching anything," I said. "But we're not fishing. We're looking for an old farm house along this stretch where some military guys might be staying."

"Well there's all kinda military places around here but nothin' on this side of the inlet. If ya head south down there at Ostrich Bay you'll find the military."

"Yeah, we know about that. The guys we're looking for are ex-military. Sort of a militia group, you know what I mean?"

The guy sitting back by the motor spoke, "Say buddy, what's your name? You look kinda familiar."

He looked familiar to me also. We both remembered at the same time. The New Lotus Bookshop. He had been one of the two DOG members in attendance. The one who hit on the female

FBI agent. Before I could even open my mouth, I found myself staring at a semi-automatic pistol. My palms started getting sweaty and it felt as if my heart was pounding two hundred beats a minute. If my bladder had been full, I probably would have peed in my pants.

"You're that writer who wrote all that crazy shit that old fart called Mike has been upsetting' people with."

In a very scared voice I said, "Yeah. I'm Scott Hunter. I was paid to write that stuff. That's how I make a living." My brain started to kick into gear. Mike had said most of these guys are Baby Souls, so I had to figure out something fast. Shit, I'm standing on a pontoon of a seaplane, I can't swim, and some asshole with an IQ below the mean was holding a gun on me while the other guy had a gun aimed at Jim and Pudgy. A wave of anger swept over me. I was pissed at my own stupidity. I'd forgotten about sentries. These guys are guarding the hideout from a water attack and I'm too dumb to have figured that out.

The one in the front, with the gun on Jim and Pudge, yelled at Jim, "Keep your hands offa that fuckin' radio or you, the fat boy, and this fuckin' atheist are all gonna be fish bait."

Jim looked scared and slowly pulled his hands away from the controls. "I'm just the pilot, I don't wanta get in the middle of any argument you guys have. That's strictly between you guys."

"He's right. I just hired him to fly over this area." By now, my initial fear had worn off and the adrenaline was kicking my brain into overdrive. "Look fellows. I'm glad to find you. I wrote that book you mentioned but now I want to write another explaining your side. That's why I been trying to find you guys. But you just disappeared."

"Shut your fuckin' mouth, hotshot." Then turning to his companion, "Hey, Snake, Call HQ and tell 'em what we got us here. Ask 'em if I should just plug these fuckers and sink this fuckin' plane or what."

The guy called Snake pulled out a cell phone, dialed a number and explained the situation. He grunted a few answers then disconnected. "Drake's sendin' another boat. I'm supposed to bring mister hotshit writer to HQ. Sez for you to taxi the plane across the inlet to Chico Bay and tie it up at that old deserted pier. The other boat'll meet ya there, then bring the pilot and the fat guy back to HQ. Drake don't want the plane near here but said don't sink it. We might need it for our escape if things get hairy. He's a smart dude. I forgot about that deserted pier over there."

While Snake's buddy crawled around me and up into the plane's cabin, Snake moved to the back, then I carefully eased myself into the small boat. Non-swimmers are always extra careful getting in and out of boats. I didn't see any lifejackets, and considering the situation, thought it was better to keep my mouth shut rather than giving them one more easy way to kill me.

I sat in the bow facing Snake. He laid his gun down so he could use both hands on the engine. Spotting my eyes on the gun he said with a sick laugh, "Go ahead fuckhead. Ya think ya can grab it, go for it." I could figure out I didn't have a chance. This guy more than likely was in the military recently and a highly trained killer. Probably kicked out of Special Forces like some of his buddies for some racial incident. "Hey, man, you're in charge. I'm not about to try anything stupid."

Damn, I thought to myself, I had been stupid enough to walk right into their trap. Of course they'd be watching the water, since that was one of the borders of their hideout. What was I thinking? Now, here I was captured and headed into their hideout with nothing but a single-edged razor blade in one of my sneakers and a small can of mace stuck in some goop behind my balls. A hell of a lot of good that was going to do. At least James Bond always had a small arsenal of powerful weapons that could save his ass when the bad guys caught him.

Snake appeared to be mid-twenties. Pale skin, lots of tattoos and a head that looked like a serpent. His eyes were deep-set, tucked under heavy brows that scrunched together in the center over his nose. There was a gap between his two top front teeth. A scar, still red in color, ran from just under his left ear to the edge of his nose. He appeared to be about five eleven, one seventy to one eighty, and in great shape. I tried to guess his Soul Profile. I guessed Baby Soul. His eyes had the same intensity as many Baby Souls. His Role was clearly a Warrior. This was not the guy to try and sway, so I kept quiet as we closed on land.

Chapter 32

As we approached, I could see a boathouse to the left of the pier, right on the water's edge. At the pier, I noticed there was another motor boat tied up. Counting the one that was going out to the seaplane, there were three.

Up the hill, about thirty feet above sea level, slightly to the right of the pier was the main farmhouse. Just to the right of the house was a tower, about three stories high with a windmill attached—apparently placed there decades ago to generate power from winds swirling around the inlet.

The tower had a small window in it and I could make out the silhouette of someone up there, who I guessed was a lookout. To the right of the windmill tower, and slightly behind it was a small outbuilding that probably was once a chicken coop. Behind it was a large barn that looked tired but was still intact, although it clearly needed a major scrapping and new paint job.

Two guys dressed in military garb met us at the pier and helped me out of the boat as Snake gave me a shove, almost knocking over the guys on the pier. Grabbing me by the arms, one said, "Hey, Snake, ya search 'em?"

"Naw, I'll leave that up to you pussies." Then with his sick laugh he said, "He's probably got a grenade hidden up his ass. You guys can flip a coin and decide who gets to reach in and pull it out."

Ignoring Snake's comment, the guy on my left said, "Let's go." We walked up the small slope towards the farmhouse on an asphalt pathway, cracked in places where weeds had broken through. The yard had been recently mowed but consisted mostly of crabgrass that had long ago ganged up on the healthy grass blades and forced them out. The farmhouse looked pretty rundown, and like the barn, in desperate need of scraping and painting. Once white with blue trim, it was now a dirty cream with the blue trim faded to a pale watery blue. I would have guessed it as deserted except for some smoke coming out the chimney. All around the area were evergreens—forty to sixty year olds mostly with dense underbrush under them. The land had been cleared between the buildings and the woods, leaving at least fifty yards between the buildings and woods. If the FBI tried to rush the place they'd be sitting ducks once they left the tree line.

I noticed black cable running from the farmhouse to the tower, and other cables running between all the other buildings. I guessed they had done temporary wiring for a communications system. Lights were on so they had tapped into nearby power lines.

They stopped me just short of the porch stairs and one said "Put your hands on your head and spread your legs." I complied, then one of them frisked me exactly as Pudgy had said. Just a light brushing over the crotch area—thank God. When done, he said, "He's clean. Go ask Colonel Drake what we do with 'em."

Before the guard could open the battered screen door, a man I guessed to be Drake pulled the front door open and pushed the screen door outward and stepped out on the porch.

I found myself looking up at a trim athletic man, forty-something, maybe six foot one, two hundred pounds, broad shoulders, with narrow hips, with a .45 in a polished black leather holster on his right hip. Drake had a black beret on his head and wore heavily starched and pressed green camouflage fatigues, with a silver eagle insignia of a full bird Colonel on the beret and each shoulder. His black boots glistened from a recent spit shine. His face was narrow, high cheekbones, olive complexion with a thin, neatly trimmed mustache. He exuded an air of arrogance and supreme confidence as he stood with his feet apart and hands on hips.

"Well, well. Mr. Scott Hunter I presume. Isn't it a little early to be out selling books?"

Realizing that I wasn't going to trick him, I responded directly, "No, my book isn't published yet. I was looking for Connie Kamura. I thought by now she would have been scared enough and you'd let her go."

"So...you think I have Ms. Kamura. How did you come to that conclusion?"

Not wanting to tip him off to the search that was narrowing in on him I decided to try and convince him I was playing Lone Ranger. "I went to a psychic and she said you had her. The cops laughed at me so I decided to look for you on my own. The psychic gave me clues that led me here."

Slowly stepping down the stairs, Drake stopped directly in front of me. His dark brown eyes only a foot away from mine, looked directly at me. He was testing me for any signal I was lying. The slightest flinch could blow my story. Without blinking, and maintaining perfect eye contact, I said, "the cops might not believe it, but I'm convinced you've got her and you're hiding her here. Isn't that right?"

His left hand shot up instantly, grabbing me around the throat. "You expect me to believe that some phony bitch on some stupid Psychic Hotline gave you directions to get here?"

Struggling to breathe, I croaked out a feeble, "Yes, but it was a real psychic, not some Hotline."

Releasing his grip he said, "Tell me, what did she say?"

Choosing to follow the path of telling the truth, just withholding selected information, I told him the truth starting from calling Temera and meeting her at Wendy's in Ballard, and following her clues from there. I omitted mentioning the FBI, and Mike. I said the cops weren't interested so I hired the seaplane so I could look over here.

I could see I had him puzzled. My story was goofy enough to be real. He was confused. If I was telling him the truth, he had another hostage and nothing to fear about an attack. If I was lying, he might be in big trouble. He kept staring at me, furrowing his brow, and stroking his mustache and chin.

Turning to one of my guards he said, "Corporal, send a Red Alert to all troops and conduct a search of the perimeter immediately. If the perimeter is secure, take two vehicles and mount a north-south search of the nearby area. First make sure Tracyton Boulevard is clear at least two miles in each direction. Then push east to Brownsville Highway. Report to HQ every five minutes."

The guard, fired off a loud "Yes, Sir," and rushed up the stairs and disappeared into the house. In a matter of seconds, bodies were running around inside. Doors were opening and shutting as Drake's well-trained militia sprang into action.

"Follow me," Drake said as he turned on his heels and reentered the house. I felt a shove in the back from the remaining guard and quickly followed Drake. Inside, the house was missing all the normal furnishings, replaced by several folding tables, chairs and boxes of what appeared to be ammo. A couple of grunts were busy dismantling and oiling some firearms at a far table.

"In here," Drake said as he entered a back room that in grander times probably had been the master bedroom. The walls were covered with various maps of the region. A large three feet by six feet oak desk faced the door. Drake slid behind it and gestured for me to take one of the three metal folding chairs facing the desk.

The guard spoke, "Colonel Sir, Reamer and Snake request permission to interrogate the prisoner. Sir!"

"I'll decide later. Right now Mr. Hunter and I are going to have a little chat. No—I take that back. First send Snake in here—with one of his assistants."

"Yes, Sir."

A thousand thoughts raced through my head. I tried recalling from some old movie or book what to say or do. Should I lie? Try to trick him? Be a smart-ass?

I decided my best bet was to use the knowledge in my book that Mike had taught me. I had never applied it before under such a pressure situation but it seemed like my best bet. I knew my Soul Profile by heart—I was Sixth Level Old Soul with a Role of Scholar, Goal of Growth, with Impatience my weak point.

I remembered Mike giving us Wolfe Drake's Soul Profile— 2nd Level Young Soul. Role of Warrior with a Priest Essence Twin. Goal of Dominance and his Chief Obstacle is Arrogance.

Whereas most DOG members were Baby Souls he was not. As a Young Soul, he was in DOG for power. Mike had said Drake's Priest Essence Twin influence makes it easy for him to buy into the group's dogma and spew it out with the best of them, but deep inside he's marching to a slightly different drummer. Because he's in Dominance, this lifetime is about developing leadership skills. He's a strong leader who will be ruthless in making his men follow. Any disobedience will be dealt with harshly. So his men will be in fear of his wrath if they disobey orders. Where he is vulnerable is his Arrogance. He can't stand being thought of as normal or mediocre. Also, since his inner allegiance to the cause is not as strong, he is more susceptible to being pulled away over issues of money and power.

I hoped to Hell Mike was right because if I misjudge Drake and piss him off I'll soon be a dead man and Karen a widow.

Drake said nothing. Just stared at me as if he was trying to decide the best way to torture me. Then behind me I heard footsteps. "Colonel, Sir, you requested me?"

"Yes, Snake. Perhaps you'd be kind enough to introduce Mr. Hunter to one of your assistants."

"Yes, Sir!"

I heard some rustling around me and as I turned my head slightly I found myself staring at the fangs of a hissing diamondback rattle snake. I leaped back in fear, knocking my chair over and falling to the floor. Snake, holding the rattler by its head, dangled its body over me, the rattles almost touching me. Pushing frantically with my feet and hands I scooted backwards in a near panic. Snake kept pressing towards me dangling the rattler over me, relishing my fear.

"Okay, that's enough," barked Drake. "I think Mr. Hunter will now feel free to discuss what he knows with me."

I was out of breath, gasping for air while my heart was pounding so hard I was afraid it might rupture. My body was drenched in sweat. Sweat that reeked of intense fear. I'll admit it—when it comes to poisonous snakes—I'm scared of them.

Drake, in complete control, with a sly grin on his face, picked up the chair I had knocked over, and said, "Please have a seat Mr. Hunter. I believe there were some things you wanted to share with me."

Totally disoriented, I stammered, "Ahh, ahh, yeah, okay. Sure. What do you wanta know?"

"Let's go back over that bullshit you gave me about the psychic. What's the real truth? What do the cops really know?"

"Look, Colonel, I sat in on a briefing the FBI held shortly after you grabbed Connie. They're positive it's you. They gotta tire print from the van at Wendy's that matches the tire print from the attack on the gays. They're convinced you ordered the gay attack, the bombing at the Times, the death threat to my former literary agent, the attack at the Space Needle, and the kidnapping of Connie Kamura. They're still gathering evidence and I don't know everything their crime lab has turned up, but I know they think if they can find your hideout they'll get all the missing proof they need to arrest you.

"Mike, the spiritual guy I wrote about, called up a psychic and some remote viewers—you know the guys the U.S. Government uses—to get clues about where you were. What I told you about the clues was correct. That's exactly what she said. The remote viewers said to look for something that looked like an anvil. Here let me show you."

I got up and walked over to his map of the region. "See right here. See where these streets form a shape that looks like an anvil. Then we spotted the other clues. Sherwood—Oaks—Ostrich—Mud—Bass—mountains to the west. Last night we told the FBI what we had. They said they'd split their task force up and keep half up near your old hideout in Snohomish and send the rest over here.

"We had some observers on the ground this morning that saw the seaplane go down and probably saw you capture me and the others. So I guess it'll only be a matter of hours before they find you. They now know you're hiding in a farm house in this general area and since there are only three farm houses along here as soon as they eliminate the others they'll know exactly where you are."

By now, I was regaining my composure and Drake was starting to listen, so I decided to start applying my knowledge of his Soul Profile.

"Colonel, there's something else."

"Well, what is it?"

"They think Calvin McCallum's setting you up. They think it's funny."

"What do you mean?" snapped Drake.

"Well, I'm just a writer so I don't know all the details but what I heard is McCallum thinks you're selling drugs on the side. I heard McCallum finances DOG with money made off selling stolen credit card numbers internationally and doesn't wanta mess with drugs. The Feds have been putting a lot of pressure on McCallum so he figures if he sets you up they'll go after you. Right now he figures you're getting too powerful. Figures you might be a threat to him. With drug money, you could grow big enough to take over the whole operation. The Feds think he ordered you to attack the gays, the black couple, do the bombing and the kidnapping. They also said something about he ordered you to kill some wetbacks crossing the border.

"The whole country is upset over these recent incidents. Everyone is demanding that the government do something. Hell, right now, back in Washington, DC, at the Justice Department, DOG is on the top of the daily briefing agenda. They've pulled in the ATF and the DEA to help the FBI. Not only the Feds, but state and local cops have a lot of heat on them to catch you. Colonel, I think you're too smart to end up a dead martyr for DOG.

"Look, I'm telling you the truth because I don't wanta die, and if you go down, I'll go down too. Remember Waco? Ruby Ridge? Remember the Simbionese Liberation Army, the SLA? The group that kidnapped Patty Hearst? You know the Feds don't negotiate. They're going to come in here with enough firepower to wipe this farm off the face of the earth. Hell, by this time tomorrow the Coast Guard will have the inlet barricaded and gun ships hemming you in. I mean, look at this building. It's old, the wood is dry and brittle. When they blast us with stun grenades and tear gas, this place will catch on fire in an instant. After they've leveled the area, they'll come in and sift through the ashes and claim you had killed Connie Kamura, me and the others before they attacked. They'll look like heroes saving the public. There won't be any survivors to talk. And old man McCallum, he'll be sitting back in Mississippi drinking a mint julep chuckling to himself how he not only got rid of the only man smart enough to take over, but he'll be able to use the death of you and all your men to increase his fundraising among the right wing in this country."

"So Hunter you actually think McCallum is setting me up to take the fall?"

"Yes, and you can go along with the plan or you can outsmart him. I think there's a way you can come out of this whole mess and show McCallum who's the smartest.

"Look at reality, Colonel. This hideout and your men are enough to protect against an attack by some rival drug gang, but we're talkin' the whole damn government. You're big time now. They'll spend the bucks—whatever it takes to destroy you. Shit, you know the U.S. military or CIA can't wage war on you, but they'll loan the FBI, DEA, and ATF whatever they need to blow up this place.

"Colonel, you've been around. You know exactly what's going to happen. Within 24 hours, this place will be surrounded. Power will be cut off. Water will be cut off. Your radio transmissions to your men will be jammed. Then in the middle of the night flood lights will light this place up like the middle of the day. Some FBI negotiator will start talking to you over a bull horn telling you to give up. You'll refuse and the standoff begins. But remember, they don't really want you to give up. They wanta destroy you—make an example of you—they wanta show the world that you can't mess with them and get away with it.

"They'll let you stew for awhile. Then you'll hear the roar of the engines of armored personnel carriers. Helicopters will start buzzing overhead. They'll start taunting your men, hoping to draw fire because once you fire the first shot they'll have the excuse they need to blow you to pieces.

"There's gonna be over five hundred guys out there, all as good or better than your men, and they'll all be itching to squeeze the trigger. Even if your men don't fire, at some point the Feds will launch their stun grenades, tear gas and smoke bombs. Even if you have gas masks, the place will catch fire and your men will be slaughtered or cremated. Believe me, they won't take any prisoners. All your men die. Connie Kamura dies. I die, and you die. McCallum lives."

I could see I was getting through to him. Everything I said made sense and tied into the belief of the right-wing militia groups that the Feds wanted to wipe them out. I knew he wouldn't just surrender and go to prison. As a Young Soul, he wanted money and power too much to spend the rest of his life locked up.

"You've got one chance—give up McCallum."

"What do you mean by that, Hunter?"

"It's simple. You know enough about his entire operation to bring him down. You know how the credit card scam works. You must know the details of lots of illegal acts. Killings that he's ordered. You might even have hard evidence. Documents, tapes, whatever. The Feds will give you a walk if they get the head honcho. You know how they do it."

"Right, then McCallum sends a hit squad after me."

"How's he going to find you? You'll be part of the Federal Witness Protection Program. A year in Brazil getting plastic surgery and not even your mother would recognize you. Hell, you probably have several million stashed away off shore someplace right now from drug sales. The Feds aren't going to press you about that. They've been after McCallum for ten years. They'll do whatever it takes to get him.

"Colonel, you're a smart man and an outstanding leader. You've got charisma. After the plastic surgery, have the Feds set you up in some real estate development business over in a small town in central Washington, Oregon, or California. In no time at all, you'll be one of the leaders in the community. You could become a politician. Who knows you might end up as mayor and have your own police force."

Bingo. I could see Drake's eyes light up as he envisioned himself a wealthy and powerful political figure. He probably was figuring that if he controlled the law enforcement, he could continue his drug business.

I remembered hearing Connie, Wes Conners and Tyrone Willis talking about sleazy criminal lawyers and they were arguing who was the best of the sleazeballs. The name Arnold P. Wexler popped into my mind. "Look Colonel, you don't have much time. I can connect you up with a lawyer who'll work out the deal for you. If you use DOG's lawyers, they'll rat on you to McCallum and you'll be a dead man."

Chapter 33

There was a sharp rap on the door, then it opened. "Excuse me, Colonel. I thought you should know. I'm picking up lots of radio transmissions. Something big is happening. The Kitsap County Sheriff's department is calling in all off-duty personnel. Something about going to a tactical alert. Ferry traffic to Bremerton is being delayed. I can't figure out all the messages."

"What have you heard from our RECON units?"

"First perimeter is secure, Sir. No sign of the enemy. Second perimeter shows signs of increased police presence. Both marked and unmarked vehicles. A county water department truck has set up a barricade at Fairgrounds Road and Tracyton Boulevard. It might be a fake repair."

"Damn it," shouted Drake as he pounded his fist down on the table. "That fucking asshole set me up. Private, alert Eagle's Nest. I want them at Red Alert. Do it now, damn it."

Turning back to me he said, "Okay, Hunter, it appears you might be telling the truth. It looks like the Feds are closing in. What's to keep me from killing you and the other assholes and escaping before they close in?"

"Nothing, Colonel, but how do you figure McCallum knows about your drug dealing? Can you trust everyone of your men? What if one of them is a spy for McCallum? If you take off, the spy will tip off McCallum and your location will get leaked to the Feds. Then, it'll be the same scenario as now—only without me, it'll be harder to work a deal with the Feds. The public won't be too wild about making a deal if Connie Kamura dies."

There was a knock at the door and one of the thugs stuck his head in the door. "Colonel, Sir, we have a problem. Somethin' strange is goin' on. The bouncer at the bar who wants to buy goods from us. Well, Sir, it turns out he was on the same seaplane as Hunter. What should I do?"

Drake stared at the guard for a moment, then turned to me and said, "What the fuck's going on, Hunter?"

"I hired the big guy to tag along—for protection. He was recommended by a friend. I never met him before today. You mean he's part of your drug operation?"

Drake glared at me angrily. "Nick, take this lying piece of shit and put him with the other prisoners. I'll talk to this other asshole in a few minutes and find out what the Hell's going on around here."

As Nick led me off, we went through the kitchen into a room that had obviously been an add-on to enclose the old storm cellar that in old farm houses was located outside. The old-style double doors that angled up from the floor surface were still in use. Nick removed a two-by-four that had been rammed under the door handles to lock it. The stairs going down were steep and rickety. At the bottom there was an opening about ten square feet. The ceiling was low, barely six feet, with a single forty watt bulb dangling from an old electrical cord that was covered with cobwebs. The cellar had a damp musty smell to it. Off to the right, was a door with a padlock. A guard standing by the door, unlocked the padlock and kicked the door open. The room was dimly lit with three candles placed on a card table centered in the room with four chairs. I guessed the room was about twelve-by-twenty. The damp concrete floor was partially covered with rough wooden planks that looked like little wooden pathways to a series of army cots lining the outer walls. Sitting on the cots, with their arms tied behind their backs were Connie, Pudgy, and Jim the pilot. Off to the right, I spotted a big pile of old wooden milk bottle crates, left over from the days when milk only came in glass bottles. The pile went almost up to the ceiling.

"Arms behind the back, hotshot," said the guard. He quickly tied my hands with some clothesline rope. "Ya gotta go...latrine's over there," he said pointing to a filthy white five gallon plastic pail sitting in the corner.

"But how do I get my pants unzipped when I have to go?" I said.

The guard grabbed me roughly by my neck with his left hand and reached down with his right hand and jerked my zipper down with a couple of rough tugs.

"I just solved your zipper problem little boy, you figure out the rest. If you start whining and ask me to pull your fucking dick out for you, I'll yank it off. Understand?"

"Yeah. Okay. Okay. I'll take it from here," I blurted out quickly, not relishing the thought of having my penis ripped off.

"I'll be outside if any of you little cupcakes need room service."

The guard left I heard the padlock slam shut.

"Oh, Scott, I'm so glad to see you," said Connie. "Pudgy told me what's been happening. What are our chances?"

"I don't know. I'm trying to use some of Mike's Soul Profile knowledge to convince Drake to let us go but I don't know if it's working.

"Pudge, if Drake interrogates you just say you first met me this morning. Say you were recommended to me by the owner of the bar when I was inquiring around about some muscle to help out if I ran into trouble. Play dumb. Stick to your drug deal story. Say it's a coincidence. Say you didn't know the drug people were the same ones who grabbed Connie. Maintain that you still wanta do business. Give him a sob story. Talk Nam. Talk about how the VA fucked you over—You know whatever it takes. Oh, by the way—one of his men, a guy named Snake— scared the shit outa me with a live rattle snake he's got somewhere upstairs."

"Oh man, why'd ya have ta say that—I hate snakes," said Pudgy with a grimace.

We heard someone fumbling with the pad lock then the door opened. "Hey, Harley, the man wants you—NOW!"

Pudgy got to his feet, and walked, hunched over to avoid the ceiling, out the door. As soon as we heard the padlock snap shut I moved over to the cot next to Connie's cot. She said, "Pudgy told me about the razor blades and mace but until a few minutes ago they had a guard in here with us and he couldn't get them out."

"Now's our chance. I'm gonna lay down on the cot with my right foot behind you. You'll have to untie my shoe."

Connie twisted awkwardly around and after a little struggle pulled the laces apart. "Now go to the outer side of my foot and line up with my ankle," I said. "Good, now feel around for a piece of duct tape inside of the shoe. Good. Now be careful. Under it is a single edge razor blade. The safe side is pointing up. Careful. Careful. Good, you got it. You wanta cut my ropes first or shall I cut yours?"

"No, you cut mine. I'm shaking so much I'm afraid I might cut your wrists," said Connie.

We turned our backs to each other and Connie carefully handed the razor blade to me. I slowly felt her ropes and found a spot that was as far away from her skin as possible, then started sliding the blade back and forth. It seemed as if nothing was happening for the longest time. Finally, I could hear some strands popping. Then I was through the rope. I dropped the razor blade and started pulling the cut ends of the rope until things started to come undone. Success. Connie grabbed her wrists and started rubbing them to restore her circulation. She picked up the razor blade and quickly sawed through my ropes then Jim's.

Poor Jim. He was confused. He had gone from what appeared to be a routine sightseeing charter to being tied up in a cellar and not sure if he was going to be killed or not.

"Now, Scott, where's the mace?" said Connie.

"In my pants, in a very sensitive place."

As I reached in my pants I said, "the guard was kind enough to unzip me, I'm just grateful he didn't go digging around."

I located the mace cylinder and ever so gently started to remove it which I discovered was a lot harder than I had been led to believe. I could now understand how Poligrip could hold a set of false teeth to the roof of a person's mouth. Only there are no hairs growing in your mouth. I finally discovered that if I concentrated on disconnecting the mace from the goop it was better than trying to remove the goop and the cylinder at the same time. I figured I could always take a bath later and get the goop off. At last, I proudly held the little tube up, "Success!"

I quickly wiped it off and handed it to Connie. "Here. You keep this. If something happens, I'll try and distract the bad guy while you mace 'em. Remember, don't shoot it in my face. Are you up to this?"

"I think so, Scott. But I'm really scared of these guys. When I took a woman's self-defense class it was nothing like this. I never thought I'd be defending myself from highly trained military guys with nasty weapons."

Connie was still wearing a navy blue suit coat with matching slacks. Her silk blouse looked beige in the flickering candlelight. A single gold chain with a cross hung around her neck. Her face and clothes had some dirt on them and there was a little mud on her low heeled shoes. There was a red welt on the left side of her face but other than that she looked okay physically. Emotionally, she was hurting. I just hoped that if things turned rough she would be tough enough to fight back.

I grabbed one of the candles and started surveying our cellar prison. More than likely it had once been a dirt cellar a hundred years ago. Now the dirt walls had been covered with one-by-twelve planks nailed horizontally onto the eight-by-eight support posts. The boards I tested seemed solid. When I got around to the milk bottle crates, and held the candle up so its light would shine between the narrow cracks between the crates, I thought I saw a different type of wood behind them. Being careful not to make any noise I gently lifted a few of the top crates and moved them to the outer edge of the pile so only the most observant guard would know anything had been moved. I was right. The wood behind the pile ran vertically and seemed to be more finished than the other wall boards. I pulled out another crate just enough to reach my hand behind it and trace the edge of the wood. My hand ran into what felt like a cabinet door hinge.

Jim got excited. "Hey man, if it's a door it must lead somewhere. Let's make a run for it."

Connie, who had been standing with her ear to the padlocked door, suddenly whispered, "Scott, someone's coming."

We all rushed back to the cots, grabbing our ropes and crudely wrapping them around our arms behind our backs. The padlock clanked open, then Pudgy, with his hands still bound, returned, hunching over to avoid hitting the ceiling, and plopped down on his cot.

After the guard left and we heard the padlock shut, Pudgy, looked at the three of us and said, "Whew, that friggin' rattler damned near made me shit my pants. He had the friggin' thing six inches from my face—I was looking down its throat—those friggin' fangs were drippin' venom."

"What did Drake say?" I asked as I turned Pudgy around so I could use my razor blade on his ropes.

"Hey, man, just like you said. I laid out the whole story. I said one of my kids has leukemia and my wife can't work. Said that ever since Nam I can't hold no regular job. Bouncin' don't pay shit. Said I need money bad. Said you offered me $200 just to ride on a plane and be backup if anything bad happened. I told 'em you said you were hopin' to get some reward money for findin' Connie Kamura. Said you'd pay me $1,000 if we got a reward. I didn't know the guys who took her were the same dudes I was hopin' to partner up with on weed. Said there's no way I woulda said yes to you if I'd known.

"We talked a lot about Nam. Seems none of his thugs served over there. All too young. He saw a lot of the same shit I did. I really got through to him when I bitched about the VA. He hates them too. I said they refused to give me any decent counseling—just dumped me back out into society.

"I told him my regular weed supplier got whacked and I got no stuff to sell. Said I don't care about no reward money if I can get a new supplier. The friggin' leukemia treatments cost a friggin' fortune. The only way I can keep my head above water is dealing. I said I could buy a hundred pounds a month of the regular weed and a hundred of the primo sensimilla. His eyes got big when I said that. I could see the wheels turnin' in his head."

"I'm curious," said Connie, "what does a hundred pounds cost? I thought people bought it by the ounce?"

"Yeah, the end user does. But the middleman, to get the best price, pays between $400 and $600 a pound for regular and $1,000 to $1,200 a pound for the good stuff."

"Pudgy...that's between $40,000 and $120,000. That's a lot of money. You don't have that kind of money."

"Right, Connie, but Drake doesn't know that. If he was going to do business with me, the DEA was gonna put up the bread.

I'm hopin' to get reward money—but from the DEA. The important thing, between Scott and me, is we got him tuned into his Young Soul instincts. He ain't thinkin' about the Scriptures. He's thinkin' money and power."

I was about to tell Pudgy about the possibility of some kind of door behind the milk crates when we heard footsteps and the padlock being unlocked. In walked Mitch, the driver of the van I had seen months ago at Green Lake, and Reamer.

"Hey, Mitch, look at all the sad people," said Reamer. They ain't got nutin' ta watch. No fuckin' TV. They got no way a knowin' what fuckin' lies the media is sayin' about us. And that's because they tried to fuck with us."

Mitch, who earlier I had guessed outranked Reamer, dragged one of the cots over to the side of the room opposite the three of us, said, "Ease off, Reamer. Drake said we gotta get some rest. We might have a big night ahead of us."

"Ya know, Mitch, you remind me of my fuckin' high school football coach. He kept sayin' go to bed early before the big game and no pussy. Said it drains your energy. I told him bullshit. So, the night before the big game I stayed up all night long fuckin' these twins—Sandy and Mandy. Ya know what happened? I had my best game ever."

"Well, ain't no one gettin' any pussy here tonight so forget about it."

"What the fuck ya mean?"

"Come on, Reamer, you know what the Colonel said. No one gets to fuck the Jap until he says so."

"Yeah, well that's a crock a shit. Drake just wants her first. Why should I have ta settle for sloppy seconds? I'm the one that grabbed her."

Reamer, puffed his chest out and walked over to where Connie was lying on her cot. Slowly he pulled out his combat knife, twisting it slowly in Connie's face so the flickering candlelight reflected off it on the walls and ceiling. Connie started to tremble. I could feel Pudgy shift ever so slightly on the cot we both were sitting on. Reamer lowered his knife to the bottom of Connie's slacks then in a sudden jerking motion shoved the knife under the fabric and slit one leg up to the knee. Connie screamed and jumped backwards as far as she could go. Reamer laughed. "What's the matter bitch, never had a real white man before?"

"Reamer—God damn it. I said knock it off."

"Go fuck yourself," Reamer responded as he quickly cut the other leg of her slacks. He grabbed the neckline of Connie's blouse and slit the fabric, then with a sudden jerk tore it open, exposing a beige bra underneath. Connie was quivering in fear and I could feel the tension increasing in Pudgy's body.

"Reamer—Reamer—Damn it. Knock it off. That's an order!"

Ignoring Mitch, Reamer grabbed the waistband of Connie's slacks, slit them, and tore the fabric exposing Connie's thighs and beige panties. Relishing his sexual feast, Reamer's eyes opened wide, staring at Connie's body while he started to pant in anticipation. Reamer quickly undid his belt, zipper, and dropped his trousers and shorts to his ankles. His penis was already half-erect. Mitch leaped to his feet, pulled his .45 pistol out of his holster, and shouted, "God damn it, Reamer. That's enough."

Mitch grabbed Reamer's left arm to pull him back from Connie. In a rage, Reamer spun around and rammed his knife, all the way up to the handle, into Mitch's chest. Before he could even pull the blade out, Pudgy sprang forward grabbing Reamer from behind around the neck. We heard a sickening crack as Reamer's neck broke. Pudgy stepped back as Reamer's body collapsed to the ground.

"Oh shit," said Pudgy. "We have a problem. Even with their two .45's, we can't out-shoot everyone upstairs. We gotta bluff our way out. Make it look like a double killing. Scott, turn around. I'm gonna retie your hands but there's a slip knot so just yank on this part and you'll be loose. Got it?"

"Yeah, but how are you gonna explain Reamer's broken neck?"

"Watch."

Pudgy bent down, picked up Mitch's limp hand, still holding the .45, and pointed it at Reamer's neck. The sound of the gun going off in the low-ceiling cellar was deafening. First one bullet in the neck and the second in the chest. Pudgy lowered Mitch's arm and jumped back on the cot, wrapping the rope around his arms and hands behind his back as best he could.

Chapter 34

All Hell broke loose. Suddenly footsteps were running everywhere upstairs and in a matter of five seconds, the door crashed open and two guards with UZI's rushed into the room. Their eyes darted from the two bodies on the floor to us and back again. Drake, with pistol drawn rushed into the room. "What the fuck's goin' on here?"

Pudgy spoke, "That guy with the pants down went crazy, Colonel. He was gonna rape the woman. The other guy kept saying no way. Said your orders were hands off. The one guy cut the lady's clothes off and the other guy grabbed him. That's when the first guy spins around and stabs him. The guy with the knife in him got off two rounds before he died."

Drake's intense eye's scanned the room. Pudgy, Jim and I appeared to be still tied sitting on one cot. Connie was untied, but her clothes were in shreds. The two bodies were overlapping on the ground. The gun and knife were clearly visible.

The cellar filled with more of Drakes' men, staring at the bodies of their fallen comrades. Apparently Drake bought the story. He turned to one of his men and said, "That fucking Reamer. I knew he was gonna screw up sooner or later."

Then, strolling to the center of the room he, waved the men to gather around.

"Listen up. Here's the situation. RECON patrols indicate we've been located. In a matter of hours, we'll be surrounded and outnumbered. Remember Waco? The Feds want to do the same thing to us. We aren't strong enough to outlast them so we're gonna beat them using guerrilla tactics. Keep shifting our base and keep attacking them and running.

"I want two men to go to the barn and pack our arsenal in the two Humvees and drive them up to Eagle's Nest, only go south first, towards Tacoma then cut over to the 101 and circle in from that direction.

"Next, get some military clothes for the woman, the pilot and the writer. Some fatigue jackets and trousers. We don't have anything big enough for the biker. If the shooting starts I want them to look like us. Then if we all get killed, at least the Feds will get blamed if they find the Fibbies bullets in the hostages' bodies.

"Pull up Reamer's pants and drag him and Mitch upstairs. Prop 'em up by a window. So when the firing starts it'll look like the Feds killed them.

"Set the explosives so this place will go up when they enter it. Booby trap everything.

"We start a staggered evacuation the moment it's dark. We go in teams of six plus two returning escorts. I'll lead Alpha team. I'll take Nick and the four hostages. We use the tunnel and the eight-man raft. We cross the inlet to Chico Bay where the seaplane is and take it to Eagle's Nest. Tim and Nevada will be the two escorts who'll bring the raft back to this side for the next team. If you spot the Coast Guard or any suspicious boats use the black tarps and paddles only, otherwise use the outboard. If anything goes wrong, come ashore wherever you can and work your way back to Eagle's Nest. Sergeant Craig will give everyone $200 in small bills so you'll have cash if you need it. We can't risk a loose tongue giving away the location of Eagle's Nest."

"What about the hostages?" said one of the men.

"Once we get away, we'll keep 'em for a few days then if the Feds haven't discovered us, we can get rid of them. Except for the biker. If his story checks out, he lives. Once we're ready to dump 'em, you boys can all get your rocks off. But until then, my order still stands. Keep your hands off the woman. Understood? Now let's get moving."

Several of the men grabbed the bodies of Reamer and Mitch and dragged them out of the cellar and up the stairs. When all the men were gone, Drake turned to me and said, "Hunter, follow me."

Not knowing what to expect, I gave Pudgy, Connie and Jim a quizzical look as I got off the cot and headed out the door after Drake.

Upstairs he led me into his office and pointed at a chair. "Sit down." He closed the door, walked over to the edge of his desk and sat on it. "I've been thinking. McCallum is a fucking lunatic. For over forty years, he's been spouting off this Bible and God crap. At first, I listened to him. It made sense, you know, about the White race being superior and all that stuff. Well, he still might be right, but what the fuck has it got him? After forty years, he's got maybe a few million in the bank and less than three hundred troops nationwide.

"He talks about growing DOG until we're so powerful we can take on the government. Hell, his credit card scam doesn't bring in enough to do much more than cover overhead. Drug dealing brings in a hundred times as much. But, he's too fucking dumb to see it. He thinks drugs are an 'abomination in the eyes of God.' I say what the Hell, if the public is willing to pay for them why not benefit. That's what capitalism's about. So, here I am, raising more money in a month than he can in a year and the old fart wants to wipe me out. He should be kissing my ass."

As Drake meandered on with his stream-of-consciousness ramblings, it became apparent that he was throwing off his Baby Soul imprinting from his parents, and the real Wolfe Drake, the aggressive, money-hungry Young Soul was emerging like a butterfly from its cocoon. Given a choice between the religious ideals of McCallum's Baby Soul world, and the chance to live life as a rich drug tycoon he was rapidly sliding towards the latter.

"You said you know a good attorney. How can I get in touch with him?"

"His name's Arnold P. Wexler. From what I've heard, he's the best defense attorney around. Just tell him you'll give up the hostages and turn in McCallum. I'm assuming you got some documentation that can be used against McCallum. Right?"

"Yeah. I got plenty. He called the shots on all the murders and attacks. My job was to execute his orders and recruit new members."

He pulled a small recorder out of middle desk drawer. "I recorded all my conversations with him...just in case."

He turned and unlocked a lateral file cabinet and removed several file folders, placing them in a military backpack, then pulled open a desk drawer and grabbed two boxes full of microcassettes, sealed in plastic wrap, and dumped them into the backpack.

"Here's the plan, Hunter. Once we get to Eagle's Nest, I'll call Wexler. If everything goes as you claim it will, I'll set you free as soon as I get my guarantee of immunity."

"Why not pick up the phone and do it now?" I asked.

"No way. All but four of my men, it used to be five before Mitch got it, are fanatics as crazy as McCallum. They'll kill all of us before we could get halfway out the front door. My plan's the only way to pull this off."

"But what about the others? They'll be right behind us in the evacuation. They'll be at Eagle's Nest too?"

"Hunter, you worry too much. Just follow my plan and make sure Kamura, the pilot and the biker don't try anything funny that could screw up the works. Got it?"

"Yeah. I got it. We'll be cool."

"Good. The moment it gets dark we're outa here."

Drake walked to the door, opened it and spoke to a guard. "Here, put him back in the cellar with the others. Make sure he's got some fatigues."

When I walked back into the cellar, everyone was relieved to see that I hadn't been singled out for any punishment. I quickly filled them in on what was happening.

While we waited for darkness, we explored the cellar some more and discovered that there was a door behind the milk crates. It was padlocked, but if we were left alone long enough we could easily have opened it. Unfortunately, we thought it probably just led to another storage area so we ignored it.

With no windows, it was hard to tell how dark it was getting, but my watch said 10:00 PM so we figured things would start happening soon. We had all agreed to play along with Drake, since it appeared he would make a deal to swap us and turn in McCallum for immunity. It wasn't the best of all worlds. Jim was skeptical but agreed to play along for a while longer. Connie was the most upset. "I hate to see a killer like Drake going free," she said.

"Connie, after all you've been through, I don't blame you," I replied, "but Drake could come in here, blow three of us away, grab Jim and take off anyway. McCallum would still be spewing out his hatred and recruiting more sickos to join DOG. McCallum is the big cheese. Remember, the best way to kill a snake is to cut off it's head. McCallum is the head. Even if Drake could somehow manage to take over the organization, he's a Young Soul. His heart isn't into it anywhere as deeply as McCallum. If he brings down McCallum, for all practical purposes DOG will be dead."

"Yeah, Connie, Scott's right," said Pudgy. "What we gotta do now is stay alive during the evacuation. By now Wes and the FBI boys and every other damned law enforcement dude within fifty miles are closing in on us. These guys have been made fools of by Drake. They're pissed and they want revenge. At night, you guys are gonna look just like two of Drake's men."

"So what do we do?" I asked.

"Well, they got some kinda boat that we're going in to get to the other side. If the water is patrolled by the Coast Guard, we could get caught out in the middle. If Drake's boys start firing, we could be blasted outa the water. Our only chance is goin' overboard and hoping the Coast Guard will pull us out. If the Coast Guard is in a 'take-no-prisoners' mind-set, we're goners."

"I got news for you, Pudge, if I have to jump overboard, I'm a goner. I can't swim."

"Oh shit. How bout you, Connie? Jim?"

"I'm okay, I can swim," said Connie. Jim nodded in agreement.

"Then, Scott, I'll try and keep my eyes open for you. I can't promise, but I'll do my best. Okay, man?"

"Yeah. Thanks."

Our conversation was suddenly ended when we heard the crackle of gunfire.

"AK-47's," said Pudgy. "Sounded like it might be coming from Drake's men. Could be the cops were getting too close and got spotted. No return fire. That's good. Means the cops are bein' cool. I figure they'll do the loudspeaker thing first. You know the drill, 'Put down your weapons and come out with your hands up.' At least Wes should know that most of these sick-ass fanatics won't stop until they run outa ammo."

We heard footsteps coming down the cellar stairs. Drake dashed in followed by two of his men who immediately went over to the crates and moved them, exposing the door in the wall. They unlocked the padlock and we suddenly realized that it wasn't another storage room, it was a tunnel.

One guard shined a flashlight down the tunnel. It looked to be about six feet high by three feet wide and had been reinforced by wood, some of which was half rotted away, exposing the dark damp soil behind it.

"Quick," said Drake, "get their makeup on."

A guard responded by opening a can of face paint and rapidly smearing black paint over all our faces and on our hands. He then handed us all black skull caps to wear.

"Let's go," said Drake. "Nick, you take the lead. Then Nevada and Tim. Hostages next. I'll bring up the rear."

Nick, crouching low with a flashlight in one hand and his UZI in the other, started moving forward. Soon we were all in the tunnel slowly moving forward. Pudgy was the only one having trouble. He was clearly one size too big to fit comfortably in the tight space. I heard a couple of boards collapsing behind us and wondered for a moment if Drake was deliberately pulling them down to seal off the tunnel. I tried picturing in my mind where the tunnel led, but all I could figure out is we were headed south. I vaguely recalled that there was some rough terrain and some trees south of the property, near the water.

After what seemed like fifteen minutes, the tunnel widened to ten feet. Nick stopped as if he was listening, then turned and said, "We're at the end. No more talking. No lights. Let's go."

I could feel a breath of fresh night air as he slowly opened a hatch in the ceiling and climbed out. It appeared we were in the middle of a thick forest with heavy underbrush. Tim and Nevada quietly climbed out, motioning for us to stay put. They disappeared in the darkness. A few crickets were chirping and nearby I could hear the sound of water lapping gently against the shore. We waited for what seemed like another fifteen minutes, then Nick appeared out of nowhere, without making a sound. He tapped me on the shoulder and motioned to me to follow him. I quickly climbed out of the tunnel and turned to help Connie and Jim. Pudgy, for a man of his size, had no trouble getting out. Just by standing up he was half out. Holding hands we followed Nick through the trees and brush. Near the water, the terrain curved out slightly creating a small jetty that shielded us from the farm. Nestled into the bushes I made out the outline of a large black raft. It was covered with a netting of some kind and had been camouflaged with tree branches and brush. A large piece of driftwood was lashed to one side of the raft.

Tim grabbed a handle on the raft and pulled it toward us and motioned for us to get in. Drake positioned himself in the bow. Nick, Connie, Jim, Pudgy and I crouched behind him, while Tim and Nevada took the stern area. They gently pushed the raft, with the attached driftwood, out into the water. There was no moon and I couldn't see more than ten feet ahead. Drake put something on his head that looked like night vision goggles. Suddenly he raised a hand and everyone froze. "Boat coming."

After a moment I could hear an engine and suddenly saw a spotlight sweeping back and forth. The boat appeared to be coming from south of the farm, and headed in a northerly direction, monitoring the shoreline. It kept getting closer, its engine getting louder. We crouched as low as we could get in the raft, then the spotlight swept over us, hesitating for just a fraction of a second then moving on. Everyone breathed a sign of relief. Tim and Nevada put down their AK47's and picked up paddles and started softly paddling, first going south along the eastern shore of the inlet. As we approached the lights of Tracyton, they switched on a small outboard motor and turned west. A hundred yards or so off our port side, I could see the lights at Rocky Point. Several minutes later I could see some lights on shore, which I guessed were on Erlands Point. As we slowly circled the Point, Drake ordered the engine cut. The escorts, Tim and Nevada, picked up the paddles again and slowly brought us into Chico Bay. We followed the shoreline until we reached a dark isolated section of the bay. We paddled under some overhanging tree branches and tied the raft to a large branch.

We waited in the dark, hearing nothing but water lapping against the shore, and crickets chirping in the underbrush while Nick left to check out the seaplane. After about ten minutes, he returned and gave us a thumb's up.

We quickly walked along a dirt path to the dock where the seaplane was tied up. Jim hopped in first and started going over his pre-flight checklist while Nick stood on a pontoon helping everyone aboard.

Once we were all in place, Drake told Tim and Nevada to untie the seaplane and take the raft back for the next team. He then turned to the pilot and said, "Get this bird outa here fast!"

Jim turned the plane around facing the north and pulled the throttle. If only the commercial airlines could board, and takeoff so fast.

Drake pulled out his cell phone, punched in a number and said. "Eagle to Nest. Fledglings in the air. Coming home." Then he disconnected.

As we gained altitude, Drake ordered the pilot to fly in a large circle. Looking down we could see what appeared to be weapons fire coming from the area of the farm. Drake pointed, "Look—grenades. Those dumb shits, are using the grenade launchers on the cops. They're as good as dead. That's what the Feds have been waiting for. Now they can attack. See that heavy weapons fire on the left side of the farmhouse, now from the right. Those assholes don't have a chance. See, a fire has started in the barn. Now the farmhouse roof has caught fire. Man, look at that ground fire. There must be hundreds of cops pumping rounds into that house."

The sky started lighting up as the explosions went off giving the area an eerie, almost surreal, look.

Turning to Nick, Drake said, "That's what McCallum did. He set us up big time. We're just damn lucky we were on the first boat out. Hey, look down there. To the right. Out in the water."

I looked and saw what appeared to be the Coast Guard boat with its spotlight on the raft. Gunfire was going back and forth then as quickly as it started the firing stopped.

"Well, it looks like Tim and Nevada are gone too. Damn, they were good men. We're all going to miss them. If I had that double-crossing asshole McCallum here right now, I'd cut his guts out and dump his body out from ten thousand feet up so we could watch him go splat when he hit the ground. Let's get outa here. There's nothing left down there."

Chapter 35

Jim banked the plane to the north and started heading to Eagle's Nest. After a short time, Drake told him to alter his course heading to the northwest towards the Olympic Peninsula. The Peninsula is a vast wilderness area with the massive Olympic National Park and National Forest occupying most of the land mass. Finding a hideout in this area would not be easy. Although Temera had impressed me with her ability in finding the last hideout.

Finally, Jim started banking to the left, going into a slow circle. Drake punched a number into his cell phone and said, "Eagle to Nest. Activate strobe now."

Everyone was peering down into the darkness when the pilot said. "There. It's over there." He quickly adjusted his flight path and started dropping, then lined up on the strobe and went in for his landing. Once on the water, he followed the strobe light until a dock appeared. He cut the engine as the seaplane came to rest gently against the dock. A guard grabbed a rope and lashed a pontoon to a piling.

As we all climbed out of the seaplane, a guard said, "Colonel. I gotta call from Sergeant Craig. We're getting massacred back at the hideout. The fuckin' place is on fire and the Feds keep pourin' in the ammo, smoke and tear gas. Sergeant Craig said he was goin' try and run for it but didn't think he'd have a chance. Colonel, what happened?"

"We got problems. Let's get everyone inside for a briefing," said Drake.

Up from the dock, I could see a cabin with lights on inside. We followed a pathway made of sawdust and wood chips up to the cabin. It appeared to be a fairly large wood cabin with high beam ceilings and a large fireplace at one end. Drake motioned to Connie, Pudgy, Jim and me to take seats on the raised hearth. He motioned to Nick, and the guards named Otto and Hawk, to sit at the large oak table.

"Men, we were setup by General McCallum. He ordered me to do the attack on the gays, the black couple, the Seattle Times bombing and the kidnapping. Apparently, he had a spy planted among us who kept him informed of our nice little side business.

"We tried to evacuate before the Feds attacked but we only got our first group out. Tim and Nevada were ferrying the men from the tunnel to the other side of the inlet. But the Coast Guard got them before they could get anyone else out. We just lost a lot of very good men. From the air it looked like another Waco."

"A couple of men took the Humvees and some weapons from the barn earlier in the evening. I don't know if they made it yet. They headed south towards Tacoma. They'll be circling around the Peninsula and coming up through Hoquiam and Forks. So, if they haven't been caught they'll be here later tonight."

"How'd the Feds find us so fast, Colonel?" asked one of the men.

"According to the writer over there, they used a psychic and some remote viewers. And, they're damn good. I figure they'll find this location in a few days, too. So I have to make some decisions.

"Yesterday, we had three eight-man squads, plus me. Twenty-five total men. Mitch and Reamer killed each other fighting over the woman. I'm here. The three of you are here, and MAYBE two men will get here with the Humvees. That means we've got either four or six men left out of twenty-five. And, when the Feds realize we got out and have the hostages, they'll be right back on our trail. And, I still don't know who McCallum's spy is."

"Hey, Wolfe, I'm your brother you know it isn't me," said Otto, "and I'll stake my life on Nick and Hawk here. We're tight. And ain't no way they'd rat ya out. I don't know about the guys in the Humvees. Maybe it was one of the guys who didn't make it?"

"Otto, I know you, Nick and Hawk are with me. But stay alert in case the Humvees show up. I don't know which two guys are driving them. One of them could be a spy. Now I gotta make some calls and see what I can find out before I decide our survival strategy.

"Otto, you cover the hostages. Hawk, you go patrol the perimeter. Keep your eyes open for the Humvees. Hunter come with me."

I got up and followed Drake into a bedroom that had been set up as his office.

A simple portable folding desk was set up facing the door. He motioned me into a chair facing the desk while he took a seat behind the desk. He pulled out his cell phone and said. "Get a hold of the hotshot lawyer. What'd you say his name is?"

"Arnold P. Wexler."

"Okay. Get a hold of him."

"I don't have his number. Do you want me to call information?"

"Whatever. Just no tricks."

I dialed information, got the number and handed it to Drake. He dialed and got a voice mail greeting and hung up.

"I just got a fucking voice mail. Time's running out. His home phone must be unlisted. Any ideas how we can get it before the Feds find this place and turn it into another bonfire?"

"Yeah. I could call Wes Conners, he's the FBI Special Agent in charge of this case. I could lay out the details. Tell him the hostages are safe. Right now he probably thinks we're all dead and that he's about to get some heavy heat dumped on him by Washington, DC. Besides, he needs a few hours to clear things with the Attorney General on the immunity deal. It'll be cell phone to cell phone so there won't be a trace on the line."

"Okay. Do it. But no tricks. If I'm going to die, everyone up here goes with me. Got it?"

"Yeah, I got it. Don't worry—I want to live."

I quickly dialed the cell phone number for Wes.

"Conners," he answered in a stressed voice.

"Wes, it's Scott Hunter. We're okay. Connie, Pudgy, and Jim, the seaplane pilot. We're all alive. Drake's got a gun pointed at my head so listen carefully. Drake claims all the shit that's happened, the gay killings, the bomb, the Space Needle attack, the kidnapping, even the border killings were all ordered by McCallum in an attempt to set up Drake to take the fall. Drake wants to turn on McCallum in exchange for immunity. Federal Witness Protection, the whole bit."

"Does he have any hard proof? We've been trying to nail McCallum for ten years. He's slippery as Hell."

"Yes. He's got a backpack full of documentation—written orders, e-mails, even taped recordings of phone conversations. He wants to contact an attorney before he comes in. Can you get a hold of Arnold P. Wexler for us? I don't have his home number."

"Old Arnie Wexler, that slimy weasel. Yeah, hold on." I could hear him talking to someone nearby.

"I'll have it in a minute. I'm assuming you can't tell me where you are, but when will you be coming in?"

"Let me ask Drake."

"He's getting Wexler's number. When are we coming in?"

Drake grabbed the phone from my hand and said, "Conners this is Wolfe Drake. As soon as I talk to Wexler and you and he work out the deal with the Attorney General, we'll come in. The sooner the better. You got Wexler's number? Okay, I got it. We'll be in touch. No tricks."

He disconnected the phone and dialed Arnold P. Wexler's home number.

"Mr. Wexler, this is Wolfe Drake. I assume you've been watching TV and know who I am."

Pause.

"No, I'm very much alive however I could use a good lawyer. Are you available?"

Pause.

"Good. I want you to work out a plea bargain. In exchange for total immunity and relocation in the Federal Witness Protection Program, I will turn over enough incriminating evidence to convict Calvin C. McCallum, the national head of the Defenders of God, of several counts of murder and credit card fraud."

Pause.

"Yes. I have the evidence in my possession."

Pause.

"As soon as possible. Tomorrow morning at 9:00 AM would be perfect if you can get the deal worked out."

Pause.

"I'll bring four hostages with me. Also, I want the search called off for any of my remaining troops. They're small fry. The FBI wants McCallum badly. Get him and the whole organization goes down the drain. Call me the moment you get the deal worked out. I'm paying you, and you'll be getting massive press coverage. Call Wes Conners, the FBI Agent in charge. He's waiting for your call. Call me the moment we have a deal. I don't care if it's three in the morning." Drake gave Wexler his cell phone number and the cell phone number for Wes Connors and disconnected.

"Hunter, this had better work."

"What about your men?" I asked.

"I trust my brother Otto 100% and I'm 95% sure Nick and Hawk are okay. I'm not sure about the guys with the Humvees. If one of them is the fucking spy, we could be in trouble."

"Yeah, but what if they get pissed because you're getting immunity and they're not?"

"You heard what I said to that asshole lawyer. He'll get them to call off the search. They can just disappear into the woodwork, besides we got some extra cash from our business operations. I'll pay some bonuses."

I assumed he was referring to his drug trafficking business. I wondered if this hideout was the base for the drugs. Located in an isolated area yet near a major metropolitan area. Close to the Pacific Ocean, the Straits of Juan de Fuca, and the Canadian border. Heck, the Olympic Rain Forest was nearby. I wondered if pot would grow well there. The evergreens sure do. Oh well, I was sure Drake wasn't going to share any of his secrets of the trade with me. I just wanted to get home to Karen. I hoped she hadn't seen TV and assumed I died in the inferno at the hideout.

We could hear the sound of a cell phone ringing in the other room, and one of the guards answering, Drake got up and opened the door. "What's going on" he asked Hawk, the guard on the phone.

"It's the guys with the Humvees. It's Farley and Sanders. They made it. They're about ten miles out. They want to know if it's safe to come into the Nest."

"Hawk, tell 'em to use the green light for signaling. Flash twice, wait three seconds and repeat until we give them a solid green."

Hawk repeated the instructions and disconnected. Turning to Drake, he said, "I'll go get our green light and wait for 'em."

Drake disappeared back into his office and a few minutes later re-emerged wearing a black leather vest over fatigue shirt. Under the vest I could make out the harness for a shoulder holster. Since he already had his .45 in a holster on his right hip, he apparently had decided to add a backup weapon. A hunting knife was in a sheath built into his boots.

Soon we heard the sound of the Humvees pulling into the yard. The engines died, doors opened and shut and we heard some muffled conversation as the drivers were greeted by the guard.

Ron 'Razor' Farley was the first one through the door followed by Sanders, then Hawk.

Farley spoke first, "Colonel, what the fuck happened? We heard on the radio that the whole camp had been destroyed and everyone in it."

"That's about it. What you see here in this room is all that's left of DOG's west coast operations," said Drake. "I ordered an evacuation, but the Feds struck before we could get everyone out."

"Yeah, well I see the fucking hostages got out all right. They're alive and my buddies are all dead. That ain't right, Colonel. I say we kill these fuckers now." Farley turned towards all of us, pulling his .45 out of his holster. "They're the ones that got my buddies killed."

"Take it easy, Farley. Put your .45 away. We still need the hostages to get away. Once the Feds find out we slipped out they'll be after us again. We're going to have to split up and disappear. I'm disbanding DOG's west coast operations."

"Does General McCallum know?"

"You tell me? He seemed to know a lot about what we were doing. The old fart set us up big-time for the Feds."

"You blamin' the General? That ain't right. If it weren't for the General there wouldn't be no DOG. We can't run out on him. We're doin' God's work. We gotta drive the commie devils outa this country." Farley was getting agitated. His eyes started darting around the room frantically. "Ain't that right, Sanders?"

"Shit man, we're outnumbered. It's time to throw in the towel and split," said Sanders.

"NO. Damn it," screamed Farley. "We ain't runnin'. We got God Almighty on our side." Before anyone could react Farley pulled his gun and ordered everyone to drop their weapons. I could see Drake thinking about going for his vest gun, but he decided against it. He pulled his gun out of the hip holster hoping Farley wouldn't spot the shoulder holster. It didn't work. "Colonel, drop the shoulder gun too, and the knife in your boot. Nice and slow. No tricks."

"General McCallum told me you was a traitor, Colonel. Said you don't care about God. Said all you want is money. You out buying drugs from wetbacks and sellin' them to Americans. Gettin' our youth addicted so there ain't no way they can tell right from wrong. We're bein' overrun by wetbacks, gooks, niggers, and now even the damned commies are comin' here to America since we won the fuckin' cold war. Seems more than half the damned cabbies don't even speak American. Fucking foreigners are taking our beautiful country away from us."

Farley backed against a wall where he had a commanding view of everyone. "Okay, who's with me and General McCallum? Who wants to fight to protect America from traitors? What about you, Sanders?"

"Hey man, just relax. We all had a rough day. We all want a better America."

"Look, Farley," said Drake, in a soothing voice, "I want to split up the money we've got here so every man gets enough to get away safely. You get $50,000. That's enough to get you back to Mississippi. If you decide not to keep all the money you can give it to General McCallum to further the fight against the enemies of DOG. How's that sound?"

"Fuck you, Colonel. You think I'm some kinda fucking Judas? That I would betray Jesus Christ our Lord for some gold or silver? God speaks through General McCallum and he said you are evil and you must perish for your sins against God. And that goes for the rest of you fuckin' heathens. If you sin against God, you must die.

"Sanders, are you with me or not?"

"Hey man. You know we're buddies."

"Are you ready to kill the enemies of God with me?"

"Yeah, you know. What ya got in mind?"

"First, we kill the Jap bitch. You, the fat-ass biker. Yeah you. Stoke the fire up and get that poker red-hot. Before she meets the devil, we're going to give her a little taste of what's in store for her in Hell."

Connie squirmed uneasily as Pudgy slowly got up and moved over to the huge fireplace. He carefully added some logs to the crackling fire. Then he placed the poker in the center of the fire.

"Sanders, do you wanta do the honors on the Jap? I was thinkin' ah writing D-O-G on her chest with the poker. Whata ya think?"

"No, you go ahead. It was your idea. I wanta save myself for Drake."

"Hey, lard-ass, is the poker ready?"

"Yeah, I think so," said Pudgy bending over and reaching in to check and see if the poker was red-hot or not. I noticed from my angle that Pudgy quickly used the hook on the end of the poker to pull the damper shut.

"Yeah. It's good and ready."

Farley, motioned with his gun for everyone else to move so he could still keep them in his line of sight as he moved towards Connie. He reached down and yanked her to her feet. "Okay, bitch, take off your clothes."

Connie hesitated and started shaking in fear, dreading the thought of being burned by a red-hot poker. Farley smacked her across her face. Fighting back tears she started to slowly unbutton her fatigue shirt.

"Damn it's gettin' smoky in here," Farley said while coughing.

"Maybe I put on too much wood. It should be okay in a minute," said Pudgy.

As Connie continued unbuttoning the shirt I could see that she had somehow regained her composure and was no longer playing victim. She was ready to fight back. Before Farley realized what was happening she reached one hand inside her shirt and pulled out the tiny canister of Mace and sprayed it at point-blank range directly at his face. Screaming in pain, he waved his gun wildly around in the air squeezing off two rounds. Pudgy spun around with the red-hot poker and drove it point first into Farley's chest. Farley staggered backwards and with a coughing last gasp of breath, collapsed into a heap, smelling of seared flesh. By now the room was filled with smoke. Pudgy placed one massive booted foot on Farley's chest and yanked out the bloody poker, then turned and reopened the damper. Otto, Drake's brother, had an UZI aimed at everyone except Drake.

"Whew, I was hoping we could disband in a more amicable manner," said Drake. "But at least we know who the spy was. Now, if there's anyone else who disagrees with my plan, now would be the time to step forward. No one? Good."

Drake whispered to his brother, who immediately left the room while Drake motioned for the other two DOG members to have a seat at the table.

"Listen up, men, here's the plan. Nick, Hawk, Sanders—each of you get $50,000 plus take half of the merchandise in the shed and split it up between the three of you. The three of you get one of the Humvees. My brother will take the other.

Otto returned with three paper bags with rubber bands around them. He dumped them on the table and nodded to Drake. "I checked the merchandise. We got about two hundred pounds. Plus a shit load of weapons and ammo."

"Okay, Nick? Hawk? Sanders? Here's $50,000 each. Plus load one hundred pounds in your Humvee. Take as much ammo and weapons as you can load. Bury anything that's left. You have enough to set yourselves up in business somewhere. Best bet is to pack up now, then grab a few hours sleep and head out before dawn. Don't tell any of us where you're going. Just disappear. Is that okay with you guys?

"Well, yeah, man. It's great. Hell we might just up and sell off everything and go straight. After seein' what happened back at the hideout—shit man—maybe go to one of them trade schools and learn computers. Hey, now those computer dudes make a bundle and don't have the fucking Feds chasing 'em either.

"What you gonna do, Colonel?"

"I'm gonna try and work out a deal with the Feds so you boys can get away. McCallum sold us out to the Feds so I think it's only fair to pay him back. If they stick me in prison, I'll be dead in a week, but if the Feds will deal, Otto and I will move somewhere and start over. It's kind of risky but I don't see as I have much choice."

"Colonel, sir, all I can say is you got guts. Standin' up to Mc-Callum and all. What I hear, he's one mean son of a bitch"

"Thanks. You men better start packing."

Nick, Hawk and Sanders picked up their respective bags of cash and headed out to pack. Drake turned to his brother and said, "Otto, go with them. Take a few weapons, only legal stuff, and a little ammo, and make sure they're all okay with the deal. We'll have to sleep in shifts and keep an eye on them until they leave. I don't want one of them getting greedy and deciding to take everything when we're sound asleep."

"No problem, Wolfe," said Otto as he got up to follow the others outside.

"Now," said Drake, turning to face us, "the same rules apply. I hope no one is stupid enough to try anything funny. If everything goes according to plan, you'll all be back with your loved ones at 9:00 AM. Go and grab some mattresses and bedding from the bedrooms. Everyone sleeps here in the main room on the floor where we can keep an eye on you. If you need the toilet, either me or Otto goes with you. That applies to you as well Miss Kamura."

Chapter 36

By now, as the hour grew late, everyone was too drained from the roller coaster events of the day to even consider escape. Sleep was all we craved. We dragged mattresses and blankets out of the adjoining bedrooms and spread them around the room. Within minutes of laying down I faded away. I slept like a rock until I was jolted awake by the sound of a cell phone ringing.

I heard Drake talking to someone who I presumed was Arnold P. Wexler. My watch said 2:45 AM.

"Good. Good."

Pause.

"Yes, I have proof of that."

Pause.

"Yes, tapes and signed orders."

Pause.

"Yes. What about the media? Do they know the hostages are alive?"

Pause.

"Good. I thought so. That'll keep the pressure on the Feds and keep them from backing out of the deal."

Pause.

"What are the Feds going to do about McCallum?"

Pause.

"They did? Already. That was fast. Good."

Pause.

"We'll be at the Seattle Seaplane dock on Lake Union at exactly 9:00 AM. Make sure the media is there. I want cameras rolling so there's no double-cross. Make sure they don't stick me in some jail holding cell. I need to have protection and be hidden in some place like the Westin Hotel—in a nice suite."

Pause.

"That's right. Great job. I'll call you when we're thirty minutes out. You've earned your money, Mr. Wexler."

Some of the others were awakened by the phone call. I heard Nick, Hawk and Sanders decide to get up and get ready to take-off. Still exhausted, I fell back asleep. By the time Pudgy nudged me awake it was 6:30 AM. Nick, Hawk and Sanders were gone. Otto was packing his gear. It was agreed that Connie and I would handle breakfast. Fortunately, the place was well stocked. Fresh ranch eggs, a huge slab of lean bacon, several pounds of sausage, pancake mix, English muffins, jam, genuine New England Maple syrup, real butter and several pounds of Starbuck's coffee.

The stove was an old-fashioned wood-burning, cast iron model. Connie directed me to crack open the eggs and scramble them. Unfortunately, my egg cracking skills are not equal to my keystroking. After my sixth egg, Connie took a look at my handiwork and screamed, "Scott, for God's sake, you're ruining the eggs." I looked down into the cast iron skillet and saw little chunks of egg shell floating among the yokes and whites.

Pudgy appeared out of nowhere and said, "Hey dipshit, give me that. I ain't eating no friggin' shells in my eggs. Go see if you can figure out how to set the table. Plates up in that cupboard. Forks in that drawer."

"What about napkins," I asked.

Pudgy roared like a bull and started laughing so hard tears came into his eyes. "Hunter wants napkins. Jesus Christ. Hunter, you're too friggin' much. Napkins! Everyone burst out laughing. I could feel the flush as my face turned beet-red with embarrassment. After grabbing a stack of plates and utensils, I set the table quickly and busied myself picking up mattresses and blankets until the breakfast was ready to eat.

To get everyone's mind off my limited kitchen skills, I turned to Drake and said, "Colonel, Wexler's call woke me this morning. What's the word on McCallum?"

"The Feds nabbed him back in Mississippi around 4:30 in the morning. Dragged him out of bed, cuffed him and hauled him off to jail in his pajamas. He was screaming like a stuck pig—babbling about the Constitution and separation of Church and State. By now, they're swarming all over his office grabbing every scrap of paper and computer file. Most of his key men are behind bars too. All they need now is the information I'm turning over in a few hours."

"Colonel," said Connie, "what are the chances of an exclusive interview? We have a little time left. It could help make sure the public sentiment backs you instead of McCallum."

Connie's professionalism amazed me. She had endured a bomb threat, kidnapping, attempted rape and torture with a red-hot poker to be followed by execution, and now she was bouncing back from the horrible terror she had been subjected to and was seizing the moment to grab an exclusive story from the leader of DOG's west coast operations. She was one gutsy lady who deserved the Pulitzer Award.

Drake thought about her remarks for a moment and said, "Yeah. Why not? I can get the facts out before his spin people start smearing me in the media."

"Great," responded Connie, grabbing a pad of paper and a pen and moving her place at the table so she was sitting directly opposite Drake.

"First, tell me a little background information about yourself Colonel. Is Wolfe Drake your real name?"

"Yes, it is. My mother was German and my father was English. Drake means dragon. I'm forty-five. My brother, Otto, who you know, is two years older. Otto and I were raised in a very strict religious household. Discipline, usually in the form of beating with a leather shaving strap, was a daily routine. I got excellent grades in high school and was good in sports. At eighteen I was so glad to get away from home that I joined the Army. The war in Viet Nam was just coming to a close but I got in on some combat duty. I went to OCS and became a Second Lieutenant. Served in an Infantry outfit then got transferred to Military Intelligence. By the time the Gulf War rolled around, I was a Major in Intelligence. After I hit the twenty year mark, I decided it was time to try the civilian world.

"By that time, Otto was running a small painting business in Mississippi. I wasn't sure what I wanted to do so I worked with him for awhile—as a painter. What a crappy job. Breathing toxic fumes all day.

"One night, we're having a beer in some joint and in comes ol' man McCallum. He starts talking about Affirmative Action and...let's see...how'd he put it? 'The damn commies have taken over the country. Nowadays a good, hard-working, God-fearing, white man can't even get a decent job. They give niggers all the good jobs even if they flunk the tests.'

"Well, at the time, I hadn't been able to get a decent job. Twenty years in the Army doesn't always train you for a lot on the outside. I'd worked around plenty of blacks and other minorities in the service and didn't have any real problems with them, but I started listening to McCallum and believing him. He's one of them old-fashioned hell and brimstone preacher types.

"Next thing you know, he's standing on a wooden soda pop crate next to the bar, just screaming at the crowd. He attacked the government, Jews, blacks, Asians, communists, you name it—he had a list a mile long. The crowd was with him and the booze was flowing. If some minority would have walked into the place, he would've been stomped to death in a minute.

"After about a half-hour of working the crowd up to a frenzy, he demands to know who was with him and who wasn't. Only the way he presented the choice it was more like you're either with him or against him. He wanted to know who was ready to join his army, called the Defenders of God, to drive Satan out of America.

"Most of us raised our hands. Next thing you know some guys start circulating through the crowd passing out a sign-up sheet and directions to his headquarters. Otto and I signed up and took a flyer. We were both sick of smelling paint fumes.

"Next morning we had a small painting job to finish up so we did, then after we cleaned up we decided to check out his operation. He was located on the outskirts of Vicksburg, Mississippi, on a large estate with a security fence around it. A guard wearing military fatigues was on duty at the gate. The estate was hundreds of acres in size with several buildings.

"We were taken to an Orientation Building where we filled out some paperwork then we went to a Recruiter. The pay wasn't much but board and room was included and it seemed a lot like the good old U.S. Army. We had three days to wrap up our personal affairs then report for duty.

"The first day McCallum called me into his office. He was sitting behind this huge oak desk with an American flag on one side and his own, the Defenders of God flag on the other side. He points to the American flag and says 'That's half of what we are defending. The United States of America, from all invaders and traitors, both foreign and domestic.' Then pointing to the other flag, which had a white background with a large red cross with a gold shield on the cross, he said 'This is the other half. God. We are all God-fearing Christians defending His Almighty Word against all the atheists and false religions in the world.'

McCallum had on a dress uniform covered with medals. He recited his impressive military history, saying it ended in Viet Nam when, as he put it, 'Some uppity niggers accused him of giving them all the tough assignments. Imagine that. Any real American patriot wouldn't question a senior officer's order, or they'd be shot for insubordination. I tried to keep my true red-blooded Americans together and put the niggers and other trash in their own units. And, of course, more of them got killed. Hell the original version of the United States Constitution clearly states a nigger's only worth $3/5$ of what a white man is worth. So, ah course more ah them is gonna get killed—they ain't worth as much. So, just because a bunch of near worthless niggers up and get themselves killed, I get forced out of the army. Hell, I was next in line to be a General. The damn Jews, niggers and commies have even taken over the U.S. Army.'

"He pointed to the stars on his shoulder, four on each side, and said 'So I left the bastards and formed my own army. God came to me and appointed me four star General. God promised me the fifth star when I have defeated all the heathens in the world.'

"He rambled on for awhile then told me he had looked over my application and was impressed. He said most of his men only had a few years of experience as enlisted men. They were loyal but lacked the leadership skills he needed.

"McCallum got up and went over to a map of the United States and pointed to Mississippi. 'Here we are. Two hundred men.' He pointed to Maine. 'We have twenty-five men up here.' He pointed to Texas. 'Nearly a hundred down here and growin' fast.' Moving his pointer up to Montana, he said, 'close to seventy-five. Now that's give-or-take four hundred red-blooded American boys willing to lay down their lives to protect our beautiful country and defend the Word of God. But tell me there, Mr. Wolfe Drake, since you is an experienced military intelligence man, where's my weakest point?'

"I said, General, that all depends on your mission. You know that. If you're trying to disperse your troops to make your army less vulnerable, you've done a good job of dispersal. If you want to be near pockets of likely sympathizers you've picked good areas to start. It would be smart if each unit was trained to function as quasi-independent guerrillas, targeting local objectives. Basic strategies and routine intelligence could easily be shared via encryption over the internet. But I don't see any units in the major media centers. Public relations is nowadays a big part of winning a war. Asians are entering the west coast in droves from Vancouver, British Columbia to Los Angeles. You have a unit in Texas, but millions of Mexicans are crossing the California border too. A lot of angry whites are losing jobs to the foreigners. You could recruit a lot of them.

"Hell, isolated down here in Mississippi, no one knows you exist. Until the other night, I didn't know you existed.

"Another problem you'll have if you don't already, is funding or financing. It costs a lot of money to house, feed, train, and equip an army. And I know you don't have a grant from the federal government."

"McCallum smiled at the mention of financing the operation and said, 'Well now it seems we've found a way to raise money. At least enough to keep us growin'. What I need Mr. Drake is for some smart young man like yourself to head up my west coast operations. Ya know what I mean. Start it from the ground up.'

"Then McCallum comes over to me, looks me in the face, and asks, 'Are you the man, Mr. Drake?'

"I didn't know what to think. I had enjoyed being a Major in the army and getting all the extra perks and respect that went with the rank. It sure as Hell was a lot better than life as a house painter. So, I said yes."

Drake had just confirmed what Mike had told us. Drake is clearly a Young Soul acting like a Baby Soul. The key difference is he was raised by Baby Soul parents to have Baby Soul values, and he even chose a Baby Soul profession—the Army—but deep in his heart he was a Young Soul. He wanted power and money. Had McCallum understood the different Soul Profiles, he could have prevented, or delayed, his downfall.

Connie spoke, "How did you recruit members?"

"That was easy. McCallum set me up with six of his most experienced troopers, guys who were all zealots and believed 100% in his cause. I had decided to locate in the Pacific Northwest, particularly close to Seattle because of the heavy concentration of military bases. Hell, look at the Seattle-Tacoma area. All the air bases, naval bases, army, coast guard. It's a gold mine for prospecting. And the perfect age. The older a person gets the more likely they are to challenge what they're told. Someone seventeen to early twenties, tends to believe what their parents taught them. Their minds are a lot more malleable. After a tour of duty in the military, they're ripe to be recruited.

"The men McCallum assigned to me found recruiting a breeze. About 95% of the recruits were 100% believers."

"Let's talk about 'Operation Chili Dip' where your men were required to kill illegal aliens crossing the U.S.-Mexican border." said Connie.

"That was one of McCallum's craziest ideas. The paranoid old bastard thought someone might have infiltrated my group—it had happened to him a few times in other areas—so he set up a loyalty test. Kill someone to prove you're one of us. Street gangs do it a lot. Sort of a rite of initiation. I argued with him that it was too risky, but he said most true Americans would be glad to get rid of some wetbacks. I got worried he would turn on me so I carried out his orders."

"You ordered your men to kill innocent, unarmed people, just because they were crossing the border illegally?" asked Connie, shaking her head in disbelief.

"Yes, I did. Those were my orders."

"Did you personally kill one of them?"

"I don't think so. As the leader, I felt I had to take the first shot. I'm an excellent marksman, so I aimed for the shoulder of an alien about one hundred yards away from our location. We heard a scream and he dropped. My men thought I had made a kill. Over a three month period, we executed over twenty-five illegals."

"How did you feel, Colonel?"

"Sick to my stomach. The men—most of them—got a kick out of it. After all their military training, a lot of them were hungry for real action."

"There was an attack on two gay men on Capitol Hill in Seattle. The FBI believed your men were responsible. Were they?"

"Yes. McCallum was looking for some kind of an incident to stir up trouble with the gay community. He felt they were getting 'too cocky' no pun intended, and wanted to create fear. All the various DOG units around the country were on the lookout for opportunities. Since Seattle has a large gay population, it was only natural that we would have the best chance. My orders were to find some gays and rough them up, but no killing.

"As it turned out, Reamer and Ernie got a little too enthusiastic. Their zealousness forced me to pull back from some merchandising activities I was working on and more or less go into hiding. The FBI was swarming all around us. Things were getting pretty hot."

"When you say merchandising activities are you referring to your drug dealing?" asked Connie.

"According to my attorney, Mr. Wexler, that's not a subject open for discussion. Let's just say I had developed alternative sources of revenue that involved multi-level marketing."

Connie persisted, "Do you mean like Amway?"

Drake burst out laughing at the thought of his thugs selling Amway products. "No, and it wasn't Avon or Mary Kay either. Let's just say I discovered some opportunities to supply goods that were in high demand by a certain large segment of the population. McCallum did not approve so I tried to keep it low-key. I wanted him to think all we were doing was the credit card scam he favored."

"Tell me more about that," said Connie.

"McCallum hated Jews. Claimed they controlled the world's banking system and were slowly taking all the money from the pockets of the poor hard-working Americans. He figured that by ripping off the credit card industry he was directly attacking the Jews of the world. So we would steal credit cards or get credit card numbers from insiders working in retail establishments. We would funnel the cards or numbers to McCallum. He has a complex international scam that rakes in millions by running up illegal charges, transferring money back and forth between cards, doing cash advances, whatever. I don't know all the details, I just followed orders. My unit would get a monthly report on how much we made. I did just enough to look like a team player."

"Now, getting close to home," said Connie, "Why did you try to kill me with a bomb? You nearly succeeded and some of my closest friends were injured."

"Nothing personal, I assure you Ms. Kamura. McCallum gets newspapers from all over the country. He even subscribes to a news article clipping service. He gets a copy of any article written about hate groups, or right-wing militia or right-wing Christian groups. The man has an unbelievable file system set up and an enemies' list of people who write the articles.

"Every week a new, updated 'Top 100 Enemies of the Defenders of God' list goes out to all regions. Your name was at the head of the list. Rewards are given to units that silence those critics. Any soldier who kills a 'Top 100 Enemy' gets a promotion, a $5,000 reward and a week of R & R—all expenses paid. Almost every man in my unit wanted to go after you.

"I felt, at the time, that it would draw too much attention to us so I ordered my men to put the idea on hold until the gay attack died down. Unfortunately, Otto and I had to go to Northern California to complete a large merchandise transaction and while we were gone, two of my men, Sergeant Reamer and Private Tony Amado, decided to go ahead. Fortunately, the timing was off and you survived.

"The kidnapping was a direct order from McCallum. He was testing my loyalty. If I refused his direct order, he probably would've had his spy, Ray Farley, kill me when I wasn't looking.

I knew the kidnapping would bring in the Feds. That's when I knew for sure he was setting me up to take a fall and become a martyr for the cause."

"Are you prepared to turn yourself in?" asked Connie.

"I don't see as where I have much choice. Otto and I were planning on taking off and leaving the country. But eventually the money would've run out and we would always be worried about extradition or some over-zealous bounty hunter showing up. This plan makes a lot more sense. But it's now time to get ready to meet the world."

Chapter 37

We all looked horrible. No showers, no shaves, no clean clothes. But at least we were alive and headed home. By now I knew that Karen had been told I was alive—that was a huge weight lifted off my mind.

One last look around at the 'Nest.' It could have been the spot where I died if Ray 'Razor' Farley got his wish. The number of close misses was more than enough for a lifetime. In the movies, close brushes with death are frequent, but in real life, I felt I had exceeded my quota for the next three lifetimes.

Pudgy put out the fire and we all headed down to the dock and boarded the seaplane. Drake sat in the front next to the pilot while Connie, Pudgy and I were in the back. Otto remained behind on the dock and tossed us the docking rope. Jim looked relieved when the engine took hold on the first try. After a quick check revealed that no boats were in the way, he turned the plane into the wind and opened the throttle. We started bouncing along on the water as we gained speed, finally he pulled back on the yoke and we were airborne. As we gained altitude Jim turned to an easterly heading into a rising sun fighting to break through the light morning cloud bank that covered the Puget Sound region.

After about ten or fifteen minutes, the pilot called his base and alerted those on the ground that we were about thirty minutes out.

Drake picked up his cell phone and called Wexler. "Mr. Wexler, Wolfe Drake here. How's everything on the ground?"

Pause.

"Good. Very good. We should be touching down in less than thirty minutes. I'll be looking forward to meeting you. Good bye." He disconnected and stared out the window deep in thought. Here was a Young Soul escaping with his life from Baby Souls, who would just as soon rip him to shreds. He was just following his Young Soul instincts of wanting power and money, not realizing that the true Baby Souls believed the dogma they spouted. To them it was a religion—not just a way to make money.

The silhouette of Seattle loomed dead ahead. The world renown Space Needle, barely visible through the cloud layer, told me we were almost there. Jim brought the seaplane around for a landing from the south heading north. The landing was uneventful. We taxied slowly toward the Seattle Seaplane dock where we could see the flashing lights on the police and emergency vehicles. The media and their satellite trucks were stationed up the steep hill behind the seaplane dock. Standing on the dock was Wes Conners and a dapper looking gentlemen with flowing white hair. Undoubtedly, Arnold P. Wexler. Behind them fifteen to twenty feet were several FBI agents and Seattle Police—all holding various kinds of weapons. Two helicopters from competing television stations buzzed over head jockeying for the best camera angle.

As we approached the dock, Drake opened the door and tossed the line to one of Jim's dockside assistants. Then Drake stepped out, pausing for an instant to slowly sweep the crowd with his eyes—soaking in the high drama of the moment. With a dramatic flourish, he saluted the crowd, crisply bringing his hand up to the edge of his black beret. Dropping his arm he walked up to Wexler and said, "Arnold P. Wexler, I presume?"

Wexler, with a huge smile on his face said, "Yes. And am I correct in assuming you are my new client, Wolfe Drake?"

"That is correct."

Wexler turned to Wes Conners and said, "Mr. Conners, per our agreement, my client, Mr. Wolfe Drake hereby surrenders to the FBI."

Tyrone Willis stepped forward and applied handcuffs to Drake, grabbed him by the elbow, and led him away with Wexler walking along side cautioning Drake not to say anything unless he was present.

I hopped out, then turned and took Connie's hand and helped her step from the pontoon onto the dock. A roar of applause went up when she was spotted. Pudgy emerged, but stayed in the background while the crowd was focusing on Connie. Lastly, Jim stepped out and waved to the crowd.

Wes, restrained by the formality of the moment just shook hands with us, quickly introducing himself to Jim, the pilot.

"Damn. Am I ever glad to see all of you. I was afraid when the shooting started over at Dyes Inlet that you were all killed.

"Lee Chou, Karen and Mike are waiting in my car. After you say hello, we need to get all of you downtown for debriefing. What about injuries? Anyone need medical attention?" Wes asked while pointing to the paramedic trucks with flashing lights.

"Hell no," said Pudgy. "all I want is a six-pack of beer and a long hot bath."

"Sounds good to me," I said.

"Me too," said Connie, "but first, Wes, I need to get an exclusive interview I did with Wolfe Drake to my editor at the Times."

"No problem. I think he's waiting back near my car. Is everyone ready for the media?"

"Oh my God. I look like a mess," said Connie. "Scott, do you think Karen will have any makeup?"

"Are you kidding? Of course she will, but it'll make you look a little pale," I laughed.

As we strolled towards Conner's unmarked car, Karen, Lee Chou, Temera, and Mike all jumped out and everyone started racing towards each other. Karen and I rushed into each other's arms and gave a big hug while the tears streamed down our faces. There wasn't a dry eye in sight. We all understood how close we had come to being killed. It made me feel even closer to Karen than I had dreamed possible. Finally, when we broke off our long embrace, I hugged Lee Chou, Temera, and Mike. Tears were streaming down the old man's cheeks.

The next few minutes were a blur. The four ex-hostages and loved ones were loaded into three FBI cars and we slowly started driving through the media crowd. I had never seen anything like it. There were over a dozen different radio and television stations present plus what seemed like a hundred journalists and photographers. Everyone was pushing and shoving—jockeying for the best vantage point. The police were shoving people back from the vehicles and clearing a path. Finally, we were on Eastlake Avenue and able to escape the hordes.

Downtown, at the FBI headquarters, enterprising reporters and camera crews had already gathered. As we emerged from the vehicles, we were hit with another barrage of blinding flashes from cameras. Scores of microphones were shoved in our faces and question after question were yelled at us. Mostly I just smiled and shrugged my shoulders, sometimes using the old Ronald Reagan trick of pretending I couldn't hear the question.

Once inside and past the reception area, we found quiet. What a relief. I was not cut out to be a rock star if this is what they have to put up with on a regular basis.

Each of us went off to a separate room for our debriefing. Tyrone debriefed me and was kind enough to let Karen stay in the room. After about two hours, he finally said he had enough for the time being. Thank God.

Ty led us to a back corridor where we caught the private elevator to the garage. An FBI Agent named Rogers drove us to Lynnwood and offered to stay around for awhile, but I felt we were safe and so far the media didn't know where we lived.

Once inside, with the door securely locked, I headed upstairs to the master bedroom and adjacent bathroom. I peeled off my grimy clothes and hopped into the shower. Amazing how nice soap and shampoo feel after you've gone a few days without them. By the time I had finished shaving and brushing my teeth, I could hear the beginning melody of the Carpenter's song, *Close to You*, coming from the bedroom.

I slipped on my robe and opened the door. Karen had dimmed the lights, lit several candles, and stood, dressed in a stunning black nightgown, holding two glasses of champagne. As our bodies moved towards one another, I could see nothing but pure love radiating from her eyes—I know that's what I was projecting to her from my spirit as well. Coming close to prematurely losing someone you love deeply hurts—even if you intellectually know he/she is still alive in spirit form.

I took one of the glasses of champagne, raised it and said, "To love, today, tomorrow and for eternity." We both sipped the chilled bubbly. Then Karen gently took my glass and hers and placed them on the night stand. She reached her arms upward, around my neck and pulled our bodies together. A rush of white hot passion swept over me as I felt her breasts brush gently against my chest. My hands found her waist and gently moved downward floating over her firm hips. I could feel the energy between us intensifying.

My hands went up her neck around her ears and through her hair. We looked in each others eyes—not at Karen or Scott—but seeing the purity of our two souls coming together. We were in another time and place. Deep back into a past life. Two distant lovers reconnected together on Planet Earth. Our bodies quivered as a wave of orgasms swept over us. Floating in a timeless void, we continued our lovemaking. There was no hurry. We flitted from past lifetime to past lifetime. We would look in each other's eyes and then through touch and intensity recall how we had made love in those past lifetimes.

I awoke hours later. Still in bed, Karen had turned on the news. Needless to say, I was part of the big story of the day. Connie was clearly the star of the media frenzy and she was clearly handling it like the consummate professional that she is. She gave credit to all the people involved and promised that she would have a series of articles exploring all aspects of the conflict.

She used the situation to give my book some great plugs and, judging by the media's appetite for more details about the entire story, I knew it was only a matter of a day or so before I would have a dozen microphones shoved in my face and a crowd of hungry reporters pelting me with questions—hoping I was capable of delivering a slew of crisp sound bites.

I turned to Karen and said, "Honey, do you remember that initial order I placed for twenty five hundred copies of my book?"

"Yeah, you mean with the print-on-demand publisher?"

"Right. Any word on the delivery of the first one hundred?"

"I forgot during all the excitement. There's a copy over there on the dresser. They were delivered here the day you were captured. I didn't know what to do with them so I had all but one of them stacked in the basement storage room."

Excitedly, I jumped up and went over to the dresser. There it was, a printed copy of my book. I picked it up and just stared at it for a minute, flashing back on all the events that had transpired in the process of getting it written. A feeling of pride swept over me. It was by far the hardest job of writing I had ever done.

"This is great! I'm sure with all the publicity there will be a demand for copies before we can get an agent and publisher to handle a big enough run for a national rollout.

"Oh, Scott, while you were sleeping, Lee Chou called. Everyone is getting together at their place at 6:00 PM. No reporters—just the people closest to the whole situation."

"That's great. I've had my rest and a wonderful welcome home from my beautiful wife so it only makes sense to end my hibernation and get ready for the next step in this saga. It's amazing how much ground we've covered just since late-March when I first met Mike."

Chapter 38

Later, at 6:02 PM to be precise, Karen and I walked into Pudgy's and Lee Chou's home. Hugs and more hugs accompanied with an outpouring of tears from everyone turned the get-together into an impromptu therapy session. Each person retold his or her part of the event, filling in many of the details the others were not aware of.

Temera scolded Wes and Ty for ignoring her clues and wasting time searching up in Snohomish county. I gave her another hug and told her she saved the day and had it been necessary she would've easily found the Eagle's Nest hideout.

Mike had, as I had correctly guessed, spotted the seaplane getting captured by Drake's men. He immediately called Wes and convinced him to shift the search to Dyes Inlet. Temera had been so accurate that it only took an hour to narrow the search down to the correct farmhouse. Also, during the entire crisis she kept everyone's spirits high when she kept insisting that we were all alive.

Wes apologized for the FBI spending so much time searching the wrong area. He said he pushed hard for going with Temera's clues but his more cautious superiors decided to take the more traditional approach and follow their clues.

I asked Wes why they had attacked the farmhouse so quickly since it appeared reasonable to assume that it would quickly go up in flames—with all of us in it.

Wes, turning very serious, said, "I feared that would happen. But by the time we barely had the farmhouse surrounded,

DOG started shooting. And, as you know, there are lots of homes nearby. The chance for civilian casualties from a stray round or two was quite high. Two of our men took hits—both minor wounds, but the situation was clearly going to be resolved by firepower not diplomacy.

"As we sifted through the ashes I dreaded finding any of your bodies. The thought of how I'd live with the memory haunted me. Temera kept saying you were alive but I must confess I had my doubts. When we didn't find your remains, I felt better, but until I got Drake's call I wasn't a complete believer."

Later, as we started relaxing and splintering off into smaller groups, I found myself sitting alone in the back yard with Connie.

"Scott, I want to thank you. If you hadn't gotten captured who knows what would have happened to me. Some of those creeps are pretty scary, but once you and Pudgy arrived I knew that somehow we'd figure a way out."

"Well, Connie, Pudgy deserves most of the credit for keeping us alive during captivity." I said.

"I know, Scott, but most important in dealing with DOG psychologically was your ability to make use of Mike's assessment of their Soul Ages and Soul Profiles. The Baby Souls acted like Baby Souls and the Young Souls acted like Young Souls. By your knowing this information you were able to understand what to expect from each group and how to best communicate with them."

"Thank you, Connie. Mike's teachings were correct. Thank God Drake was a Young Soul. If we had been dealing with Mc-Callum, we might not have been so lucky. What's next?"

"You better get ready, Scott—whether you want it or not, you're about to become a star of the media."

"You mean the time for my fifteen minutes of fame has arrived?"

"That's right. Only it might last longer than the proverbial fifteen minutes. "

"Connie, I'm an Old Soul—fame in and of itself means nothing—but I do have an important message—actually our friend Mike's message—to share, so whatever degree of fame is necessary to get his message out to the world, then I'm willing to play along. But if you ever see me starting to believe any of the hype and getting a swelled head, just remind me that I'm the world's worst cook, and not someone to be trusted preparing scrambled eggs."

Pudgy strolled over, catching the last bit of our conversation. "Ain't that the damned truth. Hunter, it's a good thing you got a smart talented wife because on your own you'd starve to death."

I knew staying humble would not be a problem.

"Scott, the next few days are going to be pretty intense," said Connie. The national, as well as the local media, have tons of questions. I've already given them lots of the kidnapping details and the events leading up to it, including the attack on the gays, the black couple, and the bombing at the Times.

"Just focus on your message—reincarnation, karma, as well as understanding each other's Soul Age and Soul Profiles. Once everyone understands that we all play all of the roles we will become more tolerant. Just imagine when the red-neck white male discovers that he has been black in several past lives and the urban black male, with a chip on his shoulder, realizes he has been white and might even have been a member of the Ku Klux Klan in his last lifetime."

By 10:00 PM everyone was ready to call it a day. Karen and I said our good-byes, hopped in the Lexus and headed home for a good night's sleep, ready to tackle whatever came next.

On the way home Karen broke out in tears and started sobbing. "Oh, Scott, I was so scared that I had lost you. If Temera hadn't kept saying you were alive I think I would have cracked up. I felt so helpless."

"Sweetheart, I'm so sorry you had to go through the agony of not knowing. At times I think I was better off because I knew exactly what was happening." I reached over and grabbed her left hand and held it for the rest of the trip on the freeway.

At 7:30 the next morning the phone startled me awake. Karen was already up and picked up the phone downstairs. I heard her talking excitedly as she came up the stairs holding one of our cordless phones. "I'll wake him up and tell him. He'll be excited to hear the news." Seeing that I was already awake, she said, "Oh, he's awake. I'll let you tell him. Here, Scott, take the phone, it's Debbie Windsor."

When I first wake up I'm always a little groggy. It took me a few seconds to realize that Debbie Windsor was my publicist in Chicago.

"Good morning Scott, sorry to wake you so early, but it's 9:30 here and I need your approval for a media appearance."

"Well sure, Debbie. What's up?"

"Scott, are you ready for this? The Oprah show wants you on as soon as possible.

The mention of Oprah's name snapped me instantly awake. "When is the earliest date they could put us on?"

"How does one week sound?"

"That's sensational. We'll be there. Just get the details and Mike and I will be there. He is going to be excited. This has been one of his dreams for communicating his message to as many people as possible. Thank you, Debbie. We'll see you in Chicago in one week."

Chapter 39

Chicago

The week had passed quickly. Appearing on the Oprah show had been a fantasy dream. A one-in-a-million shot. A chance to share Mike's message with Oprah and her vast audience. Just being on her show meant millions of people would be exposed to profound spiritual truths that could change their lives for the better.

While I was intent on getting our message across, my daughters, were just excited about the chance to meet Oprah. Alison, the fifteen year old, who dreams of becoming an actress, asked if she could be on the show also. I told her no, but said she might get to be in the *Green Room* before and during the taping. She replied, "Naw, I'd rather be in the audience so I can be on camera whenever they pan the studio audience."

Alison, and my older daughter Joni, decided that they would go shopping first and meet us at the studio. Mike, Karen and I had a leisurely breakfast in the hotel dining room then I changed into a suit.

Harpo Productions, Oprah's filming company had sent a white limo to pick us up, and it was waiting as we walked out of the hotel.

"Ya know, Scott, this is a little fancy for me," said Mike. We're not that far away. We coulda hopped on a bus."

"I know, Mike, but for the next couple of hours we're celebrities so sit back and enjoy it."

The limo driver closed the doors after he had ushered us in and went around to the driver's side and got in. He pointed out to us that the mini-bar was well stocked with both alcoholic and non-alcoholic beverages and some assorted snacks, then he rolled up the window between him and our section. He shifted into gear and pulled out into the traffic for the short ride to the studio. I was starting to feel the usual nervousness I get before public appearances. Over the years I had done over two hundred media interviews and countless speeches, and had learned that being a little nervous was good—it tended to help me perform better. But today I was more nervous than normal. It didn't get any bigger than the Oprah Show.

"Look, everyone, there's Joni and Alison," said Karen as we turned the corner approaching the studio. "It looks like Alison found the new lacrosse stick she wanted to buy."

I looked and waved but realized that they couldn't see us, so I rolled down my tinted window and shouted at them. They waved back then Joni pointed a finger at us, then at her camera, letting us know she wanted to capture a photo or two of us in the limo or getting out of it. The driver pulled over to the curb, right in front of the studio's main entrance. A few people strolling by turned to look at the limo and to see who got out. To their disappointment, when the driver came around to open the door, I stepped out. Since they didn't recognize me as a celebrity they continued walking.

Joni had her camera up to her eye focusing, then all Hell broke loose. Mike and I were standing on the curb waiting for Karen to be helped out of the limo by the driver, when I heard Joni scream, "Dad, duck. He's got a gun!"

At that moment I heard a series of shots from a pistol with a silencer on it. Phutt, phutt, phutt, phutt, phutt. Suddenly Mike collapsed against me, blood streaming down the side of his face. I grabbed him as he fell, then felt a searing pain in my upper right arm, then two blows to my back that felt like a horse had kicked me. Still gripping Mike, I staggered against the limo. I spotted the gunman, a white male wearing a medium blue jogging outfit, only twenty feet away. Then, rushing towards him I saw Joni and Alison. I screamed at them to go back, but they ignored me.

Joni grabbed her big 35mm camera by the sturdy thick rainbow colored carrying strap and swung it at the gunman's hand holding the pistol. The pistol fell to the sidewalk, then as the assailant bent over to pick it up, Alison swung her new lacrosse stick at the back of his head as hard as she could. He screamed as the force of her blow drove his head into a parking meter, where he collapsed into a heap. Security personnel from the studio came rushing out and quickly grabbed the unconscious gunman.

I knew I had been hit several times but between Mike's blood and mine I couldn't tell how badly. Then I realized I had my Kevlar vest on—a habit I had continued at Mike's insistence. The first bullet caught me in the arm. The next two—in my back—were stopped by the vest. I lowered Mike to the pavement, propping him against the white limo, now smeared red with our blood. He was unconscious but his wound appeared to be a scalp wound where the bullet grazed the side of his skull without penetrating it. Karen had fallen back into the limo, unhurt, but was severely rattled. She jumped out, and once she determined I was going to live she grabbed me and hugged me as hard as she could.

Sirens were sounding and soon the street was a tangled mess of emergency vehicles. I just sat on the street leaning against the limo holding Mike in my arms while Karen pressed a stack of cocktail napkins from the minibar against Mike's wound. He coughed, then his eyes flickered open. A tiny smile formed on his face as he said, "Well, Scott, it looks like the Universe was looking out for us once more. You're okay aren't you?"

"Yeah, I think so. I took one in the arm and the vest stopped a couple more. It looks like your thick skull saved you."

The paramedics took Mike from my arms, bandaged his head, and put him on a stretcher. Another paramedic helped me ease my injured arm out of my suit coat, commenting that the bullet had apparently gone completely through my arm. Satisfied that nothing was broken she bandaged the wound.

By now, staff members from the Oprah show were out on the sidewalk. Once they realized what had happened they located Mike and me quickly reassuring us that we could reschedule the appearance. I looked at Mike, and he said, "No, we're going on today, I've waited too long. I won't let McCallum stop us."

"Mike, you've lost a lot of blood. But if it's okay with you I can still go on." I said.

"Scott, just so one of us gets the message out. Go for it."

The paramedics were insisting that both of us go to the hospital. I refused. After several minutes of arguing, they finally agreed to make a sling for my arm and leave me, taking just Mike to the hospital.

As the paramedics, under the watchful eyes of the police, loaded the gunman on a stretcher, I noticed the DOG insignia tattooed on the back of his right hand. He had been sent by McCallum. Baby Souls have a tenacity that is almost beyond belief. They just keep coming and coming.

The real heroes, Joni and Alison, gave their statements to the police then were mobbed by the media. Alison, seeing that several TV cameras were on her, upstaged her more reserved sister, and gave a blow-by-blow reenactment of the attack, focusing particular attention to how she swung her lacrosse stick and knocked out the gunman.

Finally, the Oprah staff led us inside. A doctor, who had been called, arrived and gave me a mild sedative after I refused a heavier duty pain killer. The last thing I wanted was to go on national TV zonked out on pain pills and come across like some stupid zombie. I pocketed the heavy duty pills for after the show.

The door opened, and I heard a gasp. I turned and saw Oprah standing in the doorway. Except for her startled look, she was everything I had expected. As she surveyed the situation, her brown eyes projected a deep, caring, sympathetic look. I shook hands with my left hand. She again reasserted what her staff had said, that we could reschedule, but I said if it was okay with her I wanted to go on today. "Oprah, the message is too important. I can't let people like the Defenders of God stop the message from reaching the people."

"I understand, Scott—I read your book. It is vitally important. I'll put you on today."

Alison pushed forward and extended her hand. "Hi, I'm Alison Hunter. I'm the one that knocked out the creep with the gun."

Oprah ignored her hand and gave her a big hug instead, saying, "Alison, you are one brave young lady. Would you like a tour of the studio?"

"Sure."

"Okay. One of my staff members will give you a private tour."

"Super."

After making sure everyone and everything was under control Oprah excused herself and said she would see me when I went on camera.

My clothes were a mess, but fortunately the wardrobe people were able to find a pair of slacks and a shirt for me. Karen insisted that I lay down and led me to a couch in the Green Room.

As I rested, my mind flashed back to the first meeting with Mike in the Pike Place Market. So much had happened in such a short period of time it was almost beyond belief. Now, here I was about to share Mike's powerful spiritual message with millions of people. Mike and I had never figured one appearance, even on a show as popular as Oprah's, could trigger an immediate movement of peace and harmony—but it could start a national and even international dialogue debating the points Mike made. It could get people to step beyond their comfort zone, beyond what they had been taught, replacing dogma with openness, and a willingness to find the truth. Once that happens humankind will be able to accelerate its spiritual evolvement.

"Five minutes, Mr. Hunter."

Then finally the moment came. I kissed Karen and walked out into the bright lights, oblivious to the throbbing pain in my arm. An immense feeling of warmth and love swept over me as I looked into Oprah's beautiful eyes. I was enveloped in a spiritual glow of light that transcended anything I had ever felt before. We had succeeded in letting the genie out of the bottle—nothing was going to stop the truth—not DOG or anyone else.

THE END

APPENDIX A

Self-Scoring Quiz
to Determine Your Personality Traits

The following self-scoring quiz, called The Essence and Personality Profile, was created by Jose Stevens and JP Van Hulle and is reprinted here with their permission in abridged form.

The Essence and Personality Profile

The Essence and Personality Profile is designed to give you a wide-screen overview of who you are and how you act. It attempts to assess three major characteristics that form a profile of your personality. These three characteristics are:

Essence Role

Goal

Obstacle

The qualities assessed here provide a guide for understanding your unique approach to life. Your particular style reflects and contributes to the rich variety that life has to offer. The more you know about yourself and your unique style, the more effective you become in leading a satisfying and joyful life.

You will find the personality profile on the following pages. Try to answer the questions all at one sitting during a quiet, uninterrupted time of day. There are no right or wrong answers. It is important to tell the truth about yourself rather than trying to reply according to who you think you might like to be.

The simple scoring code can be found at the end of the profile. For each section, simply match the number of your reply with the number that corresponds to it in the code sheet. This will give you your specific qualities.

When you have finished scoring your answers you can go back and re-read the parts of Chapters 17, 18 and 19, that correspond to your answers. You will discover some interesting things about the role and personality you picked for this lifetime.

Role

Your Role reflects your deepest essence. However, it can be obscured by who you think you ought to be.

Here are some statements that reflect styles of *being* in the world. You may identify with more than one of them. This can be because you were conditioned in childhood to be a way that is different from who you truly are. We are looking for who you are beneath the social fabric or veneer.

It is perfectly common to be one role innately and also trained to function in another role as well. Reading about the roles in depth in Chapter 17 will provide clarity as to the talents and skills you provide to society.

Instructions

Circle as many statements as you closely identify with. Then go back and choose the GROUP that feels the most like you.

1. I like to work behind the scenes making sure every thing runs smoothly.
   Nurturing people is what inspires me most in life.
   Sometimes I feel trapped into a caretaking role.
   I like to quietly arrange situations to make other people happy.
   I frequently perform little services that go unnoticed.
   I love to take care of people and see to it they are comfortable.
   I'd make someone a perfect wife or househusband.

2. I often feel a strong urge to tell people what I see is best for them.
   My spiritual path is of higher importance to me than my relationships or material needs.
   Sometimes I get pretty zealous in my efforts to set others on the right path.
   I feel responsible for the spiritual guidance of my "flock," even if I am not a minister.

I have a natural ability to see where people are blocked and I have the urge to save them from themselves.
Compassion is the force that motivates me to relate to the world.
My friends consider me to be an inspiration to them, even if I'm not sure why.

3.   I am most stimulated by inventing and remodeling.
I love to influence the mood or flavor of what's going on.
If I can't express innovative ideas I feel blocked and frustrated.
People see me as artistic and doing things with an unusual flair.
I like to invent things in my mind that have never been thought of before.
I am fascinated with how different elements combine to make a cohesive unit.
I love to create new projects from old materials.

4.   I hate to have my communication misunderstood.
I love to have the last word.
I secretly (or not so secretly) love to be on stage and to be noticed.
I often mentally correct others' communication, whether written or verbal.
I have a little voice in my head that almost never shuts up.
I am renowned for my wit and sense of humor.
People can't really hide the truth from me. If there is some juicy new gossip around, I won't feel comfortable until I've heard the details.

5.   I like to get things organized.
I don't mind taking charge of situations to get results.
The one thing that really makes me furious is an attack on my principles —even an unwitting one.
I get so focused in one direction that I sometimes do

not see the side paths.

When people irritate me they see my sword come out.

I will quietly but relentlessly work towards some thing I know is right.

I know I'm basically a strong person, and I am quick to defend the weak and innocent.

6.   I expect to be the person who is put in a leadership position or ultimately responsible for a project.

I like to grasp the big picture and then delegate chores to see that everything is accomplished.

I don't stop until I've mastered what I'm attempting.

I get frustrated if I cannot do something perfectly the first time.

I am responsible for the action flowing smoothly in whatever situation I'm in.

When things go wrong, the buck ultimately stops here.

I am only interested in "A plus" experiences; "A minus" is not quite enough.

7.   I am innately curious and I love to study what interests me.

I am known for being objective, and I make a good mediator.

I pursue knowledge avidly.

I don't like important information to slip away unrecorded.

People value my opinion because they know that I can see any point of view objectively and fairly.

I have an inner compulsion to experiment and risk for new knowledge.

I like to research before deciding anything.

Goal

The Goal is the underlying motivator in life. It is what you are always striving to accomplish, over and above your career goals and other interests.

Instructions

Read over the statements below. You may see a bit of yourself in all of them. Select the *one group* of statements that most accurately describes your motivations.

1. Life looks competitive to me.
   I always want to find a scenario where everyone wins; but if there is a loser it won't be me.
   If things are not going my way I look for where I've lost control.

2. I want to be dedicated to a cause of great importance.
   I'm most comfortable when I feel devoted.
   My own needs are often of lower priority to me than those of people I love or owe loyalty to.

3. I hate criticism and am deeply wounded by rejection.
   I try to accept people and situations as they are.
   I would rather try to get along with others, than argue about who's "right."

4. I am very discerning about what I wear, and what I do.
   I have refined or sophisticated taste, and would make a good critic. I am an acquired taste; not friends with just anyone; and I like it that way.

5. I like to be constantly learning, experiencing things, and changing.
   Just when I get my life settled, I seem to start some thing new.
   Often I get overwhelmed, confused, and have to stop and sort things out.

6. My life seems to revolve around the same issues over and over.
   I have a disability; or a significant issue in my life that affects every other part of my life on a regular basis.
   My life is very simple in most respects.

7. My life is basically pleasant.
   Things seem to work themselves out, even if they're difficult at times.
   I do not feel a big drive to accomplish anything really major during my life.
   If I just relax and 'go with the flow," solutions to my problems always appear.

Obstacle

The Obstacle is your primary stumbling block. It is your knee-jerk response to anger, frustration or difficulty. You will find a bit of yourself in all of the obstacles because most likely you have done them all from time to time. We are looking for your most instinctive reaction, however.

Instructions

Select the GROUP that portrays your most typical response to the situation described below.

When I get very upset or I am under stress I tend to...

1. have a drink, light up a cigarette, or take a drug to unwind.
   lose control or will power and do something I know I'll regret later.
   "cut off my nose to spite my face."

2. eat or drink something to fill the void I feel.
   feel deprived and believe I can't have what I want to fulfill my needs.
   go shopping because buying things makes me feel better.

3. withdraw.
   feel like I'm incompetent.
   blame myself for whatever went wrong.

4. internalize the problem and put barriers up.
   become shy and hide behind a competent mask.
   get critical or act a bit superior in defense.

5. feel trapped in my situation and helpless to get free.
   feel depressed, because there is no escape.
   resent whoever manipulated me into this negative situation.

6. become very intolerant and try to rush to solution.
fear I'll not have enough time to get things done.
become irritated and sometimes act rashly.

7. become more determined to tough it out.
tend to become obstinate.
tune out others' feedback even if I think it might be right.

Self-Scoring Code

Role

1 Server

2 Priest

3 Artisan

4 Sage

5 Warrior

6 King

7 Scholar

The group that you chose indicates your Role. If you circled a number of statements in another group, then you were probably heavily conditioned by a parent of that Role.

Goal

1 Dominance

2 Submission

3 Acceptance

4 Discrimination

5 Growth

6 Re-evaluation

7 Relaxation

The group you chose is your Goal in life. You will occasionally use its opposite. If you chose relaxation, you will occasionally use any one of the other goals if it makes life easier.

Obstacle

1 Self-destruction

2 Greed

3 Self-deprecation

4 Arrogance

5 Martyrdom

6 Impatience

7 Stubbornness

The Obstacle you chose is your biggest stumbling block. You will often use its opposite; but everyone experiences most if not all of the Obstacles sometimes.

Special Note to Readers

For a more comprehensive and accurate personality profile and report, you are encouraged to take the PERSONESSENCE PERSONALITY PROFILE at:

Personessence.com

This enhanced profile is offered to readers for a nominal fee by Jose Stevens, Ph.D.

APPENDIX B

Channelers
of the Michael Teachings

The following individuals are highly experienced long-time channelers of the Michael Teachings and have made major contributions to this book. All of them are available for private readings. Appointments can be made for in-person or telephone readings. For prices, and available times, please contact them directly at the phone number, address or website listed below:

Emily Baumbach, (415) 456-7696
Causalworks, 32 Porteous Avenue, Fairfax, CA 94930
Website: www.causalworks.com

Jose Stevens, Ph.D., (505) 982-8732
Pivotal Resources, Inc., P.O. Box 272,   Santa Fe, NM 87504
Website: www.pivres.com

JP Van Hulle, (707) 748-7715
Michael Educational Foundation, P.O. Box 1806, Benicia, CA 94510
Website: www.mef.to

Michael Books
by the channelers listed above:

Celebrities: Complete Michael Database by Emily Baumbach

Earth To Tao by Jose Stevens, Ph.D.

Michael: The Basic Teachings by JP Van Hulle (coauthored with Aaron Christeaan and M.C. Clark)

Michael's Cast of Characters by Emily Baumbach

Michael's Gemstone Dictionary by JP Van Hulle (coauthored with Judithann David)

Parallel Universes: Your Other Selves by Emily Baumbach

The Michael Handbook by Jose Stevens, Ph.D. (coauthored with S. Warwick-Smith)

Tao To Earth by Jose Stevens, Ph.D.

The Personality Puzzle by JP Van Hulle and Jose Stevens, Ph.D.

Transforming Your Dragons by Jose Stevens, Ph.D.

Additional Resources

In addition to the channelers and books listed above you can find additional resources online. Simply keystroke *The Michael Teachings* into your internet search engine.

Author's Notes

Several celebrities are mentioned in this book, along with their respective soul age, soul level, and personality traits. All of this information was obtained, with permission, from Emily Baumbach's book:

Celebrities: Complete Michael Database.

The information was obtained by channeling and while every attempt was made to ensure that it was accurate there still is the possibility of some error creeping in as most channelers claim an approximate 80% accuracy rate.

If any person mentioned feels their information is wrong they should contact one of the channelers listed in Appendix B and schedule an in-person appointment where the data can be verified or corrected.

About The Author

W. Lawton Brown has been called an eclectic and a renaissance man... experiencing much that life has to offer in his quest for a deeper meaning to human existence. His life began in abject poverty during the infamous midwest dust bowl years. Along his life path he has held many varied jobs including: dishwasher, janitor, gardener, Boeing factory worker, professional cartoonist, professional astrologer, metaphysical teacher, Merrill Lynch stockbroker, and an international award-winning direct marketing/advertising creative director and writer.

As a brash 14 year old teenager he challenged his Baptist minister's fire and brimstone sermons, saying that many of them made no sense. That led to a 40 year study of other religions and metaphysics in his tireless quest to discover the truth. Lawton's research took him into a myriad of metaphysical fields—astrology, automatic writing, the Edgar Cayce readings, channeling, hypno-regression, the I Ching, mental telepathy, numerology, past-life regression therapy, psychic recall, pyramid healing, the tarot and even UFO's.

As the years passed Lawton realized that a great deal of the information being spewed out by our most cherished institutions, like churches, schools, governments, and the medical field, whether by design or ignorance, was far from correct. But how does one find the truth?

Describing himself as an *open-minded skeptic,* he urges readers to be open-minded rather than close-minded and skeptical rather than gullible. The close-minded person who denies the existence of anything that's not in a government endorsed school text, or fits under the scientist's microscope, or a part of one's religious belief system, will only be limiting his or her intellectual and spiritual growth. The open-minded skeptic is not afraid to look, searching for ultimate truths rather than erecting a truth-obscuring brick wall around metaphysics.

How To Contact The Author

W. Lawton Brown can be reached through the publisher:

NEO Books, P.O. Box 2402, Lynnwood, WA 98036-2402.

Or, through his website: **www.clashofsouls.com** where links will be provided to reach his fascinating and thought provoking Blog website.